SURRENDER

"Alys, do you want me?" Piers asked, his voice low.

"I do." She brought her fingertips to the clasp at her throat and undid her cloak. "I've wanted you since the night you came to me in the Foxe Ring."

No sooner had the whisper escaped her lips than Piers claimed her mouth with his own. He wrapped his arms around her and half lifted her off the floor, as if trying to absorb her.

His mouth was slick and cool and wet, and she met his passionate need with one of her own every bit as fiery and demanding . . .

Books by Heather Grothaus

THE WARRIOR

THE CHAMPION

THE HIGHLANDER

TAMING THE BEAST

NEVER KISS A STRANGER

Published by Kensington Publishing Corporation

Never Kiss a Stranger

HEATHER GROTHAUS

ZEBRA BOOKS
KENSINGTON PUBLISHING CORP.
http://www.kensingtonbooks.com

ZEBRA BOOKS are published by

Kensington Publishing Corp.
119 West 40th Street
New York, NY 10018

All Kensington titles, imprints, and distributed lines are available at special quantity discounts for bulk purchases for sales promotion, premiums, fund-raising, educational, or institutional use.

Special book excerpts or customized printings can also be created to fit specific needs. For details, write or phone the office of the Kensington Special Sales Manager: Attn. Special Sales Department. Kensington Publishing Corp., 119 West 40th Street, New York, NY 10018. Phone: 1-800-221-2647.

Zebra and the Z logo Reg. U.S. Pat. & TM Off.

ISBN-13: 978-1-4201-1242-9
ISBN-10: 1-4201-1242-2

First Printing: March 2011
10 9 8 7 6 5 4 3 2 1

Printed in the United States of America

In memory of the girl who made lists

Chapter 1

December 1276
Fallstowe Castle, England

The monkey ruined the feast.

Outside of the king's own court, Fallstowe's winter feast was the most lavish affair in all of England, and had been since before Alys Foxe was born. Every nobleman in the land coveted the yearly invitation, and most spent the summer and autumn months leading up to the celebration wracked with worry that they would be passed over. Alys had to admit that her eldest sister had outdone herself this year.

Yards and yards of shimmering, ivory fabric billowed down from the domed ceiling of the great hall, gathered to the side walls by evergreen ropes festooned with bunches of bold holly and deer antlers, giving the cavernous room the appearance of some rich, fantastical tent. The north balcony was peopled with no fewer than twenty musicians, the swelling sounds from their strings and percussion overflowing the granite railing into the stone receptacle below, drowning attendees who clutched at each other, bobbing and spinning within its seductive, melodic tide—beautiful ladies in exquisite striped brocades and long veils, powerful noblemen sporting their finest velvets and woolen hose. Balladeers meandered through the guests, strumming lutes along with the symphony above, and adding their voices in perfect, ringing tenor harmonies.

The rich perfume of melting beeswax and smoke from the hundreds of lit candles warmed and scented the air like the prelude to a storm. Endless trays of food boasted openly of the decadence of both the occasion and its hostess. It came from every corner of England—fish, quail, venison dressed with sage and onion; and far beyond—pork with oranges and lemons, goose with saffron and pomegranates. There were thick custards bejeweled with coarse, sparkling sugar, apples studded with cloves. Wine of every shade and fortitude from the most costly casks Bordeaux produced, ales and meads, and the most noxious spirits ran like streams, like bawdy rivers.

So although there were no doubt countless men gnashing their teeth in jealousy in their own plain halls this night, Alys wished most sincerely that her eldest sister would have forgotten to include *her* in the winter feast. She was bored to tears, not at all interested in dancing or drinking herself into a simpering, giggling fool like most of the other young ladies in attendance.

Her rich blue gown, made of the finest perse directly from Provence and commissioned specifically for the event upon Sybilla's direct command was quite lovely and made Alys the envy of many of the women, but she took no pride or enjoyment from it. Even when Sybilla herself had said that the shade of blue against Alys's pale skin and blond hair would cause many to mistake her for an angel, and Sybilla was never, ever coy. Alys would have been more comfortable in her plain woolen overdress and leather slippers.

She cared not a fig for the prancing young men who trailed her, obnoxiously proclaiming—and inflating—their family's importance to King Edward in hopes of winning Sybilla's approval as a match for one of the wealthy and notorious Foxe sisters. Since Mother's death more than a year ago, it seemed Sybilla's most fervent wish was to see Alys married as soon as possible, likely so that she could be quit of the devilment that was the youngest lady of Fallstowe. She'd even gone so far this night as to pointedly introduce Alys to Lord John Hart, a paunchy, somber widower who was three score if he was a day.

But marriage—especially to a wealthy, spotted adolescent, or wealthy, senile old lecher—held not the appeal that perhaps it should have since she had turned eighteen. Alys sensed she would never find a husband to suit her within the circle of Sybilla's rich and boring contemporaries.

Thus, Alys would have happily forgone the entire feast in favor of following grumpy old Graves though Fallstowe, rousting would-be lovers from the darkened stairwells, or playing with the foals in the stables, or spending the evening in the corridor outside of the garrison, listening to the soldiers curse and tell lurid tales of sex and murder.

Until the arrival of the monkey, of course. And then the evening had become immensely more interesting.

It caused a delighted commotion among the guests as it accompanied Etheldred Cobb, Lady of Blodshire, into the hall, riding on the old widow's fat, rounded shoulder. A small, grayish-brown animal with a pink face, it wore a ridiculous skirt about its waist, which seemed to be fashioned from several sheer, colored scarves, and was yoked to the old woman by a long, fine lead of hammered gold attached to a leather collar. Lady Blodshire's entourage followed meekly: her son, Clement, and her personal maid, who Alys had always fancied looked more like a man than did young Lord Clement himself. It was common knowledge, although never spoken aloud, that Lady Blodshire had carried on a raging love affair with the masculine maid Mary since Lord Blodshire had fallen ill and died a handful of years ago.

Alys had no love for her mother's acquaintance, Etheldred Cobb, especially since her son, the pale and winsome Clement, had taken more than a passing interest in Alys. But the monkey was drawing her—along with everyone else in the hall—to the mustachioed old woman like beggars to a fallen purse. Because Fallstowe was her home, the crowd reluctantly gave Alys passage at her impatient "Pardon me, excuse me."

"Yes, she's quite keen," the old woman was saying in her gravelly voice, and pivoting her rotund body so that all gathered around her could admire her pet. "A gift from one of our valiant knights upon his return from Crusade." She craned her neck awkwardly to look up at the monkey and waggled a finger toward it with a cracking coo. "You're keen, aren't you? Make your bow, now. Go on."

As Alys neared, she saw the monkey flinch and move its pink face away from Etheldred's finger warily, small teeth flashing for an instant.

"She has yet to be properly trained, of course," Etheldred sniffed, her lips settling into a habitual knot. "Still quite wild, I'm afraid, even with my firm hand." She forced her face around to look at the animal once more. "Bow, Monkey. *Bow!*" She jerked sharply on the golden leash and the animal tumbled to the stones. It scrambled to its feet and gave a halting bow, cowering and casting its eyes up Lady Blodshire's skirt warily.

The crowd broke out in applause and admiring "ooh's."

Alys's footsteps hesitated for in instant at the harsh treatment, and 'twas then that she noticed the slender, golden switch in the old woman's other hand. Alys stepped before Etheldred Cobb.

"Lady Blodshire," Alys said and lay a bright smile over her grimace. "Welcome to Fallstowe. I daresay we have been too long without your company. Sybilla will be so pleased."

Etheldred's eyelids lowered in a mass of folds as she attempted to look down her nose at Alys, and Alys felt a pinch of gratitude toward her sister for the blue perse gown she now wore, as she caught Lady Blodshire's quick appraisal of it.

"Lady Alys. You seem a bit more grown since last we met, true. At least you are dressed appropriately, although I cannot say that particular hue suits you at all. And I'm quite certain Sybilla *should* be pleased with a visit from her poor, dead mother's oldest friend."

"Yes, you were Mother's *oldest* friend, by far," Alys quipped the emphasis and then looked quickly to the floor, dismissing the dumpy beast's sly insults. "It seems we have a unique guest at Fallstowe's winter feast—is it a female?"

"It is. And what horrid manners you possess, child— Amicia weeps," Etheldred sneered and then jerked the monkey's leash once more. "Monkey, up!" She raised a nonexistent eyebrow at Alys. "Did you not notice Clement?"

"Of course I did, my lady. Forgive me." Alys wanted to kick at the old woman's shin, but instead turned to the pale young man hovering at his mother's shoulder, a dreamy expression on his thin face. "Good eventide, Lord Blodshire. It is certainly a pleasure to host your delightful family once more."

"Lady Alys," he said in a disappointed whisper. "Have we only just met? Please, I must impress upon you once more how 'twould thrill my very heart were you to address me as *Clement*." Alys was forced to surrender her fingers to his outstretched palm and he leaned over her hand and pressed his dry, cold lips to her skin, where they lingered. "Fallstowe's gay ornamentation wilts next to your sweet beauty! 'Tis as if I am in the presence of an angel!"

Alys pulled her hand free to dip into a shallow curtsey. *An angel? Oh, yes, thank you, Sybilla.* "You are too kind, Lord Blodshire."

"Monkey, *up!*" Etheldred screeched and stamped her wide foot.

But the monkey only screeched in kind reply, sounding very much like its mistress, and tried to bolt from the leash. The crowd had drifted away as Alys was welcoming the Blodshire trio, but now those closest to the old woman glanced over once more with bemused and indulgent smiles for the unruly pet.

"You devil's animal," Etheldred hissed and brought up the gold, corded switch. She swung it with a whicker of air before Alys could stop her, but instead of landing on the monkey who now hunched near the stones, the switch broke against the length of golden links, pulling the leash from Etheldred's fat fingers.

Alys squealed as, in the next instant, the monkey clambered swiftly up her own skirt and scrambled over her back to perch on the shoulder farthest away from Etheldred Cobb. She could feel the animal's tiny fingers in her hair as it clutched at her circlet and the flicking vibration of its heartbeat through its feet. Alys brought up a hand to steady the small creature. Its hair was soft and radiating heat, its limbs feeling both delicate and powerful beneath her palm.

"Come here, you little bitch," Etheldred growled and made to grab the monkey from Alys's shoulder.

Alys instinctively stepped back, steadying the monkey with her hand, her fingers wrapping protectively around its slight forearm.

Lady Blodshire's eyes narrowed to slits. "Mary?"

The mule-faced maid, heretofore nearly forgotten by Alys, stepped from behind Etheldred and toward Alys with outstretched—and bandaged, Alys noticed—hands. "Be still, my lady, lest it bite you."

Alys was not certain whether the maid meant the monkey or Etheldred Cobb, and it took a mustering of all her decorum to not turn from the Blodshire group and flee with the monkey. She could feel the animal's trembling increase in the instant before the maid's hands claimed it. Alys was forced to assist the maid by prying the monkey's fingers from her circlet, lest she lose a goodly portion of her hair along with the small animal.

"It is beyond my understanding," Etheldred began when Mary had stepped behind her once more, "why my son thinks you worth a moment of his time, as forward and gauche as you are. Amicia spoiled you to ruination, I daresay."

"Mother," Clement whispered, his thin brows lowering.

Alys's stomach clenched. "Do not trouble yourself over Clement's affections, my lady—I'm certain it is only Fallstowe's wealth he admires. 'Tis most costly to outfit as many knights for Crusade as Blodshire has so piously promised. Perhaps someone fears for her soul?" Alys let her eyes go deliberately to the homely maid over Etheldred's shoulder, and Mary dropped her gaze while her face flushed scarlet. Alys looked boldly once more to Etheldred, and noticed that the group held the other guests' attention once more.

"How dare you slander me so, you little heathen!" Lady Blodshire quivered with rage. "I should strike you where you stand."

"Oh, do allow me to have a stool fetched for you so that you might reach me properly, you fattened old—"

"Lady Blodshire, I thought it must be you when the guests gathered into such a knot. Welcome to Fallstowe."

Alys's words were cut off not only by Sybilla's gracious welcome, but by the sharpened points of her fingernails digging into Alys's tender upper arm.

"That . . . *girl*," Etheldred sputtered, and pointed a gnarled finger at Alys.

"Is young and foolish," Sybilla supplied.

Alys jerked her arm free and looked up at her sister, the sparkling-cold, beautiful Sybilla. "She is cruel to that animal, Sybilla. The poor thing is terrified of her!"

Sybilla flicked her ice-blue eyes—so unlike Alys's own rich brown—toward the monkey, and then returned her disapproving stare to Alys with a cool blink. "Should you one day possess a monkey of your own, you may treat it however you like. Until then, you will do well to remember that others' possessions are of no concern to you. Apologize to Lady Blodshire. *Please*," Sybilla added quietly, and Alys heard the dire warning in her outwardly benign tone as if her dark-haired sister had screamed it.

Alys swallowed. She was a grown woman. And Sybilla seemed to forget of late that she was not their mother. "I will not," Alys said, lifting her chin and telling herself her voice sounded strong and sure. "She flung the first barb, and this is *my home, too*, Sybilla. I'll not allow for such disrespect."

"The only lady at Fallstowe owed respect is its head, which is me," Sybilla said calmly, quietly, with a smile, even. Alys knew she was as good as dead. "And you will allow for whatever I deem appropriate. I'll not have our guests ridiculed."

"Heavens, what are you two about?" The middle sister, Cecily, now joined the group. Dark-haired like Sybilla, but sharing Alys's brown eyes, Cecily was the anomaly of the Foxe family, meek, sweet, and more devoted to God than any young woman had reason to be, in Alys's opinion. She dressed plainer than even Alys did, although her beauty was as striking as Sybilla's, even with her own rich hair hidden beneath a drab, shortened veil.

"Apologize, Alys," Sybilla repeated, ignoring Cecily's arrival. "Or be gone to your rooms for the remainder of the feast."

Cecily sighed. "Oh, Alys, what have you done now?"

Alys felt her chin flinch, and her eyes flicked to the scores of people staring at her. She was humiliated yet again before the all-powerful matriarch of Fallstowe, Sybilla. Even silly Clement Cobb now looked at her with uncomfortable pity in his watery blue eyes. She had never missed her mother so desperately.

"I will not apologize," Alys said quietly. And then, louder, *"I will not!* Clement, you are a dear man, and I am sorry for any embarrassment this may cause you, but I will not apologize to a vain old harridan who belittles others and boasts of her piety out one side of her mouth and then kisses her own maid with the other side!"

The crowd gave a collective gasp and Sybilla's already pale face went cloud white. Even the musicians and servants had quit their work.

Lady Etheldred sagged toward Mary, and the monkey leapt free as the maid's arms came around the old woman.

"My sweet Etheldred!" Mary cried.

Clement whispered, "Mother!" before falling to his knees at her side. "Are you dead?" Alys couldn't help but think she heard a note of longing hope in his voice.

The monkey clambered over the pile of bodies on the floor and launched itself at Alys, who caught it by the arms and swung it up on her shoulder as if she'd performed the action a hundred times before.

"Leave the animal," Sybilla said in a low, deadly voice, "and go to your rooms. I will join you after I have returned the feast to some sense of order."

"The monkey stays with me." She was already in enough trouble—why not add thievery to her list of supposed transgressions? Alys was certain God would forgive her even if Sybilla did not.

The Foxe matriarch's perfect, slender nostrils flared. "Go. I will fetch it when I come, so be prepared to say your good-bye then."

"Come, Alys." Cecily took the arm opposite the monkey, and her grip was firm, but so much more gentle than Sybilla's had been. She leaned in close to Alys's ear. "Please, darling—'twill only be so much more the worse for you if you struggle against her, and I wonder already what she might do."

Cecily was right. Alys had defied Queen Sybilla and now she would pay. Her oldest sister thought her a child still, and cared naught that she had just humiliated Alys before half the English nobility. There was no foretelling the lengths of the punishment that was to come.

Alys pulled free from Cecily's grasp easily. "I tire of this mundane feast, and its equally boring guests," Alys said loudly, tilting her chin lest the tears threaten once more. "I think I shall retire for the evening and work at my stitchery. I bid you good night."

She swept through the crowd with the monkey clinging to her shoulder gamely, the guests parting for her as if she had been touched by a curse.

Alys could not help but think to herself that perhaps she had been.

The only stitchery that was worked on in Alys Foxe's chamber was done by Cecily, who chose to stay with her younger sister rather than rejoin the dubious and scandalized festivities below. Alys was quite surprised that Saint Cecily had not spent the past hour on her knees, praying for Alys's very soul. Instead, the middle Foxe sister sat in an upright chair near the hearth and a table of oil lamps, working on one of her endless tapestries, and chastising her sweetly every few moments.

"I know you feel you have your reasons in most instances, Alys," Cecily broke the silence yet again. "But I fail to see why it is so difficult for you to at least try to get along with Sybilla on the occasions where she actually requires it."

"My quarrel was not *with* Sybilla until she stuck her pointy nose in it," Alys argued petulantly, sounding to her dismay, like the child Sybilla accused her of being. Her eyes flicked to the beamed canopy above her bed, where Lady Blodshire's liberated pet sat munching a dried fig happily, sans skirt, leash, *and* collar. "That beastly Etheldred Cobb—"

"You embarrassed Sybilla terribly with your behavior."

"I embarrassed *her* with *my* behavior?"

"Yes," Cecily agreed quietly, quickly tying a knot and then biting off the thread with her teeth. "Sybilla gives you free reign most of the time. Her view, I'm certain, was that because you are of a higher rank than Lady Blodshire, your breeding should have persuaded you to rise to your station when faced with her venom. Any matter, we are to honor our elders, even when we feel their actions are not particularly honorable."

Alys rolled her eyes and turned her face back to the window, seeing very little of the night-blackened countryside through the wavy and clouded glass.

"I would think *you* to commend me for showing mercy to the poor creature unfortunate enough to be in the care of that old bitch." Cecily gave Alys a look of dark warning, but Alys ignored it. "And for defending myself—as well as our family—against such unwarranted slander! She may as well have called Mother an idiot. I am well aware that all *Sybilla* cares about is appearances. Ironic, since she plays the whore for any man who dares cross our threshold."

"Alys!" Cecily said sharply.

"'Tis true, and well you know it. Why, I would wager that Sybilla's had no fewer than a hundred men in her bed. If you feel it your duty to lecture one of your sisters on Godly behavior, Saint Cecily, I would hope it to be Sybilla rather than me."

"She's not had that many . . . friends," Cecily said awkwardly. "And don't call me Saint Cecily, Alys—'tis a blasphemy and mean spirited. You wound me."

Alys did feel a pinch of regret for speaking aloud the popular nickname for her middle sister. "Oh, Cee, I *am* sorry for that. Forgive me. I'm only so frustrated I could tear at my hair!"

"Please, allow me."

Sybilla had entered Alys's bedchamber as stealthily as a cat on the prowl, and one look at her eldest sister's sparkling eyes and squared shoulders left Alys little doubt that she was the intended prey. Behind her, like a dusty old shadow, stood Fallstowe's steward, Graves. As usual, he stared beyond the group toward a corner of the chamber, as if completely disinterested in the women keeping his company. Employed by the Foxe family since before even Alys's father was born, Graves was as much a part of Fallstowe as the mortar between the stones.

"I will not apologize, Sybilla," Alys stated flatly before her eldest sister had even come to stand before her. "To you or to that vicious dragon below. You were horrid to me before our guests, and I am not sorry the tiniest bit for anything I said to Etheldred Cobb."

"I have had quite enough of your insubordination, Alys Foxe," Sybilla said, trapping Alys where she sat at the window. Now even should she desire to stand, Sybilla's powerful physical presence made it impossible. "Your behavior this evening was the final insult."

Alys slapped the stone seat at her hip. "Insult? You would speak to me of ins—"

"I said I have had enough!" Sybilla repeated loudly, as close to shouting as cool Sybilla ever came.

The two sisters stared at each other for a tense moment, and then suddenly, Sybilla turned to grab a wooden high-backed chair, the twin to the one Cecily still occupied. She swung the piece around before Alys and sat down, positioning herself directly beneath the stone window seat.

"Alys," Sybilla began, more calmly now, but a snowflake landing on Sybilla's tongue would have still frozen to death. "You and I have had our quarrels, true. But I do hope you recognize that as—"

"Head of this family," Alys supplied in the same moment as Sybilla. Her eldest sister paused, her lips drawn together in a thin line. "You've made everyone very aware that you

rule Fallstowe, Sybilla, so get on with whatever punishment you've conjured in your power-drunk mind."

"Alys!" Cecily gasped again from her seat by the hearth.

Even before Cecily's chastisement, Alys realized she had once again let her tongue run away without her good sense, as any small glimmer of mercy was now gone from Sybilla's blue eyes.

"I have always wanted the best for you, whether you believe that or nay. I understand that, as her youngest, Mother indulged you, and allowed you to claim your happiness by whatever means you chose. Running about Fallstowe like a rough squire rather than a titled young lady. Passing your time with the peasants. Saying what and behaving however you pleased. She did it out of love, I recognize, but I believe that she has done you a grave disservice."

"Do not speak poorly of Mother, Sybilla, I warn you," Alys said quietly.

"Not intentionally," Sybilla placated. "And I loved her too, and miss her more than you will likely ever know. But she is gone. And I can no longer try to control you on my own. Mayhap your future husband will fare better than I. We will all pray that he does."

"We're not going to discuss finding me a husband again, are we?" Alys rolled her eyes. "Cecily is four years my senior, torment her."

"I shall likely take the veil, Alys," Cecily reminded, still seated in her chair, but now her stitchery lay forgotten in a jumbled heap on the floor.

Graves, now stoically studying the monkey who was leaning over the canopy in a crouch and returning his appraisal, sniffed loudly.

Alys had to agree.

"Oh, you will not, Cee," Alys scoffed. "You've been saying that for years now. Sybilla is the only one who likely believes it anymore."

"Nay, we are not going to discuss finding you a husband," Sybilla said, as if the interchange between Alys and Cecily had not occurred.

"Thank God," Alys sighed.

"For I have this night secured your match."

Alys's stomach tumbled. "What? Who?"

"Clement Cobb has asked for your hand, and I've given my blessing, as has Lady Blodshire. As a token of peace, she's offered to let you keep the animal you absconded with as a wedding gift."

"You promised me"—Alys slid off the window seat—"to *Clement Cobb?*"

"Yes. It was either him or Lord John Hart, and I took it upon myself to choose the match most appropriate to your age and temperament. Lord Hart is more than two score your senior, and a widower with no heir. Although he seems anxious to marry quickly, I believe he would have little patience for your immaturity and fits of temper, and would most likely beat you or send you home in shame. As it is, your rash behavior this evening is costing Fallstowe handsomely with your dowry to the Cobbs."

"Sybilla," Alys croaked. "No! No, I refuse to—*no!*"

"It is already done." Sybilla rose from her chair. "You will be married in thirty days, here at Fallstowe. I will make the formal announcement personally, this night. If you like, and promise to behave, you may accompany me and receive everyone's well-wishes. It is a fine opportunity to redeem yourself and show that you are not the child everyone thinks you to be." She turned her back to Alys and made to cross the bedchamber.

"Sybilla, you must not have heard me," Alys said in a

shaking voice. "I will not marry Clement Cobb. I would rather take my chances at the Foxe Ring."

Sybilla's laugh rang out before she stopped and turned to face Alys once more. "Oh, Alys—you *are* such the child, still. To put faith in a superstitious set of crumbling old rocks, for shame."

"'Tis how Mother and Father met," Alys said defiantly.

"It is a tale. That's all," Sybilla chuckled. Then she glanced toward the window, and her expression grew contemplative. "But the moon *is* full this night. The weather kind for December. Hie yourself to the ring, if it shall give you some sense of control of your future. Sit there for the entire month if you like. Should a man appear—not only in the middle of Fallstowe lands, but within the very ring of grown-over stones itself—and take you for his bride, my best to the pair of you. I shall be so moved as to pay equal dowry to both Blodshire and your new husband, quite happily."

Cecily stood. "Sybilla, don't tell her such foolishness! You know she will attempt it!"

Sybilla shrugged. "I care not how she passes the month. But you will be married in thirty days, Alys." She paused for a moment, and then lifted one of her rapier-slash eyebrows. "Are you coming below, or nay?"

"Nay," Alys's voice shook. She swallowed and gathered all of her hurt and anger. "I hate you, Sybilla."

Alys saw Sybilla's faint smile. "I know." Then she turned to Cecily. "Would that you join me, Cee. I'd have at least one of my sisters at my side this night."

"Of course, Sybilla." Cecily gave Alys a disappointed frown but then an instant later, crossed the floor to embrace her tightly. Alys did not return the gesture, letting her numb arms hang at her sides.

"Don't fight this so," Cecily whispered into her hair. "You yourself said that Clement is a dear man, and—God forgive me—I do believe you might find him quite biddable after his mother is dead." She leaned back, grasping both Alys's upper arms. "And *don't go to the Foxe Ring*. 'Tis cold and damp, and naught will come of it but further disappointment for you. If any should find out, they will mock you."

Alys stared past Cecily's shoulder to the fire in the hearth. "I cannot believe you of all people would stand against me on this."

Cecily sighed. "I do love you. And I am happy that you are to marry." She kissed Alys's cheek, and then swept past Sybilla out the door. Alys turned toward the window once more, so that Sybilla would not see her childish tears.

From behind Alys, Graves spoke to Sybilla. "Would you have me bolt the door, Madam?"

"Nay, Graves," Sybilla said. "Alys is now free to go where she would."

"Shall I accompany you, then?"

"Of course. You are family as well, dear friend. This announcement will be a joyous one for Fallstowe."

Alys heard her bedchamber door close.

Alone at last, she sank to her knees and dropped her head to the stone window seat with a sob. She barely heard the skittering behind her of the monkey clambering across the floor and then leaping up to sit near her head. The animal started picking at her veil and hair beneath.

The damned monkey! It had ruined the feast, ruined her life!

She gave a long sniff and rose up to gather the animal close to her, rubbing her cheek against its soft hair, staring, staring out the window.

Sybilla would not win. Not this time.

Likely the Foxe Ring was naught but a silly tale. So be it. But she would go there to make a point. Alys was not a child, and she would not be treated like one.

She would simply run away with her monkey, instead.

Chapter 2

Every bone in Piers Mallory's body ached as he trudged up yet another hillock in the dark, wet night. Perhaps, as the monk had warned him, he was not yet well enough to travel. His wounds were not completely healed, and even now, Piers's head throbbed so that his stomach roiled.

Spill his brains onto the ground! I want to see them seep from his skull and wash downstream, the filthy bastard-beggar!

He paused, blinked painfully against the pressure of the woman's shrill voice, swallowed. He could all but taste the green water of the River Arrow on the back of his throat once more. Thankfully, he did not vomit again. So, indeed, perhaps he was not yet well.

He began to walk slowly once more. London seemed very far from his vantage point over nothing more than his own two feet, and he must reach the King's Bench in a fortnight. If he did not, Bevan would win Gillwick Manor.

Bevan is no brother to you, Piers.

His father's words were quieter, but the torment they inflicted was no less severe and so he had to stop again—the pain was threatening to turn his insides out. He was certain he could move more quickly if only he could stop reliving that hell-filled night over and over again inside his bruised brain. The night his father had died. The night Piers himself had nearly lost his own life. The memories squeezed so, twisted, in his head and in his guts.

Why, Father? Why now do you weep?

My son, my son! Can you ever forgive me?

The night went red behind his eyelids, and Piers thought for a moment that he might pass out. But then a heavy fog rolled through the valley and misted his already damp neck with a sweet coolness. The red faded slowly, the pounding behind his eyes lessened enough so that he could open them once more. He straightened with care, and onward he went, the hateful voices gamely giving chase.

Slovenly peasant! Son of a whore! Nasty little bastard! Someone ought kill you in your sleep!

His stepmother, the conniving Judith Angwedd, would be at court as well, of course. How she had terrified him as a child, barring him from even sleeping inside his mother's humble cottage. She had done everything in her wicked power to be certain that Piers never saw Gillwick again. She and Bevan thought him dead even now.

But Piers lived. He lived, and he walked. To London, in the night, where he would not be discovered by any who could report to Judith Angwedd. Time when he could heal, and think, and plan the exact moment when he would appear in Edward's court and make his claim for Gillwick. When he would at last stand before his half—nay, not half. When he would stand before his *step*-brother, look him in the eye as an equal.

And then Piers thought he might kill Bevan Mallory. Perhaps with a blade. Or perhaps with his bare hands, as Bevan had tried to do to Piers. All the years of Piers's life, he had denied himself of his revenge on the man he had known as his brother. No matter how belittling Bevan had been, how cruel. How quick to point out to Piers at every opportunity the life that Bevan enjoyed and that was denied to Piers. Piers had never retaliated. But now, he thought he might savor the moment when Bevan's evil soul departed his body. Piers would laugh and laugh and laugh . . . perhaps until he was mad with it.

Or perhaps Piers was already mad.

But now he was simply tired. So tired, and hurting.

Ahead in the foggy gloom, he could see the skeletal ruins of some old keep. Unless he had truly lost his mental capabilities, the decrepit standing ring rising to the foreground in silhouette against a jagged, crumbling central tower indicated he had arrived at the old Foxe family hold. From village gossip, Piers knew the great Fallstowe castle was nearly an hour away by foot, and he was certain that none from the keep would be about the grounds at this hour in the damp cold.

He looked at the sky, the fat, white moon little more than an impression behind thin, high clouds, then back to the ancient remains. A chill kissed each droplet of sweat on his forehead. Were he a superstitious man, he might fear the old place, rumored to be magic. But Piers Mallory did not believe in magic. Or miracles, or tales of wild people living in the forests, or unicorns. He no longer believed that right always triumphed, or that perseverance made you strong—it only made you weary. He harbored no faith in a benevolent maker, and therefore no fear of demons.

And so he would rest at the old Foxe Ring. He would rest, and then tomorrow, he would march again.

Are you certain he's dead? Hit him again.

"Oh, I will be certain, Judith," Piers muttered aloud

as he climbed the last hillock leading up to the ruin. "I will be quite certain he is dead."

Alys passed the lonely, still time at the Foxe Ring by alternately crying and shivering on the fallen-down slab of rock in the center of the ring. She fancied that perhaps it had long ago been used for pagan sacrifices, and she thought how fitting the idea was as gooseflesh overtook her. She was offering herself up this night, partly in faith, partly in desperation.

Her newly acquired monkey now kept residence with her other quickly gathered possessions inside the drawstring sack, snuggled up against Alys's belly. She'd packed a spare amount of clothing, food, and miscellany for herself and the monkey, quite certain that the two of them were hardy enough to spend as many as three nights at the ruin—long enough for Sybilla to feel the shameful pinch of what she'd done and apologize.

But now Alys cried more out of self-pity than anger at her sister. 'Twas dreadfully cold—much colder than it had seemed when she'd departed Fallstowe through the herders' gate. And much colder than she could ever remember being while scurrying about the bailey with her friends in her disobedience to Sybilla. Alys suspected she'd never really felt the cold then because she had no reason to fear it. There was always a warm, comfortable shelter only steps away from wherever she chose to adventure and she'd never given a thought to the idea that she might be unable to retreat to a warm haven once she'd felt the desire.

She felt like a fool. Like the child Sybilla accused her of being. And so she also cried because she knew she would not last longer than morning at the ruin. She would return to Fallstowe once the gates were open for the day, defeated, humiliated, and likely with Sybilla never even knowing Alys had spent a cold, lonely night at the old keep. Her defiance had been for naught. Her will, weak. Perhaps simple, watery, whispery Clement Cobb was her ideal match, after all.

The sack shifted and a small hand poked out of the drawn opening. Alys rose to sit on one hip while she liberated her pet.

"I'll wager you won't like it out here any more than in there," she said ruefully, pushing the sack aside as the monkey clambered up her chest. "'Tis colder than Sybilla's frozen heart."

The monkey clung to Alys's bodice with warm hands and feet, and tucked its head under her chin.

Alys sniffed and then sighed. "What are we to do then, little monkey?" She paused, tucked her chin to look down at the small, pink face. "Hmm. I can't continue calling you Monkey, now can I? 'Tis what that dreadful, nasty, ugly witch called you. Let's have a good look at you."

Alys held the animal away from her for a moment, liking the way it curled itself around her hands. "From the Holy Lands, are you? A girl," she mused, tucking the animal back into her body when it leaned that way. And perhaps because of her melancholy, Alys called to mind a sad romance from Persia itself, overheard while listening outside the soldiers' garrison.

"How do you fancy 'Layla'?" Alys asked the monkey, feeling very much like old Graves who only ever spoke in questions. The monkey didn't try to bite her, so she took that as agreement. "Very well, then. You shall hereby be known as Layla. A fine choice, and my congratulations to you."

That important detail resolved, Alys now appraised the

ring of stones tossed seemingly haphazardly around her, trying to keep her mind off of the incessant shivering of her body. Still no heavenly glow from any of the towering gray pillars, no ethereal music, no shimmering voice of wisdom calling to her through the ages, heralding the arrival of her true love.

The fabled Foxe Ring was no magic place, after all. Yet another thing Sybilla had been right about. Alys had been in the very center of the frigid circle for ages it seemed, the moon lighting her like a beacon, and the only visitor she'd received was some sort of nocturnal animal scurrying out of sight in the ruined keep's interior.

It seemed everyone in the land had either tried the Foxe Ring, or knew someone who'd used it, as a last desperate act to find love, and all the stories had told of its wise success. Men and women, brought together alone within the circle of standing stones upon a full moon were fated for a lifetime of love together. So respected was the belief that many couples who met in the Foxe Ring never even bothered with an official ceremony. They entered the ring alone, but they departed a couple, for the rest of their lives and even into eternity, if the tales were to be believed fully. The ring had brought her own mother and father together, and so Alys did believe, God help her foolish, girlish heart.

But for Alys, it was a failure. Or perhaps 'twas she who had failed. Perhaps the stones felt her unworthy of a magical, forever union. Or perhaps Clement Cobb and old Lord John Hart were simply the only two remaining eligible men in the whole of England. Any matter, Alys couldn't so much as slink back to Fallstowe to crawl into her own bed at this hour—she'd be forced to beat at the gates for someone to admit her, and her pride could not tolerate another stiff blow this night. Better to sneak back in with the sun, and simply avoid meeting with her future husband for as long as Sybilla would allow.

"Alys Cobb, Lady of Blodshire," she said aloud, and then pretended a retching sound. "Horrid."

Alys reached for her sack with one hand and plumped the contents. Then she lay down on her side once more, snuggling Layla into her midsection and cushioning the monkey with her arms. She pulled her cloak around them both, flicked up her hood with one finger, and then rubbed her face against Layla's soft hair. Her nose was numb. She closed her eyes lest they begin to leak once more.

There was a girl sleeping inside the ruin.

A golden haired girl, lit up with moonlight until it seemed to Piers that she glowed. Asleep on a cold slab of rock as if it was her royal fairy bed, her hood shielding all but a sliver of her creamy face and a single, thick lock of yellow hair trapped beneath her cheekbone.

He closed his eyes tightly, took a deep breath, and then looked again.

He blew out his breath in a weak huff. She was still there.

Piers's eyes narrowed and he quickly looked around the standing stones and over both shoulders, even spinning around to take on any would-be attackers. He had gained enough experience in brawling for coin that his instincts for ambush were sharper than most men's. Piers knew there was almost no level too low for an opponent to sink to when a heavy purse was the wager.

But no, he was alone, standing just outside the ring, looking at the enchanting golden girl asleep on the stone slab.

Perhaps the final blow from Bevan had rattled Piers's brains irreversibly—by all that was holy, his head still hurt like the very devil, the healing wounds itching on his butchered scalp. There could be little other explanation for the girl's presence save madness. Certainly she wasn't a fairy—there couldn't be fucking fairies on Fallstowe lands. That was absurd. And he couldn't see any wings, any matter.

Piers recognized that he was debating the existence of a mythical woman-creature in an unlikely area of England, as if there were other regions more hospitable for the fey. This disturbed him enough so that he squared his shoulders and stepped into the ring fully, determined to either discover the woman's origin, or jump entirely over the farthest edge of insanity.

The atmosphere within the standing stones seemed oddly thick, and Piers didn't think it was his imagination. Warmer here, too, although the fallen and standing stones—most two yards wide and twice that tall—were no shelter from the now burst open, sparkling sky. Piers hadn't noticed the clouds disappearing, but now the moonlight seemed to rival the very sun in its brightness. He reached up to the cowled neck of his borrowed monk's robe and pulled it away from his skin. He was starting to sweat.

"Ho there," he called out, dismayed at the timid whisper that barely stirred the air in front of his face.

Her arms, crossed in front of her bosom and covered by her cloak, shifted.

Piers moved slowly to the stone slab, until he stood over the woman. She seemed very small to Piers. Curled on her side, the toes of her dainty slippers peeked out from beneath the hem of her fur-lined cloak, and he fancied he could scoop her up from the slab with one swipe of his arm. The tips of her profile—browbone, nose, lips, chin—seemed like polished ivory in the moonlight, and her dark lashes rested on her cheeks like the smallest black under feathers of a tiny bird. He shrugged out of his pack and let it slide soundlessly to the ground.

"Hello?" he called again, and this time, he reached out one hand. He intended to pull back her hood and experience her full beauty—imagined or nay—at once.

A blur of movement stopped his heart, and before he could jerk his arm away, the first two fingers of Piers's left hand were laid open by very small, very sharp teeth.

As he roared and began to fight off the thing that was attacking him, Piers no longer thought he was insane.

But he did think it somewhat ironic that he was wearing monk's clothing while in a battle with the devil.

Alys came fully awake at the shout that seemed like thunder in the heretofore stillness of the Foxe Ring. Layla had clawed from her embrace and Alys could no longer feel her small warmth, although she could most certainly hear the monkey's wild shrieks. She sprung upright on the slab.

Someone was trying to abduct the monkey she had rightfully stolen!

"Layla!" she cried, and then immediately scrambled down from the stone to launch herself at the dark, hooded mass of a creature that was presently trying to flog Layla with a forearm. "Let her go, you beast!"

"Get it off me!" the hooded figure boomed. "It's biting my fucking fingers off!"

"Stop hitting her! *Let go!*"

"*I'm not holding it!*"

"Layla! *Ow!* That was *me,* you bastard!"

At last Alys managed to work an arm between the monkey and the hooded man, and wrench Layla away from the cloaked villain. She marveled at the amount of effort it took to remove such a relatively small animal.

"My goodness, Layla," Alys gasped, bending over at the waist to brace her hands on her knees now that Layla had taken up watch from her shoulder once more to chatter angrily at the man. "You're a strong girl, aren't you?"

"Son of a *bitch*!" the man hissed, grasping his left wrist tightly in his right hand. His cloaked head came up, and although Alys could not see his face clearly in the shadows of his hood, she could imagine his ugly, furious countenance. "I'll have that beast's hide!"

Alys straightened and knew a moment of unease. He was a large man, and obviously quite angry at the injuries Layla had visited upon him. There was no one around the old ruin as far as the eye could see. Who knew what he was capable of? Although he was dressed in the garb of a pious man, his vulgar language quickly gave truth to the fact that he was almost certainly common. Cecily would faint into a puddle at the very thought of the phrases issuing from such holy vestments.

"She was only protecting me," Alys said, lifting her chin and striving for an air of superiority. "What business have you sneaking up upon a woman whilst she sleeps and molesting her?"

"Moles—" the man broke off. "Just what is a young girl doing about a desolate ruin in the dead of night with only a monkey for protection?"

His summation of her as a young girl stung Alys's already battered pride so that her courage experienced a rebirth. "That is absolutely none of your affair. Besides, this is Fallstowe land, and as I am none other than Lady

Alys Foxe, I go where I please. 'Tis *you* who are the trespasser. Layla has gifted you with but a sampling of the punishment you shall receive once my sisters hear of your assault."

The hooded figure snickered. "Oh, so I am to fear your *sisters* now, am I?" His mirth grew into a round laugh. He looked down at his injured fingers and flung blood away. "I cow to no *lady*." He said the word as if it were a foul thing.

Alys frowned at being laughed at. "You very obviously have never met Sybilla, then. She is completely vicious, I assure you."

"I have heard of Sybilla Foxe," the man acquiesced. "And I am most familiar with vicious women. But I can assure *you* that I have already met the worst of the lot, so forgive me if I do not quake and tremble." He paused. "What are you doing out here alone? 'Tis unsafe for a girl, even if on your own lands. After all, I came upon you, and there would be no help for you should I have wicked intentions. A monkey is only so much against a blade and a quick hand."

"Well, she's already taken care of one of your quick hands. And I am not a girl. I'm ten and eight."

"Oh, well then, my apologies, matron." His hood turned slightly as if he looked at the stone slab. "I see you have your bags packed. Running away from vicious Sybilla, were you?"

Alys felt her face heat in the cool moonlight. Observed by an outsider, her actions did seem that of a young girl rather than a grown woman. But he simply didn't know how desperate she had been to leave Fallstowe for the Foxe Ring. And now Sybilla was going to see her married to *Clement Cobb* because the old legend had turned out to be nothing more than—

"Oh, my God," Alys breathed, realizing that her impossible wish had come true and she hadn't even noticed it, so busy had she been arguing with the man. "Take down your hood."

The cloaked figure drew back slightly. "Why?"

"Because"—Alys licked her cold, numb lips—"because I want to see your face." Her heart pounded and she forced a nervous laugh. "You've seen mine after all. And I've only just realized what is happening."

"I don't see what that has to do with anything, but I'd rather not. I'm not very pretty of late."

"Please," Alys breathed. "We are in the Foxe Ring, at the full moon. We will both remember this moment for the rest of our lives."

He stood silent for a moment, as if unsure. The silly man—he was shy! How perfect!

He tried to back away at the last moment, but Alys took him by surprise when her arm shot out and shoved back his hood. He cried out indignantly.

The moonlight hit his face and Alys gasped. He looked like he had been very recently run over with a cart. His skin was pale around fading bruises ringing bloodshot eyes, a cut over one eyebrow healing, but still scabbed and red. His lips had been split by a heavy blow, their scars visible even within the tangle of uneven beard. His hair was of a darker shade, although in the night it was hard to tell the exact hue, but the cut of it was in no recognizable fashion: long in spots, hanging down to his shoulders, and missing in other patches, as if hacked off in great chunks.

He looked quite mad, Alys had to admit, and more than a little unkempt. Perhaps he was even a bandit, wearing monk's clothing as his disguise. But she quickly dismissed these trivialities. After all, a mad, disheveled outlaw was better than Clement Cobb. And now Sybilla would be forced to keep her word.

"What happened to you?" Alys asked, trying to pull her mouth out of the grimace she knew had to be apparent.

"Whatever do you mean?" the man replied with a snide lift of his mouth.

To her own surprise, Alys giggled. And the man's sneer faded into something akin to a grin. Still perched on Alys's shoulder, Layla clapped her hands. The Foxe Ring at last felt like the magical place it was rumored to be.

"You didn't tell me your name," Alys pointed out.

"Didn't I?" the man taunted. Then he paused, looking at her contemplatively for a moment. "Piers, and that's all you need know. I was going to shelter here for the night, but as it is obviously already occupied . . ." He shrugged, bent to pick up the pack at his feet and then nodded his head toward her courteously. "I would not risk us being found together. 'Twould ruin you and possibly put me in great danger."

Alys was intrigued. "Danger? Are you fleeing from someone?"

"More like fleeing *to* someone." He shrugged into the pack. "Good luck with your sister, Lady Alys." He only glared at Layla and then turned as if to leave.

"Wait!" Alys called, reaching out her hand and taking a step toward him. "Uh . . . Piers! Where are you going?"

"Not your concern," he said over his shoulder.

"It is my concern. You can't go without me."

Now he turned toward her once more. "I can't go without you?"

"Of course not," Alys scoffed. "It's fate!"

"Fate," he repeated flatly.

Alys rolled her eyes and sighed. "We're in the Foxe Ring. At a full moon . . . ?"

"And . . . ?"

She growled in frustration. 'Twas as if he didn't know the legend of the ruin! Or he was being deliberately obtuse. Perhaps he thought she was the one who was unlearned of the old tales. "*And,* you can't just leave me here now!"

"Why the bloody hell not?"

Alys beamed at him, happy to speak the miracle aloud. "Because, silly—we're *married*."

Chapter 3

Piers shook his head as if perhaps the motion might clear it, for surely the girl had not just said that they were married.

Had she?

He squinted and leaned toward her slightly, pointing to his ear. "My apologies, but could you say again? I've just recently taken a sharp blow to the head. Several blows, actually."

The little golden-haired thing leaned in, giggling, her monkey sitting surely on her shoulder. "*We're married.* You know"—she spread her arms and looked around the circle of stones briefly—"here in the Foxe Ring."

Piers stood upright once more, completely perplexed. "As I understood the situation, you were cross with me for trespassing on your family's lands and nearly getting my fingers bitten off by your ridiculous animal."

"I was waiting for you, Piers," Alys said, her face softening in a manner that caused an uncomfortable sensation in Piers's gut. "Only I didn't know 'twas you, of course. It could have been anyone, any man in the whole of the land, but"—she took a deep breath and let it out happily around her bright smile—"it's *you*."

Then Piers felt his eyes narrow. Surely this could not be a trap laid by Bevan and Judith Angwedd. Regardless, he would not take any chances.

"You obviously have me confused with someone else," he said to the still-smiling girl. "Good . . . er, night, Lady Alys."

"Wait!" she called to him again, but this time, Piers kept walking, out of the ring and down the opposite side of the hill to the south east. He had no time to decipher the riddles of a female just out of the nursery. She was obviously anathema to her family, having been sent off to the old ruin in the middle of the night alone. Perhaps they *wanted* someone to abscond with her, and take the brat off their hands. Well, it would not be Piers.

Christ! He was exhausted enough to drop, but now it looked as if his rest was yet miles away. He was not relishing sleeping in an open forest again.

"Would you *wait*?"

He glanced over his shoulder and was surprised to see the girl running to catch up with him, dragging her sack behind her with one hand and holding on to her monkey with the other. Her fine, long cloak flapped around her legs. Clearly, she was not dressed for foot travel.

"Go back to the ruin and wait for morning, Lady Alys," he commanded, never slowing his pace. "I'll not wait for you, and should you become disoriented and lose your way, you'll die in the open alone."

"Won't you at least accompany me back to Fallstowe?" she gasped exasperatedly.

"No." Absolutely not. As he had already told the girl, he had heard tales of the powerful Sybilla Foxe. And he also knew of her cat and mouse with King Edward. The lady would demand his name and then likely imprison him as a kidnapper and defiler of women. Or mayhap she would listen to his tale and then turn him over to Judith Angwedd. Any matter, Piers doubted Sybilla Foxe would want the slightest connection with a man who had serious business with the monarch sniffing around Fallstowe's walls, looking for a chink in which to topple the woman's hold on her family's demesne.

Piers had enough problems of his own to deal with. He only needed to get to London, as quickly as he could, and alone.

"I'll not go back!" she called the warning to him while still struggling to keep pace. "You can't leave me—I'm your *wife*!"

Piers didn't answer her, only kept walking. His head started to pound again. She was clearly unstable. If she continued to follow him, she would be parallel to Fallstowe again within the hour. Having likely fallen far enough behind as to become frightened by that time—not to mention cold and tired—she would see her family home and give up.

Good-bye, Alys Foxe. And good riddance.

The forest was dangerously bright when Piers found a suitable den in which to sleep the majority of the daylight away. In the juncture of two massive, fallen trees, a dam of old pine branches and dead leaves had made a natural lean-to and Piers threw his pack into the fortuitous shelter with a sigh. He would not risk even a small fire now.

He stretched his arms above his head, hearing every muscle in his body moan. He would climb into the den that looked just big enough to accommodate his body, eat some of the old bread and the last bit of the cold, salted fish from his pack, and then gratefully fall into unconsciousness.

At least he had shaken silly little Alys Foxe. She had disappeared from Piers's rear horizon along with Fall-stowe's dark, foggy silhouette, and he was relieved that he would not have to contend with her disjointed ramblings about the two of them being married.

Piers shook his head in disbelief as he crouched down to inspect the wounds received by the unusual Layla. The bites weren't as deep as he'd first feared, although they throbbed like black hell. The cuts were already scabbed over within rings of vivid bruises, and so he simply wrapped them tightly in some of the bandages given to him by the monk.

Married. Lady Alys Foxe, married to Piers Mallory, common dairy master and notorious bastard son of the lord of Gillwick Manor. If little Alys had only known what a close call she'd had, she'd likely have wet her underdress. And he was certain Lady Sybilla would not have been amused in the least.

Married! Ha!

No one would marry you save a goatherd, or mayhap one of the goats. Crude, penniless bastard.

So now he was to contend with the voices in his head alone, but at least with them Piers felt no compulsion to answer. He heaved a great sigh as he rocked from his heels to his backside, drawing up his knees and pulling his pack toward him, rifling through it for his sustenance.

Warin was to have you drowned upon your birth, but his heart had been softened by our little Bevan. He chose to simply forget all about you! Isn't that amusing? You should thank my son for saving your life!

Even though Piers was relatively certain that his father'd had no such malicious intentions toward him after his birth, it was true that Warin Mallory had largely forgotten his second son was alive. Piers's mother had died when he was only six, and Warin had the decency to keep him in the manor's dairy. Now he was master of that enterprise, but he knew it was not a courtesy stemming from the circumstances of his birth. He was simply the best at what he did, and even cruel Judith Angwedd had made begrudging mention of his talent.

"Peasant blood will tell," she'd sneered.

He could still remember that first, traumatic year without his mother, leaning his face against the warm side-belly of a cow and sobbing soundlessly while he milked. Sleeping with the other village orphans in the lofts of the stables, learning to fight for what was his out of necessity, and then later, for coin. There had been no one to protect him after his mother was dead, and there was no one to aid him now.

He choked down the last bite of the day's ration of bread—the stuff was like eating wet wool—and took a swig of wine from his jug. He sighed and corked the jug, replacing it in his pack and shoving the bag deep into the tree den. At least now he could escape into sleep.

He had just crawled into his makeshift bed when he heard a horrendous crashing through the underbrush of the forest. Satisfied that his hiding place would not be discovered by any happening by on the road just beyond the tree line, Piers squirmed farther back into the shadows and closed his eyes.

He heard a squealing chattering, and more rustling of leaves.

Likely just some forest creature, out to break the fast, he told himself and squeezed his eyes shut more tightly.

"Piers! Piers, where are you? Do you see him, Layla? Neither do I. Pie—eers!"

His eyes snapped open. *Surely not.*

"Piers, I'm tired and I'm cold and I'm frightened."

Piers frowned. She did sound rather fearful.

"Where are you, dammit?"

Or perhaps she wasn't.

He couldn't let her wander farther into the woods to die. Well, no, he *could*, but then he would be no better than Judith Angwedd. He would point her back toward Fallstowe, grudgingly give her a bit of his dear supply of bread and wine, and send her on her way. 'Twas full daylight now, and she would be on Foxe lands within the hour. Two, at most, should she wander a bit from the straightaway.

He was just about to undertake the massive task of moving his exhausted body when the monkey dashed into his den, scrambling over him to sit on his bicep, and then screaming like the devil, bouncing up and down and flailing at him with her long, surprisingly powerful arms.

Piers shouted with surprise and, yes, a bit of fear—he didn't want the fucking thing to bite him again. He threw the beast out of his den with a swipe of his arm that sent the monkey rolling with an outraged shriek and then fought his own way out of the shelter. Better to face the fiery little thing out in the open.

The monkey, as well.

When Alys saw Layla streak from beneath the fallen trees, chattering indignantly, she knew her wayward husband was found. She dropped her sack, crossed her arms over her chest, and tapped her foot, waiting for him to emerge from behind his curtain of curses.

He was still in his monk's robe, but as he gained his feet in a cloud of crumbling leaves, twigs, and colorful phrases, Alys noticed that he seemed much larger in the brightness of day. And the dappled sunlight was not kind to his face, bringing out in sharp relief his injuries against his obvious fatigue. His hair was a worse disaster than she'd been able to glimpse in the moonlight—as if he'd fallen into a den of blade wielding badgers. She thought he was older than she'd originally guessed—possibly thirty. And while perhaps in other circumstances he could have been described as pleasant looking, to Alys he looked dirty and hairy and hardened and bitter. And quite possibly very angry.

But no matter for that—so was Alys.

"You mean-hearted bastard!" she said to him before he could have chance to speak. Layla ducked her small head under Alys's veil and into her neck. "I could have been killed following you like that!"

"I know!" Piers shouted. "That's why I told you to stay behind!"

"How could I stay behind not knowing where my husband was going, or when he would be back for me?"

"I *wouldn't* have been back for you," Piers growled.

"See? And I don't know where our lands are, or even my family name!"

"Your name is *Alys Foxe*," he said very slowly and distinctly, as if speaking to someone not in possession of their right mind. "And I have no lands." He paused and then muttered, "Yet."

"No lands? But"—she broke off, frowned, and then realized what he was saying—"I've married a commoner?" Alys howled with laughter and clapped her hands, causing Layla to clutch at her head to keep from being toppled to the ground. "Sybilla will be completely furious!"

"I fail to see why marriage to a commoner would

please you," Piers said, and then he shook his head and stuttered. "We're not married!"

Alys rolled her eyes and sat down, still chuckling. Oh, Sybilla would just turn *blue*!

"We *are* married. Don't pretend you don't know the legend of the ring—everyone in the whole of England knows it! Do you have anything to eat?"

"I do doubt everyone knows it," Piers sneered. "And didn't you pack food in your run-away-from-home-sack?"

Alys wrinkled her nose and felt her cheeks tingle. "Well yes, some biscuits and honey with a bit of milk in a jug. And some chicken and ham. And two boiled eggs. But I've already eaten them."

He stared at her, a hint of concern creasing his brow. He didn't look quite as dreadful when he wasn't shouting or cursing. "How long were you at the ruin?"

"I don't know, exactly." His frown increased while Alys tried to think. "Ah, 'twas most likely near midnight when I arrived."

Piers blinked. "Midnight. Of . . . *last night*?"

"Yes, that's right."

"And you ate everything before I arrived?"

Alys felt her cheeks glowing now. "I was arguing with Sybilla and missed my supper. And I didn't eat *everything*, as you so crudely put it—I have some dried figs and a pomegranate left."

"A *pomegranate*?"

Why did it seem like he was mocking her? "Yes. I'm saving it for Layla. I've read that monkeys prefer fruit."

"You've read that—" He broke off, seeming too furious to form words. He closed his eyes, bowed his head, and Alys could see his nostrils flaring. In the pose he almost looked like a monk at prayer.

Perhaps a monk with a mangy dog on his head.

After several moments he looked at her once more, having seemingly regained his composure. "It is winter in England, Lady Alys. You and I are on the cusp of a barren forest where, despite the tales of magical wood people who roam through it unseen, survival is not only difficult, 'tis unlikely. You have followed me against my advice and now expect me to care for you because you have no rations, save a few pieces of exotic fruit that likely cost more than what I see in a year, and which you are saving for a monkey."

"Well, I'm sorry you were so poorly compensated at your work, but she has to eat, Piers."

"I'll eat her *and* her fucking pomegranate!"

He looked so outraged that Alys couldn't help but laugh, especially since Layla took that moment to voice a timid and worried-sounding yip. Perhaps it was only fatigue, but she was finding him to be quite witty when he was angry. She laughed and laughed until tears rolled down her cheeks.

"'Twould be . . . only fair . . . since"—Alys gasped around her peals—"she's already . . . had a taste of *you!*"

To her surprise, Piers started to chuckle. In a moment, they were both grabbing their stomachs and wiping at their eyes. Layla scrambled down from Alys's shoulder and removed herself to the sanity of the fallen trees, wringing her hands and chattering nervously. It was several moments before their chuckles dwindled, and Alys sighed contentedly, pleased at how much better she felt. Besides being hungry, of course. But she daren't bring up that subject again to her prickly husband so soon.

"So, do we sleep now?" she asked, pleasantly, she thought.

He shook his head. "I sleep. You walk." He pointed a

long arm toward the way she'd come. "That direction. 'Tis unsafe for you here."

"Why is it unsafe? I daresay I'm much less likely to have misfortune befall me while I'm under your protection than if I should be traversing the countryside alone."

He again shook his head, more emphatically this time and with a pained-looking grimace, as if the mangy dog on his head was beset by fleas. "*No*. See you the scars I bear? They were given to me by a man who meant to see me dead. If he is not already looking for me, he shall be soon enough. 'Tis why I travel at night. Alone," he added with a stern frown.

"My, that *does* sound dangerous. Where are you going?"

"That is not your concern."

"As your wife, I think—"

"You are not my wife!" Alys jumped at the ferocity of his words. "You are a spoiled little girl who has had a row with her sister and thinks to spite her by running away."

"I am not spoiled," Alys said, completely offended. "And I am not a girl."

"Look at you," Piers demanded, gesturing to where she sat in her puddle of skirt and cloak. "Your gown is fit for royalty—what is it? Perse?"

Alys was too shocked to answer. Any matter, he continued.

"That looks to be sable inside your cloak. You've run away from grand Fallstowe Castle in your jeweled headdress with your exotic pet and an embroidered silk bag, likely because your sister wouldn't let you have a new pony or some other nonsense. You've convinced yourself that you're married to me, a commoner who doesn't have two coins to rub together, and you're *happy* about that because it will perturb your sister. You would thoughtlessly risk a vast fortune such is your family's out of childish, petulant spite. You *are* a foolish *girl*, and I take no responsibility for your asinine judgment, or lack thereof."

Alys had been on the receiving end of stinging dressing-downs since her mother had died, so Piers's lecture should not have fazed her. But it did. Here he was, a veritable stranger, and yet he had used many of the same words her sister had. Spoiled. Childish. Foolish. Somehow, the terms stung more coming from this man than they ever had flicked from Sybilla's cool tongue.

"I am only dressed this way because Sybilla and I had a falling-out during the winter feast. I didn't take time to change. I don't wear clothing like this all the time—I even brought my everyday gown with me."

"Oh, your *everyday* gown! What is it made of? Gold?"

"No, it's woolen," she said calmly. "And I didn't leave Fallstowe because I was denied a pony, you heartless ass. Sybilla is to see me married to the Lord of Blodshire in thirty days because I would not cow to her unreasonable demands. If anyone acted out of spite, 'twas her."

"I know of Blodshire. 'Twould be a noble enough match for you, a younger sister. Why would you take such a pairing as spiteful?"

Alys blinked. "Have you *met* Clement Cobb?"

"I've not had the pleasure of Clement's acquaintance in some years, but I do know of his mother. Nasty old bitch."

"Isn't she?"

"Indeed."

She shrugged. "Well, at least we have something in common. Sybilla only did it because I refused to bow and scrape to her in front of our guests. Because I would not stand to be insulted by Clement's awful mother. Because I would not allow Etheldred to further abuse poor Layla.

And because I would not apologize for speaking the truth. So if that is childish, then I suppose I am."

"You're certainly headstrong. And yes, it likely is childish."

"Go to hell, Piers Whatever-your-name-is."

There was pity in his eyes. "Go back to Fallstowe, Alys Foxe."

"I won't. Not today," Alys hurried when Piers lowered his brow. "I can't face Sybilla and what she's done today. I'm too weary, by far. I must think of some way to change her mind before I confront her."

"As you wish, but find somewhere else to think, eh?"

"You really intend to send me off alone, don't you?"

"Yes." He put his hands on his hips and stared at her. After a long moment, through which Alys was determined to hold his gaze, he cursed softly and dropped his eyes. "Fine, dammit. You may rest here for the day."

Alys smiled triumphantly.

"But don't think for one moment that this"—he waggled a finger between them—"is to continue beyond the time it takes for the sun to set over yonder hills. I am no child's nurse."

Alys raised her eyebrows. "And I am no child."

"Well, that is debatable, isn't it?"

"Not at all. Very well then, crawl back inside your hole and get your own rest. You look as though death wouldn't have you—I do hope that's due to your fatigue and injuries, and not how you look all the time."

"You shan't have to worry about that though, shall you?"

Alys shrugged and gestured to the monkey, who was picking beneath the peeling bark of one of the trees. "Layla and I shall fare quite well with my cloak to shelter us." She couldn't help but add, "'Tis quite warm—lined with sable, you know."

Piers shook his head, letting her playful goad pass ignored. "No, you take the lean-to. If your hair or gown should peek out, you'd be a banner to any passers-by. Your very presence here is a grave liability to me, Alys."

"Oh, come now," she scoffed with a smile as she passed him. "It can't all be so dire. Who would care so much to see a simple commoner such as yourself dead?"

Chapter 4

"He's not dead."

It was quite obvious to Judith Angwedd Mallory, Lady of Gillwick, that the peasant was petrified of delivering this piece of news to her. And if 'twas true, then right he was to be frightened.

Judith Angwedd did not adhere to the tradition of sparing the messenger.

She calmly leaned back in her chair at the dining table, her chalice still in her hand. There was no need to become alarmed as of yet. She dismissed the only servant from the room with a practiced wave of her other hand, leaving her and the messenger alone save for the new "steward" who stood behind her. Judith Angwedd had only hired the enormous man with the shaved head two days ago, when he'd come 'round the manor looking for work. He had no experience running a hold—she suspected he was some sort of criminal by the old and multitudinous array of scars across his wide back, but Judith Angwedd was confident she could train him properly in her preferences for running Gillwick. Especially since the majority of his duties would take place in her bed.

She asked the messenger, "How can you be certain he is not dead?"

"The body was gone," the man began in a stutter, his eyes seemingly unable to meet his mistress's.

"It's been several days. Perhaps 'twas washed away by the river," she suggested. "Or carried off by animals."

It looked as though it pained the man to shake his head. "No, milady. When I couldn't find him, I went 'round to the abbey, making as if he was a dear friend o' mine."

Judith Angwedd ran her tongue along the front of her teeth behind her lips, swallowed. "And?" she queried quietly.

"They'd had him. The monks," the messenger clarified. "One of 'em found a man calling himself Piers by the river and took him in to nurse him."

Judith Angwedd took a deep breath, but so slowly that her chest didn't seem to move. It was important to stay calm. "He is no longer at the abbey?"

"No, milady. He left only yester morn."

She rolled her lips inward, stretched her cheek with her tongue. "I see. Do they know we seek him?"

The man shook his head rapidly. "I give 'em a false name, milady. Said him and me was just travelin' companions what had been separated."

"Wise," she praised coolly and nodded once. She almost smiled when she saw the messenger visibly relax. "No one will be able to trace you to Gillwick Manor—or to Bevan or me."

"That's right, milady. I done everything just like you said."

Judith Angwedd's nostrils flared, and she nearly lost her composure. If the man had done as she'd commanded, her dead husband's bastard would be in pieces, burning on a pyre at this moment, instead of running loose about the land, likely in a straight line to the king. But she smoothed her tongue along her fine teeth again, and it calmed her enough to summon a hint of a smile for the doomed man.

"Of course you did. Well done. *Well done,*" she praised.

"What shall I do now, milady?" the man asked, wringing his cap all the harder, obviously anxious to please her.

"You have done quite enough," Judith Angwedd assured him. "You are dismissed. Phineas will meet you at the road with your payment."

"Of course, milady." The man began backing away, bowing the entire time. "Thank you."

When he was gone, Judith Angwedd turned her face slightly to speak to the fierce looking man still standing behind her chair. "Send for Bevan right away, Phineas. He must come no matter how drunk he is. Mayhap the bastard Piers is still bothered enough from his wounds that we might gain him, but if not, we shall inquire of the holds from here to London to see if any might have given him refuge. He will not hide from me, the cowardly filth."

The man bowed.

"And Phineas?"

"Yes, my lady?"

"That messenger who was just here . . ."

There was only the briefest pause. "You mean the thief, my lady?"

"Yes, Phineas. That is exactly who I mean. That man was most certainly a thief." She held her chalice up near her ear and in a moment it was taken from her hand. "He has stolen my favorite cup."

"I know how to handle thieves, my lady. Think upon it no more."

Judith Angwedd listened to Phineas's hollow footsteps as he left the room, and she waited for her son.

* * *

Sybilla Foxe watched from the comfort of her bed as the man dressed himself. She liked the way the long, thick muscles to either side of his spine swelled and bunched as he bent over to pull up his pants. The morning sunlight streaming through the bank of windows in her bedchamber lit him afire—his dark hair, his hollowed cheeks. Lord Bellecote was a beautiful specimen of a man, and he had proven himself to be an enjoyable and adventurous lover. August had become a welcome friend and confidant, and so Sybilla was glad that she had put off sleeping with him these many months—the anticipation had been quite delicious—but at the same time, she was feeling a bit melancholy now before he left her.

She would never have the pleasure of him in this capacity again. By her own edict, true, but that was the way things were.

He was lacing up his blouse now, his tunic folded in half over one thick forearm, and smiling at her. She let herself smile back, if only to enjoy these last moments, and to perhaps pretend that there was a chance she and August Bellecote would meet under these circumstances again. Sybilla's dark hair was undone over her shoulders, and she could still catch a whiff of the fresh cologne the maid had dressed her with before the feast last night. The silk pillows beneath her bare back were warm and smooth and deep, her coverlet weighty and smelling of sunshine. Beyond the stone walls of her chamber, all of Fallstowe waited for her to emerge from her rooms and direct the day. Sybilla should have felt like royalty. Instead, she felt damned and burdened.

She would have to face Alys today. Her youngest sister, still so naïve and fiery in her youth, who resented Sybilla for taking their mother's place. Headstrong, reckless Alys, whom Sybilla was only trying so desperately to protect before time ran out for all of them.

Lord Bellecote picked up his boots with one hand and strolled toward the bed, that sleepy, sexy smile still on his sculpted lips. His lashes were so dark, his eyes seemed to be lined with kohl. He sat on the edge of the bed to don his footwear, causing Sybilla's hip to roll toward him and her coverlet to threaten to slide from her breasts. She clutched at it and covered herself once more.

"No point in being shy now, is there?" August teased, lacing his boots with firm pulls and jerks.

"Not shy, only chilled," Sybilla said.

"Hmm. Well"—he dropped his booted foot to the floor and turned to lean over her, bringing his face to her neck—"shall I warm you up a bit before I go?"

Sybilla placed a palm against his chest and turned her face away. "I have many duties to attend to this day, August. The remainder of my guests depart, and I must see to my sister."

"The nun or the heathen?" he asked jokingly.

Sybilla's small smile dropped from her face and she pushed at him more firmly. "I don't believe either are any of those things."

"Sybilla, I tease you," August cajoled. He raised a hand as if to caress her cheek, but she moved her face away from his reach. "I'm sorry. Let's not quarrel."

"We're not quarrelling," she replied coolly. To quarrel with a man would imply that Sybilla held passionate feelings for him, and she could not afford that, not even with a man such as August Bellecote.

"Good," he said emphatically, although his lowered brow betrayed his doubt in her sincerity. "Good, for I would not want this beginning to be marred by resentfulness over some silly thing I said in jest."

This beginning. Sybilla would have laughed were the whole thing not so very sad.

"Shall I call on you tomorrow?" he continued. "After your guests are departed and Fallstowe is once more at peace?"

At that she did laugh. "Fallstowe is never at peace, August. But no, my schedule is quite full for the next month."

His frown deepened on his handsome face. "The next month? Surely you cannot expect me to wait that long to see you."

And off we go, thought Sybilla. "There is much to do before Alys's wedding. I do hope you and Oliver will come."

August laughed. "My brother would not miss a chance at a hall populated by women whose heads are full of domestic notions. He feels it makes them romantic and reckless, therefore bettering his chances of a conquest. He was sorely put out at missing the feast due to the unfavorable winds that kept him abroad."

"I shall look forward to seeing him—and you—in one month, then," Sybilla said.

At her words, her meaning quite clear, August sat up fully, his wrists resting on his lap. His expression was almost incredulous.

"So that's it, eh? I am no better than the others?"

Sybilla turned her face away, so as not to have to meet his eyes.

"I thought perhaps you waited so long because we would be—"

"Different?" Sybilla supplied, looking at him now. He would become angry now, and Sybilla could accept anger. "You thought that one night with you would cause me to fall helplessly in love with you? That we would be married and have children and live out our joined lives in incomparable bliss?" Sybilla forced a laugh. "'Twas good, August, but not that good."

His chiseled face ruddied and he stood from the bed. "You care for me not at all beyond one night of sex, is that what you're saying?"

"I'm sorry if you thought it to be more. We are still friends, of course."

"I don't believe you," he said quietly. "In fact, Sybilla Foxe, I think you're lying through your teeth."

Her eyes flew to his, and she could feel the shivery panic in her belly. God, what she would give to have a man like August Bellecote at her side permanently.

But she was spared from what he was to say next by an insistent rapping on her chamber door. That was no servant's polite query.

"Sybilla! Are you awake?"

'Twas Cecily.

"You should go, August." She would not look at him again. "Yes, Cee."

Her chamber door opened and her younger sister rushed into the room with a demure swish of drab skirt. As soon as Cecily saw August Bellecote standing at the bedside, she gasped and brought a hand to her eyes.

"Oh my! I am sorry." Cecily turned bright red and her eyes were directed to the rug under the bed. "Sybilla, why didn't you tell me you weren't alone?"

"He's not naked, Cee. And you didn't ask if I was alone, only if I was awake. It's alright—Lord Bellecote was just leaving."

"Lady Cecily, lovely to see you again." August bowed toward her sister.

"Lord Bellecote. Er . . . ah, good morning," Cecily stammered.

August turned back to Sybilla. "I will be back, Sybilla."

Sybilla met his eyes then, although she had been determined not to. It was the only way. "Don't bother," she said flatly and succinctly.

He stared at her for a long moment and then bowed to Cecily. "Good day." Then he stormed through the still-open chamber door, slamming it closed after him.

Cecily jumped at the crash.

Sybilla only sighed. Then she turned to Cecily. "What is it, Cee?"

"Alys isn't in her rooms. It doesn't look as though she's slept there, either. You don't think she actually went to the ring, do you?"

"Oh, probably." Sybilla threw the covers back and lighted from the bed nude, crossing the floor to her wardrobe. "Where else would she be?"

"I'll send a rider to fetch her," Cecily said and then turned to go.

"No." Sybilla's command stopped her sister.

"No? Sybilla, 'tis December. She'll freeze. Or starve!"

"Oh, Cee, she will not. If she gets hungry enough or cold enough, she'll come home. And I'll wager that when she does, Blodshire's comfortable manor will have begun to appeal to her. Let her teach herself a lesson for once. I tire of it."

"That's mean hearted, Sybilla."

"It is not. It's quite fair, and Alys needs learn that not everything goes according to her wishes. This match is the best thing for her. You know it as well as I."

"I do agree that Alys needs . . . handling, but . . ." Cecily bit her lip for a moment. "Even now, Etheldred Cobb is near to shouting down the hall because her future daughter-in-law has insulted her by not joining her and Clement for breakfast. I do believe the old woman wants to show off her son's prize. God forgive me for being malicious, but that woman tries my charity, Sybilla! She or Alys will kill the other one inside of a fortnight."

"They'll come to an agreement, I'm sure," Sybilla said over her shoulder as she searched through her clothes for a robe.

"What should I tell Lady Blodshire, then? She's said she won't go home until she sees Alys. Clement, too, but for entirely different reasons, I suspect. And I have to be at chapel again in a half hour, so I can't entertain them. I'm certain with as engaged as you have been entertaining our guests that you have simply forgotten that it is the Sabbath."

Another rap at her door. "Your tea, my lady."

"I'll get it." Cecily turned to the door and admitted Sybilla's personal maids. There were three. One carried the silver tray bearing Sybilla's typical light breakfast, one hugged an armful of bolts of cloth, and the other wielded a thick, bound ledger—Sybilla's dragon of a schedule.

Sybilla buried her face in two handfuls of gown and steeled herself against the scream that wanted to explode from her throat. Could she not have one single moment of peace? A bit of privacy to mourn what might have been with the man who'd just left her room?

She raised her head when she felt the silk of her missing robe drape over her shoulders—one of her maids was wrapping it around her—and Sybilla pushed her arms through gratefully.

"Thank you," she said quietly.

And, just like that, her armor was donned.

Sybilla cinched the belt of her robe tightly about her waist and turned to face her sister. "Go attend your obligations, Cee. I shall deal with Blodshire myself. If Alys has not returned by supper, I shall send Clement after his beloved. Mayhap they will have a romantic encounter and she will fall hopelessly in love with him if only because of his enthusiasm and semi-daring at riding his horse for a quarter hour through the drizzle to fetch her. I'll engage Etheldred in the fabric selection for Alys's dress. That should please the old toad."

Cecily smiled her pleasure at Sybilla's words and Sybilla could not help but think again how lovely her sister was. Out of the three girls, Cecily was the best, by far.

"I'll pray for you and your sharp tongue, Sybilla," Cecily teased, and then blew her a kiss as she departed the chamber.

"Pray for us all," Sybilla whispered under her breath before turning to the work her maids had brought her.

Chapter 5

Piers grumbled to himself as he lay the fire, making use of the shrinking, gray December daylight. He was still cold, he was still tired, he was still hungry, and now the first two fingers on his left hand hurt like a pair of devils.

He moved stealthily—and muttered only under his breath—to avoid waking Alys Foxe and put off her impossible presence for as long as he could. 'Twas because of her that Piers had leaned against a hard log all of the day, his head jerking up painfully whenever he would nod off. As exhausted—both mentally and physically—as he was, he could not allow himself to relax while in the open daylight. Let the girl get her sleep, for when she woke she would have no excuse now not to leave Piers to his lethal mission. Once he was rid of her, he would be able to rest. Hell, even keeping up his torturous pace would seem peaceful without her inane chatter following him.

Gray smoke curled up from the tinder, birthed by the orange sparks beneath the twigs, and Piers lay the side of his face to the ground to blow up the flames. A satisfying crackle promised that at least soon he would be warm. He sat up on his knees once more and brushed his hands together.

"Are you going hunting?"

Piers looked over his shoulder at the girl, just now crawling from beneath the natural lean-to. She looked all of eight years old then, her cheeks creamy around the soft pink blooms of sleep. Her eyes were brown like a young calf's, her hair now adorned with twigs and bits of dry leaves in place of the fine headpiece and veil she'd worn that morning. She could have been a child of the manor emerging triumphant in a game of hide and seek.

Piers guessed that was likely an apt description for the game she played with her sister now, and the idea of it made him resentful and cross.

"No," he sneered. "Are you?"

She laughed as she gained her feet, her absurd pet taking up post on her shoulder while Alys shook out her outrageously costly blue skirts. Simply looking at the monkey seemed to make Piers's fingers throb all the worse. And now that she was standing, and Piers could see the swell of her small bust, he no longer thought of her as eight years old. His mood went from sour to black, and what little patience he had vanished.

"We would be in dire straits indeed were the food gathering left up to me. I'm fast, and I can be quite stealthy, but alas, I have no weapon save Layla." She reached up to scratch the beast's hairy head and the monkey leaned toward her adoringly. "Perhaps you could be my hound, eh, girl? Could you scare up a deer for us? You've already cornered a boar." She looked at Piers with a mischievous grin.

He turned his back to her to add some slender sticks to the fire. To Piers's dismay, she came to stand beside him.

"If you're not going hunting, what shall we eat? I'm famished."

"I'm certain there is no want for food at Fallstowe," Piers said. "It shall motivate you to walk faster."

"Back to that again, are we?"

Did nothing faze this silly child?

"We are. If you leave now, you will have some daylight for the whole of your journey."

"You want me to leave now?" she asked, as if doubting she had understood him properly.

"Yes."

"*Right now?* Immediately?"

"Start walking."

Alys Foxe sat down near the fire. "Piers, I've been thinking . . ."

Piers closed his eyes and sighed. "No, don't think. *And don't sit!* Sitting moves you no closer to Fallstowe and no farther from me!"

"Do you truly find me so annoying?"

"Yes!"

"Well, I'm quite sorry to hear that. But, as I was saying, I've been thinking, and—"

He gained his feet and strode into the trees.

"Wait!" He heard her scramble to her feet. "Where are you going? Why did you walk away from me?"

"In part to look for more wood for the fire," he said, his eyes scanning the forest floor. He leaned down and snatched limbs from the ground as he walked. "And also to keep from strangling you."

"That's rude," she said, from not very far behind him.

"I'm certainly not forcing you to put up with me."

"True," she conceded. "Any matter, I know you wish for me to leave you alone with your miserable and quite secretive plans, but there is a problem."

Piers came to an abrupt halt, so quickly that Alys ran into his back. The monkey chattered and bounded to the leaves underfoot.

He did not turn. "What problem?"

"I . . . I don't know the way back to Fallstowe."

Piers whipped around to face her, darkly pleased when she took a step back. "What do you mean, you don't know the way back? You've lived there the whole of your life, have you not?"

"Indeed, I have." She nodded agreeably.

"And yet you cannot find your way home little more than an hour from your own keep?"

She flushed, pursed her lips to the side and her eyes flicked nervously to the trees surrounding them. "No, I don't think so. I'm afraid not. Sorry."

Piers's own eyes narrowed. "Bullshit."

"I beg your pardon?"

"Bullshit!" he said more loudly and began walking back toward their primitive camp. "I may be mostly of common blood, but—"

"Mostly?" Alys asked, intrigue high in her voice as she skipped along behind him, and Piers winced inwardly.

"—I do know how gentle-born ladies behave: riding their ridiculous show mares, going visiting to their neighbors, skipping to market, insisting on accompanying hunts. You will not convince me that a female as sporting as yourself, who would adventure to an old ruin in the middle of the night alone, can not manage a short walk back to her home."

"You think I'm sporting?"

Piers rolled his eyes. "Just go, Alys. No more stalling, I beg of you. Apologize to your sister and take your punishment like a big girl. I don't want you here." He threw the small bundle of sticks to the ground near the fire and then looked up at her, prepared to see her properly chastised.

She was looking back at him boldly, swinging Layla around her body, hand over hand. They both seemed to be enjoying their little game.

"*You* have to take me back, Piers."

He blinked at her. "What?"

"I'm sorry, but that's the only thing for it. I already *told* you that Sybilla has promised me to Clement Cobb!"

"So?" Piers ground out expectantly.

"Well, when Sybilla and I had our row, I told her that I would rather take my chances at the Foxe Ring than marry him, which is where I was fortunate enough to meet you, dear husband."

"Alys . . ." Piers growled.

"Sybilla told me that if I happened to meet a man at the ring, she would pay Blodshire my dowry and I would be free to do as I chose."

He approached her then, causing her eyes to widen and Layla to scamper off to the safety of the lean-to. He grasped her upper arms. "Alys, this is most important, and so I want you to listen carefully: *we are not married.* I will not tell your sister that we are only so you don't have to be related to Etheldred Cobb."

"I know you think we're not married, Piers," Alys said quietly. "But I do. My parents met at the Foxe Ring, and I believe in the legend's purpose with my whole heart. You don't have to tell Sybilla that you *accept* that we are married, necessarily, but Sybilla always, always keeps her word. If you only corroborate my story of how and where we met, I shall be free. Please. Please, take me back to Fallstowe, Piers."

"And if I refuse?"

Her pink lips thinned as she set her mouth. "I shall continue to follow you, for as long as I can keep pace."

"And when you can no longer keep pace?"

She shrugged. "I don't know what, then."

He realized he was still holding on to her slight biceps and he let her go suddenly. He didn't know how it was possible, but the girl actually seemed to smell of nobility. Sweet and clean. It offended Piers, used as he was to manure and sweat and nothing.

"Please," she followed him as he walked away from her again. "This is my life, Piers. I need your help. I believe there is a reason you came to the ring last night, even if you do not."

"Your life is imposing on mine, Alys Foxe, and I am in a terrible hurry."

She hesitated. "I shall give you forty pounds if you will agree. And . . . and my own horse. I swear it. They should aid you on your journey quite nicely."

Then it was Piers's turn to pause. Forty pounds was a veritable fortune, not to mention the outrageous luxury of a mount. He could be to London in days, even with traveling through the forests. Perhaps returning Alys Foxe to her home was worth the risk.

In days, he could have his revenge on Bevan and Judith Angwedd.

He could claim his rightful place as lord of Gillwick.

Not a fortnight. *Days.*

He turned to face her. "Your sister—would she not seek to detain me?"

Alys appeared perplexed. "Likely she will wish you away from Fallstowe as soon as possible, if only to prevent me from *legally* marrying you. I hope you're not offended, but I do doubt Sybilla would consider you a catch."

Piers stared at the girl for a moment. He could feel the weight of her foolish hope from where he stood.

"Get your monkey and your bag."

Alys had never been so nervous and excited in the whole of her life as she skipped-ran to keep up with Piers, Layla unwillingly riding in Alys's drawstring sack. They were retracing the way back to Fallstowe, together.

Now all Alys had to do was to figure out a way to convince Piers that they were truly meant to be together, forever, as the stones had very obviously decreed. Difficult, as he had refused to respond to her attempts at conversation for the past hour. She didn't have much time left, but she was confident that something would intervene. After all, it was the Foxe Ring at work. One might even venture to call it fate.

"Where are you going once you leave Fallstowe?" she tried yet again.

He merely shrugged.

"You're in a terrible hurry, and yet you have no destination in mind?" she teased.

"London."

"Oh, I adore London!" Alys said happily, thrilled to her toes that he had at last responded. "I haven't been in ages though—since before my mother died."

Piers, ever the skillful conversationalist, grunted.

But Alys was undeterred. "Are you to visit family there?"

"I have no family."

"Oh. Friends, then?" She giggled. "No, don't tell me—you don't have any friends either."

"Right."

She reached out an arm to snag a fold of his robe and gave it a playful tug. "I'm your friend."

"You're a ninny."

Alys laughed. She was quite certain Piers was in possession of a wonderful sense of humor if she could just coax him to open up a little bit wider than a shoe seam.

"My favorite activity by far is to market. The markets in London are so very entertaining! Why, I'd wager that you can buy anything at all there. What is your favorite thing to do in London?"

"I don't know. I've not been."

"Really?" Alys was shocked. "Then how do you know where you're going?"

"I simply plan on looking for the very biggest palace in the city and then going there."

Alys's mouth fell open. "You're going to see the *king*? How exciting! I've never met the king. Were you summoned?"

"Somewhat, I suppose."

"Sybilla herself is dreading another summons from Edward."

Piers grunted.

"Do you want to know why?"

"Not especially."

Alys let her voice lower dramatically. "He wants to take Fallstowe from her."

"So I've heard. Terrible luck, that."

"Yes, it is actually. He thinks our mother was a spy and that after my father died, she held Fallstowe illegally. So of course, now that Mother is gone, he is outraged that Sybilla—a lowly *daughter*, no less—refuses to surrender the castle to the crown."

"Your mother was a spy?" He shook his head with a

˙snort. "Obvious now where you get your tenacity from, then. And your recklessness."

Alys drew her head back and smiled. "Why, thank you, Piers."

"It wasn't a compliment."

"I shall take it as one any matter."

The day was only the faint sliver of a memory now, night's blanket lying orange and pink and soft on the faraway hills as Fallstowe came in sight. Its towers and walls rose solidly in black relief out of a gentle purple and indigo mist, and a group of riders rode toward the keep on the road ahead of them, their figures as black and muted as the stones.

The thought crossed her mind that, if they hurried, she and Piers could gain entry along with the mounted party before the portcullis was lowered. Alys's mood soured. Yes, she had lived at Fallstowe all of her life, but now that her mother was dead and Sybilla was at the family helm, the grand castle had lost that comforting feeling of home. Alys felt almost adrift on the waves of rolling hills surrounding the keep, as if she was being sucked relentlessly closer to a certain and deadly whirlpool. That whirlpool was her cold, demanding sister, ready to sacrifice Alys to the depths.

Perhaps the enigmatic man who accompanied her would somehow become an anchor. So far though, there had been no sign that he would remain steadfast.

The harker called out from the watch, his words little more than a whisper from such a great height. "Who approaches? Declare yourself under threat of death!"

Piers came to a halt well before the road leading to the drawbridge, and turned to look expectantly at Alys. Even in the gloom of evening, she could see the look of wariness on his face, and sense the change in his posture.

"Would they fire upon us?" he demanded.

Alys stopped as well, setting Layla's conveyance on the ground. She'd let the monkey out in a moment, now that she wasn't being forced to practically run to keep up with Piers. "*Would* they? If we were both strangers and proceeded, then certainly, yes. I doubt he's even noticed *us* yet at such a fair distance, let alone expects to hit one of us with an arrow. His warning was for the riders ahead of us."

She cupped her hands around her mouth, readying to shout up to the wall to hold the gate for them, but before she could announce herself, another voice called out of the night from the mounted party already before the drawbridge.

"Lady Judith Angwedd Mallory of Gillwick Manor, and her son!"

Alys rolled her eyes with a groan and was turning to lament the visitors to Piers when he snatched her around the waist from behind and threw her to the ground. She started to cry out that Piers was crushing her, but his hand came up to clap over her mouth, and then his lips brushed her ear.

"Unless you wish me dead in the next pair of moments, lie absolutely still, Alys."

The rumble of chain and wood soon shook ground beneath Alys's smashed bosom, and she could feel Piers's shallow breathing against her back. He really was taking this secret mission of his seriously, to be worried about such lesser nobles as the Mallorys. Why, Judith Angwedd hadn't even been invited to the winter feast!

And although he truly was a weighty man, Alys began to enjoy the feel of Pier's body atop hers. She wiggled a bit to test him and, to her delight, his hold on her tightened.

"Shh," he breathed into her ear. "Alys, please. I'm trying not to hurt you."

Her stomach clenched and she closed her eyes to savor the sensations his body and words were creating within her. One thick forearm was pinned between the ground and her navel, while his opposite hand now cupped the back of her head, ensuring that she remained completely prone. His face pressed against the side of hers through the window his arm created, and his legs were to either side of hers, holding her tightly. Alys struggled against the temptation to ease her bottom upward. She'd experienced more excitement and adventure since meeting the man atop her than she had the entire eighteen years of her life before him.

"That's it," he whispered. "Easy now. Almost over."

Alys gave a disappointed little whimper—she didn't *want* it to be over. But a moment later, the ground shook again as the portcullis lowered on the hoof beats that were fading away into the barbican. Piers lay very still atop her for several more breaths before whispering in her ear once more.

"Our deal is off."

Then, in a blink, his weight was gone from her, and she was alone on the cold, wet ground.

From within the sack still on the ground an arm's length away, Layla gave a questioning little coo.

"I haven't the slightest idea," Alys sighed.

Then she gathered her limbs beneath her and pushed up from the ground. Snatching the sack up, she turned and fled from Fallstowe's wall toward the blackened wood once more.

Chapter 6

Sybilla had no earthly idea what Judith Angwedd of simple and bucolic Gillwick Manor wanted from her, and normally she would have had Graves play the go-between for the unsavory lady and her strange son, but after an entire day of placating Etheldred Cobb and the vapid Clement, any distraction was heartily welcome.

Sybilla hoped the woman wasn't there to present her son as a match for one of the Foxe sisters. The very idea of a Mallory and a Foxe was absurd.

Judith Angwedd swept into Fallstowe's great hall and down the center aisle created by the dining tables as if she floated rather than walked on two legs, her son lumbering along behind her. She was a tall woman, on the spare side, and of the eccentric habit of wearing her dull red hair long and straight down her back, but short and rolled into perfect, thumbsized curls on the sides and top of her head. Her face was paunchy and waxen, like the thick butter Gillwick manor was known for producing, and her dirt-brown eyes sat in fatty folds not matching the rest of her thin figure. She had extremely large teeth, wide and long and white, and was quite proud of them by the way her tongue constantly attended to their polishing. Judith Angwedd could in no way be called a handsome woman.

Her son was her male counterpart. Tall like his mother, but blocky and wide, his large, flat face was surrounded by the same childish, fat, red curls. His eyes, too, were like Judith Angwedd's, enveloped in swollen flesh to the point that they seemed to be in danger of being swallowed by his face. And Bevan Mallory's face appeared just hateful enough to do it. The purple-red hue of his nose emboldened rather than detracted from the brown freckles splashed across his cheeks. Sybilla thought he looked mean and stupid, and she wondered if he would prove her suspicions when she first heard him speak. Although the Mallorys had been in attendance at a handful of functions at which Sybilla had also been present, the two families had never had cause for direct conversation. The strange Gillwick clan had never been invited to Fallstowe castle, as far as Sybilla could recall.

"Lady Foxe." Judith Angwedd floated to a stop before Sybilla's dais and sank into a deep curtsey. Behind his mother, Bevan bowed sloppily. "I do beg your pardon for arriving so unannounced, and I must confess straight away that my appearance is in part to ask for your assistance."

Sybilla's eyebrows rose. The woman obviously thought much of herself to request anything from Fallstowe. She was little more than a commoner. Perhaps if Gillwick lay in a town, Judith Angwedd would be considered a burgess's wife, but the announcement of requested aid was very strange any matter, and set Sybilla immediately on alert.

"Indeed? Our houses are not well connected, but of

course I am always willing to offer what I can in the spirit of Christian charity. What troubles you, Lady Judith?"

The woman's brow gave a flicker of displeasure at being reminded of her station, but she continued. "As you likely have heard, my husband, Lord Warin Mallory, died only a fortnight ago."

"No, I hadn't," Sybilla replied mildly, not caring in the least. Perhaps Judith Angwedd was to ask for money, then. "May God receive his soul."

Judith Angwedd's color was high now. "Thank you, my lady," she gritted out. "Unfortunately, his death caused his other son a great deal of distress, to the point that I'm afraid he went quite mad."

"You have another child?" Sybilla asked, her eyes going to Bevan, whose face was now entirely covered by the purplish tinge.

"Piers is not my child," Judith Angwedd hissed, and even to Sybilla, who was known to be cool of nature, the words were icy. "He is a bastard born by a common whore of our village. A farm hand. No one of any consequence."

"I see," Sybilla said, although she did not. "What has this to do with Fallstowe, Lady Judith?"

"Upon Warin's death, Piers was overcome with the mad notion that it should be he who inherits Gillwick Manor rather than Warin's older and *legitimate* son, *my* Bevan. So possessed was he by this idea that he attacked Bevan, and tried to kill him."

Again, Sybilla's eyes flicked to the heretofore silent Bevan. "He looks fine to me."

"Well, Bevan overpowered him, of course," Judith Angwedd simpered proudly. "But now Piers is nowhere to be found, and we believe him to be quite dangerous. He isn't here, is he?"

"No," Sybilla said without hesitation. "I would have been informed had a troubled man come upon Fallstowe's gate. Why would you think him to come here?"

Judith Angwedd looked uncomfortable for only a moment. "Bevan and I are to appear before the court of King's Bench in less than a fortnight—perhaps Piers travels there with the idea that he will plead his delusional cause with Edward. Fallstowe lies directly in the path between Gillwick and the crown, and so I thought . . ." She paused, letting her wide teeth flash for an instant. "You haven't had any horses stolen, have you? Chickens? Anything of the like?"

Sybilla laughed out loud. "I've not counted them myself, but no, I've not heard that our henhouses have been breached. I'm sorry I cannot be of any help to you, Lady Judith."

"I see. Well, if you would happen to—"

At that moment, Graves leaned close to Sybilla's shoulder, so that the visitors could not hear him. Sybilla held up a palm to Judith Angwedd, signaling the woman to petulant silence.

"Has there been word from Lady Alys, Madam?"

Sybilla's brow creased. Likely this Piers had wandered into the forest or the river and was either dead or had in some other way made himself of no consequence to Fallstowe or its inhabitants. But as far as Sybilla knew, Alys had yet to return to the keep, and the youngest Foxe sister was just foolish and headstrong enough to engage anyone she came across to her own cause now that she was to wed.

"Shall I send a rider?" Graves asked when Sybilla had yet to answer.

Sybilla gave only the briefest nod, and Graves made not a whisper of sound as he left to do her bidding. As Sybilla turned her attention back to the fuming Judith

Angwedd and her purple son, she heard the approaching cackle of Etheldred Cobb. A sharp pain began throbbing beneath the delicate tissue of her temples. Sybilla wanted nothing more than to dismiss Judith Angwedd from the hall and retire to her rooms for the evening, leaving the Cobbs to a lonely supper. But she would not, as long as there was even the slightest chance Alys could have run upon a dangerous person.

"Lady Judith," Sybilla began, seeming to have to force her mouth to form the words. "Fallstowe entertains other guests this evening." She stopped, and Judith Angwedd's face fell into an offended scowl. The woman's discomfiture suited Sybilla, but she forged ahead with the invitation. "But I would be pleased if you and your son would join us for a meal before taking your leave."

Judith Angwedd's padded eyes widened to the best of their ability, and after one stunned moment, she curtsied.

"It would be our honor to dine in such a grand hall as Fallstowe's, Lady Sybilla," the woman simpered.

"Why, Judith Angwedd, it's been three years, I'd wager." Etheldred Cobb entered the hall with Clement and maid Mary on her heels, and the old woman seemed unreasonably pleased to see the Gillwick party.

Judith Angwedd straightened and her brows rose. "Lady Etheldred, Lord Clement. What a lovely surprise. You remember Bevan, of course. What brings you to Fallstowe?"

"Yes, ho there, Bevan. Eating well, I see." Etheldred Cobb pulled her own sizeable mass onto the dais and took a seat at Sybilla's table as if the chair had been inscribed with her name, while her maid moved alone to one of the common tables on the floor. "Clement and I decided to stay on a bit after the winter feast. Strange—I don't recall seeing you among the guests." The slight flew through the air with the surety of the straightest arrow. "And, of course, with Clement and Lady Alys soon to wed . . . well, pray God one day you may know how loathe young people in love are to part from one another, eh Bevan?"

"Oh, Mother," Clement admonished as he helped to push Etheldred's chair in with an affronted screech to the stones beneath. He turned to the Mallorys. "Hello, Bevan. A good year for sweet grass, was it not?" He nodded politely toward the redheaded woman. "Lady Judith, you're looking well. My condolences on the loss of your husband."

Sybilla was feeling nauseous as Judith Angwedd preened girlishly. She hoped that whoever Graves sent to the ring would hurry. A serving boy came from the kitchen bearing a tray, but upon seeing Sybilla's nod toward the newest guests, he ducked back through the doorway with rolling eyes. She made a mental note to reprimand the lad for his indiscretion later.

Sybilla's toes curled in her slippers as she gestured to the empty chairs at her table. "Please, join us."

Even when Piers had been wracked by pain from the beating he'd received, when he'd had his skin sewn up, his wounds painfully scrubbed, when his head had felt that it would explode while he vomited blood, he'd never felt as scared as he did now, running through the gloam from Fallstowe to the cover of the wood. The bite he'd received from Layla throbbed in time to his pounding footfalls.

Judith Angwedd and Bevan had followed him. They knew he was alive, and were at his very back now.

"Piers, wait!"

He ran faster. This was *her* fault! Had silly, childish, senseless Alys Foxe not chased after him in the first place, had she not lured him back to her home like he was some biddable pet no more intelligent than the monkey, Piers would not be so close to the two people who were trying with all their might to steal from him what was rightfully his, and see him dead in the process.

He charged into the apron of underbrush before the forest, crashing into the cover of trees. His boot caught on a vine and he fell. He lay very still in the black night that had finally yielded up its shelter. It was only a pair of moments later that he knew she yet pursued him.

"Piers? I can't see a bloody thing, but I can hear you breathing, so you might as well show yourself instead of hiding like a common thief."

Anger filled him then and he did gain his feet, finding her so quickly that she hadn't had time to gasp properly when he seized her arm and spun her around. From within the sack, Layla screeched.

"I *am* common!" he shouted in her face. "And you nearly got me killed just now!"

"I did no such thing," she argued. "I lay still when you asked, I was quiet. Although, if you would have let me speak, I could have told you that Judith Angwedd was no one of any consequence—she couldn't possibly know who you were running from. Now, let's go back before we kill ourselves in the dark. I'll have your coin and horse readied and you can leave in the morning."

"It's her and her bloody son that I'm running from!" Piers shook Alys. "You stupid child!"

She slapped him then—Piers thought as hard as she was physically able. He released her, his body shaking.

"Don't ever dare to call me stupid again," she said, her voice cold and even. "And never put your hands on me in anger. If you do, 'twill be I who is most likely to see you dead."

He had lost control of himself, and he knew it. But he had neither the time nor the inclination for an apology. The girl had no idea the threat he was under, couldn't possibly fathom what was at stake.

"For the last time, go back to Fallstowe, Alys. This is no game."

He bent and dug around in the tangle of brush for his pack. Seizing a strap, he swung the bag onto his back and began walking.

"If you leave me here, I *will* go back," she called to him.

"Good. Go," Piers threw over his shoulder.

"And when I do, they will send riders through the wood until they find you."

Piers stopped in his tracks. "They wouldn't, unless you betrayed me."

She approached him now. "Piers, listen to me: I know you think that stumbling upon your enemies at Fallstowe was a near disaster. But, where as before this day you might have grown complacent in your travels, now you know that they are at your heels, and you can take even greater care to avoid them. I know the roads from Fallstowe. I know the way they are likely to go if they are indeed following you. I can help you, Piers. Let me."

He couldn't see her face in the black, but he could feel her presence, trembling with youth and heat and ridiculous optimism. He could feel the warmth of her, as if she was a stone oven hidden in the shadows of the night forest, keeping secret her blazing fire. Such a little fool. She could not help him. He wanted to kiss her then, to show her the very real folly of becoming involved with such a desperate man.

But she was right—now Piers knew exactly how high the stakes had risen. He was confident he could find the way through Fallstowe's thick wood and then along the roads to London well enough. He could travel more swiftly alone. He didn't think Alys Foxe would set his enemies to his trail, but he could not be certain. If he left her behind, he might never know the depth of her resentment at his refusal of her help until it was too late. He could not tarry to debate the matter—his foes were too close.

"I do not trust that you wouldn't betray me," he admitted. "But I will not be responsible for you should you insist on following me. If you cannot keep pace with me, I will not wait. I will not feed you, tend to you like some servant."

"I won't hold you back," she promised, her voice carrying a hint of breathlessness. "Only let me change my gown and shoes."

He cursed under his breath and then nodded curtly, feeling as though he had just sealed his fate as a traveling corpse. She was already holding him back. "Hurry up."

She rustled through the underbrush, away from him. Her voice went periodically muffled as she continued to talk to him while she undressed. Piers tried not to think of her firm, compact body naked just steps away from him. He had been a long time without a woman.

Too bad Alys Foxe was still a girl.

"We'll find the road and cross it to travel the south side. A river follows on the north, and most of the way to London it's filled with washes and ravines—largely impassable. Turn it loose, Layla—give it! Yes, yes, alright—get out then." A pause, a shuffling and sliding of cloth. "We'll go as far as you wish tonight, to put as much distance between us and Fallstowe as possible. But then I do think you should consider traveling in the daylight. Oh! Dammit, Layla! I've dropped my slipper."

Piers rolled his eyes. "Come on, come on!"

"I'm trying! It's black as the devil's ear here, Piers, and my shoe is brown."

"If you hadn't brought your entire wardrobe you wouldn't need look for an additional shoe."

He heard her sigh of exasperation. "You could help, you know, as opposed to standing there berating me uselessly. It's rather difficult going, hopping about on one foot."

"Oh, for Christ's sake." He walked toward the sound of her voice. "Does milady loathe the feel of dirt on her sole?"

"We're standing in a briar, half-wit. Take off *your* shoes and walk about and see how you fancy it, eh?"

Piers kicked though the tangle of vines with his boots, knowing he was near her when he could once more feel her heat and hear her breathing. He bent over.

"Did you find it?" she asked.

"Certainly. I'm only seeing how long I can stay bent over in such a manner before I am beset by cramps."

He heard her hop closer. "Piers!"

"Shut up, I'm looking." His hand brushed smooth, supple leather. He snatched up the shoe and rose. "Here it—"

He collided with Alys and she began to fall backward, shrieking and windmilling her arms. Without thinking, Pier's left arm shot out and went round her waist, pulling her to him in the next instant.

"—is," he finished, more quietly now that her face was only inches from his. He pressed the slipper into her hand.

"Thank you." She sniffed. "You smell like a cow."

Piers felt his face heat. "I work a dairy."

"It's nice," Alys said lightly.

"I'll steady you while you put on your shoe." His fingers kept a loose grasp on the curve of her waist as she leaned to the side. He held her weight easily, unable to ignore the limberness of her back and stomach. She was like a young, green reed, strong and pliable and smooth. Bent as she was, the monkey on her shoulder was now face to face with Piers. Layla reached out of the black and tweaked his nose hard. Piers slapped at the air before his face with a growl.

"I'm finished." Alys stood aright once more.

"Good," he said gruffly. "May we continue now, milady?"

"Only if you turn me loose," she said in a teasing voice. "Unless you'd rather we—"

Piers released her in a blink, walking away from her surprised cry and ensuing crash as she fell to the forest floor.

"Ouch! You bastard," she muttered, and the monkey chattered madly in accord. Piers kept moving as she gained her feet noisily and caught up with him. "That was unnecessary. I think I've got a thorn in my bottom."

"Now you know how *I* feel," he muttered, as his face crawled with heat.

Although, were he to be honest with himself, the uncomfortable sensation he felt was not in his bottom at all—more to the front side, actually.

Sybilla had done little more than push her food about her platter throughout what had to be the longest supper ever known. Her head pounded, her stomach churned, her ears rang from the incessant, nonstop, eternal, and relentless posturing and boasting of her begrudged female guests. With every utterance, each woman backhandedly insulted her dinner mate. Bevan Mallory had said not a word, only belched wetly on occasion. Clement was the only civil one at the meal, including Sybilla, if she was to be honest about it. She knew she was behaving imperially, not deigning to take part in any of the conversation, but she didn't care. That was her reputation, and this night, she was happy to live up to it.

Just when she thought herself to go mad and murder them all with her eating knife if only to make them *shut up*, Graves appeared through her private door located in the wall behind the dais, a sweaty soldier on his ancient and sure heels. He came to her at once. Her rude and noisy guests were completely uninterrupted by the servant's arrival.

"Should we be alarmed, Madam, that, while Lady Alys was not at the Foxe Ring, a bit of blood was found on the center stone?"

Sybilla's entire body went icy cold.

Alys!

"Yes, Graves," Sybilla said quietly. "Yes, that is indeed cause for us to be alarmed." She rose from her chair and turned to face the people at the table. Clement looked to her attentively, wiping his mouth with a cloth. Bevan's face was still in his platter like a pig at trough. The women remained oblivious in their haranguing of each other over the rude clatter of cutlery.

"I will have silence in my hall!"

Etheldred Cobb and Judith Angwedd both turned their faces toward Sybilla, owl-eyed and affronted.

Now that she had their attention, Sybilla continued, speaking around the knot in her throat. "I fear I have potentially very grave news to share that concerns each of you."

Chapter 7

Alys wondered if she would ever see daylight again.

It was hard traveling through the seemingly eternally dark forest, even in the wide wake of Piers's crashing passage. Each score of steps found one or both of them tripping, stumbling, or completely falling over some unseen obstacle. Although the moon was still largely ripe, the thickness of the bare branches of the deciduous trees as well as the full and towering evergreens threw deceptive shadows on the tangle of forest floor, disguising downed limbs and rocks and burrows. They had been walking for hours, and Alys's feet and knees and buttocks ached. Layla was an additional liability, riding atop Alys's shoulder once more, but the monkey had refused in quite an impolite manner to continue the journey in the relative safety of Alys's bag.

Even though the terrain was nearly impossible, she was glad they were not on the open road—the silent man she followed would have already left her far behind by now. Alys Foxe had no desire to become separated from Piers, the dairy hand, or whatever he was, and she thought mayhap it had little to do with them being in the thickness of a dangerous forest.

He'd nearly kissed her in the briars near Fallstowe. The way he had held her, his breathing going shallow and ragged, his arm tightening almost imperceptibly around her middle. Alys had only been truly kissed once, by a lad from the village this past May Day, so it wasn't as if she had much experience at it, but she had known when the young village man had been about to kiss her, and she had known tonight with Piers, although the two sensations had been worlds apart.

She'd *wanted* Piers to kiss her, and so in hindsight she thought that perhaps she should not have commented that he smelled like a farm animal. But Alys had been honest when she'd said his scent was nice. She spent much of her free time in the company of Fallstowe's beasts and so the fragrances of barn and stable were comfortable friends to her. Cows and horses did not stare at you coldly like Sybilla, or lecture you on brazen behavior like Cecily. They were warm and calm and happy just to have someone nearby for company. They didn't mock you for wishing for adventure and variety outside of the stifling gray stones of Fallstowe, where the sad, empty space left by your mother's death screamed at you. They didn't care that you were a Foxe. They didn't care that you were a girl. All they cared about was the stiff brush in your hand, or the oats in your apron pocket.

So now Alys knew that Piers worked a dairy. He was "mostly" common—whatever that could mean—and he was running away from Judith Angwedd of Gillwick Manor to see the king on a highly secretive mission.

Alys was completely charmed by her new husband.

And, with each tripping step, Layla bobbing along contentedly on her shoulder, Alys moved farther away from

Sybilla, from Fallstowe, and from Clement Cobb. She could not have been happier.

Ahead of her, Piers stopped abruptly, and seemed to scrutinize the small clearing they had passed into. A thick, naturally curved wall of briars footed by two large stones shielded the clearing from the north. The ground sloped gently to the south, eventually rolling off in a shoulder into a black nothing. Alys assumed it was a ravine.

"This will do," he said, and shrugged out of his pack.

"Thanks be to God," Alys sighed and dropped her own bag. Layla hopped down gamely and began worrying at the ties of the sack. "I know, love. You'll eat in just a moment." Alys took the time to stretch her arms above her head with a groan. Her back was in knots. "Will we have a fire?" she asked Piers.

"No," he said curtly. He pulled a long piece of cloth from his pack and wound it around his forearm to fashion a pillow of sorts, which he tossed against the seam of the boulders and ground. He sat, and began digging through his bag.

"Of course not." Alys sighed and dropped to her knees, rescuing her own sack from Layla before the monkey had the drawstring in a hopeless snarl.

She reached inside and withdrew the last piece of fruit, an only slightly bruised pomegranate. She held it for a long moment, thinking wistfully of the figs she'd handed up one at a time to the monkey while they had been on their way back to Fallstowe. Her stomach gurgled and twisted around its emptiness, and Alys considered digging her thumbs into the fruit and dividing it in half. But in the end she surrendered the juicy treat over to Layla, who sat back on her haunches and began to turn the fruit rapidly against her teeth. Alys's mouth watered at the slurping sounds, and so she moved her attention once more to Piers, who was tearing into a piece of foodstuffs of his own. By the way his fist jerked away from his mouth, it was quite possibly saddle leather he was eating.

"Are you going to tell me why you are frightened of Judith Angwedd?" she asked.

"I'm not frightened of Judith Angwedd," he said while he chewed. He fished a jug from his bag, released the cork with his teeth, and took a long, noisy drink.

"Then why are you running from her?"

He shrugged one shoulder. "I simply need to reach London before she or Bevan does."

"Why?"

He stopped chewing and stared hard at her, likely thinking to intimidate her into silence. Little did he know that Alys was well accustomed to hard stares, and they no longer affected her in the least.

She stared back, making her eyes wide and pulling her mouth down at the corners—a silly attempt to disrupt his solemnity. It failed, and she gave a frustrated huff. "If we are to be in this together, I would know exactly the danger we face."

"We don't face it. They're behind us, for the time being."

"Piers . . ."

"I don't wish to talk about it tonight, Alys. I'm beyond tired and my head pains me, as does my hand, thanks to your idiotic monkey."

"Must you be such a boor about the whole thing?" she exclaimed. He offered neither comment nor apology. "Alright then. Fine. I won't ask you again."

There was silence between them for several moments.

"You'd better eat if you're going to," he said at last, his tone carrying a bit of unease, as if he was not used to making conversation.

"I'm not very hungry," she lied. "I had quite a large meal last night, remember?" Alys would have rather married Clement Cobb on the spot than remind Piers that the pomegranate Layla was now polishing off was the last piece of food she had. He had already made it clear that he thought her a stupid girl and that he would not take responsibility for her. Alys would not ask him for food.

She chose not to think about what would become of her resolve in a day or more.

"How could I forget?" Piers said snidely. "It is beyond me still why you would choose to run away from a home and inheritance such as Fallstowe."

"Of course it is beyond you, because you don't know what it is like there," Alys said, rummaging through her bag now for some sort of pillow of her own. The only thing large enough to give her any comfort was the blue perse gown. She wound it around her arm with a vengeful smile, thinking of the extravagant amount of money Sybilla had paid for it. "The castle is horrid; Sybilla, worse."

"Oh, come now," Piers scoffed, re-corking his jug and shoving it down in his bag. Alys wondered briefly if it contained wine. "What was it? Too much money? You couldn't walk the corridors without tripping over a pile of it?"

Alys went still. "Don't mock me, Piers. Everyone envies Fallstowe, and they think Sybilla the epitome of beauty, power, wealth, charm. But my sister cares for no one save herself, her own advancement. The retainment of her station as ruler of Fallstowe. She would do anything, crush anyone, to keep hold of all she now has. She would even deny our king. You can't possibly know how vicious she is." She was horrified to hear her words thickening. "I consider myself lucky to have escaped."

He was quiet for a moment, and when next he spoke, his voice had changed, gentled. "It was bad for you?"

She nodded. "She . . . Sybilla tried to smother me."

"My God," Piers breathed. He was intent on her now, and Alys felt his appraisal like a warm wash of water. Gooseflesh sprang on her arms as he continued. "It was the same with me, with . . . with my stepbrother."

Her eyes widened, and hope burst into her chest. "Is that why you work a dairy? Why you say you are only mostly common? Did you leave to escape your family?"

"No. My father sent me there," he admitted.

"Oh!" Alys gasped. "That's outrageous!"

"It was the best thing," Piers assured her. "It likely saved my life. But what of you? I had no idea the Foxe family was such a den of treachery."

He was not mocking her now, and so Alys was happy to continue the conversation. "Sybilla has always been cool natured, from what I can remember of my earliest memories of her. But when mother fell ill some four years ago—stricken so that her right side was completely without use—Sybilla began receiving instruction to take our mother's place. 'Twas then that her evil found its head."

"Power?" Piers guessed, sounding more interested in Alys than he had the entire time of their strange acquaintance.

"Indeed. Power and status. And she exercises both well." Alys dropped her eyes to her lap, picking at the folds of her gown. "After Mother died . . . Sybilla became less than human. Bitter. Demanding. I was a trouble to her, and so she sought a way to put end to me disrupting her cool order of things."

"Jesus. Little wonder you were so eager to escape." He leaned forward a bit. "What did she use?"

Alys opened her mouth but then quickly closed it again, confused. "I beg your pardon?"

"Was it a cushion? A rope? *Her bare hands?*" He sat up fully now, engaged and animated. "Bevan tried to hang me from the loft once when we were young, but the rope was too thin—old and rotted—and it snapped before I passed out."

Alys was horrified. "What *are* you talking about?"

"Your sister smothering you," Piers said.

"I don't mean she actually tried to *kill me!*" Alys cried. "My God, what kind of—" Alys stopped abruptly. "Wait! You said Bevan. Bevan Mal—you work a *dairy! Bevan Mallory is your stepbrother?*"

"You *said* she tried to *smother* you!" Piers accused. "You meant only that your sister wouldn't give over to your every whim, didn't you?"

"No! Well, perhaps I should have used 'stifle' rather than 'smother,' but—Bevan Mallory tried to kill you? More than once?"

"This conversation is over," Piers growled. He turned away from her and lay down.

"I disagree," Alys said, scrambling to his side. "Is Bevan the one who gave you the marks you now bear?"

"Go to sleep, Alys."

"How can I? Is Judith Angwedd your mother?"

He whipped around so quickly that Alys jumped. "Don't ever dare to compare Judith Angwedd to my mother!"

"I wasn't comparing them—I don't know!"

Piers flopped back onto his side.

Alys's eyes narrowed and her mind whirred. "If Judith Angwedd isn't your mother, then your father would be Warin Mallory." She frowned. "But, no, you said 'step-brother,' and Bevan is Warin Mallory's only son, so—"

"Don't be so certain," Piers growled.

"But that's just it—I'm not certain at all!" Alys slapped her palms onto her thighs, and Layla took it as an invitation. Alys gathered the small animal to her bosom. "It is a long way to London, Piers. Can you not confide in me the tiniest bit?"

He was still and silent for so long, that Alys was nearly resigned to the idea that he would not answer her. When he did speak, his words conveyed no satisfying resolution.

"You may as well try to get some rest. We'll be off not long after sunrise."

"But—"

"Good night, Alys."

She sighed, her lips pressed tightly together. After a moment, she reached over to snag the bundled perse gown, Layla clinging to her front, and stuffed the makeshift pillow against the rock next to Piers's. She lay down on her side close to him, the monkey snuggled between.

He raised up slightly and turned his face to look at her over his shoulder. "What are you doing?"

"I'm trying to get some rest, as you commanded," she snapped. "'Tis cold, Piers. I know you'd likely prefer I freeze to death, but I rather enjoy living."

He laid back down. "You're young. Give it time."

"You are the most cynical person I believe I've ever met."

"Thank you."

"It wasn't a compliment."

His shoulders jerked, and for an instant, Alys thought he might have chuckled. "I shall take it as one any matter."

* * *

Everyone was gone from Fallstowe's great hall now in the smallest hours of the morning, save for Judith Angwedd and Clement Cobb. The disgustingly lavish hall had been a flurry of grim activity up until several moments ago, with her highness, Sybilla Foxe, organizing a thorough brigade of soldiers to search for the youngest Foxe girl, Alys.

And Piers, Judith Angwedd thought to herself with a smile. The most powerful house in England was now to do Judith Angwedd's work for her. Lady Sybilla herself—that rich, cold, pompous bitch—had been quite clear that should her men find Piers Mallory in possession of her sister, his life would be forfeit.

Delightful!

The Fallstowe soldiers were on the trail, commanded in no uncertain terms to search every road, every wood, every rough animal path for sign of the little wayward princess. Judith Angwedd hoped the soldiers found two cold, dead, scavenger-gnawed bodies—'twould serve Sybilla Foxe justice for treating the lady of Gillwick and her fine son so poorly. But that was only the beginning.

With the chore of finding the bastard Piers delegated nicely, Judith and Bevan would soon carry on to London, to pay homage to Edward and once and for all secure their hold on Gillwick Manor, whose lands very soon after would more than double in size. And while they were in audience with the king, Judith Angwedd would be sure to bestow upon Edward any detailed morsel that might aid him in knocking Sybilla Foxe from her lofty, self-appointed throne.

Before they were off though, she would enjoy Fallstowe Castle's luxuries and have herself a spot of fun, since Phineas had been left behind at Gillwick.

She approached the distraught Clement, sitting at a common table, his fine, white hair falling over his fingers where they grasped his head. His narrow shoulders were hunched, the perfect figure of despair. She placed her palms near his neck and squeezed lightly.

"Sweet, young Clement," she cooed. "My darling, you must not mourn so. It saddens me to no end to see you in such pain."

"My Alys, my angel!" he cried in a strangled voice. "She is alone out there, with that . . . that—"

"Low-born killer, yes," Judith Angwedd said lightly, and she smiled while she said it because Clement could not see her. She sat down next to him on the bench, facing away from the table and letting her hand trail down his arm to his elbow. "And, as troubling as it is to think, we must all prepare for the very, very worst."

Clement whimpered.

Judith Angwedd sighed toward the vaulted ceiling. "A young girl such as Alys—innocent, trusting—she stands no chance against a base criminal such as Piers. She is likely already dead."

There was a muffled cry from the vicinity of Clement's hands.

Judith Angwedd turned on her hip to wrap her arms around Clement's shoulders. "Oh, but my darling, you must not mourn your own life away! You are so young yet, Clement—my sweet, comely Clement! You will marry another and put this sadness behind you." She pressed her lips to his hair, kissed him and then whispered, "Oh Clement, I adore you so—and your kind and gentle mother, my dear, dear friend! How I regret to have played a part in your distress."

"You have shown great honor, Lady Judith, and courage to

come to Fallstowe with your warning," Clement whispered. "We are all in your debt."

"Perhaps," Judith Angwedd acquiesced lightly. "But I feel so very guilty, lovely Clement. Would that I could comfort you in your sorrow!" She stroked his hair, pulled him closer, her breasts pressing into his arm. "A widow such as myself, I am most familiar with loneliness and heartbreak."

He turned into her embrace, as she'd known he would, and Judith Angwedd pressed her lips to both his damp cheeks. "You must not mourn for poor Alys, who is surely dead and cold and stiff now. You must live, Clement!" She kissed his mouth. "Live!"

He leaned into her and kissed her, his mouth wet and eager, his tongue snaking thickly past her teeth. Judith Angwedd moaned deep in her throat.

But then he pushed her away with a cry. "Oh, I dishonor the memory of her, my betrothed, my sweet and innocent beloved!"

Judith Angwedd pulled him back to her roughly. "She would not wish for you to be alone this night, Clement. Not her greatest love, alone and weeping. She would want *this*, want your friend to comfort you. Let me, Clement. *Let me*." She drew his face to hers again, and he did let her.

And a moment later, he let her pull up her gown and mount his lap in Fallstowe's darkened great hall, sitting on a bench at one of the common tables. He let her, until he cried out her name and it echoed off the stones.

Chapter 8

Piers had never gained so much insight from someone he was doing his best to ignore.

All the long day they had walked, breaking camp early that morning when the sunlight was only a silver sliver on the horizon through the crowding, skeletal gray trees, the fog of his breath hanging solid in the frozen air. Alys Foxe had awoken cross and tightlipped, perhaps still feeling the sting of his rebuff from before they had gone to sleep. After a pair of hours though, she was back to her usual loquacious self, commenting on this or that, relating various bits of gossip from her noble circle of acquaintances, slyly phrasing questions to Piers, to which he remained steadfastly silent. Then she would grow piqued at his lack of response and let him be for the next hour. But it was not long before she was chattering again.

And Piers was finding it increasingly difficult to not answer her. Without any interrogation of his own at all, he was learning quite a lot about the youngest Foxe sister, and to his dismay, he was beginning to wonder if she was as shallow and silly as he had first thought. Her remarks were witty and well formed. Her opinions substantial.

It was unsettling.

For as much as Piers was determined to keep a mental if not physical distance from the wayward lady, his psyche was being increasingly pulled toward her. She was enchanting, engaging, and quite intelligent. There had never been anyone in Piers's life—noble or otherwise—who had wanted to speak with him at such length. And her chatter had the added benefit of occupying his mind to thoughts other than his throbbing, burning fingers or the dangerous pair who hunted him.

For an instant—and just that most fleeting instant—Piers wondered what it would be like between them should he and Alys Foxe be of similar station. He laughed darkly at himself. Even were they of equal rank, she would not so much as glance his direction in his current state—filthy dirty, scarred and still bandaged in spots. She was obviously a lover of tales, was her monkey's moniker any indication, and so she likely would think him more akin to monstrous Grendel than brave Beowulf. He was surly, disrespectful, and had, at times, been physically intimidating to her. They were not meant to be friends, and that was for her own good whether she realized it or nay.

But that didn't mean Piers had to continue in the state he was. He could barely stand himself any longer, and he knew that he had become at least partially accustomed to his odor. He couldn't charge into Edward's court looking like some ghastly beast—his claims would be difficult enough to prove. Lucky for him, he could hear the rush of the river not far from where they walked. The road must have wound back to meet it once more.

"We're crossing the road," he tossed over his shoulder as he headed to the bank on the left. His voice was gravelly and cracked from disuse.

"Why? Is someone following us?" He heard the slight

rise of intrigue and excitement in her words, matched by the increased crunch of the leaves under her foot as she sped up to keep pace with him up the incline.

"That's the whole point of keeping to the wood, isn't it?" He reached the top of the rise and stopped, still in the cover of trees, and held a forefinger behind him, signaling for Alys to be quiet. He continued in a low voice as he scanned the long dirt avenue as far as his eyes could see in the afternoon light. "I believe the river is just over the far side."

"Of course it is," she replied brightly, and, Piers thought, a bit loudly. He frowned and brought his finger to his lips. She complied by speaking next in an exaggerated whisper. "We're nearly upon the village of Pilings. Were we to continue on, we'd run straight into the butcher. He's at the river's edge."

"Pilings?" he asked. At her game nod, he winced. "Terrible name for a village, isn't it?"

"Yes. But they are known for their pork."

"I see." Piers squatted down next to the packed surface of the road, both to stretch his tight muscles and to listen a moment longer. He heard nothing but the hollow wind, the rush of nearby water, the whisper and creak of the winter trees. He stood. "I hope for their sake that they've brought their pigs in to shelter for the night, for if I see one rooting about the leaves, I shall have his side meat for my supper. Come on."

They crossed the road at a run. Once they were safely to the other side and into the wood proper once more, Alys spoke.

"We could wait for nightfall then go into the village and steal one."

He looked sideways at her, and couldn't help his snort

of laughter. "Steal a pig? Have you any idea how difficult they are to catch?"

"The piglets, yes. But a full grown one is a bit harder to miss."

Then he truly laughed. "I'd like to see you try to steal a six hundred pound pig. They'd find your little flattened body under one the next morn and then throw you in a beggar's grave for a thief."

"Is that so?" she said haughtily.

"It is." He stopped at the broken edge of earth that capped a steep ravine down to the churning water. No getting down this way lest he wished to be drowned. Piers turned to his right and began to walk south once more, Alys following him, obviously quite offended.

"You underestimate me, husband. You think I can't do anything save for lie about and be waited on."

"Stop calling me husband. And I do believe you can do more than lie about and be waited on."

"You do?" He heard the shock in her voice.

"Yes. Well, not useful things, such as outfitting your-self properly for a journey, or listening to reason, but you're actually quite good at walking."

A clod of wet dirt whisked past his left ear to sail harm-lessly into the ravine below.

"You certainly have terrible aim, so no future at all in archery." Piers felt his spirits lifting merely through the act of speaking aloud. It was rather enjoyable to spar with Alys Foxe. He spied a path down the ravine wall. "Here we are." And he dropped down over the side with what he himself even thought of as a rather spry hop, leaving Alys to get down through her own devices.

"*Ooph!* Oh, hold on, Layla! Why are we going to the river again?"

"I need water," was all Piers was willing to disclose as

his feet touched the wet and pebbled strip of ground at the river's edge. His spirits lifted even further when he spotted the rocky overhang ahead of them, perhaps a third of the way back up the ravine. It would be a perfect shelter for the night—no one looking down from the road would be able to see them. The clouds blanketing the whole of the dark gray sky looked heavy—'twas likely to rain, or perhaps even snow should it grow colder. They would at least stay dry, if not completely warm.

"We'll camp up there," he called to Alys over his shoulder, and pointed toward the overhang as he walked past.

"Where are you going?"

"I'll be back."

"Oh, I think not," he heard her mutter. He glanced behind him and saw her hurrying along the river bank at his heels.

He stopped. "What are you doing?"

"I'm going with you."

"No, you're not. You can't."

"Yes, I can. You're not leaving me here alone. I'm not a complete idiot, Piers."

"What are you talking about? I said I'd be back."

"The oldest trick in the history of trickery!" she cried. "Don't think I haven't realized how early in the day it is to be making camp. You think to abandon me here while you go on your merry way with enough daylight to get as much distance between us as possible. *Voila*! No more Alys."

"That isn't my plan at all," Piers said, and he meant it. But actually, her idea was a rather good one, and Piers wondered why he hadn't come up with it himself. What better way to be rid of her than to just walk away into the woods on other pretenses and never return? She'd not realize she'd been abandoned for a good hour, and Piers knew he could run a fair distance in that amount of time, even with his whole hand now aching and itching.

"You can't follow me," he continued. "It's a . . . private matter."

Her eyes narrowed for a moment and then she flushed as she caught his meaning. Or the meaning he meant for her to catch. Let her think he meant to go find a nice comfortable log over which to move his bowels.

But then her face went suspicious again. "I don't believe you."

"I give you my word, I shall return."

"Not good enough," she said. He noted her eyes roving over his body and then she smiled. "Leave your bag as ransom."

"What?"

"Your pack. Leave it with me so that I will be certain of your return."

He rolled his eyes but then began to shrug out of his shoulder straps. He swung the bag in front of him and thrust his hand under the flap to find his only other clothing, the rough linen shirt he'd been wearing when Bevan had attacked him. Although the tears had been inexpertly mended by his savior, the old monk, the raggedy thing was stained a horrible brown from Piers's own blood, even after being boiled at the abbey.

"Oh, no," she said and then before he could stop her, she had snatched the bag from his grasp, his shirt stretched between his fist and the pack. "If whatever you're searching for is that important, you'll return for it."

He frowned at her and considered taking the bag back by force. He also considered strangling her. But the first would only assure him that he would be followed and have an audience for his bath, and he was not capable of the second, although right at that moment he was quite willing. So he simply jerked his shirt free.

"'Tis naught but a clean shirt," he said, shaking it at her before turning and beginning to walk along the riverbank, and continuing to rail at her. "I'm not going to ride it to London, for Christ's sake! Just afford me a bit of privacy, would you? And take care with my pack."

"Gladly!" she called after him. "Don't miss me too much! Enjoy your 'private moment!'"

Piers winced and turned to shout back at her, "You're quite crude for a girl, do you know?"

She smiled and waved and then turned to scramble up the bank to the rock overhang.

"I might be a bit," he called loudly. "Don't worry."

She threw up a careless hand, indicating that she had heard him, but didn't bother to look at him this time.

Piers missed her already.

It didn't take Alys long to set up her part of the primitive camp. She had nothing to unpack. The sounds of the river below swirled inside the mock cave with a hollow echo, and she dropped her bag near the back of the overhang, where the dirt was bone dry and soft like flour. She tossed Piers's pack next to hers, and then a moment later fell upon it, ripping at the ties. She leaned back once, looking down the river for sight of him. She saw none, so she turned her attention back to the pack, jerking it open fully.

She tried simply rifling through the contents, but they were jumbled together in the shadows of the deep leather bag, and so she finally resigned to pulling them out one by one and setting them on the ground.

A small roll of what looked like old, clean but stained,

bandages. His brown jug—she shook it, and at the watery rattle, uncorked it and turned it up. The droplets tasted faintly of soured wine, and Alys wondered how long it had been since the jug had contained proper fruit. Her tongue was barely moistened, but the jug was now emptied of all but air, and so she recorked it and set it in the dirt.

The remaining items were of even less interest: a small pouch containing a flint and steel; a pair of woolen hose that looked at if they had been half eaten by a wolf, and stained the same terrible brown as the bandages. Those she dropped into a pile with a wrinkle of her nose. Two sheathed blades emerged next—one large and serrated, the other slender and fine-edged, but both looked potentially deadly. A piece of oilcloth that contained naught but the strong smell of herring and a few pebbles of old, brown bread. Alys quickly popped the crumbs into her mouth.

A small, carved wooden bowl, and a crudely fashioned cross on a string of rough wooden beads rounded out the contents. Alys grinned at the cross—it must be a part of his poorly executed costume that he'd elected to forgo. Perhaps Piers feared God would strike him dead should he wear it, the liar.

Alys looked around her at the meager collection of items from the pack. Nothing. Not one piece of anything that gave her the tiniest insight to the enigmatic man she traveled with. She knew that her sister, Cecily, would be horrified to learn that Alys had gone through another's belongings without their permission, but Piers was obviously in a desperate situation, and Alys meant to help him, whether he wanted her to or nay.

She paused as the thought reminded her of something Sybilla might say, but then Alys pushed the uncomfortable idea away, reassuring herself that she was nothing like her eldest sister.

She began returning the items to the pack with a sigh. She would have to depend on what Piers deigned to tell her. At the rate they were going, she might know his surname by London.

Alys was reaching for the only thing left—the roll of bandages—when Layla scampered over and snatched up the old ball of cloth and began to worry at it.

"It's no toy, Layla, give it over." Alys leaned forward and swiped at the monkey's hands, snagging the end of the bandage in her fingertips. "Give it, before he comes back and we're both caught."

Layla chattered indignantly and threw the ball forcefully at Alys. It bounced off of her cheek and to the ground, unrolling like a skinny rug as she held on to its end. As the last bit unfurled, it spit a small golden object onto the dirt.

After an instant of disbelief, Alys raced the monkey to the piece and snatched it up just as Layla screamed with frustration.

"Oh, stop," she muttered, holding the golden thing between her thumb and forefinger and peering at it.

It was a ring, made of thick, hammered gold. At its center was a dark, oval carnelian stone, engraved with a bold letter M.

"Em," Alys mused aloud. "Mallory, perhaps? But why would Piers have the Mallory signet ring? Bevan was Warin Mallory's only son."

Don't be so certain.

Alys frowned at Layla, working out the riddle aloud. "Judith Angwedd is not Piers's mother. Bevan is his stepbrother, and Bevan tried to kill Piers. Piers alluded to the fact that Bevan was not Warin Mallory's only—oh!" Alys gasped and Layla chattered nervously. "Piers is Mallory's son, as well! But, then Bevan would be his half brother, not step. And 'tis obvious that ugly oaf is of Judith Angwedd's issue. Bevan would only be Pier's stepbrother if Piers was Warin Mallory's son and . . . *and Bevan was not!*"

Alys let her hand holding the ring drop to her lap as her mouth hung open. She continued to advise Layla, who was now sitting on her heels with both small hands over her eyes.

"Piers is on his way to see the king, and Judith Angwedd and Bevan are desperate to stop him, even to see him dead. It all makes sense now! Piers is trying to take Gillwick from Bevan! *Piers is the rightful lord of Gillwick Manor!*"

Alys's breath huffed out of her disbelievingly as Layla scampered away to sit atop their bag and worry at the fur over one knee, as if the monkey was trying to ignore her. Alys looked down at the ring once more.

"He is noble," she whispered. "Sybilla *would* allow it." Her head turned, and she stared down the river where Piers had disappeared. "I knew the Foxe Ring couldn't be wrong."

Then she hurriedly gathered up the string of bandage and rewrapped the ring, shoving it deep into the bottom of the pack once more. She retied the flap closed and placed the pack in what she hoped was a nonchalant position against her own limp bag. She adjusted its slouch twice for effect.

Her thoughts tumbled, like the river over the rocks below. She couldn't be certain of what she suspected of course, not until Piers confirmed it. But she was just certain enough now to not give up on him.

"A celebration is in order," Alys said to Layla. She patted her thigh while she gained her feet, and the monkey came scampering, climbing her skirt in a blink to sit on her shoulder. She picked up her bag and untied the drawstring, holding the bag open by its edges.

"Go on," she said to Layla, and shrugged her shoulder. "I know you don't like it, but I can't leave you behind and you'll have a great treat once we're through."

Once Layla was safely—albeit resentfully—confined, Alys drew the strap across her body. She paused in thought for only an instant before seizing and then shrugging into Piers's too-big pack. Then she left the rock shelter and began to climb the bank.

Alys knew she was taking a grave risk by following the road into Pilings, even though she didn't let her shoes so much as touch the packed dirt. She skipped-ran along the fringe of trees in her haste, one arm around the warm lump that was Layla, to keep from offending the monkey too much with her hurried passage. But she had to find some way to be of use to Piers, to get him to trust her. Perhaps by gaining them some much-needed supplies, he would feel her more worthy as a traveling companion, and even a friend.

Alys wondered with a wry lift of her mouth if all wives struggled so to gain their husbands' confidence.

He was rough, she admitted readily. Like a field dressed side of meat, rolled around in the dirt. Show him a bit of washing up though, expose his toughened hide to a generous warmth, and he could very possibly be quite delicious. Never in her life had she been responsible for another person's wants or needs—not even her own, really, and Alys was determined to win this challenge. If she had to steal, she would steal. But she would not return to the little camp by the river without the booty she set out for.

And besides, she was starving. She hadn't eaten a morsel in two days; Layla, since the night before. She already knew that Piers's bag was devoid of anything to eat. So unless he came back from his toilette with a feral chicken, they were all in desperate need of food.

As she hurried, looking around her all the time for sign of him or anyone else following her, she was also taking stock of her appearance. Both her fine cloak and the worn woolen gown beneath it were filthy from sleeping on the ground, full of bits of leaves and winter nettle. She held out one hand to inspect her fingers—disgusting. The creases of her knuckles and undersides of her nails were packed with black dirt. She turned her hand over and saw a thick layer of dried mud—likely from when she had thrown the clod of dirt at Piers. Should she wipe her hands on her skirt, 'twould only serve to worsen her appearance. She frowned. She could see the dwellings just ahead through the last bend of trees. With the awkward burdens of Piers's pack and her own bag, her cloak could only conceal a portion of her common skirt. Anyone happening upon her in the village would indeed take her for a thief or a—

"A beggar!" Alys said aloud with a grin. Of course! Should she scamper in to town, a clean and tidy woman walking along the road alone in a sable-lined cloak, it would only serve to raise suspicion and interest. She came to an abrupt halt.

Alys slid out of the pack and eased Layla's confinement to the ground, then took off her cloak and hid it away in Piers's pack. She looked fondly at her filthy palm once more before scrubbing the crumbly dirt all over her cheeks and forehead, while Layla chattered and writhed and fought within the bag on the side of the road.

"Fear not, noble Layla—your captivity will be short. A beggar, they will want to be rid of rather quickly." She paused suddenly as another idea came into her head. She quickly jerked the tie out of her hair, wincing as several strands went with it, and then bent to the ground, swiping up a large handful of the forest floor. She raked the molding leaves and twigs through her hair, tangling and snarling her locks until they stood out from her face in crazy, dirty lumps.

"There! A *mad* beggar, they will wish gone immediately!" She reclaimed Piers's pack and hitched her sack over her head to seat the strap across her chest. "Sorry, girl. Ow! Don't pinch!" She gave the bundled monkey a light pat through the bag and then she skittered around the curve of forest and breached Pilings behind the farthest row of cottages.

The settlement was largely quiet, save for the honking of some goose across the town and the sharp ringing sound of perhaps someone banging a spoon against the side of a pot. A dog barked twice, from a safe distance away, and then all was silent.

Alys stepped carefully along the narrow avenue of daubed wall and wood, her crunching footsteps making her wince. She pulled a face as she realized there was no rear window on the north wall of this particular cottage. She came to the corner of the house and slowly, slowly peered around it. The village center was straight ahead, and empty. She bolted across the twenty or so feet to duck behind the next cottage backing the wood. She reckoned in this manner, she could make her way around the entire town without being seen.

The rear of the next cottage was also devoid of anything useful, as was the one after. She was coming upon the far corner of her current cover, growing more cross with each impatient step, when she ran full body into the woman coming around the side of the house.

The woman, matronly and kind-faced, cried out and threw up her hands, dropping her shallow basket of kitchen scraps. Alys stepped back quickly, and then, remembering her ruse, dropped into a crouch.

"Halloo, halloo! Don't 'urt me, milady, I beg of ye!" Alys was rather proud of her put-on accent.

"Good gracious, child!" the woman gasped, and took in Alys's appearance with a look of distrust. "Just who might you be, and what business have you sneaking about the backside of my house?"

"Only hopin' fer some small scrap to eat, milady." Alys bobbed her head and grinned like an idiot. It was quite difficult to keep from laughing outright at the woman's horrified expression. "Would ye 'ave mercy on a poor beggar?"

The woman's eyes narrowed. "Are you one of the wood people?"

Alys froze. She wasn't certain if the village woman truly thought her to be one of the storied rebels who, according to legend, dwelt invisibly among the trees, or if the question was some sort of test, and so she didn't know which answer would best help her mission.

"You can tell me if you are," the woman continued. "I vow I shan't turn you in."

Alys nodded her head once quickly, and waited.

"Oh, you unfortunate thing!" The woman pressed a palm to her bosom. "I just knew they were in a poor state, no matter the rumors. Did they turn you out?"

Alys nodded again, completely baffled by the conversation she was participating in. The woman seemed convinced that Alys was a character from a fictional tale.

"They says I's mad," Alys whispered. "'No food for you! Get out!' they says."

The woman pressed her lips together and shook her head. Then her face grew thoughtful. "You're Ella's girl, are you not? Your hair, it—"

Alys nodded again. The situation was growing more strange by the moment.

"I thought as much." The matron smiled sympathetically. "You'd be what? Fourteen now? I haven't seen you since you were just walking. I must say I'm not a bit surprised for the way they've treated you, the lawless heathens."

Fourteen? Alys cried to herself in outrage. But outwardly, she smiled and bobbed her head again. "Can you 'elp me, milady? I'd return to . . . to me mother and make amends. May'ap I 'ad some little thing to take 'er . . . ? A piece of bread or . . . or a pig. Or a lovely, lovely chair."

The woman winced. "Of course, of course." She looked over her shoulder quickly and then held her palms toward Alys. *"You stay here,"* she said slowly and emphatically. She pantomimed along with the rest of her words. "I'll bring you some food. If my husband sees you—*very cross.*" She frowned and shook her head.

Alys nodded, grinned, gave a sniffling laugh. "Husband cross. Mean. Grr!" Alys raked her fingers through the air like claws and tried not to laugh at the thought of her own husband being slightly put-out with her as well, if he only knew where she was.

"That's right. So you stay here." The woman backed slowly away and then turned with a swirl of her plain skirt and disappeared around the side of the cottage.

Alys stood upright with a sigh and stretched her neck by rolling her head. It was difficult work, playing at being mad. Her jaws ached and her knees trembled. She shoved her arm down into her sack, her fingers searching for the little purse. Her fingers fought with the drawn opening while Layla clung to her arm.

"Layla!" Alys whispered through her teeth at the bag, as her fingers tentatively found their intended item and she fought to withdraw her hand from the monkey's clutches. "Get off! *Let go!*"

The woman came around the side of the house, a rough sack in her arms, just in time to hear Alys's words, and see her jerk her arm out of the bag's opening. Alys quickly resumed her previously subservient posture.

"And good day once more, milady!" she keened. At her side, Layla fought and tumbled in the bag, bumping very obviously against her hip.

The woman frowned, and her eyes dropped to the writhing sack warily. "What have you in there, child?"

Alys blinked, her mind searching for a logical reply. "A monkey."

The woman's eyes widened and she rolled her lips inward for a moment. "A monkey. Of course you do."

Alys took a step forward. "Do ye wish to see 'er? She likely wouldn't bite ye."

The woman stepped back quickly. "No! No, that's quite alright. Well, then, here you are." She stretched out her arms as far as they would reach, Alys assumed to avoid coming any closer to her than was absolutely necessary. Alys reached out and took the bag with a wide grin and bob of her entire body.

"There's some meat, and a few other small things, as well. All I could lay hand to quickly without the husband seeing. May God bless us both with it, you poor child."

Alys shuffled closer to the woman, who cringed for an instant when Alys's closed fist shot out toward her.

"Fer yer kindness, milady."

The woman held up her palms with a nervous smile. "No. You may keep whatever it is."

Alys let a genuine smile replace the mad grin she had been keeping thus far. "Please. I would not be indebted to you, nor take from your family's mouths without repayment."

The woman frowned faintly and then after a moment, hesitantly held out her palm, wrapping her fingers around the item Alys placed there, never taking her eyes from her.

Alys kept her true smile as she asked, "Would you be so kind as to point me in the direction of London?"

The woman nodded absently toward the forest, the opposite side of town from which Alys had come. "Simply follow the road."

Alys gave her best curtsey. "I thank you. Good day, milady!" Then she turned and ran straight into the wood at her back.

After the little blond thing was gone, the village woman opened her hand warily. In her palm lay a shining gold coin.

She looked into the darkening wood with a frown as she heard the sound of riders approaching like the start of a landslide.

Chapter 9

Alys was gone.

Piers whipped his head around, then turned on his heel, his eyes scanning the river below, the ravine sides. His hair lay cold and dripping on his shoulders, but the chill he felt was not from the frigid water he'd washed with. He threw the bundle of monk's robe and his filthy shirt to the ground.

Alys was gone, and she'd taken his pack with her.

The Mallory signet ring—the tentative evidence of his birthright—hidden deep inside.

He wanted to shout her name through the trees. He wanted to take off at a run to the road. He stood there, turning in circles, his mind racing with the possible explanations.

She'd grown tired of him and left. No—where would she go but back to Fallstowe? And Piers knew she'd rather drown herself in the river than marry Clement Cobb, or worse, face her sister, Sybilla, in defeat.

At that thought, he looked down at the rushing water once more. No body. And Piers had been downstream. He would have seen her tumble past him as he washed.

Perhaps after a certain amount of time, she'd decided to follow him after all, and become lost in the wood. Perhaps even now, she was walking, searching, deeper into the forest.

Then he did almost shout her name. Alone, she was certain to die. But then he thought of who may be in the vicinity of the road, the sounds of their travel undecipherable to Piers over the crash of the water.

Or mayhap Judith Angwedd and Bevan had found her, found his pack, and taken her. Piers thought of Bevan, bringing him into clear focus in his mind's eye, along with all of the terrible things Piers knew the bastard capable of. He looked down: the sandy floor of the overhang was plowed with footsteps, but Piers could not decipher them.

Then he was out of the cave, charging up the steep bank itself, falling, slipping, scrambling upright, fighting his way to the road. He gained the shoulder of the ravine and sprinted and dodged through the trees to the road where he came to a skidding halt, his head swiveling in either direction.

Empty.

Piers walked to the center of the track, where fresh hoof prints churned and tilled the cold, hard dirt. He looked both ways again. Riders had passed through here, mayhap only moments ago. And now, Alys was gone.

He took a deep breath, and roared to the treetops. *"Alys!"*

Within the echo of his shout, Piers heard a crunching through the wood. He spun around toward the sound and she emerged casually from the trees as if his command of her name had summoned her. Her bag was crossed over her body, her cloakless shoulders supporting his pack. She carried a bundle under one arm, and it was upon that same shoulder which Layla rode. Alys was chewing, and passed a bit of whatever was in her hand up to the monkey. The youngest lady of the house of Fallstowe looked as though she had been in a brawl with a midden heap, and lost badly.

"You really shouldn't shout, Piers. That's a poor way of keeping our whereabouts secret." She turned her gaze to him fully then, and stopped at the edge of the road. Her jaws paused for a moment, and then she swallowed forcefully. She looked him up and down. "You took a bath!"

"Where in fucking hell have you been?" he growled even as he marched toward her. She did not shirk at his approach. Piers's heart, however, pounded and tripped at the sight of her, safe, and uninjured, and alone.

"You look . . . ah, much better, I must say. Quite . . . well"—she cleared her throat and swallowed again—"Quite an improvement, Piers."

Layla screamed indignantly as Piers reached out to spin Alys around. He grabbed the flap of his pack and began to pull it from her back. "Give me my goddamn bag! *And where have you been?* A band of riders has just come through, and by the size of the party, I do doubt they were simple travelers. They could have seen you, you little fool!"

It was either that, or kiss her for the fright she'd given him.

"My, you do curse a lot when you're surprised. Wait a moment, and I'll take the pack off and give it to you—if you rip both my arms off, I'll drop my apple!"

He let go of her. "You were supposed to wait for me. Where did you get an apple?" He jerked the pack from her hand when she held it to him.

"You didn't tell me to wait for you. And besides, you're not responsible for me, are you?" She took a crunching bite of the small blushing fruit in her hand.

"You stole my bag," he growled and then stormed past her toward the ravine again. His heart still pounded so that he could no longer look at her.

"Since I'm here and have returned your bag, you can hardly say I stole it. You told me not to let anything happen to it, so I took it to Pilings with me. My cloak is in there, by the way, and I'd like it back—I'm freezing."

He stopped and spun around. "You went into the village?"

"Yes, but your bag was with me the entire time, so don't worry—your ring is safe." She took another bite.

"Did anyone see y—" he broke off as he realized what she said. "You went through my bag?"

She swallowed her mouthful of apple. "Yes. I did. And the only one in Pilings who saw me"—she held her arms out from her body and turned her face to the side, her nose loftily in the air—"thought me a mad, wandering woman of the wood people. I came upon no band of bloodthirsty riders. Only a simple village matron."

"You had no right," he said through his teeth and turned toward the ravine again.

"Would it help if I apologized?" she called from behind him, obviously around a mouthful of fruit.

"No," he threw back. He reached the steep path to the river bank and hopped down. Turning, he held up a hand to Alys, who took it as she made her own way onto the narrow track. Her fingers were impossibly cool and smooth, slender and frail feeling, as if her bones were the tiniest dried twigs, liable to snap off in his palms with the slightest squeeze of his own clumsy, farmhand digits.

"Thank you. You needn't worry that I've outed us," she continued when he released her and they made their way down the bank. "There was but one woman who saw me, and as I've said, she thought me an insignificant beggar. Did you not notice my costume? I was brilliant as a madwoman, I tell you. You should have seen me, Piers."

"You're mad, alright," he growled, and started up the incline once more at the bottom of the overhang. "You have no idea the jeopardy in which you've placed us, Alys. We don't know who the riders are—they may return to search for us."

"You worry overmuch." In a moment, she was at his side. She dropped her bag to the dirt and her monkey scrambled down to sit at her feet, its eyes locked on the bundle under Alys's arm. She sank into a cross-legged seat, her gown falling naturally over her knees. She began opening the bundle, chattering, chattering all the while.

"Even should someone inquire of the woman about me, and even should she call me to mind with suspicion, they would not expect you or me to be *behind* the village." She withdrew her hand and tossed him an apple with a grin. He caught it, and the sweet tangy smell of the fruit caused his mouth to water, and a wave of nausea to wash over him. He broke into a sweat.

She continued, "'Tis early yet—look at the light. They'll assume we've moved through already, as I made it a point to confirm the direction of London before I left. Once away from her, I simply circled the village and"—she spread her arms with a sly smile—"here I am once more. Safe and sound and bearing gifts."

He took a bite of the apple, half of it disappearing into his mouth. He chewed and forced the hard chunks of food down his constricted throat, giving himself time to think, while she produced yet another of the precious fruits and held it up with a triumphant "hah!" before the monkey. Layla snatched it, jumping up and down with excitement, before scampering to the back of the cave-like shelter and hunkering down to eat.

She could be right. It was unlikely that anyone suspecting Alys would think her to still be in the area. He would not praise her, however.

He gestured to her roughly with the half eaten apple. "'Twas still foolish." I was worried when I couldn't find you, he said, but only to himself.

Alys held up her forefinger. "Or brilliant." She began digging through the bundle again, her blond hair a snarl of leaves and dirt. The fluffy tangles quivered with her every movement, and the sight of her, now that the imminent danger was past, was nearly enough to force a grin to Piers's mouth.

She did look quite mad. Nothing like a lady of one of the richest houses in England. He polished off the apple, core and all, in one bite. Perhaps it was only food that his body needed. His stomach did feel more settled now.

Alys gasped, and then looked up at him suddenly. "Could we have a fire tonight, Piers?"

He shook his head. "We're too close to the road."

She huffed and her fists jerked at the bundle on her lap in frustration. "Please? Perhaps later? Once it's fully dark?"

He frowned "I don't know. You've already taken enough risks for one day, I'd wager." He paused. "Why?"

"Well, because I'm cold, for one—I've been cold for *days,* and I'm sick of it. *And* you're not the only one in need of washing up. *And* we have apples"—she reached into the bag then withdrew her hands one at a time—"*and* an onion. And . . . a *pig*!"

Piers felt his eyebrows raise. In her hands were a small, blocky onion and a hunk of striped, cured sidemeat. In that instant, Piers could taste the salty pork on his tongue, the tang of the onion in the juice of the fruit. His stomach clenched. It was a feast she presented to him.

She winked at him. "Never again doubt me, fair?"

"I'll think upon it," was all he said.

Alys sighed and rolled her eyes, replacing the food-stuffs in the bundle. She reached for her own bag and began searching through it. "Very well. But I am going to the river to wash while there is still light."

"I'll go with you," he said.

"I think not," Alys said with a laugh. "Although we *are* married, I still feel we don't know each other well enough for you to watch me bathe."

Piers's face burned at the thought. "We're *not* married."

"Whatever you say, husband."

His brows lowered even further. "Is that *soap?*"

"Yes," she said mildly, looking at the items in her left hand. "And my hairbrush. How else am I to bathe prop-erly? Would you be so kind as to make use of one of those knives in your pack and cut a towel from my blue gown, please?"

"You're going to wash with perse."

"As I imagine it will feel quite smooth against my skin, yes."

Piers shook his head as he retrieved a knife and cut a long, rectangular strip from the hem of the costly gown. He handed it up to her, and noticed that while he had been mangling her dress, Alys had also retrieved her fine slip-pers from her bag and exchanged them for the worn leather shoes on her feet.

She was going to wash in a river, with a perse cloth, while standing in silk slippers.

"Thank you," she said sweetly as she took the rag.

"Don't go far," he warned. "Just below us. I won't watch."

"Very well," she conceded, and then pointed to Layla when the monkey scampered over to join her. "No, Layla, you stay with Piers."

The monkey hunkered down on her haunches as if pouting. Piers felt a bit resentful himself.

Alys turned to leave the ravine, but paused at the edge to look back at him. "And Piers?"

"Yes?"

"You have my complete permission to go through my bag." She gave him a wide grin and then disappeared down the bank.

"Holy—!" Alys shrieked when she first dipped the wadded up perse in the river. Icy did not even come close to describing the temperature of the water. Her skirts were tied into a knot just below her knees, and she'd already brushed and re-tied her hair back from her face. Unlike Piers, she was unwilling to wash her hair in such cold weather without the assurance of a warm fire to dry it by, but she was pleased to note that the smell of it wasn't completely unpleasant—rather woodsy, actually.

"Alys?" She heard Piers's faint call. She looked up and saw him standing at the edge of the shelter, looking wide and wild.

She waved at him, signaling that all was well. Then she turned back to her task grimly, wincing as the frigid water ran over her knuckles when she wrung out the perse rag.

She scrubbed at her face and neck, her skin burning both from the vigorous washing and the cold water. Then she dipped into the bodice of her dress, huffing out her breaths in "ha-ha-ha" as her skin threatened to shiver from her flesh. The spots under her arms and breasts were the worst, by far, but the fresh scent of sandalwood from her soap did ease the discomfort a bit. After her legs and private areas were swiped clean, she rinsed the rag in the river and laid it on a nearby rock while she loosened her skirts and then attacked them with her hairbrush.

Even the full-body chill that had seized her was not strong enough to shake the image of a freshly-clean Piers from her mind. She had been right at her earlier guess that a bit of washing up would do wonders for his person, but she could never have imagined the sight which would be revealed beneath all that dirt and old robes. The goose-flesh on her arms and legs were only partly due to her damp skin now.

Noble, strong of body . . .

And he had helped her down the ravine—actually extended his hand and touched her without her request. Alys could not help but think that perhaps he was beginning to soften toward her. She paused for a moment, her hairbrush held mid-stroke over her skirt, as a realization occurred to her. Alys had not known that Piers's bag contained something as meaningful as the signet ring when he'd left it in her care, but Piers had.

A sudden breeze swept through the ravine over the river at her toes and Alys smelled smoke. She turned her head toward the bank and saw Piers crouched down near the opening of the overhang, a column of smoke fluttering sideways under his hands.

He was making her a fire!

A slow smile crept over her face and she felt a warmth in her chest beneath the field of prickly flesh. Perhaps the risk of a fire was a repayment for the food she had obtained them, or perhaps he was simply weary of bearing the cold, as well. Alys hoped those weren't the only reasons, though.

She watched him pull his straggly, uneven locks of hair away from the growing flames, and an idea struck her. She gathered up the slippery soap and damp rag. Stepping gingerly in deference to her thin-soled, silk slippers on her wet and frozen feet—she hadn't wanted to get her only pair of shoes suitable for walking wet—she made her way over the rocky river bank to the ravine wall, and began to climb carefully.

Piers only glanced at her as she came into the overhang— he was busy skewering the onion between a pair of apples and situating them over the flames. The sidemeat was already leaning over the fire at a sharp angle, so that its juices would run down the slab and into the little wooden bowl she recognized from Piers's pack. Doubt came into her mind for a moment, and as much as she was looking forward to the meal and the warmth, she hoped they weren't taking a foolish risk by having a fire.

"You think it's alright, then?" she asked, as she was putting her things away, save her slippers which she had kicked off by the fire. She tried to watch him closely as she pulled the drawstring tight, having learned already that Piers's emotions were fleeting across his face. She wanted to be sure to catch them if they showed.

He looked over at her, his eyes not quite reaching hers before he brought his attention back to the food once more. "What's alright?"

"The fire." She approached him and sank to her bottom, already feeling the delicious warmth radiating from the flames. The meat popped once, a prelude of the grand meal to come.

He shrugged. "'S'fine."

"I hope so, because I don't believe I've ever felt anything so lovely," she sighed and began brushing at the bottoms of her feet with her hands before slipping into her leather shoes. "If you told me we had to put it out, I'd likely throw you from this cliff."

He snorted. "You couldn't throw Layla from this cliff."

"You underestimate me again, husband. I'm quite strong for my size." She thought he would rise to the bait of her calling him by that title, but he just huffed and shook his head. He was proving quite difficult to draw into conversation unless he was angry.

"Did you do that?" she asked, pointing to the little carved bowl collecting the drippings.

He nodded, and then after a moment, said, "It was a way to pass the time while I was healing." He glanced at her. "It's not very good, I know."

"I think it's a lovely bowl," Alys argued. "It's round, and—" She searched her mind frantically for some other quality to praise. "Not very deep, which can be bothersome in a bowl. And it's very . . . well, round. Nicely so."

He made no comment.

Oh, well. Nothing else for her to do but go on and ask.

"I want to cut your hair," she blurted.

His movements ceased abruptly and he froze for a moment. Then he turned his face slowly toward her. "What did you say?"

"Your hair." Alys cleared her throat, wondering at his hostile stare. "I want to cut it."

"That's what I thought you said. No."

"No? Why?"

"Just . . . no." He brushed his hands together and rose to his feet.

"It looks simply dreadful, Piers," Alys argued.

"What do you care what my hair looks like, eh?"

"It's not entirely for my benefit," Alys reasoned. "You can't give audience to the king looking like . . . like—" She broke off when he turned to look back at her expectantly, and then she settled for waving her hand in the general direction of his head, and pulled a frightened face.

To her surprise, he gave her an amused grin. "Grendel, perhaps?"

She gasped, snapped her fingers and pointed at him. "That's it exactly! Grendel!"

He huffed a laugh and shook his head, squatting down once more near his bag to retrieve the roll of bandages. He spoke as he pulled a length of the cloth from the ball which still held his ring tight in its center. "I had two men chop at my hair in a fortnight, neither with my permission. You'll forgive me if I don't allow you to do the same."

"Why were two men cutting your hair? And so badly, at that?"

He sliced off a length of bandage with his blade, and seemed to think on her question as he draped the piece over his knee and replaced the roll in his bag. Alys waited while dusk crept quietly around their fire, as if to sit with them and share their company. She welcomed the dark, felt more safe with each tree across the river that was lost to her sight, consumed by the advancing, hungry night. Piers turned slightly away from her while he rewrapped his fingers where Layla had bitten him, and Alys realized he was not going to answer her without encouragement.

"Of course, the style of the day is for men to wear their hair rather long," she commented nonchalantly. "But it's most oft fashioned to be straight, and certainly no longer than the shoulder. Yours is much longer—in, ah, *parts*, that is—and quite, um . . . wavy. Ish."

"Wavy-ish?" Piers teased.

"Yes. And I do believe I can see your scalp above your left ear. It's not at all becoming to you, if you'll forgive me for saying so."

He pulled the knot of his bandage tight with his teeth.

The tangy scent of cooking pork was blooming in a warm cloud around them.

"The last man to cut at my hair was the monk who saved my life," he said quietly. "He did it while I was unconscious, in order to tend the wounds on my head."

"And before that?" Alys prompted.

Piers sighed and looked to the ground between his knees. "Bevan. Before he tried to beat me to death."

Alys swallowed, shocked, but unwilling to break the spell of the conversation by an exclamation of horror. "He thought you Samson?" she asked lightly.

"Perhaps." Piers nodded absently. "He said I was always vain of my hair. It repulsed him, reminded him of the common trash I was. More likely he was envious of it, the bloody-headed bastard." He looked to her suddenly. "Do you know him?"

"I have seen him on scant occasion," Alys admitted. "His head is quite the nastiest part of him, I agree."

"If only that were true, mayhap he would not be so evil." Piers moved to the fire to adjust the meat, which was now sizzling in earnest. The wonderful smell of pork roasting over glowing coals seemed almost too pleasant, playing in accompaniment to Piers's grisly anecdote. The wide blade of his smooth-edged knife caught the fire like a mirror as he prodded the fruit.

"Any matter," he continued, "both were unpleasant experiences, to say the least."

Alys nodded. "I'm sorry. But Piers, you can't go into Edward's court looking as you do now. You're to request something of the king, are you not? That's why you're going?" She didn't want to reveal her suspicions of his mission too soon.

Piers nodded, but said nothing.

"Then you must approach him with respect, for him

and for yourself. No man worthy of audience with the king would dare enter his court looking less than his very best." She waited. "Surely you can't think to leave it like that . . . forever?"

He shook his head and sighed. "No. I've considered my appearance as well. You're right."

Alys's heart leapt. She'd never thought to hear those words from his mouth.

He looked at her again, and in his eyes, Alys saw doubt bruised with distrust. "How much would you cut?"

Alys winced. "All of it, I'm afraid. There's nothing else to do, Piers. If you could only see—"

"I know. I know how it must look, just by the feel of it." Still, he had not consented.

"You can sharpen your knife until it would cut a kiss," she encouraged. "And I have a hairbrush, and—"

He held up a hand, cutting off her enthusiastic speech. "Fine."

"Fine?"

He swiped the blade, flat side, against his thigh and then spun the knife expertly in his hand, offering it to her handle first. She took it hesitantly, worried that he might snatch it back in the last instant.

But he did not. "I must succeed with the king, Alys. If cutting my hair will help in the smallest way, so be it. I can not fail. If I do, I am truly a dead man."

"Then you shall not fail," she assured him solemnly, shaking her head. Then she cracked a smile for him. There was no need to be so dour. "I am Lady Alys Foxe, and I will not allow it."

To her relief, he returned her grin. She rose to fetch her brush from her bag once more as he relaxed fully to his backside.

She came to stand behind him, and an only slightly sinful notion occurred to her. "You should take off your shirt."

He glanced over his shoulder at her.

"You'll itch," she explained sensibly, trying to keep her eyes from going wide.

He nodded and an instant later, his broad back glowed in the firelight. Alys frowned at the old bruises, still yellow and green, painted across his ribs and lower back. *My poor Piers*, she said to herself. She wanted to touch those marks, comfort him.

Instead, she began brushing his hair, jerking the brush through the half dried snarls roughly so that he would not suspect the tears in her eyes or the weakness of her heart in that moment.

He was beginning to trust her, and that was enough for Alys.

For now.

Chapter 10

It was well past midnight when Sybilla Foxe received the first progress report on the search for Alys and the rogue commoner, Piers Mallory. And although there was no purpose for anyone else to be about the hall at this hour, she was—quite to her disgust—not alone.

Fallstowe's steward, Graves, stood at Sybilla's back, as usual, and his was the only presence Sybilla welcomed. She could be completely alone in the old man's company should she wish it, or at once have the most trusted and loyal inhabitant of Fallstowe at her council. But Clement Cobb had come running at word that one of Fallstowe's soldiers had returned, and at his very heels trod Judith Angwedd. The sight of the woman was enough now to make Sybilla nauseous, she of the large teeth, girlish coif, and sickeningly sweet mannerisms. Sybilla did not hold the reins of Fallstowe through stupidity or naïveté, and like her mother, she was an expert at knowing when someone was trying to play her false.

While others might have missed the signs, Sybilla had known that morning that Judith Angwedd had seduced Clement Cobb. It was almost as if the air in the hall had been scented with betrayal. Sybilla had ordered the entire massive stone floor and all of the furniture scrubbed with strong soap, and incense burned even now—a nod to her mother's old ways. She knew that it was likely the reason Etheldred Cobb had taken to her guest rooms all the day with her maid—she was hypocritically mortified by her usually meek son's blatant indiscretion. Sybilla didn't know where Bevan Mallory was, nor did she care.

She watched Clement Cobb, pacing below her dais, wringing his hands. Judith Angwedd sat at the end of a nearby table, her predatory gaze following him with a transparent smile of contentment. Sybilla was yet unsure as to why Judith Angwedd had bothered with the sensitive and distraught young man, and she considered the possible explanations while she waited for the soldier to be brought to her.

Perhaps she thought to marry him, increasing Gillwick's— and her son's—worth, not to mention her own station.

Perhaps she hoped Clement knew some piece of information that would aid the search for her dead husband's bastard, although that seemed too much of a stretch. Clement did not exactly socialize in the same circles as illegitimate farmhands.

Or perhaps—and Sybilla thought most likely—Judith Angwedd only sought to interject strife and despair at Fallstowe. Sybilla had felt the woman's green loathing of her the instant Judith Angwedd Mallory had first entered her hall. Should Alys be found alive—pray God— it would be no little blow to her pride for Clement Cobb to have been found unfaithful to his newly betrothed, only days after they were promised and while she was missing and feared dead.

As much as Sybilla detested Judith Angwedd, she surmised the woman was clever. Clever and mean, and it would be in keeping with her character to ruin anything she could that she deemed more or better than what she herself had.

Sybilla would never force Alys to wed a man of so obviously little discernment, but Alys would have to accept someone else quickly. Their time was running out. Perhaps John Hart would still consider the youngest Foxe sister—he had seemed quite eager to find a bride.

As soon as Alys was safely away from Fallstowe, Sybilla would press Cecily for a decision regarding her religious vows. If none was forthcoming, Cecily, too, would wed. Sybilla had ignored and then blatantly disobeyed Edward for too long. Already, the king had called his tenants-in-chief to appear with all owed military service to Worcester at Midsummer for, Sybilla assumed, an attack on the Welsh. The next time he summoned her and she refused, Sybilla knew that the king would have an endless army at his disposal with which to lay siege to Fallstowe and take it by force under charges of treason.

Or try to, any matter.

But if Alys was already dead, then all her precautions to protect her sister had been in vain, and none of it would matter any longer. She would have failed her mother, betrayed her. Betrayed them all.

The soldier approached, his quilted tunic dirty, but his steps sharp, his expression intent. In his right hand he carried a small cloth pouch. At the man's entrance, Clement Cobb rushed to the dais, his pale, trembling hand gripping the edge of Sybilla's table. Sybilla saw Judith Angwedd's ears—like some feral bitch's—practically perk.

The soldier's cracking footsteps came to a halt before Sybilla's table, and he bowed. "My lady."

"Have you found her?"

"Not as of yet, milady. We picked up an odd trail of two

persons traveling afoot from Fallstowe's gate into the wood—a large man, and someone smaller, likely a woman. There seemed to be some sort of a tussle by the way the brush was flattened, but both were well enough after to continue." Sybilla was shocked that Alys had been at the very threshold of her own home and then fled, and her mind flew with the possible reasons. But she held her tongue, letting the man finish his report uninterrupted.

"The trail led southeast, the side of the road opposite the river. We found what we think was a camp, although they had no fire. There was strange scat near the site, containing what seemed to be pomegranate seeds."

At this, Clement gasped and looked to Sybilla. "Mother's pet?"

Sybilla did not bother to look at the despicable weakling, only nodded to the soldier. "Go on."

"Several miles farther, the tracks crossed the road and went down a ravine and to a riverbank. The trail was fresh, we could not have been more than a quarter hour behind them, the daylight still plentiful. But at the river, the footsteps diverged, the man heading away down stream. The smaller footprints backtracked up the ravine and then disappeared."

Sybilla raised an eyebrow. "Disappeared?"

"The tracks were difficult to follow through the forest without the larger set to mark them," the soldier explained without apology. "She did not take to the road. But we continued on to the most likely destination for a young woman traveling alone, with night swiftly approaching."

"And that would be?"

"The village of Pilings, milady. We saw no sign of her, but there was this." He took a single step forward, deposited the pouch on Sybilla's table, and then returned to his previous stance.

Sybilla picked up the cloth bag—it felt largely empty. She pulled open the drawstring and upended the pouch into her palm. She looked down.

A gold coin, a stylized image of the king on one side. Sybilla turned it over, and her blood ran cold at the sight of the large, scripted F.

Fallstowe.

She looked up at the soldier, and he had her answer ready before she could voice the question.

"A village woman offered it, reluctantly. Said a young girl had come from the wood begging for food. The woman thought her quite mad until the end of their encounter, when she was offered this in payment for the charity, and then asked if the road through the village was the London Road. The girl left the village in that direction, but there was no trail to follow."

Sybilla turned the coin over and over in her palm with the meaty base of her thumb and fingertips. "Did this villager say what the girl looked like?"

The soldier nodded. "Hair the color of straw. Mayhap fourteen years. Carrying a bag containing something alive, allegedly"—the soldier cleared his throat—"a monkey."

"It *is* her!" Clement Cobb wailed, and dropped his high forehead dramatically onto his forearm. "Oh, my sweet angel, how I have betrayed you!"

"Shut up, Clement," Sybilla said evenly. She placed the coin on the table carefully, precisely, so that it made not a whisper of noise against the wood. She looked at the soldier again. "Think you she indeed hies to London?"

"Aye, milady."

Behind the soldier, Judith Angwedd stood with an

abrupt screech of the wooden bench. "What of the man? Did you follow *his* tracks? Where is he?" she demanded shrilly.

No one dare look at Judith Angwedd save Sybilla, who sent the woman her most level, cold stare.

"I have given you no leave to address my envoy."

Judith Angwedd's cheeks bloomed a shade akin to that of her hair, although the skin of her neck and around her eyes went snow white. "I must know," she choked on the rage in her throat.

"Fallstowe's soldiers were not sent to do your bidding, Judith Angwedd," Sybilla clarified. "You are here upon my charity, and that is all. I understand that you wish to intercept this Piers before he reaches London—for fear of what he will witness to Edward against you, likely. But you will hold your tongue while I question this soldier as to my own interest or be gone from this castle."

"You high-handed sow," Judith Angwedd hissed, all color gone from her face now, as well as all previously feigned respect from her words. "I am not the only one who should be fearful of witness against me to the king. Likely your precious little princess will have her revenge on you and see you to the executioner's block for your family's fraud against the crown. And I hope to be there to see your head roll across the green, as your lying, witch mother's should have!"

The air in the hall seemed to vibrate, like the moment before a lightning strike. The temperature dropped, or so it seemed to Sybilla. She rose from her chair calmly, her eyes never leaving the stricken face of Judith Angwedd. Sybilla walked the length of the table, her steps measured and sure. Holding her skirts up briefly, she stepped from the dais, and her heels clicked dully across the stones of the hall, her pace increasing.

Judith Angwedd's eyes began to widen. "What are you doing?" she demanded, but it was false bravado. Sybilla could hear the tremble of her voice, could practically smell the woman's sour dread.

"Stay away from me!" Judith Angwedd warned hollowly, and stumbled backward, her flight halted by the table behind her.

Sybilla's hand shot out and she struck the woman across the face before she had even come fully before her, the sound echoing like a thunderclap. Judith Angwedd's head snapped to the side. The woman had barely brought her face forward when Sybilla struck her again, and this time, Judith Angwedd cried out and tumbled down the side of the table to fall to the stones on her hip. The woman's hand came to her face, and when she looked up, Sybilla was darkly pleased to see the tears in her wide, frightened eyes, and the small trickle of blood from the corner of her mouth.

"You will remember in whose hall you stand, and to whom you speak." Inside, Sybilla was shaking with rage, and only keeping herself from falling upon Judith Angwedd and beating the life from her by the tiniest shred of self-control. Outwardly though, her voice was calm, cold, and threaded with iron. Let there be no doubt in Judith Angwedd's mind who ruled here, and what her disrespect would reap her.

"Should you ever again think to speak ill of my mother, Judith Angwedd Mallory—even to *yourself*—hear this: I will know. I will know, and I will hunt you, and I will wring the breath from your body with my own hands."

The fat curls around the woman's face danced. "You can't threaten me like that," she whispered, her face a mask of horrified disbelief, her hand still cradling the side of her face.

Sybilla smiled briefly, and the sight must have been chilling by the way Judith Angwedd recoiled. "I can do anything I please. For instance—" She angled her chin slightly over her shoulder. "Graves, give my command to the archers: once Lady Mallory and her son cross over Fallstowe's drawbridge, if they are ever again seen within range of the walls—together or separately—they are to be shot dead, without inquiry."

"Regular arrows, or flaming ones, Madam?" Graves asked sincerely.

"That is at their own discretion, Graves."

The soldier volunteered, "I shall relay the order upon my return to the garrison, if my lady wishes."

Sybilla threw up a hand granting careless permission, and soon the clicking steps of the soldier were echoing away from the hall.

Judith Angwedd gasped. "Edward will hear of this, I warn you."

Sybilla threw back her head and laughed to the buttresses above. She shook her head in mock pity. "Do you actually believe I care what *the king* thinks?" She held her arms out from her sides and looked around her hall pointedly. She raised her eyebrows. "Hmm?"

"You are what they say, aren't you?" Judith Angwedd choked, her lips trembling. "You and your mother. The whole lot of you!"

Sybilla bent at the waist in a rush, bringing her nose so close to Judith Angwedd's that their breaths mingled. Sybilla smiled.

"Care to find out?" she whispered.

The woman shook her head almost imperceptibly.

"A very wise choice." Sybilla nodded once, emphatically.

And then she grabbed a handful of hair from the back of Judith Angwedd's skull and rose, pulling the shrieking woman onto her hands. Sybilla began marching down the center aisle of the hall toward the door as if against a strong gale, dragging Judith Angwedd behind her, who was now screaming in earnest and clawing at Sybilla's hand.

"I am not a woman to be trifled with, Judith Angwedd," Sybilla said in a tone of friendly advisory, although she nearly had to shout it over the woman's terrible wailing. "And you may tell Edward *that* as well."

She only let go of the woman's hair once they had climbed the steps and arrived at the doors of the hall. Judith Angwedd was sobbing now. Without having to give signal, the two guards on either side of the entry swung open the doors. Sybilla gave a courteous sweep of her arm and Judith Angwedd began crawling over the threshold.

When she was nearly through, Sybilla planted her slippered foot on the woman's backside, completing Judith Angwedd's exit and knocking her on her face.

"Your son shall be roused to join you shortly. Good night, Lady Mallory." Sybilla turned back to the hall, and the guards threw the doors closed.

She strode swiftly back down the center aisle, calling instructions before she had reached the men still standing near her dais.

"Graves, send Lady Cecily to me immediately, and have a party outfitted for my imminent departure. Inform the lieutenant who reported that he shall accompany us to this Pilings with additional soldiers, and we will search until we pick up Lady Alys's trail." She was nearly past the table now, heading for her private door.

"All the way to London, Madam?"

"Pray we reach her before then," Sybilla sighed. "And

send several strong men to Master Bevan's room, to assist him with his and his viperous mother's belongings. I'm certain Judith Angwedd wishes to be reunited with her offspring as soon as possible, and far be it from me to cause the woman any distress."

Graves slipped soundlessly from the dais.

Sybilla had laid hand upon the door latch when Clement Cobb seized her elbow weakly. Sybilla had nearly forgotten about him. But her ire was still high and looking for further escape, and so she whipped her arm free and spun on the man.

"Lady Sybilla," Clement simpered and cowered. "'Twas wise of you to rid Fallstowe of that scavenger, indeed. But, I beg of you, let me accompany your party. Alys is—"

"I am not at all certain that Alys is anything to you now, Clement," she informed him evenly. "And until I and Lady Alys come to that decision, Blodshire will see not one farthing of Fallstowe coin. You may gather your belongings, your mother, your servants, and be gone from my home within the hour, lest you also wish a hasty departure." She looked pointedly toward the doors where Judith Angwedd had so recently taken her own leave.

"Oh, Lady Sybilla! Why? Whatever have I done to give you such cause to reconsider the betrothal?" Clement nearly sobbed and sank to his knees. "I love Alys so— adore her! She—"

"If you hurry," Sybilla interrupted pointedly, "you might yet catch one more experienced at comforting you in your mourning, although I do hold some doubt that her compassion is at all sincere."

Clement's face seemed to pull in on itself, and take on a greenish cast. He swallowed.

"Do we understand each other, Clement?"

He gave a hesitant, terrified nod. Then he whispered, his eyes pleading with Sybilla, "I beg of you, tell her not."

Sybilla turned and swept through her private door, slamming it closed behind her. While she preferred to not bruise her dignity by running to her chamber, she did walk as quickly as she could.

Everything! She had to do every damned little thing herself.

But her mother had warned her of that. That, and so many other things which seemed to be coming to fruition, one after the other, like bone tiles collapsing in a long, clicking line.

And so Sybilla gritted her teeth and, at last, ran.

Chapter 11

Alys didn't know what she found more delicious—the succulent pork, or the sight of the recently-shorn Piers, sitting a quarter of the way around the fire from her. The light played over the lean planes and hollows of his face, sparked the gold in his bristly short hair, shadowed his long, dark lashes against his skin. The look of him, clean shaven, relaxed, eating good food, had triggered a hunger in Alys's stomach that could not be sated by the meal they shared.

He was gorgeous. Gorgeous and brusque and damaged. And Alys felt drawn to him as surely as rainwater must flow down to deep, dark valleys. She wanted to touch him again, not only his warm scalp and the skin of his neck, but every part of him beyond, to satisfy her curiosity of his whole body. And she wanted to learn of him, his hard past, his desperate mission, his dreams and hopes for Gillwick Manor. She wanted to know the truth about the ring in his bag, beyond her suspicions. Alys realized she was craving intimacy of any kind, every kind, with him.

She must have been staring at him for quite some time, because at last he flicked his eyes to her and frowned.

"What?" he said around a mouthful of food.

"Promise me you'll never wear a beard again." She remembered the piece of food still grasped in her grease-slicked fingers and took a bite of it.

He swallowed. "Beard keeps me warm in the winter. I'll grow it back out."

"Then why shave at all?"

He seemed to think for a moment, as if testing his answer in his own mind first. Then he shrugged. "It was unkempt. I had no mirror to trim it into a proper shape. Reckoned I'd do better to simply start anew."

She popped the last piece of onion into her mouth—it was soft and caramelized and sweet—and then shook her head while she sucked her fingers clean. After she had swallowed, she simply said, "Don't."

He was finished eating as well, and so he picked up a long stick and began tweaking the fire. Sparks flew up in the air in a dancing, crackling spiral, and the burst of light across Piers's face caused Alys's stomach to clench. She was mesmerized by the very sight of him.

"I doubt you'd hold that opinion were it you who must venture out before dawn in the dead of winter."

Alys shrugged. "But when you return to Gillwick, you'll not have to perform menial chores yourself, will you?"

He looked at her warily.

Alys raised her eyebrows as if challenging him to deny it. "The ring in your bag—it was your father's."

He was quiet for a long time before nodding "It was. Although he never wore it, to my knowledge."

"Did you steal it?" she asked simply.

"No. He gave it to me the night he died."

Interesting. "So you have his blessing."

"I'd not call what I must do a blessing."

Alys reached behind her for her bag and dragged it to her side, between her and Piers. She leaned her upper body on it, toward him, and propped her chin on her palm. She felt sated, relaxed, in the glow of the fire and with her belly full. Layla crouched in the curve of her hip and thigh, searching methodically for abandoned morsels in the folds of Alys's skirt.

"Speaking to the king to claim your birthright is not a blessing?"

Piers shook his head. "It's more of a dangerous riddle, actually."

"Why?"

"You are better off not knowing."

Alys hummed noncommittally. He would tell her eventually. "Does solving this dangerous riddle require facial hair?"

He looked askance at her. "No."

"Then continue to shave. You're too handsome by far to cover your face in prickly bristles. I rather enjoy looking at you, Piers."

He stilled and looked into her eyes. "'Tis a bold and dangerous game you play at yourself, young Alys."

"Bold, yes. Dangerous?" She shrugged. "Mayhap. But 'tis no game. I am most sincere."

"I am a grown man. You are—"

"A grown woman," she interrupted.

"A *young* woman, with no experience outside of her sheltered and pampering home," he continued.

"Does my youth make me undesirable?" she challenged. "Or my wealth? Most men are attracted to me for both."

He frowned and turned his gaze quickly back to the fire. His poking stick had become engulfed in flame and he whisked it sharply through the air with a surprised curse that made Alys smile.

"If you had so many suitors, why is it that you are now being forced to marry the likes of Clement Cobb?" he goaded, avoiding the subject she'd raised.

"That is a fair question, I suppose. I didn't even like—much less love—any of the men who offered for me," she said honestly. "I certainly am not in love with Clement Cobb. Sybilla is only impatient to be rid of me."

"Why?" He turned his face back to her.

Alys frowned. "I suppose because she doesn't like me very much. Sybilla and I—we are very different from each other."

"That is no reason for her to be desperate to be rid of you," Piers argued. "It's not as if you are an infant that demands her constant care, or Fallstowe Castle some lowly hut where the two of you are forced to sit in each other's laps."

"True. If I'm very, very lucky, days pass when Sybilla and I don't catch sight of each other."

"Then there must be some other reason," Piers insisted. "You have another sister, also older than you?"

"Cecily claims that she will take vows. She has no desire to marry."

"Then why do you not do the same?"

Alys laughed. "Think you a convent would have me? Any matter, it's not as though I don't want a husband and children. And I have a husband now, so we must work straight away on a family."

Piers gave her a warning frown. "Alys."

She smiled in reply. "You never answered me: do you find me unattractive, Piers?"

"I'm not having this conversation."

"Why? Are you worried that I might assault your person in a fit of passion?"

"Yes."

Alys dropped her flushed face to her bag for a moment and laughed, and to her surprise, Piers chuckled. She raised her head, still smiling, and her desire was out of her mouth before she had time to consider the repercussions of it. "Will you kiss me, Piers?"

He stared at her, the smile falling away from his mouth slowly, his eyes drawn to her lips. She licked them, encouraging him without words.

"I shouldn't," he said quietly.

"But will you?" She sat up again, leaning toward him, her eyes searching his face. "I want you to, very much."

"Why?" he asked, as if the question pained him.

She leaned farther, slowly, as if trying not to frighten him away. "Because you are handsome. And courageous. And witty. And I think"—she licked her lips again, as the warmth of his face reached her—"I think I'm falling in love with you, husband."

His head was still turned toward her, her mouth a finger's width from his. She could smell the scent of him, his maleness perfumed with woodsmoke and autumn air.

"Alys," he whispered. "Don't."

"Why?" She let the question sigh from her lips and then closed her eyes.

A rude gust of cold air was all that kissed her mouth. Her eyes snapped open and she saw Piers already walking away from the fire.

"Where are you going?" she called, sitting up quickly.

"To get more wood." Then he disappeared into the dark as the sound of tumbling rocks announced his hasty descent down the ravine.

Layla scrambled up onto Alys's shoulder and began to

pick through her hair. Alys dropped her chin onto her fist with a deep frown and let the monkey have her way.

"Dammit," she said softly. Her eyes searched the dark beyond the fire.

But he had let her get closer, still. She was making progress, and that was encouraging. She knew he'd wanted to kiss her, she just hadn't been quick enough. And they still had a handful of days until they reached London. Perhaps three more nights, if she was lucky. It wasn't a lot of time, but it was all she had.

She let her mind settle on the problem, much like Layla continued to worry and pick through her tresses. By the time Piers returned, announcing his arrival by tossing a small bundle of dead wood near the fire, she had failed to work out a plan. It frustrated her, as she couldn't help but feel that the answer she sought should be painfully obvious.

She smiled up at him, hoping that kindness would gain her some ground. "Welcome back."

He stood there staring at her for several moments, his brows drawn down in his signature scowl, his long arms at his sides. The fire lit half of his face to golden, flickering brilliance, but even in that glow, Alys thought he looked paler than when he'd left.

"Don't do that again, Alys."

Her eyes went wide as she tried to feign innocence, difficult with a monkey huffing little breaths into her ear. "Do what?"

"You know what." He crouched down by the fire and turned his attention to arranging the wood fuel. He was clearly in no mood at the moment for sport.

"Oh! You mean try to kiss you?"

He threw her a glare from the corner of his eye.

"Why is it so wrong for a woman to be forthright in her

desires?" Alys demanded. "The Foxe Ring decreed that we are man and wife, and if you are attracted to me, then I see no reason—"

"Alys, we are *not* married."

"That is debatable."

"No, it isn't."

"Since we are debating it even now, I would say that it is, in fact, debatable. You are unlike anyone I have ever met, Piers."

He threw the last chunk of wood into the fire, causing an explosion of sparks. "You've never met anyone like me because you don't spend your social time with the servants!"

"Actually, I do. Quite a lot, really. Drives Sybilla mad."

He was very obviously unimpressed by her candor. "Here is why I will not kiss you, Alys, and why we will most certainly never—" He broke off and waved one hand between the two of them. "Your entire life, you have gotten everything you want. Me? I get nothing that I want. We are two different animals."

"I don't agree with that at all."

"No?" he challenged. "Look at your gown—even though it looks as though it belongs on a kitchen maid, it is still better than what I now wear. And this is my *only* suit of clothes, save the ruined monk's costume that was given me out of charity. You bade me cut up a dress for rags that would support me for five years!"

Alys simply shrugged.

He gaped at her. "See? You care nothing for the ruination of such a costly item."

"Why should I? I didn't pay for it or even *ask* for it—it was all Sybilla's doing. If you fancy it so much, *you* may have it."

"Do you blame everything on your sister?"

That stung. "Go to hell, Piers."

"Oh, poor Lady Alys," he mocked. "Forced to live as royalty, her every whim attended to. Who must run away with a commoner to have a bit of excitement. Don't think for a moment I don't know what will happen once we reach London."

"And what exactly is that?" Alys demanded.

"After your little adventure, you'll beg Edward for haven until you can be carried back to Fallstowe. You'll recuperate from your time in the wild with such an uncouth commoner and live out the rest of your days as a well tended, married lady in pampered decadence."

"The only haven the king would likely see me to is a cell should I dare step foot in his court," Alys argued. "He would hold me ransom in Sybilla's place."

"And she would come running to your rescue, no doubt," Piers sneered.

"Not bloody likely. Sybilla would not give herself up to Edward for the likes of me, I assure you."

"No? No, of course not," Piers said sarcastically. "She only sees that you live like a fucking princess. She very clearly hates you."

"She's marrying me to Clement Cobb!"

"After she gave you your choice of men and you refused them all! If she hated you, she would have married you to the first one who didn't run away screaming!"

"Oh! What's *your* excuse?" Alys went on the attack. "Why is it that you didn't claim your rightful place as one of your father's heirs before now, hmm? It's not a secret that you're Warin Mallory's son, is it?"

"No," he gritted through his teeth, and Alys suspected she was pushing in just the right area. "But before he died, I was nothing more than an embarrassing mistake to him. Bevan was his sole, legitimate heir. That was made very clear."

"So why challenge that now? Why not years ago, when you could have avoided such poverty, such humiliation, such cruelty from Bevan and his mother?"

"Because I didn't know I could!" he shouted. "My own father didn't even know!"

"He didn't know for certain that you were his son?"

"He didn't know that Bevan was not!"

There it was—the truth, at last. The crackle of the fire and the shush of the river were the only sounds filling the rock overhang. The air seemed to tremble in the wake of Piers's announcement.

He walked to the edge of the shelter and stared into the night, his back to Alys.

"Judith Angwedd cuckolded your father?" she asked quietly.

He nodded jerkily, but did not turn.

"Then who is Bevan's sire?"

"My father didn't know to tell me. He only overheard Judith Angwedd and Bevan talking when the pair of them thought him asleep. The day he died. He had just enough time to send for me, and give me his ring. He told me to carry it to the king, and to 'seek my blood' on my journey. He said that would lead me to the answer that would save Gillwick and myself. I still do not know what he meant. Perhaps the king will." Piers paused. "Once Bevan inherits Gillwick, he and Judith Angwedd plan for his true father to also claim him as heir."

"Uniting the lands for Bevan," Alys surmised.

"More likely for that greedy viper Judith Angwedd. She's always aspired to a greater station than she's ever deserved. Gillwick—and my father—were naught but stepping stones to her. And Bevan has never cared about more than his drink and his cruel perversions."

"What of your own mother? Other family members? Did they not know?"

"My mother died when I was six years old. I have no idea what she knew or didn't know. Her father—my grandfather—abandoned her in shame, shortly before I was born. He never returned to Gillwick, and my mother never spoke of him. I presume he is dead. Anyone I ever had blood ties to is dead. That is why my father's final words to me are such a riddle."

Alys's heart clenched. "And up until the day he died, your father never acknowledged you."

Piers was quiet for a long time. "I don't want to talk about this anymore Alys. It . . . it's in the past now. It doesn't matter. All that matters is that I correct this mistake with the king. Judith Angwedd will not dishonor my father's memory with this treachery—announcing to all the land that she deceived him so when he is unable to accuse her of wrong."

"You're going to Edward to defend his honor?" Alys said, shocked. "What of your own honor, Piers? Of what they have stolen from you—Judith Angwedd and Bevan and—yes—your own father?"

"I will have my justice," Piers said quietly. "And it is naught that Gillwick's lands or the title of its lord can gain me."

"What better revenge could there be?" Alys asked.

But Piers never answered the question. Instead he began banking the fire, piling up the sandy soil in a ridge, causing the flames to hiss petulantly.

"So now you see how we are so different."

Alys nodded slowly. "Yes, we are different, but we are also very much alike."

He looked to her, the question clear in his expression. Alys obliged him.

"We are both on this journey to gain what we desire. You are going to gain Gillwick."

"And you are going to escape marriage to Clement Cobb." Piers shook his head at the fire.

"That was my intent the night I left Fallstowe, yes. But now my desire has changed. Grown bigger than I ever could have dreamed." He looked at her and she swallowed, gathered her courage. "I go to London with you, for you. For *you*, Piers. *You* are my desire."

"Stop," he said curtly and turned his gaze back to the flames.

This time it was Alys who shook her head. "No. Piers, I can help you in London, I feel it."

He sighed and sat down near her, his arms wrapped around one wide, drawn-up knee. "How? By getting yourself thrown in the dungeon? I don't even know myself how I will convince Edward of the truth—all I have is hearsay from a dying man, told by his common bastard son, and a ring my father never wore, which Judith Angwedd will surely say that I stole, any matter."

"That *is* a problem," Alys admitted. "But I know that we are stronger together than apart. Our unlikely union has—" She broke off as the answer came to her with such blinding surety that for a moment, Alys's head throbbed.

"Has . . . ?" Piers prompted, a trace of humor in his voice. "Words failing you for once?"

"Piers," she whispered, her eyes wide. "You are not common any longer."

"I am until Edward decrees otherwise," Piers said ruefully.

"No. No, that is not true." Alys couldn't help the

stunned huff of laughter that came from her throat. "You are actually . . . quite wealthy, right at this very moment."

He turned to her, his face a mask of forced impatience. "What are you talking about?"

Her smile was slow, sly, and carried the weight of her imminent triumph. "You are related to the most powerful house in all of England . . . *husband*."

His frown deepened, and then realization dawned on his face. "Bloody hell," he whispered.

Then Alys leaned so close to him that Piers had to draw his head back to look down at her upturned face. Her eyes played over his face, his lips.

"*Now* will you kiss me?"

Piers had not kissed her. Instead he'd sent her to sleep like a troublesome child, which had stung her pride and hurt her feelings, Piers knew. But he needed time alone, to think without her constant chatter and questioning. Once he was certain she was occupied by her dreams, he sat at the edge of the overhang, one knee drawn up, one foot dangling into the blackness of the ravine.

Alys Foxe, Alys Foxe. She was either the greatest blessing or the greatest curse to ever have come into his life. Since the fateful night they had met at the old ring, he had been denying her superstitious claim to him, thinking to protect both of their interests. Certainly, what man in possession of good sense would refuse any one of the Foxe ladies? Not simply the wealthiest women in all of England, but ruling the most powerful house beyond the throne? Even the king himself seemed unable to command them.

Piers knew that no matter how flattering it was for a woman such as Alys Foxe to chase him, any attraction she felt for him was likely only novelty. Once she came to realize the simplicity of him, the humbleness of his birth and life and home—even should he be successful in his endeavor to claim Gillwick—she would tire of him. She would long once more for the riches of her family, the wealth and luxury. Even though she only spoke of her sisters as a burden to her, Piers guessed that the women shared a close bond. Piers had no love to show her, give her. He doubted he even knew what the emotion meant.

Perhaps his mother had loved him. His memories of her—old and gray and fleeting—were warm and smiling. But he did wonder if that was naught but a sad little boy's longing, to remember his mother as a loving protector. Had he ever been truly happy in his life? Piers could not say that he had. But he had known sadness. And loss, and anger and resentment and hate and jealousy. He had nothing to offer Alys Foxe but those things, and when she wearied of playing with him—as she undoubtedly would—his life would only be that much more miserable.

He had heard melancholy old women say that it is better to have a fleeting love than no love at all. But Piers did not agree. Having the love of his mother for those few years had only brought into stark relief the lack of tenderness and care in his life once she was gone. It had made him bitter, yes. But strong. He was strong. That was the only reason he was still alive.

Piers could not allow himself to love Alys Foxe, or to let her even think for a moment that him loving her was possible. But the opportunity she presented him now was almost too tempting to refuse. They had been completely alone together now for days, a fact that could be easily verified by her family. They had known Alys was running away to the Foxe Ring, and Sybilla herself had given her blessing upon any man Alys met at the ring who would have her. It was no secret that many in the land used the old stones to find a mate, and the superstition was so highly regarded that most of the time a formal ceremony was not even held.

Yea, 'twas likely that a professed union between him and Alys Foxe would stand before the king. And how much more weight would his accusation of treachery against Bevan and Judith Angwedd—not to mention his claim to Gillwick—then carry? Edward wanted Sybilla Foxe, and to have her brother-in-law in his court, claiming lands that would then be connected by marriage to the grand Fallstowe's, might be too beneficial to the king's own interests to deny.

Perhaps Alys Foxe was in some way the answer to his father's riddle. Piers hadn't sought out the tenacious little blonde—indeed, he had done all in his power to escape her. And yet as her husband, perhaps it was her own powerful blood ties that would save Gillwick and himself.

But if he used her so to gain what he wanted, what would happen to Alys in the aftermath? How would they ever disentangle their lives from each other's? Would Edward indeed take Alys for ransom, reining her powerful sister to him?

What would you care if he did? a nasty part of him argued. *She will leave you any matter, deny you. Have you not kept her safe in this reckless petulance she has carried out by running away from her family? Have you not potentially saved her from a marriage she did not want? Should you not be rewarded for choosing not to leave her alone to die in the wood with her damned monkey, which nearly took your fingers off? She would not die at Edward's hands—the king is not stupid. And her sisters would surely save her, any matter. Let Alys Foxe for once pay the consequences of her actions. She*

will then be free to again do as she pleases, and you will
have Gillwick. And your revenge.

Piers sat for a long time, staring into the blackness over
the river and listening to that voice, while the fire faded
and then died quietly behind him. His fingers throbbed,
his stomach roiled, his head pounded. The night seemed
to have become inexplicably warmer to him, so much so
that his face was covered in a thin sheen of sweat. He told
himself it was naught but the excitement of having his
victory only as far away as the king's court.

Some time before dawn, he sought a cool, smooth
stone for a pillow and lay down to sleep.

Chapter 12

Although he was indeed even more handsome in the daylight, sporting his new hairstyle and clean jaw, Alys thought Piers looked unwell the next day. She knew he had likely stayed up long after she was asleep, considering his newly arrived at decision to let her accompany him all the way to London and perhaps aid his plight with the king, so perhaps it was only fatigue that she saw. She hoped so. But it had been she who needed remind him of eating the last of their food before they started out once again on their long journey, and Piers had done little more than nibble at a small piece of apple before shoving the uneaten portion into his pack.

She felt a strange coolness from him, and it didn't stem from his lack of conversation. She could feel him, in the way she'd felt Etheldred Cobb's shame, the way she sensed that she must rescue Layla. Alys's mother had once told her long ago that there was a way in her family blood, of sensing certain things other people could not discern. Some might call it witchcraft, Amicia had warned her, and advised that it was best not to announce her talent. But Alys's mother had also instructed her to heed these feelings, and cultivate a notice of them. Alys had never given the idea much thought.

But as she now trudged along the forest floor behind Piers, she tried to sharpen her awareness of him—something she'd not done before in more than a purely superficial manner. Her steps fell in rhythm, the crunching leaves became a sort of heartbeat, her breath like ocean waves, rising and falling, rising and falling. He was clear in her sight—his broad back swaying with his steps, his pack bouncing, his head performing a choreographed dance of looking in turn down at the way before him and then left and right, always alert for anyone following them.

And as she stared at him, although his form was crisp and clear, the areas of her peripheral vision began to blur out. She stared for a long, long time, until at last she saw a light around him—yellow, but not the sweet gold of sunlight. It was more akin to smear of old mustard, and where it lined his body, it darkened to a fungus green. And instead of radiating from him in sharp, brilliant points, the light was rippled, like heat.

Alys blinked, and her vision cleared, although now her heart beat faster and her stomach clenched.

Was he ill? She wasn't certain.

"Piers," she called, her voice high-pitched and breaking from fear and disuse.

He glanced over his shoulder at her in answer.

"Could we stop for a moment, please?"

He kept walking. "Do you need the bushes?"

"No. I need to talk to you."

"Walking has never prevented you from doing that before."

"Yes, but I need to look at you while I do it," she insisted. "It's important."

"You can look at me when we stop. Perhaps another

hour. It looks to rain soon any matter, and we'll need make camp early." She could hear the frustration in his voice and something else, a weariness, perhaps.

And Alys was bone-cold—the air she breathed into her lungs felt loaded with ice crystals. The day was frigid. If any precipitation fell on them, it could be nothing other than snow—being a man of a farm, surely he of all people realized that.

She frowned. "Alright, Piers. In an hour then."

He walked on without reply.

She needed to look at him, yes, but perhaps it was better that they make camp first. The farther along they were, the better chance they had of coming across a village of some sort for supplies. Her knowledge of the countryside surrounding Fallstowe had run out just past the little village of Pilings, and she had no idea now where they were or how far away London lay. She did know that they would be needing more food, of course, and if Piers was ill as she suspected, perhaps herbs, a potion—she didn't know. Cecily was the sister learned in the healing arts. Alys knew little about caring for the sick, save that they needed a soft bed and a warm hearth and Cecily Foxe—none of which were at her disposal, or even within reach.

Perhaps for the first time in her life, there was truly no one for Alys to call on save herself.

Alys had the dreadful feeling that wherever they stopped for the night, Piers would not be able to leave, for a while at least. Until he got better, of course. He would certainly get better.

She concentrated on him once again as she worked her legs like machines, telling herself that the green color close to his body was simply a very dark shade of green now, and not black.

Not black.

The voices were coming to him again for the first time in days, whispering in his ear with a vividness that was frightening. Piers fancied he could feel Judith Angwedd's cold breath against his sweaty neck.

Filthy, dirty, foul little beast! Your whore mother burns in hell.

Piers's head whipped to the left—surely his stepmother must be hiding behind that tree.

But no—no one peeked around the trunk at him. Only moss and dead-brown vines.

Hit him again! The voice echoed and was so loud, Piers winced at the bright pain it caused. *Again, Bevan!*

"Stop!" He tried to shout, but to his horror the word came out as little more than a whimper. His eyes felt as though they were bleeding and he swiped a hand across his face. He looked down at his palm and saw that it was wet.

Bloody hell, he was hot. And the bandage covering his fingers was damp with yellow and brown stains. Fucking Layla . . .

"Piers?" He heard Alys call to him from leagues away, it seemed. He glanced over his shoulder at her, noticing with dread how little range his neck had with the pain. His head swam and he looked forward once more lest he fall over his own feet.

You are my only heir.

"Piers, it's been more than an hour," she called faintly.

"I do think we should stop—you don't look well. Are you feeling alright?"

"I'm fine." He tried to make his voice carry back to her, strong and certain. Each word caused his vision to pulse, the wood around him bulging with heat. "Just a bit farther."

My son, my son!

He looked around him, trying to evaluate their surroundings as to suitability for camp, but he couldn't seem to make sense of anything. There were only trees . . . and he could not discern forest floor from trunk or slope or rock. How far away was the road from where they walked? They should have come across one of Gillwick's rock walls by now, and the barn would not be far beyond. How far had they come? Where was that bastard, blistering sun hiding?

Spill his brains onto the ground . . .

Bevan is no brother to you, Piers . . .

"Piers, I . . . I think I do have need of some bushes now."

Are you certain he's dead? Hit him again . . .

My son, my only son! Can you ever forgive me?

"Piers!"

"Shut up!" Piers screamed, coming to a swaying halt and gripping his head in both hands. He fell to his knees. "All of you, just . . . shut up!" His breath roared in and out of him, sounding like great slides of rock down a mountainside. The ground seemed to undulate before his eyes.

He couldn't pass out. The cows needed to be brought in for the night still, and there had been reports of wolves north of Gillwick. The beasts were lazy in the height of summer, and he could usually frighten them away with a rock or two. Yes, he might need to keep watch, keep them safe. And Alys would need a place to sleep where Bevan would not find her . . .

"Piers?" Her slippers came into view, shifting the damp leaves in fuzzy slow motion.

"It's alright," Piers said, and his words sounded slurred. "Just give me a moment, Alys. I have work to do. Wait for me in the mew." He would gladly share his pallet with Alys, but that damned monkey would have to bed elsewhere.

Then her face was before his, her neck bent so that she could look up at him, and her fingers were like rounded icicles stroking his cheeks and forehead.

"My God, you're burning up!"

"Be cooler once the sun sets," he promised her, the spoiled girl, used as she was to her dark, stone castle. She'd never make a proper farm wife, but she was so pretty and fiery . . .

"There is no sun, Piers—and it's starting to snow," he heard her say as if she was moving away from him. But that couldn't be, because he could feel her hands gripping his arms, taking his pack from his shoulders.

"My ring," he mumbled, and tried to swipe at his bag, but the woman had the speed of a minx, darting away from him in a blur. "It's all I have."

"It's alright," she placated, and was half pulling him back against something solid. Where did she find a bed so soft to bring him? Was she so wealthy that she could conjure furniture from raw wood?

"You have me." She framed his face with her frozen palms. "Just rest here—I'll start a fire."

"No," he struggled to sit up, but was unsuccessful. "No fire. Too close to the road." The wolves would find them, and he hadn't brought the cows in yet. His father would be so disappointed.

"I have no earthly idea where the road is, but I don't think it's close." Her voice faded in and out as she seemed to move away and then near again. "I think we've gone somewhat off course."

He realized his eyes were closed, and tried to open them. It was not safe to sleep with Bevan skulking about. Little Alys bloomed into vision, her sweet brow crinkled, her pink lips in a thin line as she clumsily piled twigs atop each other. She dug in his bag rudely, eventually pulling out his flint and steel and a bit of tinder, dropping everything twice as she tried to work the tools.

"You'll burn yourself," Piers slurred, marveling at the softness beneath his head now. He was enjoying watching her move, and the pain in his head was only a dumb, numb memory.

"Shh," she chastised.

Piers chuckled. So stubborn. His eyes closed. He struggled to open them again, and when he succeeded he saw dancing flames. How long had he slept? It seemed only an instant. He was confused. And cold, now. So cold.

He looked down and saw that his legs had been covered by the bulk of Alys's blue perse gown. The dusting of snow across his lap shifted, and the monkey poked her head from beneath the cloth near his chest.

"W-whaddo you w-want?" Piers challenged through his chattering teeth. "G-geddoff."

"You're keeping each other warm." Alys's face was before his again as she crouched before him. Her cheeks were cream and poppies, her breath little white clouds in the night with the fire behind her.

When had night fallen?

"Here, have a drink." She pushed the lip of the jug against his teeth and turned it up. The water was wet and delicious as it flooded down his hot and tight throat.

She set the jug on her knee. "Piers, I can't find the road," Alys said. "Do you know where we are?"

Piers frowned. He concentrated on her face, hoping it would remind him. "G-gillwick?"

Her lips grew thinner. He didn't like the look of Alys distressed. She was always so carefree.

"Try to remember," she said. "You're very ill, Piers, and I must try to find a village or travelers on the road or something. You must try to help me decide in which direction to go."

"No. C-can't leave," Piers insisted. "B-Bevan find you. Or the wolves."

"There are no wolves, Piers. I have to find someone to help us. Can you think at all where we might be?"

His memories all boiled together place and time. Gillwick, the abbey where the monk had taken him, the Foxe Ring, the river, the road to London. He couldn't put them in correct order. He thought and thought, so hard that his head almost started to hurt and so he stopped. "We're not to London yet, are we?"

"No. No, we're not." She drew a deep breath and blew it out slowly through her lips. "Alright. Listen to me: I'm going in a straight line the direction I think is south. If I find nothing in an hour, I'll come straight back. I've built the fire so that your location is quite visible."

"No," Piers argued.

"Yes. I need all the help I can get in the dark. And perhaps God will hear my prayers and someone will find you before I return."

"If Bevan . . . he'll kill me," Piers croaked.

"If no one finds us, I'm afraid you'll die any matter," she said levelly.

He stared at her, realizing a moment of clarity as her face blurred in and out of his vision. It was too dangerous for her to go, but he knew he could not stop her. And he knew that he was quite ill.

He tried to smile. "Sorry . . . terrible husband."

She peered at him for a moment and then her lips curved upward softly. "You are a fine husband. You have taken such care of me, now it is my turn to try to do the same for you. You need me, Piers, and I will not fail you."

Her words struck him somewhere deep within his feverish body, and he tried to swallow. She was planning to walk south . . .

"Don't go," he whispered. He could barely find the strength to move his lips now.

"It will be fine," she insisted. "You'll get well and we'll gain London just in time. You'll see." She leaned forward and pressed her warm lips to his cheek for a long moment. When she leaned back, there were tears in her eyes.

"Don't," he said again, his words little more than formed breath.

"Take care of him, Layla. I'll be back as soon as I can. Two hours at most."

And then she was gone, the black night and the cold, blowing snow rushing in to fill the void she had left.

"Alys," he whispered into the wind. "Alys, the road is north . . ."

Chapter 13

The only other time in Alys's life when she had been almost as scared as she was now, was when she had finally accepted that her mother was going to die. She had not been scared for Amicia—the Foxe matron was so sure of her better reward, and had suffered humiliatingly for so long—it was a blessing upon her to finally go in peace to meet her beloved Morys once more. Then, as now, Alys had been scared for herself, but her fears were of what was to become of her happy, predictable life, how she and Cecily and Sybilla would fare with no one to lead the family and defend against the king's accusations save the cool, eldest daughter.

Sybilla had always possessed a will of pure steel, true, but she had no experience outside of her family and Fallstowe. Their mother, Amicia, had years of life behind her, coming as a young woman from Bordeaux to England, marrying Morys Foxe, standing at his side as he ruled Fallstowe in the midst of the civil turmoil that marked Henry III's rule. That experience and strength were the very reasons Amicia herself had held the demesne after her husband's death. So even though Sybilla had been in

training by her mother for hours upon hours as the end
drew near, sometimes going as many as three days without
leaving Amicia's chamber, Sybilla was no battle-wizened,
gray haired lord. Alys's eldest sister was but a score and
seven, and though her way with men was like magic, she
had never even come close to betrothal, as far as Alys knew.

Alys wondered for the thousandth time what Amicia
and Sybilla had talked about those last months, what was
so secretive and intricate that not only were Cecily and
Alys forbidden from their mother's chamber while
Sybilla was within, they were warned against simple inquiry. After Amicia's death, her personal maid—the only
other person save old Graves who had been allowed in the
chamber during these meetings between Amicia and her
eldest—had simply vanished from Fallstowe.

Alys huffed ragged breaths as she stumbled through the
forest, lit only by a waning moon intermittently filtered
through clouds which spit snow at her occasionally, as if
for sport. She'd run straight away into countless trees,
fallen over logs and into washes parallel to animal trails.
She could feel her scraped palms burning in the cold
blackness as they reached out before her, the ache in her
twisted knee, the fear spiraling up her spine with greedy
haste. She guessed she had been running in a southerly
direction for almost an hour now, and still, she had not
crossed the road.

She thought of Piers, alone and helplessly ill, lying like
so much bait before a roaring fire with only one tiny
monkey for protection, and the image caused a sob to
swell in her throat.

And so she continued to think upon Sybilla instead,
and to her surprise and regret, Alys realized that she
longed for no other living person as badly as she wanted
her eldest sister right at that moment. Sybilla would know

what to do. Sybilla would waste no time wandering around a remote stretch of deep forest in the dead of night with a snowstorm threatening. No, Sybilla would not tolerate being lost. Actually, Sybilla would have likely had the good sense to not be in this situation at all. Alys tried to think of what she could have done differently.

She should have not bothered with food in Pilings, saving her—albeit very convincing—theatrical display, and should have instead stolen a horse. She and Piers would be almost to London now certainly, even riding double. But she had seen no stables obvious in the village, and likely she would have been caught. Had she procured a mount, 'twas likely she and Piers would not have shared the night in the rock shelter, a memory already too dear to Alys to consider erasing.

Perhaps when she and Piers had been at Fallstowe's very gate, Alys should have gone ahead into the castle and gathered all the supplies they would need and caught him later in the wood. But no, at that point, he would have gladly gone on without her and she would have never found him. Then he would be completely alone now, and possibly already dead from whatever sickness was claiming him.

Perhaps she should have never insisted on following him in the first place.

Or, perhaps, she should have heeded Sybilla's wishes and not gone to the Foxe Ring at all.

Alys realized she was crying as she panted and groped her way through the maze of flurries and sudden trees. Had she listened to Sybilla, she who had single-handedly held Fallstowe better than any man could have, who had always tried to accommodate Alys's wishes, who had allowed her sisters to keep their lives and their home by sheer cunning and strength and brazen defiance to their very king, Alys would right now be in her safe, warm rooms, helping to plan her own extravagant wedding.

But no, her foolishness had led her to believe that her life was worth more than what Sybilla had selflessly struggled to give her. Alys had wanted everything and then even more. Never satisfied. Childish wishes, petulant rebellion—Alys could at last see all of her faults of which she had been accused. And she knew she was guilty. Sybilla had been right all along. Even Piers had taken correct measure of her the very first night they had met. It had been so obvious to everyone save spoiled, demanding Alys Foxe herself.

She looked back at her life up until that moment with bittersweet longing, and with the knowledge that no matter how she eventually came out of this cursed wood— whether on to London with Piers or back to the haven that was Fallstowe—that old life was no more. She no longer cared that Sybilla had commanded that she marry Clement Cobb. Alys realized now that it had been she who had backed her sister into that corner, and then railed at her for doling out the consequence, and there were fates well worse than that gentle privilege. She wanted to thank Sybilla now, for so many things, and to tell her she was sorry. So sorry, and so late.

But what she wanted more was for Piers to live. To live, and to carry on to London and see his victory, however he needed it to play out. In her heart, she belonged to Piers, and she would do whatever it took to save his life and his future, even if it meant the destruction of her own.

She still truly believed that fate had brought them together in the Foxe Ring, and that they had met—and Alys had stubbornly clung to him—for a purpose greater than either of them knew. Perhaps part of that purpose was to cause Alys to realize the folly of her own life, and to that end, it was greatly accomplished, but she still thought that it was also because she was the only one who could help Piers seize what was rightfully his. What Bevan and Judith Angwedd had so cruelly tried to steal.

When she held up her life in comparison to his, Alys was shamed to her very soul. She desperately tried to recall a time previous when she had acted wholly for the benefit of another person, and to her mortification, she could not.

"Well then, let this one count," she gasped to the trees, as if pleading with them to consider her intentions and pick up their roots like skirts to create an avenue to her rescue.

Perhaps the trees heard her, and arrived at their judgment. For with her very next clumsy step, a rope tightened around her ankle, and with a crack and a whoosh, Alys was jerked off her feet. Her back slammed against the frozen ground for an instant and then she was dragged upward, her temple scraping against the jagged end of a dead, broken branch. Her ascent came to a sudden, bobbing halt and she was left hanging upside down, swaying from the underside of a tree.

It began to snow in earnest, hinting at a silent, grim finale to Alys Foxe's grand adventure.

Alys began to scream.

Cecily Foxe paced.

Sybilla and the soldiers had been gone for almost two days, and there was no word yet, from or about her older or younger sister. The fire in the hearth closest to the lord's table roared, but still Cecily shivered as her slippers traced over a single line of seven stones, back and forth. She gripped her upper arms and rubbed at them periodically, so firmly that she knew she would be bruised the next day, but was unable to stop. She felt dizzy, and as though she was freezing.

In Sybilla's absence, Cecily was effectively head of Fallstowe, and the very idea of it had obviously made her immensely fretful—feeling sensations that were completely at odds with her reality. She knew they were naught but a side effect of her concern for her family. They were not real.

Not real.

Never had Cecily been in residence at the castle without at least one other Foxe, and as far as she knew, Sybilla herself had not left Fallstowe's lands since the day their mother had died. Cecily considered returning to the chapel to pray and keep her vigil, but the cold of that pious space at well past midnight had been what sent her fleeing to the great hall in the first place.

"Shall I keep vigil with you, Lady Cee?" Graves's deep, mellow voice came out of the darkness, and Cecily started, clutching herself even more tightly.

She turned to face the old steward, bringing the fingertips of one hand up to rub at her temple where a sudden ache had bloomed. The skeletal old man stood just inside the perimeter of firelight, his hands hanging at his sides, his shoulders pulled back in his trademark stance of attention.

"No, Graves, it's alright. Seek your bed. 'Tis unlikely we shall have any word this night, but I am not inclined to rest until we do."

He gave a nearly imperceptible nod of his gray head, his own bow of acquiescence, and then his faded eyes flicked to Cecily's fingertips at the side of her face.

"Are you unwell?"

Cecily dropped her hand immediately. "It's nothing. A headache."

"Madam or Lady Alys?"

Cecily and Graves stared at each other for several moments, one patiently waiting for an elaboration, the other loathe to give one.

"It's only a headache, Graves," she said at last. "I don't . . . I'm not like Sybilla or Alys or Mother. I don't pretend to see colors or cast spells because I can't." She shrugged, and hoped it was nonchalant. "It's a headache and nothing more. Everyone suffers them from time to time."

He gave another one of his fractional nods, but Cecily could tell he was not convinced.

"Perhaps we should pray, any matter?"

"Of course we should." She gave him a brittle smile. "We should always pray. Fortunately, it's what I'm best at. Fallstowe's spiritual conscience. The Foxe family's nod to religion."

He stared at her and she stared back. Cecily rubbed her arms again, the cold seemed to seep from the stones beneath her feet and leach up her legs into her core. Her cheeks burned as if being slapped by a sharp wind.

"You'll send for me right away should you have any need?"

Cecily turned back to the fire, so as to be able to escape those ancient, knowing eyes. She stepped closer to the hearth, holding her palms toward the flames. "I'll come myself. Good night, Graves."

There was a long moment of silence, and when next Graves spoke, his voice was low, neutral.

"Wouldn't you agree that it is likely to be Lady Alys most affected by the cold tonight?"

She didn't hear his footsteps retreat as he left the hall—

the man was like a shadow himself when he moved—
but Cecily knew he had gone all the same.

The admirable thing about Graves was that, as a trusted
servant of Fallstowe, he never assumed to have the last
word with a member of the family.

But he certainly always had the last question.

Sybilla stared at the darkened roof of her tent, her arms
at her sides atop the thick pile of furs over her body so
that she could feel the cold air on her upturned palms.

She, if not the men she traveled with, could have
stayed in any of the dwellings at the village of Pilings.
Several residents had offered—including the woman
who had given Alys food. They likely looked not only for
Sybilla's coin, but also the privilege of having nobility
under their roof. But Sybilla had declined. The cottages
were little more than huts, most appearing to be only one
room, and Sybilla could just imagine the smell. She dis-
liked strangers, strange places. The thought of lying
down to sleep in a foreign bed, next to someone she
didn't know, in their house and not hers, was enough to
make her skin crawl.

In her tent, she had her things, Fallstowe's things. A
brazier was set in the middle of the tent, and if the shelter was not quite cozy, at least it was not frigid. She had
thick, clean furs as well, and a guard standing watch just
outside the lashed flap. Here she could be alone in the
quiet of midnight, her hands exposed to the air—air
which Alys had breathed and passed through not two
days ago.

Although Sybilla believed that Alys had come into Pilings alone as the village woman had claimed, Sybilla

knew that Alys had left the area with another person. A large person, carrying a pain greater than his own size.

Sybilla could only assume this person was Piers Mallory.

It was a stomach-clenching relief to know that Alys was alive, but Sybilla didn't trust anyone related to Judith Angwedd, even if only through marriage, and she worried deeply that Alys was still with the renegade commoner. Why? What use was he to her, and vice versa? Sybilla was confident that her sister was not being held against her will—the man would have never let her go into the village and have contact with the natives were that the case. So why?

And why would Alys determine to carry on with him to London, if that was indeed Piers Mallory's destination? Could it truly be because of Sybilla's fear of the king? Of her tenuous grasp on Fallstowe? Perhaps that bitch, Judith Angwedd, was right—Alys was going to Edward, in retaliation for Sybilla binding her to Clement Cobb.

No, that couldn't be. As angry as Sybilla knew Alys had been over the betrothal, and even though she and Alys seemed to constantly be at odds, Sybilla did not think her sister would betray not only her, but the people of Fallstowe, so grievously.

Alys was young. So young and missing their mother so, Sybilla knew. Alys had been the baby, and Amicia had admitted to encouraging her youngest child in her pursuit of freedom and adventure. Alys had simply never deigned to grow up and realize that life as an adult was not filled with leisure and adventure and whimsy. There was only responsibility, and pride, and duty. The pleasures you reaped were few and well appreciated when you could steal a bit of happiness.

Sybilla wished that she could have found a way to

somehow fill the void left by Amicia's passing and perhaps help Alys realize and appreciate the duties of her station, but Sybilla was no mother figure. The very idea of it caused her brow to wrinkle in the cold air of the tent. No, she was only a leader, a ruler. Her duty in life was to protect her sisters and their home, so that when the end came—as surely it must—Cecily and Alys would be safe. Sybilla would not fare so well, but it was a promise she had made, and she accepted her fate. She may be brought down eventually, but she would not go meekly.

And she would never surrender.

First though, she must find Alys. Find her before London, preferably, so as to escape Edward's dungeon for herself. If the king captured Sybilla, Fallstowe would fall in a blink under Cecily—the middle sister always wanted to think everyone had the best intentions at heart. Attackers could be undermining one of Fallstowe's towers and Cecily would suggest they were only trying to reinforce it.

Sybilla clenched her hands into fists for a moment and then uncurled her fingers, bringing her back to the task at hand.

She began to whisper into the blackness above her face.

Chapter 14

"Help!" Alys screamed into the trees as she fought to keep her body as still as possible. She had only just stopped swinging, and with hanging upside down, she thought there was a great possibility that she would vomit should she start to sway once more.

It was difficult not to move though. Her left leg felt as though it would pull from her hip and she tried to keep her right leg crossed over and lock her ankles together. Her skirts were fallen up—or down, really—around her face, exposing her legs and lower back to the winter night. Her stomach was only spared because she had her arms held at her sides. The hem of her cloak trailed the ground below her head.

"Help!"

This was very, very bad. She must have stepped into some hunter's snare, although what he expected to catch with a trap so large was beyond Alys. Perhaps a dragon. Who knew when the man would be through this part of the wood to check his traps in the winter? Any game he secured would stay patiently frozen, waiting for him. Alys had to return to Piers. Even though she had found no aid for him, she could not let him be alone.

And the thought did cross her mind that she could die like this, feet in the air, her skirts around her face. With all the jibes Alys had sent her eldest sister about her numerous male companions, Sybilla would never let her live it down.

"Ha!" she huffed on a white cloud of breath.

She had to get loose.

Even though it worsened her vertigo, Alys craned her neck back to look at the ground below her for a weapon of some sort. There were a couple of smaller rocks perhaps three feet out from her head, but even when she let her skirts fall back around her face and stretched as far as she could, her fingertips could not reach them. She was too high off the ground, were the rocks even directly beneath her head. They weren't sharp rocks any matter. She could do little with one save beat her own brains in. Which might soon be a winsome fantasy if it became obvious she was going to hang there for eternity.

She tried to fight down the panic that threatened to step in and take control of her mental faculties. Her left foot was numb now, and an ache was crawling from her ankle to her hip, her buttocks cramping with the strain. She struggled to gather her skirts together to the side of one thigh and secured them in a large, clumsy knot. The wind seemed to tear at her exposed skin. She coughed, cleared her throat of saliva and spat to the side. Then she took a deep breath and craned her head around to find the tree she was suspended from.

It was about ten feet away from her. But even if she could pendulate herself enough to reach it, she didn't know what she would do once there. Attempt to shimmy up the trunk, upside down, and with one leg tethered? Ridiculous. It was too wide to even get her arms about.

She arched her back, her head swimming as the ground waved beneath her, and then strained with her stomach to bend her chest up to her thighs—if she could grab her ankles, then the rope . . .

"Aghh!" she screamed as her hip strained—she barely got to a ninety degree angle before falling back down. She lengthened her arms behind her head and tried again, swinging herself harder and throwing her hands toward her feet.

The pain was so that she couldn't even scream this time. She fell back down and fought with her skirts as she swung and swiveled.

When her vision was unhampered once more—save for the sickening dizziness—she noticed another tree perpendicular to that of her captor, a young tree whose girth was only perhaps the thickness of her thigh, and which had low, spindly bare branches perhaps six feet off the ground. If she could swing herself so that she could grab hold of one of those branches . . .

What? she asked herself. *You'd be stretched across the forest floor like a rabbit on a spit. What good would that do you?*

But if she could suspend enough of her weight to loosen the strangle knot, she might be able to kick the loop from her ankle with the other foot. Even if she fell after . . . well, a fall from that height wasn't likely to kill her. She hoped.

"Alright then," she growled, keeping her eyes on the smaller tree and tightening the knot of her skirts. She let her hands go over her head once more, then arched her body to begin swinging.

"Oh!" she gasped, and tried to swallow as she began to

pick up speed and distance. The blood in her head and behind her eyes seemed to slosh, her ears popped painfully. The wind swept her hair across her face and she clawed it away. "Oooh!"

She was only about three feet from her fingertips reaching the lowest branch. She bowed her body even further on the back swing, ready to launch her momentum.

She cried out as she flew forward, her fingers reaching, reaching—she was going to grab it!

Warm flesh clamped over her outstretched hands, halting her ascent and jarring her stretched body to a halt. Her hip screamed. A man's face, upside down, appeared before Alys's.

"Enjoying yourself?" he asked.

Alys's heart stopped as she looked at the doubling, tripling image of the grizzled old man before her. Her stomach, however, heaved.

"Let me go," she choked.

"As you wish." He smiled and released her hands, and Alys flew backward.

"Heeelp meee!" she cried, screaming shrilly as her head passed inches away from the trunk of the large tree.

"Oh, make up your bloody mind!" the old man admonished. He came to stand beneath the branch that supported her, and on Alys's next pass, he reached out and seized her arms, bringing her to a gentle halt. He released her, then bent to peer into her face. "What are you doing caught up in my snare?" he demanded.

"Oh," Alys gasped, and then gulped as the little contents of her stomach inched up—or down, rather—her throat. "Just hanging around. It's so comfortable, I simply can't understand why you went to the trouble to hide it."

The old man gave a snort. "Pert tongue on you, missy.

Have you had enough, or shall I leave you to your own entertainment?"

"What do you think?" she asked coldly.

The old man straightened, crossed his arms over his leather tunic, and frowned. "I think that, despite your maid's clothing, I've snared me a lady."

"Yes. Yes, I am," Alys rushed. He must be looking for coin, and coin Alys would gladly and gratefully pay him for cutting her down. "I am Lady Alys Foxe of Fallstowe Castle, and my family will reward you generously for your aid."

"Is that so?" the old man said mildly. "Well then, that bein' the case"—he gave her an exaggerated bow, one arm crossing over his middle—"I'll be happy to leave you to rot in hell, *milady*." He turned and began walking away.

"Wait!" Alys screamed, the rope beginning to twist slowly so that she was forced to whip her head side to side to keep sight of him. "Wait! Where are you going?"

"To me own warm home," the old man called back to her.

"No! Come back! You must cut me down!"

"Sod off!" he shouted merrily.

"Please!" Alys screamed. "Please, I was searching the wood for help when I got caught in your snare—there's a man very ill, he'll die if no one comes for him!" Alys could not imagine what it was about her that had offended the old man so. He'd seemed ornery but sane until she'd acknowledged that she was of the nobility.

Of course!

"He's only a commoner and has nothing!" she shouted as loudly as she could, the old man having already disappeared into the blackness between the trees. "A poor dairy farmer! Please, you must help us!"

Only silence answered her, and she began to panic. A

sob bubbled at her throat and she squeezed her eyes shut. "Please come back!" she keened.

After several moments, Alys decided that the old man really had walked away into the woods, leaving her—and Piers—to die. Anger replaced her fear.

"You son of a bitch!" she screamed, her throat feeling as though it was shredding with cold and strain and thirst. She punched the air near her hips in a fit of rage. "I would have had that branch in my grasp if not for you! *Damn* you! Damn, damn, *damn* you!"

She took a deep, shuddering breath, and tried to choke down the burning bile again. She gagged. Another deep breath, and then she arched her back once more.

"Aghh!" she cried as she began to swing. She pulled harder, her arc increasing, her fury pushing her. Tears leaked from the corners of her eyes and the wind kissed them away.

Higher. Higher. Almost. Her fingernails scraped bark. She whizzed back into the night, steeling herself for the next push. She reached her arms until her back screamed, burned, threatened to tear—

Her fingers latched around the whip-thin branch and the slender stick began to slide through her hands like a rod of fire as momentum threatened to rip it from her hold.

"No!" she screamed. The smooth bark felt as slippery as a moss covered river rock in her grip. The outsides of her palms jammed against the base of two twigs forming out of the branch and her slide stopped. She bobbed between the rope and the limber branch. Her arms were over her head, stretched as far as they could without coming loose from her torso, one ankle still bound, her other left flailing toward the ground, which looked considerably farther away than she'd originally thought.

She tried kicking the snare free, but the knot was biting into her flesh. She couldn't get enough leverage.

And now the tiny twigs keeping her hold were folding, bending onto the branch, and Alys felt her palms sliding minutely. In another moment, she would fly back over the ground.

"No!" she screamed again, as she began to hurl toward the earth.

But this time, she fell feet first. The branch ripped from her hands and she crumpled to the ground. The leaves beneath her face and palms felt so good, smelled so good. The universe was solid once more, even if her head and stomach were still swimming.

Alys raised her face perhaps two inches to look across the small clearing. She saw the head of a crude stone hatchet sunk into the dirt. She turned her face the other way and there stood the old man as well as two other, younger, men, staring at her, all three with their arms crossed over their chests.

Alys tried to crawl to the base of the young tree, dragging her skirts from the knot and down to cover her legs. She nearly made it before she began to vomit.

Alys was not coming back.

Even in his state of near delirium—which he knew could be the only explanation for what he was seeing and hearing—Piers recognized Alys's vulnerability. She knew nothing of survival, had no supplies, knew not that each step she took south carried her farther and farther from the road she sought. It had to be freezing because it was still snowing, and it was sometime during the night because it was still dark.

She was likely dead already.

Piers tried to raise his head to look at the fire—he barely caught a glimpse of tiny licking flames before his head fell back against the tree. The fire was dying, too. Fitting. He rolled his head to the left. At least his father was still there to keep him company.

Warin Mallory sat near the weakening fire, one knee bent to his chest, his other leg crooked under him for support. His gray hair was untied, swooping away from his forehead and falling over both shoulders. His beard and mustache were full and neat. His gaze was icy, but merry, as if death had been so startlingly bright as to have bleached his eyes, but he had enjoyed the experience. He was dressed in his typical dark green tunic, and was shelling what looked to Piers to be hazelnuts by hand, and feeding them one at a time to Layla.

Layla crouched at Warin's knee, her little hands clasped patiently before her mouth, nibbling and watching as each shell piece fell onto the pile growing on the ground. Lord Mallory never spoke, but he did keep a gentle smile on his face. Every now and then he would look up at Piers and nod encouragingly, or hold a nut toward him as if offering it to him to eat.

Piers had managed to barely shake his head no the first time. Now he just looked away. He had tried speaking to his father when Warin had simply walked from the snow-storm and toward the fire, but his words had been garbled and unintelligible to his own ears, even knowing what he was trying to say.

Why do you haunt me?

Is it your wish to see me die?

Was it not enough to torment me with your uncaring the whole of my life?

Can you not rest until you are certain I have died a death as lonely as my life?

But his questions had only come out as pathetic sobs, and so Piers had held his swollen and dry tongue out of pride. With Warin keeping the death vigil over him, both Judith Angwedd's and Bevan's cruel words had ceased, and that at least was a blessing.

Piers was sorry. Sorry that he had ever met Alys Foxe and unwillingly brought her into the misery that was his mission. Had he simply abandoned her, she would have eventually returned to Fallstowe, and would not be now wandering a desolate wood populated only with myths in search of nonexistent aid for him. She deserved to live her fortunate life. Everyone deserved that, Piers thought. Poor misguided child had ended up with him instead.

Piers thought he heard a crunching in the wood beyond. Likely naught but some nocturnal forager, and so he ignored it, choosing to watch his father instead. Piers believed this was the longest he'd ever been in the man's presence in his life. Warin looked over his shoulder and then to Piers. He gestured toward the sound with his head and then his smile widened slightly.

Piers nodded. It seemed what was expected of him. In death, Warin Mallory seemed to take great pleasure in such a simple thing as a mouse scampering through leaves in a lonely world painted with black and cold and quiet. And sharing his favorite treat—hazelnuts—with a little foreign animal.

"I've found him!"

The male voice cut through the night like a blade dragged through gravel. And Piers let his eyes close, knowing that now that Bevan had tracked him down at last, his moments on this earth were like the snowflakes that landed on his cheeks—little, fading miracles.

"Yes, there! I see the fire!" A woman's voice, and even

though shrill and hoarse, it was not Judith Angwedd's. "Piers!"

Could it be Alys?

Piers's eyelids felt like stiff, dried leather as he struggled to open them. The crashing sounds beyond the trees grew in volume and intensity. His chest suddenly felt crushed, and when he managed to drag his eyes open as far as they would go—barely a sliver—he saw that Layla had returned to perch upon his midsection. The monkey began to chatter in an agitated fashion, and Piers thought that perhaps she was trying to defend him from the stranger whose voice had called out. But even Layla's slight weight was proving too much for Piers's laboring lungs.

Alys's little monkey was going to smother him to death.

Piers flicked his eyes toward the fire—Warin was brushing bits of hazelnut shells from his palms, his smile seeming wise and merry and damnably eternal. He stared into Piers's eyes as Piers stared back and struggled silently to draw breath, tried to raise an arm to brush at Layla. The vision of his father began to throb as consciousness wavered.

Warin braced a palm on the ground and began to lever himself up.

Piers's view of him was blocked as a figure rushed in front of the fire, blackening his world. Layla screamed pitifully and then Piers felt as if a boulder had been dropped onto his chest as the monkey launched herself upward. But then it was gone, and air trickled into his lungs.

A breeze fell over him as Alys—wondrous, impulsive Alys—dropped to her knees at his side, holding her pet to her bosom with one arm and leaning into Piers. Her free hand stroked his forehead, his cheek, turning his face toward hers.

"Piers, can you hear me? God, you're burning up! I've found some men who are going to help us, take you back to their town."

His eyes shifted toward the fire once more and he saw four men, but only three strangers. The newcomers were dressed in leather and rough wool, and carried an assortment of weapons and tools strapped across their bodies with thick ropes. Warin Mallory looked each up and down, and then his eyes turned to Piers and he nodded, his smile crooking to one side as if to convey that the men looked likely enough.

"Alys," Piers tried to say, and it came out like the scratch of a fingernail against a piece of dried wood.

But she heard him, for she leaned closer, her tone anxious. "Yes? What is it?"

"I'd like you"—he tried to swallow, and raise his hand, but only one of his fingers twitched toward the men— "meet my father."

Alys was silent for a moment, and in that time Warin Mallory's smile grew into a proud grin. Then Alys leaned into Piers with a rush, pressing the side of her face to his, her mouth near his ear. Piers could smell the sharp scent of her sweat-wet scalp, her fear. He could feel her humid breath against his skin. He kept his eyes on his father, whose mouth now formed the words that Alys gave voice to.

"I'm sorry it took me so long, Piers."

He felt a catch in his chest, a pressure behind his eyes and they stung, as if they wanted to weep. He blinked to rid himself of the uncomfortable sensation—he had those in spades already,

When his eyes opened, his father was gone.

"Snow's comin' ice," one of the new men said brusquely. "We'd best take him now else we'll not get him up the ladders."

Ladders? Piers said to himself.

Alys pulled away from him. "Ladders?"

"Aye," the man answered. He began to walk toward where Piers lay, his hands flying over the numerous straps across his body. "I've a fair length of rope and a blanket, we can—*bastard*!" the man hissed as he stumbled. He looked first to the ground around his feet, then up toward the tree tops and at last at his companions. "We're standing in a thickness of walnuts. The whole bloody forest is walnut."

"Aye," the old man of the group growled. "So watch yer bloody step, you tenderfooted maiden."

"Walnut," the man repeated and then gestured brusquely with a palm toward the ground. "Where did all the bloody *hazelnut* shells come from?"

Piers chuckled, but only to himself, as at last he let himself slip away into oblivion.

It seemed to Alys that they walked for hours, although the old man, Ira—he of the loathing for nobility and the talent for a fine snare—had informed her that their town was just beyond the place where Alys had been strung up like game.

Piers was being trundled along between the two younger men, suspended in a sort of cocoon conveyance, all but a tight circle of his face swaddled in the rough blanket. When Alys had asked the old man if he had any idea what could be wrong with Piers, Ira had replied, "Looks to me that he's ill, woman. Not to worry, Linny will have him springin' an' spry."

Alys didn't know who this Linny was, or exactly what "springing and spry" meant, but she prayed that it meant Piers would be well soon.

She struggled and slipped up the side of a sudden embankment, bearing the awkward burdens of her own sack strapped across her body as well as Piers's pack, which she clutched to her chest. Layla clung to her head as she came at last to the top with the rest of the group. The loud and startlingly close hoot of an owl caused Alys to jump, but then at her side, Ira raised both gnarled hands to his mouth and returned the call, so eerily reminiscent of the bird he mocked that Alys was certain they were somehow related.

She jumped again as a rustling whoosh sounded, and a long tongue of rope and wood unfurled not six feet before the old man.

Ira yanked on the rope, nodded to himself and then called upward. "Send down another—we've found a sick man an' he's unlikely to go it on his own."

Then Alys looked up, and brought a hand to her mouth as she gasped.

The trees seemed to be alight with fae fire—above her and before her, the canopy flickered with little balls of light, some bobbing as if in lanterns, others dancing tall like virile torches. Along the forest floor, she could now see no fewer than a dozen fires crackling, before what looked to be rounded twig huts and pens made out of thick, crooked branches. Shadows began to coalesce from the darkness and move toward Alys and her companions, like trees that had come alive, walking wood, and her mind went back to what the woman she'd met in Pilings had asked her.

Are you one of the wood people?

Then another long rope swish-rattled down and the two younger men still bearing Piers pushed Alys aside rather carelessly to stand beneath the ladders. They looked at each other.

"Could use the lift," said the youngest, Alys thought. He had curly blond hair and a slim, pointed face.

"Whilst carrying him?" The other young man shook his head, curly blond also, but wider. Alys decided they were likely brothers. "Too large. Take some fair labor."

"No, set him down. Save our backs."

"Roll off the side. Strangle."

"Pull fast?"

The older brother seemed to consider it for a moment. "Climb slow."

The younger shrugged in agreement.

They lowered Piers to the ground carefully and then their hands moved so deftly and so fast that their motions were blurred, knotting the ends of the rope to fashion two longer loops. The brothers hefted the loops over their heads to rest on their outside shoulders and began to climb—rather quickly, Alys thought. Piers swayed between them like a swollen bridge, farther and farther away from the ground.

Ira stood at her side silently, his arms crossed over his chest once more and his face tilted back to track the progress of the brothers and their cargo. Alys's eyes flicked nervously between the old man's face and the invisible treetop, not sure what was going on or what would happen next. Would they follow the men and Piers to whatever nest was above them? Alys was anxious to be at Piers's side once more—he had looked so much worse when she'd come back to him. And he had spoken of his dead father as if the man had been standing in the camp with them.

The thought made Alys shiver.

Ira turned to her, his mouth twisted as if he'd consumed something bitter. "I don't want you here," he said without compunction. "'Tis due to the likes of you that we live as we do, and I'd as soon cut off one of me own arms than allow you above."

"Ira, I—"

"But if I turn you away," he said over her words, "'tis likely you'll only give away our place."

"I wouldn't," Alys insisted. "I couldn't find it myself—I have no idea where we are, where the road is, the river. I'm completely lost."

"Think you I believe your lies, *lady*?" he spat nastily. "I can't ken why you'd be with a commoner such as the man who lies above us but I would wager that it's not but for your own greedy gain."

"I love him," Alys said. She hadn't intended the confession, but there it was, and it was true. She wanted to tell Ira that Piers was her husband, but if Ira asked Piers, in his current state of delirium—and even once he was completely clearheaded—he would likely only deny her. "I've held my tongue in thanks for the aid you are giving us, but it is grossly unfair the horrid things you assume about me, simply because of my birth. You know me not, Ira."

"I know enough of your kind," he said, as if she were a terrible poison. "And a young woman run off from her rich family can only mean so many things." He looked her up and down and Alys wanted to cringe. "Have his child in your belly, do you?"

"No!" Alys said, horrified. Her skin crawled with stinging heat.

Ira's eyes narrowed and then he chuckled. "No? Perhaps not. But, surrounded by limp lords as you are, 'tis likely what you love about him is in his breeches, you noble whore."

Alys struck him. Ira's old face snapped to the side with her sharp blow, but when his head came round again, his whole body followed. He grabbed Alys by her upper arms, his gnarled fingers biting into her sore muscles. Layla jumped screeching to the ground, and Ira began marching away from the tree, pushing Alys backward in front of him while she struggled and flailed and tried not to drop Piers's pack.

"Let go of me!"

Ira approached the swell of ground that sloped away from where their village hid and then shoved her over, grabbing Piers's pack in the last instant. Alys windmilled her arms before falling and tumbling down the slight grade, Layla scampering through the leaves after her.

Alys slid to a stop on her side, her hips and back already weeping pain from her encounter with the old man's snare. Layla scurried nimbly over to her and crouched behind her body. Alys looked up the hill to where Ira glared down at her, and eight or so of the wood people from deeper in the village had come to flank him. They stared down at her with blank faces, as if they were not at all surprised to see her there or by Ira's treatment of her.

"Hah!" Ira growled and flung his hand at her as if he was shooing away a troublesome dog. Piers's bag was already slung over one of the old man's bony shoulders. "Get you from here, *whore*," he emphasized. "Dare you not return, else I break with the oath I swore my father and kill a woman." The old man turned and disappeared from the brink of the hill, while the wood people filled in the void of his presence, all still staring at her and none of them speaking.

"Are none of you going to help me?" she demanded, astounded.

No one so much as flinched.

Alys wanted to lay her numb face on her frozen forearms and simply cry. She felt as though she were living in a nightmare, lost in a dangerous wood, starving, injured, and surrounded by rough social deviants who now had possession of a very ill and helpless Piers, not to mention his precious ring. No one would listen to her, no one would help her.

Her brow lowered.

Alys pushed herself to stand with her palms—sore and reddened from the cold and her death grip on the branch from earlier. She stared right back at the wood people while she snapped her fingers at Layla, calling the monkey to her shoulder. Alys began to climb the hillock in stuttering strides, one arm flailing out to the side for balance, the other clutching her bag at her hip. Layla clung to her like a barnacle.

When she reached the lowly summit, the wood people gave way for her to stand. She looked around at their faces, blowing hair out of her face. Her stomach was in a knot, but she was not about to let this group of people see her fear.

"Which way did he go?" she asked.

A middle-aged looking man pointed a leather clad arm toward the tree the brothers had climbed with Piers. Alys glanced at the double rope ladders hanging down and then back at the cluster of faces appraising her interestedly.

"None of you will try to stop me?"

"Why should we?" the man asked mildly. "You want to get tossed out of a tree . . ." He crossed his arms, shrugged. "Your neck."

Alys squared her shoulders and took a deep breath. "Thank you." She began marching toward the dangling ladders as if approaching a battlefield.

"She's really going up there," Alys heard the man say to his companions, as if he couldn't believe her brazenness.

"Child, wait!" a woman's voice called from behind

Alys, but she kept walking. She would not be turned away from the one thing in her life that was important, that mattered more than anything ever had. Piers. If she had to physically fight the old man, she would.

"Child!" Alys's elbow was seized and she was pulled to a halt by a woman perhaps ten years her senior, with rich brown hair partially hidden by her hood, and eyes with kind tridents at their corners. The woman hesitated and looked askance at Layla for an instant. "Don't go above. When Ira's in a temper, he's apt to say and do aught which he heartily regrets come the morrow."

"My—" Alys again wanted to say husband, but she was unsure how the wood people would take her declaration. Would they then mark Piers as related to nobility and turn him away? "My friend is very ill, and he is up there alone with strangers, including one very mean old man, who has stolen a bag not belonging to him."

"Your friend is in fine, fine hands. No better than Linny's for a thousand fathoms," the woman insisted, her grip gentling, but becoming more insistent all the same. "Ira is not a bad man, and if he's taken your friend to Linny, no harm will come to him or his possessions by hand of those who dwell here." The woman seemed to hesitate and then asked, "Did he fall?"

Alys shook her head. "No. It's a fever."

"God have mercy! Was he cut? Bitten?"

"He was injured a fortnight ago, but—" Alys paused suddenly, her mind going at once to the bandages on Piers's hand, and then further back, to the night they had met at the Foxe Ring. Her stomach clenched.

"He was bitten. Layla"—she gestured to the monkey on her shoulder—"accidentally bit him, several days ago."

The woman frowned and released Alys's arm as she edged away from Alys and her monkey. "Well, there'll be naught you can do for him this night, as exhausted and cold as you seem." She looked Alys up and down. "And hungry, too, I'd wager?"

Alys felt her eyes well with tears and she could do little more than nod hesitantly. "I am. Layla will not bite you, mistress. She is a gentle animal, you have my vow. Piers took her by surprise the night he was bitten, and she was merely frightened. She shan't harm you."

"I see. That is often the way with animals. Well, then." The woman drew her arm around Alys's waist, steering her gently toward the heart of the village. "I'm Ella. You—and Layla—may stay with me and my family tonight, rest, and then someone will speak to Ira for you in the morning."

"No," Alys said, shaking her head. No one would take her responsibilities from her again. "I would speak for myself."

Ella paused. "Alright. But will you come with me? Take some food and drink and lie down?"

"Thank you very much," Alys said in acceptance. "I'm Alys, by the way."

"Pleased to meet you, Lady Alys," Ella said with a smile.

"No. No lady here," Alys said wryly. "Just Alys."

Ella's smile grew wider with knowing. "Come along then, Just Alys. I'll help you into the tree."

Alys balked to a stop.

"Tree?"

Chapter 15

Alys awoke with a start, her breath huffing in white rushes from her mouth. In an instant, the nightmare that had roused her was gone, like the clouds of her own steamy breath. She blew out a relieved sigh and leaned back fully onto the sagging rope cot that was her bed. It felt like the most luxurious ticking, even after a long night of hard sleeping. She looked down to check on Layla, but the monkey was not there.

Alys bolted upright in the bed, her hands reaching out to grasp the rope sides and steady the swinging her motion had set off. She'd had quite her fill of swinging from a rope the previous evening. Ella's family's hut circled a large tree, its platform perhaps eight feet wide, trunk to outer edge. She could hear the sounds of the forest beyond the skins that covered the sidewalls like a tent, and the interior was largely dark thanks to the skins and the pine boughs laid over a crisscrossing frame of skinny limbs which formed the roof. Alys guessed that the hut was used mostly as sleeping quarters, as the interior contained little else save several more of the swinging cots and clothing hanging from pegs hammered into the tree trunk.

"Layla?" Alys called softly, not wishing to call attention to any of the villagers yet—she needed time to collect her thoughts and work up a plan of action for approaching Ira. But she was concerned that the monkey was gone from her side. Although Ella's hospitality was a kindness Alys had not expected, she was still unsure about the nature of these people who chose to eke out such a rugged existence as outlaws that they had been relegated to legend. Alys herself could still scarcely believe any of it was real.

"Layla?" she whispered a bit more insistently.

"Not to worry, Lady Alys—I've your lovely pet right here."

Alys looked over her left shoulder and saw the murky outline of a person—a girl from the sound of the voice, or perhaps a very young boy. Whoever it was clearly had Layla on their lap, and was feeding her something from a bowl.

"Oh. Hello," Alys said, pushing her hair out of her eyes. She was unused to having a stranger present when she awoke. "Who are you?"

"I'm Tiny," the shadow replied. "I—and most everyone else—was asleep when you arrived last night. Good morn to you. I fancy your monkey, milady. Reminds me of me baby brother."

Alys huffed a laugh. "Thank you. She is very pretty, but also very troublesome at times." Alys didn't want to seem stingy, but she was uncomfortable with the entire situation. She patted her thigh. "Come here, Layla, and bid me good morn."

Layla's shadow seemed to turn toward her as if debating, and then Tiny spoke up again in a giggling voice.

"I don't think she wishes to leave her breakfast just yet,

milady." The shadow held forth a bowl. "Fresh turnip? I sliced it meself."

"Perhaps in a bit," Alys hedged. "Tiny, are you one of Ella's"—daughters? Sons?—"children?"

"Aye, milady. Her oldest girl, am I. Nearly thirteen," Tiny said proudly. "'Tis why Mam allowed me to sit with you."

"Oh." Alys was deciding on the best method for disembarking from her cot. She shifted one leg as if to throw it over the side, but the whole thing swayed wildly, prompting Alys to bring her legs together quickly and grip the side ropes. Her experience with Ira's snare was still too fresh in her mind.

"It's best to just roll out at once and catch your feet under you," Tiny advised sagely. "Else you'll come upon your nose." She set the bowl on the hut floor and then stood, and Alys saw Layla hop onto the girl's shoulder easily. Tiny took a step toward the bed and held out her palm. "Take my hand, milady—I'll steady you for your first time."

"Thank you," Alys mumbled and was surprised at the delicate feel of Tiny's small hand—the child had been named suitably. Holding her breath, Alys rolled, and was grateful when she was able to catch her feet under herself with a huff of breath. She stood fully upright. "That wasn't so bad."

"Well done, Lady Alys," Tiny praised in her little girl voice. Standing next to the child, Alys was shocked to see that she—no giant herself—was likely a full foot taller than Tiny. Layla looked like a mighty griffin perched on the girl's slender shoulder. "We can go to ground now, if you wish—I'm certain Mam's put back some porridge for you if you'd prefer it to turnips."

"Yes, thank you." Alys began following Tiny around the perimeter of the platform, to the other side of the tree.

"I hope you don't mind using the lift," the girl called back over her shoulder. "I'm disallowed from using the ladders 'cause of me being spindly—Papa fears I'll slip and break me very back. He's likely right. The lads, they simply swing down from ropes more oft than the ladders, but not me and Mam." She paused. "But I reckon you could go on down the ladder yourself." The girl seemed reluctant to offer this courtesy.

"I must confess that I was not fond of the ladder last night." In fact, Alys had been scared for her life, feeling that the rope conveyance would buck out from beneath her feet at any moment and spill her to the ground. Spindly or not, it would not have been a comfortable landing.

"You'll fancy the lift then," Tiny said. "And since we're together, we can lower ourselves and not have to wait for one of the lads."

Alys frowned to herself as Tiny and Layla ducked through a fold in the skin-wall. Then a triangle of forest appeared as Tiny pulled the covering aside. It looked as though Alys was about to step into the thin, cold air between the gray branches.

"Don't fear, milady," Tiny encouraged. "We carry Mam and all the littlest ones up it in a go—it will for certain hold three wee girls such as us."

Alys stepped onto a square wooden platform butted up to the hut floor, and her breath caught in her throat at the view around her. They were truly in the trees, the ground at least twenty feet below. The breeze stirred her hair, scented with wood smoke and winter and the perfume of the trees themselves. Under their feet, villagers crossed to and fro attending to their chores, several carried bundles of long branches strapped to their backs, two men suspended a large buck on a spit, a woman herded bright red chickens with a switch. Children ran among the busied in play, fires crackled under tripod and bubbling cauldron. All around them in the surrounding trees, other huts had their skin walls pulled aside, and long ropes strung from branch to branch supported laundry and several woven rugs.

Alys's attention was torn from the fantastical view by Tiny's polite instructions. "Just undo that rope there on your side, milady—take it from the peg, that's it—but hold on tightly lest we spill sideways!" The girl seemed to find the idea of this amusing—Alys did not. And so she gripped the rough rope in her palms until her fingertips tingled.

"Now just let us down easy. One hand, then the other. Hold tight to me, little Layla!" Tiny began to release the rope into the carved pulley over her head, and Alys did the same, her eyes flicking to the girl periodically and also over her own shoulder at the ground that was inching up to meet them.

The ride was smooth and slow, and by the time the platform came to rest on the forest floor, Alys had decided she much preferred the lift to the twisting rope ladder. She watched as Tiny tied off first her own rope and then Alys's—presumably to keep the machine out of use to younger hands—and then followed the miniature girl off the conveyance and toward the nearest fire.

Ella was nowhere to be seen, and Tiny went without hesitation to a small black iron pot set near the side of the fire. She lifted off the lid with a hooked instrument and peered inside. In those brief seconds, Alys took the opportunity to study the girl in full daylight. Her hair was straw colored, much like Alys's own, and she immediately recalled the village woman in Pilings's mention of Ella and her daughter. The Pilings woman had alluded to the fact that there was something wrong with Ella's girl, but all that Alys could tell was that she was of unusually small size for her age—more along the lines of an eight-year-old.

Tiny turned her face toward Alys with a smile, and Alys was fascinated by the girl's impossibly light colored, gray-green eyes. In the forest light, with Layla on her shoulder, she indeed looked to be a figure from folklore, a fairy, an elf. She was enchanting.

"I was right—here's some porridge if you'd be wantin' it, milady."

"I would love some," Alys said.

Tiny went to the base of the tree, where one of the small, rounded huts crouched and walked straight in, whereas any other person her age would have needed to duck. She emerged a moment later with a wooden bowl and a spoon, as well as a clay jug. The earthen vessel seemed a burden, and so Alys approached her with her hands out.

"Let me help you—"

"Not at all, milady," Tiny said cheerfully and swerved around her toward the fire. "'Tis unwieldy more than heavy. And I don't need as much help as you would reckon." She set the jug by the fire and Layla hopped to the ground, at last coming to greet Alys. Tiny removed the lid of the pot once more and began scooping its contents into the bowl.

Not knowing what else to do, Alys sat on the ground. Obviously it was the right choice, for Tiny brought the bowl and jug to her, without directing her to any proper seating. Alys took the offered meal with a smile of thanks.

Tiny stood above her, beaming down, her hands folded

at her waist. Alys was not used to being watched so closely whilst having a meal, but she knew not what else to do, and so she saluted Tiny with the spoon and tucked into the bowl of warm grain.

It was bland, with perhaps a hint of some sort of sweet syrup, but it was hearty and heavy in her stomach, and Alys thoroughly enjoyed the first hot breakfast she'd had since leaving Fallstowe.

"Did Ira really throw you down the comin'-up?" The question burst from the girl, as if it had been growing and growing inside of her and she could simply no longer contain it. "And did you really get caught in his snare?"

Alys forced the mouthful of porridge down her throat when it threatened to stick somewhere halfway. "The comin'up?"

"The hill on the edge of the village. When someone approaches, they have to climb it, and they always call out—"

"Coming up," Alys finished with a wry smile. "Clever. And yes, he did, and yes, I did. Is that how he usually behaves toward visitors? String them up and then throw them out?"

"Mercy, yes," Tiny giggled. "Although most don't make it past the snare. We haven't had a proper visitor in ages, and never a true *lady*." There was a hint of awe in the last word. "Were you a lad, Ira'd most likely had the brothers hand you a sound pummelin' and then taken anything you were carrying."

"I see," Alys said, her hopes for any sort of amicable relationship with the old man being whisked away into the treetops with Tiny's words.

"He's simply protecting us, you see," Tiny rushed to assure her. "Ira's not cruel. He knows that for us to keep on living here like we are, intruders must be dealt with."

"Well, he's not been exactly welcoming," Alys mumbled.

"It's your title, milady. Forgive me, for sayin'." Tiny stepped toward Alys and then sank into a cross-legged seat across from her. Layla immediately went to the girl, who produced nuts from her apron pocket as if she'd put them there earlier for that exact purpose. "Ira doesn't fancy anyone of noble birth."

"Neither I nor my family has ever wronged Ira, that I'm aware of."

"Of course not," Tiny said mildly. "But the village where Ira is from was ruled by terrible people. We've all come from such places. Ira simply wants us all to be able to live here in peace. He's a good leader."

Alys was quiet for several moments, trying to comprehend Tiny's explanation. "So all of you here—the wood people—are from villages that turned you out for one reason or another?"

Tiny nodded. "Turned out or they left for fear of punishment. Some couldn't pay their dues, others were accused of crimes—it's different for us all."

"What of your family?"

Tiny smiled impishly. "Guess."

"I couldn't," Alys said, shaking her head. "Your mother has been so kind to me, and you are a darling."

Tiny laughed. "It's me, though. We lived in a place called Pilings when I was born. I was very, very small—never grew much after. The folk were feared of me for a curse. The pigs took ill, and they blamed me."

"Blamed you? When you were a baby?"

Tiny nodded and held out her arms. "Don't I look like a changeling?"

"No!"

The girl shrugged and looked away into the forest.

"Mam and Papa wouldn't have the talk. Papa had heard of Ira and his little village, and they welcomed us. It's been a good home. All I've ever known."

The truth of this little knot of people in the wood became stranger and stranger the more Alys learned.

"So you owe fealty to no overlord?"

"Oh, I'm certain we owe it, we just don't pay it." Tiny stood, and Layla hopped up on her shoulder. "Ira says we own these woods, and I believe him. Come, milady, and I'll take you to your man. I'm certain you're wanting to see him, and Linny's just come down from her tree."

Piers felt as if every muscle in his body had been stretched beyond its limit and then snapped back. His head pounded and his left hand felt as though it was smoldering. He opened his eyes and saw thatch above him, rolled his head to the left to look at his hand and saw that it was contained in a sort of package that looked like wide, flat leaves, glistening wet and heavy. His arm was angled up on a crude bolster.

He couldn't feel his first two fingers at all.

He didn't know where he was—in some sort of a hut, obviously. He vaguely remembered Alys coming back for him, with strange men, but he did not recall walking to a village, or having his wounds tended to. Where was she now? Where was *he*, and what had his caregiver done to him? Why couldn't he feel his fingers? Had the bite Layla'd given him festered? His heart pounded. He couldn't tend a dairy properly with one hand, couldn't milk.

Piers heard his own whimper as he tried to bring his right hand across his body, frantic to remove the organic bandages.

"Still there, me friend," a rough voice said, startling Piers. "Although for how long, I know not."

The old man sat on a stool not two paces from where Piers lay on the floor of the hut. Piers had not noticed him, blending into the dark skins that made up the walls as if he too were comprised of old, tanned leather. The man worried a small object in one palm.

"Where am I?" Piers asked hoarsely.

"My village. Linny's tending you best she can, but the bites were old, sealed over, trapping the poison inside." His deep set eyes seemed to bore into Piers's. "The monkey?"

Piers nodded. "Where's Alys? The woman who was with me?"

The old man shrugged. "You mean *Lady* Alys, do you not?"

"Where is she?"

"What are you doing with the likes of her, friend? She told me you were a dairy farmer, and though I was not obliged to believe her, your hands tell a clearer truth than any of her kind would recognize—the calluses, the scars. It was me own life's work, many years ago. Does she have aught to accuse you of? What is your worth to her?"

"I don't owe you any explanation. *Where is she?*"

"I beg to disagree, friend. Were it not for my Linny, you'd likely be dead right now. I am showing you a great deal more hospitality than most would a stranger, so aye, you do owe me a bit, and I'd collect. Why are the pair of you together in the thickness of my wood?"

"We're only passing through. On our way to London," was all Piers would say. He didn't care what this Linny had done for him, he wanted Alys, and he wanted her now.

The old man whistled a high note. "London, eh? What business would the likes of a poor farmer such as yourself have that would call him to London?" When Piers only glared at him, the old man pushed. "I can see that you're not the sort of man who takes easily to being questioned, but I have me own interests to protect. You ken?"

"I don't make bargains, old man. Tell me where she is."

The old man's eyes narrowed and he looked sideways at Piers. "Even under threat of your own life?"

Piers stared at him. "Don't bluff. Kill me or tell me where she is. I'm tired of talking to you, either way."

The old man looked at Piers a long while, a faint smile on his thin lips. "I know not where her highness is at this moment. I threw her out on her titled arse last night, her filthy animal with her. No need to thank me."

Piers tried to sit up, his hand throbbing in time to his pounding heart. Alys alone in the wood? He would kill the old man himself if he could just get up.

"Don't get yourself in a lather," the old man admonished gruffly, and half rose to push Piers gently but firmly back onto his makeshift bed with one wrinkled and stingy palm. "A kindhearted woman of the village took pity on her, and I'm certain her ladyship is but a stone's throw from us. If she cares aught for your welfare, 'tis likely her voice will abuse both our ears before long."

Piers lay back, but only because he was truly too weak to continue the ruse of a struggle. He realized how very vulnerable he was.

"Of course she cares for my welfare. She was the one who found you, wasn't she?"

"Why *would* she care so for you, that was my question, lad! Is she your lover?"

Piers turned his face away. "No."

"Are you her escort? Hired to gain her the city?"

"No. I go to London for my own purposes."

"And those would be?"

"Fuck you, *friend*," Piers sneered.

"So that's how it is to be, eh?" the old man said mildly. "Well. I have my own idea as to why you're going to London, and my wager would be that it has aught to do with this pretty little bauble in my hand. Would you agree?"

Piers turned his head back toward the old man and saw his father's signet ring pinched between leathery finger and thumb.

"I'll kill you," Piers breathed.

"You're in no condition to be making such threats. But, what you will do is tell me how this ring came to be in your possession, and what you plan to do with it once you're to London."

Piers struggled to rise once more.

"Now, if you keep on with that nonsense, I'll just rap you on your skull and you can go back to sleep until you're feeling more cooperative."

"Give me back my ring," Piers demanded, his words coming out like hacking barks before he deteriorated into a fit of coughing on the woolen ticking.

The old man waited patiently until Piers caught his breath. "You stole it, thinking you could sell it?" The old man chuckled. "Any fool would know that this ring belongs on the hand of a noble. A commoner come to the city with it would be jailed before you could name a price."

"I didn't steal it. It's mine."

The old man shook his head and tsked. "No need to lie to me, friend."

"Give it back! It's all I have."

"Piers?" Alys's voice seemed to call from below him, if that was possible, since he was nearly certain he was lying on the ground.

"Alys," he tried to shout back, but his voice had wearied to a faint whisper.

"Now see there? It's not all you have," the old man said, all trace of smile gone from his face as he stood with a slight groan. He stepped to the bottom of Piers's cot and looked down at him, Piers's signet ring disappeared into his tight fist. Small, hollow footsteps sounded from the other side of the hut.

"I'll not leave here without that ring. It belongs to me," Piers whispered.

"I don't know how you came across it," the old man said quietly, gravely. "But this ring will never again leave my possession. I know you stole it, you see. I know, because it once belonged to me own daughter, now dead a score and four years."

He turned and walked into the shadows that draped the corners of the hut.

Alys approached his cot with a noticeable limp, and Piers nearly wanted to weep at the familiar sight of her golden hair and her bright smile. She glanced nervously at the old man as he passed, but neither one spoke to each other.

In a moment, Piers heard a rolling rattle and then he was alone with Alys.

She dropped to her knees at his side, her small hands reaching for his face. "Piers, how are you feeling?"

He looked up at her, his breath caught painfully in his chest. He didn't know what was happening, or what the old man meant.

Seek your blood on your journey to the king, my son. There you will find the answer which will save Gillwick and yourself.

"What is it, Piers? Did Ira say something to upset you?"

Ira. The old man's name was Ira.

"My ring," he managed to whisper.

"Your ring?" Alys's face scrunched into a confused frown. "Do you want me to fetch it for you? Where is it?"

Piers tried to shake his head and his eyes went to the stool where the old man had been sitting.

. . . *it once belonged to my daughter, now dead a score and four years.*

A score and four years ago, Piers had been six years old.

Chapter 16

"Piers?"

He was staring at an old, three-legged stool on the far side of his makeshift bed. For several moments, he said nothing. Then at last he turned his head toward her.

"Nothing," he whispered. His eyes roved her face, her shoulders. "Layla?"

"She's taken a fancy to a particular village girl," Alys said with a wry smile. "I must admit I'm rather jealous, even though the child is a delight. How are you feeling?"

"Poorly," he admitted, his voice faint and his eyes far away now, as he turned his gaze to the ceiling above.

Alys nodded. "I've met Linny—the woman caring for you. She told me that you have a fever in your hand where Layla bit you, and that it's spread to your blood."

Piers blinked, but said nothing. Part of Alys wanted to explain to him how serious his condition was, how frightened for him she was, but she recognized that her desire to share the burden of his illness was entirely selfish, and so restrained herself, and only gave him the optimistic part of Linny's opinion.

"She's drained the wounds, dressed them with a salve

that will draw the poison out. You'll rest here, try to eat and drink and sleep as much as possible, and you shall be well soon." *We hope,* she added to herself.

"How long?" Piers whispered, the question meant for her, but his words were directed toward the ceiling.

"I don't know," she said honestly. His face looked so gaunt in the darkness of the tree house, Alys felt a shiver flutter over her. "I don't think anyone could know yet."

"I must get to London." His eyes closed.

"You will. We will," she emphasized.

"Not without my ring," Piers said. "The old man has it."

Fury sprang to life in Alys. "Ira stole your father's ring?"

Piers nodded, his chin barely twitching downward.

"That miserable old thief!" Alys rushed to her feet. "I'll get it back for you Piers, I swear. I'll—"

He held his right hand up slightly from the ticking. "Alys," he whispered.

"No! He cannot think to take advantage of you while he has us both as little more than his prisoners! How dare he?" Alys seethed.

"Alys," Piers said, raising his voice to a raspy hark. He fell into a coughing fit, and Alys rushed back to her knees, her hand supporting his back.

"I'm sorry, Piers—I didn't mean to upset you. I'm sorry." She tried to think what her sister, Cecily, would do in this situation. When he began to calm, she reached for a hollowed gourd resting in a bucket of water. "Here, have a drink to soothe your throat."

"Thank you."

She replaced the dipper, pleased that she had done something right for once. Piers leaned back onto the ticking, his face pale save for the two scarlet patches on his sunken cheeks. Alys could see the sheen of sweat through the stubble on his jaw and neck.

"Will you still carry on with me to London?"

Alys swallowed, tried to quell the rush of emotion she felt. "To London, yes. To the very ends of the earth, Piers. Even should we fall off the edge and land in God's palm, with you is where I want to be."

He turned his head to look at her. "Why?"

It was too soon, Alys knew. He would think that she was still the spoiled child he accused her of being, rushing to cling to him. But Alys knew how dire his condition was, and how it was equally as likely that he would die in this wood rather than carry on. She wanted to tell him how she felt in her heart. And he needed to hear it, whether he believed her or nay.

"Because I love you, Piers."

He turned his face back to the ceiling and was silent for several moments, his chest rising and falling with his shallow breaths. "Will you do something for me?"

He hadn't returned the sentiment, and in truth, Alys hadn't expected him to. It was enough that he had not chided her for speaking the words aloud.

"Anything," she insisted.

She saw his throat work as he swallowed and forced the raspy words past his lips. "Find the old man."

"Yes, alright. I have a few coins left in my bag—shall I buy your ring back from him?"

He looked at her once more, his eyes full of dumbfounded accusation. "You have money?"

"Not much, but yes."

"You didn't tell me."

Alys gave him a smile. "You didn't ask."

He gave a short sigh. "No. Ask him not of the ring. Just send him to me. Alone. I need to speak with him alone."

Alys winced. "Are you certain that's wise? He's a stranger to you, Piers. And he's obviously already upset you greatly this morn. You need your rest." She didn't trust the old man any farther than she could pitch his stringy body from the tree. Less, actually.

"He won't harm me," he said solemnly. "Will you send him to me?"

Alys thought a moment before answering. "Yes. Yes, I will do as you ask." She hesitated at first, but then let her fingers slide beneath his palm. She squeezed.

Piers's fingers twitched weakly. But that was all.

"Shall I go now, or would you rest a while first?"

"Now. Better to get it over with." He turned his face to hers. "I know I might die, Alys."

She shook her head, fought the tears that threatened. She squeezed his hand again. "No. Linny said—"

"Likely a great deal more than you are telling me," he finished for her. "Working a farm, I understand the seriousness of a blood fever better than most would. I promise I shall do my best to improve, though."

She gave him a smile that she knew must be watery. "You always do."

"You hold a high opinion of me," he said, and his mouth crooked wryly. "A lot to live up to."

She raised her left palm to smooth over his forehead and the top of his scalp. He was running with perspiration. She leaned over and pressed her lips to his fevered brow. "See that you do. You know how we titled ladies are—you must live. I command it."

Then Alys was nearly certain that Piers did squeeze her hand.

"Go," he said, sliding his fingers free from her grasp. "I will send for you after."

Alys swallowed hard. "As you wish it, Piers. I'll be waiting below for when you call me." She rose and turned to go.

"Alys."

She turned back, her heart springing with foolish hope. Would he now tell her he loved her too?

"Yes?"

"Are we in a tree?"

"They are here." Sybilla stared through the gray morning light at the darker gray tree trunks, her mount shifting nervously under her. She stilled the stallion with a touch on his neck. Although no stable master would dare chastise her, Sybilla knew the horsemen of Fallstowe thought her choice of mount dangerous: a dappled destrier with a skittish nature and barely better than wild. But he was powerful, and sensitive to the very air he breathed, and he and Sybilla trusted each other.

The soldier standing nearest her slipper looked up from the remnants of a fire to which the increasingly wild and haphazard trail had led. "Indeed, my lady—there was a camp here. The coals are cold, but the ground beneath still holds a bit of heat."

Sybilla nudged gently with her heels and leaned to the right. Octavian obeyed immediately. Sybilla let her eyes roam the ground as her horse carried her in a wide circuit around the perimeter of the clearing. There was little else to see save for a litter of nutshells dusted with snow. She breathed deep, trying to taste the air on the back of her throat. She squeezed her thighs and her horse came to a stand.

"What is the nearest village, and how far?"

"No place of significance until the abbey at St. Albans, milady, perhaps five miles from here."

They hadn't gone on to St. Albans, Sybilla was certain. The fire was too cold to have gone out with the rising sun, and they wouldn't have tried to breach the thickness of wood in the middle of the night with blowing snow upon them. Any trail they might have left was now largely covered over with white. It was as if Alys had been spirited away from the earth, snatched up into the air by invisible hands. There must be shelter elsewhere in this wood. Hidden shelter.

"Make camp here. They came less than a quarter of the distance in one day than they have previously. Someone is wounded or ill. Something is slowing them. They are here," she repeated, almost to herself this time.

The soldier nodded and began barking orders to his underlings, directing the search. Sybilla urged Octavian away from the camp slowly, letting the stallion drop his head as he wandered. But his mistress was alert, her gaze taking in the tiny dust motes, the color of the moss on the trees, the lean of the trunks.

Where are you, Alys?

"Ready to tell me the truth now, are you, friend?" The old man took his time lowering his bony backside to the stool once more, his hands bracing on his knees. The signet ring was nowhere to be seen.

"You say that ring belonged to your daughter," Piers began. "And I say it belongs to me. There is little chance that the object possesses a twin, would you agree?"

The old man nodded once. "Aye."

"I think you lie. I think you have stolen *my* ring with intentions of selling it on your own."

"I told you that *my daughter's* ring will never leave my possession, and that is my solemn vow," the old man said in a careless manner. "Your belief of it or nay makes little difference to me."

"You do not look as though any in your family would be of means to possess such a jewel." Piers forced himself to continue breathing easily, lest another coughing fit overtake him. "Convenient solution, that she's dead and cannot claim such valuable property herself. Clever."

"It's not convenient for me that my daughter is dead, you lying, sickly bastard," Ira hissed through his teeth. "Further comments of that nature will find you a ready grave."

"When?" Piers asked without comment to the threat.

"When what? When will I kill you?"

"Tell me again when she died."

Ira's jaw worked, as if his mouth was trying to prevent the words from escaping. "A score and four years ago. My only grandson with her."

Piers closed his eyes for a long moment.

"Buying time until you can think of some way to trick me out of my girl's ring?" Ira accused in a pained, growling voice from beyond Piers's eyelids. The old man's words grew louder, as if he leaned toward Piers. "My very *life* was stolen from me! All I can hope for now is a bit of peace in these woods in which we hide, and now this—the only thing that is left of the girl I loved so. One whom I betrayed and never had chance to make amends to."

Piers opened his eyes. Ira was in the process of leaning back on his stool. His rapidly rising and falling chest and the steely glint in his eyes the only evidence of his fury.

"Would you tell me about her?"

Ira's busy eyebrows drew downward, and his gaze flicked away to the floor.

"You have the ring," Piers reasoned, trying to keep his raspy voice neutral. Nothing was certain yet. "You have said yourself that I am in no condition to take it from you. Tell me the story of this daughter you betrayed, and say no names, no places. I must know the tale of a ring such as that one, which I thought to be mine by rights, less than a month ago, when it was given to me."

"So now someone *gave* you the ring, and that's how it came to be in your possession?" the man mocked.

"That's right," Piers said levelly.

"Who gave it to you?" Ira demanded.

"Tell your tale, old man. And at the end of it, I will answer you what you have asked me."

"You only seek information so that you might justify your thievery."

"You will tell me no names," Piers reiterated. "Not even that of your daughter. But *I* will answer *you* with a name, and that is my solemn vow."

Ira seemed to be debating Piers's bargain in his head, and so Piers asked, "Does any other know this tale?"

"Not the whole of it," Ira admitted quietly.

"Tell it," Piers said.

Ira was quiet for a very long time before he finally began to speak.

"I came with . . . my girl, to"—he paused for a moment—"to a new manor with our village's mistress. The lady was to marry the lord of the manor, and I was part of the bargain." Ira tapped his gray temple. "My knowledge, for the farm. I was the best in the land. All the houses sought me, tried to buy me. My learning was worth more than this." He patted his vest, and Piers suspected the signet ring lay inside, over the man's tired old heart.

Ira clasped his hands in a loose fist and let them dangle between his knees as he stared at the floor and continued. "The new marriage was not a good one. The lady was a shrew, demanding—never content with all she had. The lord regretted his pact with her father before a moon had ripened over their marriage bed.

"I recall so clearly the day he saw . . . my daughter. We were in the barn, and she—not quite seventeen yet— was helping me with an animal what had took sick." Ira's eyes had flicked to Piers's. "We thought we'd have to put the animal down, that mayhap the disease was a catching one, and so the lord come down to see himself. She was a beautiful girl."

Ira was quiet for a moment. "The lord saw her comeliness right away, of course. He coaxed her into speaking to him—she was a shy one. Wouldn't say geddoff to a flea. And she was taken by him, his title, his money, his attention to her, a poor man's daughter.

"The lord gave her a position in the house, to attend his wife who had only just borne a child. I should have known then. I should have, and maybe I did, although I denied it to myself for far too long. By the time I realized what was going on beneath my very nose—and the lady's nose, too—it was too late. My daughter was carrying his babe."

"What happened?" Piers pressed.

"My daughter confessed. Came to me in tears because the lady had found out and banished her back to the village. My girl told me that she'd stood up to the woman, for two reasons: one, the lady was still in her childbed and unable to attack her, and two, my daughter was certain that the child her mistress had borne was not of her lover's issue."

"How could she know that?"

"While she was tending the woman in her childbed, my girl saw the babe had a mark on his chest," Ira said bitterly. "One that neither the dam nor the lord shared. The lady bragged once that the babe's sire might have signed him with ink, so surely was the child his issue."

"Did the lord himself suspect that he'd been cuckolded?"

"My daughter never said. And she held her own opinion from him, not wishing to overstep her place."

Piers winced. This tale was more painful than he had anticipated. "Go on."

"I confronted the lord. I was mad with anger. I felt betrayed. Here was my girl, so young, so innocent, ruined by one of his station. He couldn't have truly cared for her to have spoiled her for any other man who might have taken her for his wife." Ira paused for a breath. "I tried to kill him. Would have probably succeeded too, had I not been drunk."

"What did he do to you? The lord?"

"He showed me great mercy," Ira admitted quietly. "He could have had me put to death, but he only banished me from the town. He showed me mercy, but my daughter did not. She was much aggrieved with me that I had tried to kill the man she loved, the father of her unborn babe. I begged her to leave with me, but she would not."

"She stayed?"

Ira nodded. "She didn't care that she had been put to the village in shame. It was enough for her to be close to him, the little fool. He gave her a cottage, sent care for her when the child came. A lad. My grandson."

"How do you know this if you were banned from the town?" Piers asked.

Ira frowned. "I had my friends, those who would look after her and send word. She was angry at me still for what I had tried to do. Mayhap she thought that if I had only held my temper . . . I don't know what she thought. The lord had her this ring made when the lad was born." He touched his chest again. "As much as I know, she wore it until the day she died."

"How did she die?"

Ira shrugged. "Illness. I was told the lad caught it too,

and so 'twas the end of both of them at once. And the end to my fancy that one day I would have them both back. Likely the bitch that ruled there was mightily pleased, though."

"I'm quite certain she was."

Ira looked up at Piers as if just now realizing he spoke to a man in the present. His face, which had grown haggard and sad during his tale, hardened into its previously callous façade.

"So that's my tale, although what good the telling of it is to you, I cannot say." He stared at him. "So now, tell me the name you promised—who gave you my daughter's ring? I would have thought she took it to her grave."

Piers tried to take a deep breath, but he couldn't force his lungs to fill. His chest seemed cut in two with anger, and sorrow, and longing . . .

And hope.

"My"—he had to clear his throat—"my father. He gave it to me."

"Did he steal it?" Ira accused suspiciously. "Want you to sell it in London?"

Piers shook his head. "No. He gave it to me the night he died. Told me to take it to the king, to prove what was due me. What I have been wrongfully denied all the thirty years of my life."

Ira grew still, and Piers thought the wind beyond the hut's leather walls seemed very loud. The old man waited, waited.

Piers swallowed, but it did little to smooth the hoarseness of his next words. "My father, the man who gave me that ring . . ."

Ira started to shake his head.

"His name was Warin Mallory."

Chapter 17

Alys and Piers had been in the woodland town for six days, and in that time a thick snow had steadily fallen— more snow than even Ira said he could ever recall seeing in his long life. Piers's health had steadily improved, almost it seemed, with each depth of snow that built on the ground and huts and tree houses. If the village had been hard to see before, now it was nearly invisible unless you looked up. The trees seemed pregnant with large, snowy nests, and smoke from the necessary braziers within the sleeping quarters seemed to mingle with the cold fog.

Alys thought it must truly be a magical place, filled with magical people. It was the only explanation for the change in Piers, both physically and mentally. He had called to her as he'd promised he would, after meeting with the old man, Ira. And although he'd had little to say about what the two had discussed, he'd held Alys's hand for a long time, the two of them only sitting quietly together high in the tree. It had seemed to Alys to be a threshold, a turning point in her relationship with Piers, in which she had changed from an unwelcome burden to valued companion. Alys could not lay finger to the exact moment or cause for it to happen, but happened it had and she would not question it.

As for Ira's attitude toward her, he made no move to throw her from the town again, which was a great improvement, although he seemed to treat her with an even greater sense of distrust than before. He spent many hours with Piers, alone in the tree house during and after his treatments with Linny, but he rarely spoke directly to Alys. Sometimes she caught him watching her from across a fire or from the heights of Piers's sleeping quarters. He stared at her intently, and with a hostility that was almost palpable.

Alys put the old man from her mind, and turned her attention fully once more to the dough she was kneading. Ella and Tiny flanked her at the narrow workbench inside of one of the ground huts, and the little shelter was humid with the musky smell of yeast and spice. Layla was occupied on a high shelf and worrying at a ball of twine Tiny had knotted into a piece of old cloth. Tonight there would be a feast—Piers would join Alys and the rest of the town in the celebration. She knew it was to be his own test, to see if he was strong enough to leave the town and carry on to London. They would have supplies this time, and be rested as they could be. Piers had guessed with Ira's direction that they could reach the king in two days.

As if reading her mind, Ella spoke. "You'll be leaving us on the morrow, then?"

Alys nodded and then smiled at Tiny's sad whimper. "I shall miss you all so. I feel as if I've lived here for years."

"You don't have to go," Tiny said. "You could stay here with us. No one would ever find you, and you'd never have to marry that ghastly lord."

Alys reached out her arm and stroked Tiny's cheek

with the back of her wrist—the only part of her hand not completely covered with dough and flour. "I can't, love. Piers has something important he must do in London, and then I must return home, at least for a little while. I have worried my family terribly, I'm afraid. As much as I would love to pretend that the betrothal never happened, my sister gave her word, and I must try to help her find a solution that will please everyone involved. I only hope it does not cost her as dearly as I fear it will."

"Will you marry Piers instead?" Tiny asked with a mischievous grin.

Alys dropped her eyes back to the workbench and shrugged, trying to contain her smile. "One can never know."

Ella snorted. "Perhaps one who doesn't know you're as good as married already."

Alys gasped and Tiny giggled.

"What?" Ella demanded, wide-eyed. "Your man told Ira the story of how the pair of you met, and Linny overheard. The whole of the village knew by your second day here."

Alys was stunned.

"Did Piers truly come upon you in the Foxe Ring whilst you was sleeping?" Tiny asked breathlessly. "Did he awaken you with a kiss?"

Alys laughed. "Actually, no. I *was* sleeping, but I was awoken by his screams when Layla bit him."

All three women shared a chuckle—even Layla chattered happily—and then they were quiet for a moment. Ella broke the companionable silence.

"Will you state your claim to him before the king?"

Alys borrowed time before answering by placing her round of dough in a bowl and covering it with a cloth.

"No," she said lightly at last. "I love Piers, true. I don't think that is any secret here to those who have seen me with him. But I will not press my issue. If Piers wants me, wants to honor the tradition of the Foxe Ring, then I will gladly accept."

Tiny's small face looked worried. "But what if he doesn't?"

"Tiny!" Ella whispered disapprovingly.

"It's alright, Ella," Alys said mildly. She glanced at the girl as she began to pour another hill of flour on the table before her. "If he doesn't? Well, you can't force someone to love you."

"Surely he'd do no such thing," Ella said brusquely, turning her own dough into a bowl and covering it. "After all the two of you have come through, how well you have cared for him, stayed by his side. One would have to be simple to not recognize the way he looks at you."

Alys wanted to grab the woman by her arms and shout, "How? How exactly does he look at me? Please explain it to me, for I must be simple!"

Instead, she only shrugged and said, "We are very different."

"Two jugs of water are only good for so many things," Ella said enigmatically. "But, now, a jug of water and a stick of flame . . . ? Well, those are the very things that together give life. You have water and fire, you can make a meal, a home. With two jugs of water—"

"You could have a very large drink," Tiny finished cheekily.

"Or take a bath," Alys added.

Tiny laughed. "I'd trade one jug for a chicken!"

"But how would you cook it if you had no fire?" Alys was warming to the girl's play.

Tiny didn't hesitate. "I wouldn't eat her at all—we'd go swimming in the other jug!"

"You could use the jugs as weapons."

"Roll them each down a hill in a race and see who's the winner!"

"Alright, you two," Ella laughed. "Enough jesting. We have many loaves to bake if we are to feed the feast this night."

Alys nudged Tiny with her elbow affectionately, and the two shared a sideways glance and a smile. She realized how very much she would miss this young girl, and was saddened by the thought of leaving her and the rest of the villagers behind to their harsh lives in exile.

Her hands paused. "Ella, why don't you and Tiny and the lads come back to Fallstowe with me?" she asked impulsively.

"Oh!" Tiny gasped. "Verily, Lady Alys? Could we, Mam?"

Ella glanced at her. "Now why would we do that?"

"I'm certain Sybilla could find a place for you, after all that you have done to help me." She was warming to her impromptu idea, thinking it through as she spoke. "It's difficult here for Tiny, being in the trees. You could have a real home again, an easier life."

Ella's voice grew almost imperceptibly cooler. "You are very kind to offer, Alys, but we have lived in a proper village before. Everyone is either better than or lesser than another person. Here, we are all equal. And I hope you're not offended, but I do consider this a real home, although I'm sure it's not up to your standards."

"Mam," Tiny said. "Lady Alys didn't mean—"

"Ella, no!" Alys was aghast. "I was only trying to—"

"Think nothing of it," Ella interrupted and waved a hand. "Thank you for your offer, but no. Ira has sacrificed his life to afford us all a place to live in peace. We would not abandon him simply for the promise of more grand accommodations."

"I'm sorry if I insulted you, Ella," Alys said, her eyes stinging with anger at her hasty, poorly chosen words. "That wasn't my intention. I was simply looking for some way to repay you for the kindness you've shown me."

"You can thank me by not revealing our existence to other outsiders once you leave here," Ella said mildly, still kneading the dough.

Other outsiders. It was a reminder: you don't belong here. Alys felt that she had committed a grave error, and she didn't know how to correct it. "I would never," she said solemnly. "Never. Ella, I—"

"Why do you not go and ready yourself for the feast?" Ella interrupted. "Perhaps Piers needs your assistance. Tiny and I can finish up what little is left here on our own."

"Mam," Tiny chastised softly. She looked up at Alys. "I'd go to Fallstowe. For certain, I would, Lady Alys. I'd go anywhere with you."

"You hush, Tiny, and don't be burdening the lady with your pleas. She has a man to tend to, and we have work to do yet."

Alys's hands froze over her mound of dough. She was being turned out once again. "Are you certain, Ella? I want to help, and—"

Her words were cut off and the woman pushed her way between Alys and the workbench. "I'm sure. Just go, Alys."

Tiny looked over her shoulder and gave her a sad smile. "I'll see you at the feast, Lady Alys. Can we sit together?"

"Of course, Tiny," Alys said past the lump in her throat as she saw Ella give her daughter a discreet pinch. "I'd like that very much."

Tiny nodded and turned reluctantly back to her work.

"It's alright, Alys," Ella said quietly over Tiny's head. "I know your heart only wants good for us, and you're used to getting what you want. But you can't fix everything. And you shouldn't try."

Alys felt close to tears. Ella made it sound as if Alys was a meddler, instead of someone genuinely offering to help.

Was she a meddler?

"I'm sorry," she said again, picking up a cloth and wiping her hands.

"Think naught of it," Ella said, returning her attention to her chore. "It will be a grand feast to see the two of you off. I'm certain we'll all remember this evening for many years to come."

Alys ducked out of the hut, her brow furrowed, her confidence more shaken than it had ever been. What kind of woman was Lady Alys Foxe?

Or, perhaps more importantly, what kind of woman did she *want* to be?

Piers finished dressing in his clothes that Linny had cleaned for him. He felt almost like himself again.

At least he thought he did. He wasn't quite sure who he was anymore. In the span of little more than one month, he'd been a motherless, half-noble bastard; orphaned; married; and then discovered he had a grandfather. A living grandfather, who was at once mean as hell on a summer's day, sharp as any learned scholar, and generous as though he were the richest man in the land.

That Alys had gone in search of help and found Ira was more than just a coincidence that had saved Piers's life. She had given him another chance at saving Gillwick from Judith Angwedd and Bevan, true, but she had also given him something that he had, for all purposes, never had in his life: family. Someone he shared a blood bond with, a history. Ira was his mother's father, and through him, Piers was beginning to know the woman who had left him so long ago.

Family. Something that Alys took for granted, and something Piers would not let her forsake. Not for him, for what she thought she felt for him, not for anything. Alys needed her family. And she would be a fool to disobey the Foxe matriarch in her wishes for Alys to marry. The opportunities that Alys's family ties would present to her and her future children were too many and too great for Piers to let her throw it all away with idyllic dreams of becoming a dairy farmer's wife. She deserved more than that.

He would tell her tonight about Ira and his mother and father; tell her that while he still intended to go to London and attempt to secure Gillwick, he would not use Alys or her name to try to sway Edward. He would tell her that he wanted her to go back to her sisters at Fallstowe. That was all he could do.

He didn't want to hurt her. In honesty, he didn't want her to go back to Fallstowe, and he most definitely did not want her to marry Clement Cobb. There was something about Alys that pulled at his insides. That twisted his thoughts from their previously logical course. She was unpredictable and impulsive and reckless. And passionate and strong and brave. He felt pride at the idea that she could love him, that perhaps there was something worthy of him to love after all.

The best he could hope for was that she would heed his wishes for her to return to her family. She had changed during their adventure together. Piers could easily see that. Perhaps she would listen, this time.

He heard faint drumming below—sounds of the villagers readying for the feast—and then a moment later, Ira called up: "Lad! Are you coming down or nay?"

Piers stepped toward the seam in the skin wall of the house and ducked his head through. He saw the old man directly below him, his white hair and beard reflecting the dusk-blued snow glowing in the long shadows of the trees. Deeper into the village, a great fire roared, and Piers could see the black outlines of revelers already engaged in the merrymaking. Alys was there somewhere, waiting on him.

The woman who could be his wife. Wanted to.

The woman who belonged to someone else. Belonged to another life.

"Only a moment longer," Piers called to Ira.

"What—does your gown not suit you?"

Piers smiled. "I have to get Alys's gift."

"I'll not wait for such nonsense."

Piers raised a hand in acknowledgement and ducked back through the wall. He walked to his cot and pulled his pack from underneath. He flipped open the straps and then plunged his hand down inside, digging around for the object with a nervous ripple in his stomach, and then pulling it from the bag.

He'd not had enough time to work on it, he knew. But even had he another week to perfect the carvings, he was no craftsman. He only hoped that she would recognize what he'd intended to create, and that she would like it.

Piers had never given anyone a gift in his life.

He put the thing he had made inside his tunic and walked back to the flap in the tree house wall, where the ladders hung. He climbed down slowly, testing his strength and balance. Both good. He hopped to the ground three rungs high and landed squarely.

"A mite early to be so prideful of yourself, is it not, lad?" Ira had waited on him, despite his earlier threat.

"I'd know the measure of my strength before leaving on the morrow." The two men turned and began walking toward the center of the village. Children ran around and past them on fast feet, their footfalls and laughing shrieks muffled by the deep, packed snow. It seemed the village was cocooned now, safe from all outsiders.

"Mayhap you should wait a day or more," Ira suggested brusquely. "You're just from the sickbed. Would not aid your cause were you to catch croup just outside of London and die. Devil knows that noble woman of yours couldn't care for you."

Is she mine though? he wondered to himself. "She'd do her best," Piers defended Alys aloud as they neared the bonfire, as big around as one of the ground huts and nearly the height of two grown men. "I won't catch croup, any matter, Ira. I'm well now, and rested." He paused, wondering how much to admit to the old man before he left, and then decided someone else should know. "I'll send Alys back to her family once we gain London."

Piers saw the old man's face turn toward him out of the corner of his eye, but didn't need to look at him to imagine his shocked expression.

"What of the Foxe Ring?"

"It's no law."

"That it's not," Ira agreed, rather mildly, Piers thought. "Think you she'll heed your wishes?"

Piers shrugged. "It's best for her that she be with her own people. And 'tis likely she'll want nothing more to do with me once this is all over."

"Perhaps. But perhaps not," Ira mused. "Any matter, 'tis the smartest thing you've said since coming here."

"She needs be with her family," Piers repeated. "As do

you." He stopped, and Ira did the same, turning to mirror Piers's pose. "I want to come back for you when I'm through in London. I want you to return to Gillwick with me." He glanced toward the bonfire and saw Alys sitting with Tiny.

"I sorely want to, that is the truth. But I can't leave them, Piers," he said quietly. "All us here, we're all we've got."

Piers looked back to Ira. "I know. That's why I want you all to come back. There is a place for you. If you tell them the truth—that I am your grandson—they will follow you."

Ira stared at him for a long moment, and then he too, looked away toward the leaping flames, his old face streaking red and orange and black in rhythm with the merry fire. "It is hard for a man to consider returning to a place that holds such sorrow. And could be, the king will deny you, since you have no proof of Bevan's true sire, save an old rumor of a birthmark. 'Twill be that hoary bitch's word against yours."

Piers nodded. He saw Alys wave to him and give him a smile. He raised his hand in reply.

"I've seen the mark upon Bevan's chest myself, so it is not simply an old rumor. But it's true that I have no proof to compare it to. Should I be denied then, I would like to think that I would be welcome here with you, in your village."

Ira's head swiveled back. He stared at Piers and then nodded once, sharply. "Upon your wish, lad. Triumph or defeat. Should you ever desire to make your home with me, it would gladden my heart."

"And mine," Piers added gruffly. "So I hope you will consider my offer. Talk to the folk. Think upon it."

Ira nodded again. "I will."

Piers reached out an arm and clapped the old man on his bony shoulder. Then he turned to find Alys in the crush of villagers once more. She stood up from where she had been sitting beside Tiny, and Piers felt his stomach lurch.

She wore the blue perse gown under her fine sable-lined cloak. She'd sewn the ragged hem of the skirt smooth again, and even missing the wide swath Piers had cut for a rag, it still grazed the tops of her slippers. Her golden hair was braided above each ear and around the back of her skull in an intricate circlet, and sprigs of mistletoe decorated the twist at her nape. Her hands were clasped in front of her waist, holding a large, reddish cloth-like bundle. She smiled at him, her lips pink and perfect, and Piers no longer thought she looked like a child.

He walked toward her, and had almost reached her when the villagers took up a cry that caused both he and Alys, so intent on each other, to jump.

"Huzzah! He lives!" They smiled and applauded, and Piers realized they were all looking at him.

Alys laughed and then, tucking the fabric in her hand away under her arm where he could not see it, she began clapping, too.

Piers chuckled and looked to the ground. Then he gave a bow toward the crowd. "Thank you," he said. "Thank you all for your kindness."

The applause died down and then the revelers seemed to all look toward Alys expectantly. Piers did the same.

She fidgeted and blushed before retrieving the item beneath her arm and holding it out to him. "I know 'tis early, but since we're not certain what will happen once we reach London . . ." her voice trailed away and her eyes flicked to the ground for a moment. She shrugged, likely not wishing to speak the unknowns in her head—and in

Piers's own—aloud, then gestured with the bundle again. "Merry Christmas, Piers."

He held out his palm almost reluctantly. In addition to never having given a gift before, Piers had never received one either.

A thin rough string was tied into a bow around rich, burgundy cloth. He pulled one end and then shook out the material. Piers felt his throat constrict, and his eyes went to Alys's.

"I thought mayhap you should have a suit of clothes more fitting to your station for your audience with Edward," she said quietly, and Piers could see the doubt in her eyes. "Do you like it?"

Piers looked at the tunic again—thick, quilted velvet, trimmed in gold braid. A black leather belt and sturdy, black hose to match. He had never seen anything so fine, even on his own father.

"Where did you get it?" he asked, knowing the question sounded gruff and demanding, but he could not help the tone of his voice. He was shocked beyond measure at her thoughtfulness, and overwhelmed by the richness of the gift.

"I bought it from one of the lads," she admitted.

"Stolen?" he asked.

She grinned and nodded.

Piers looked down at the plush velvet again, rubbing his thumbs over it, feeling his rough skin catch on the costly material. He thought of the primitive gift he'd made her, hidden away inside his poor tunic, and he was ashamed. He could not give her some crude, handmade thing now.

But that is how it would always be, a voice in his head advised. *Her wealth could buy all the clothing in London.*

What could you ever give her that would be enough? How could you ever please her?

"I have something for you as well," he said in a low voice. "But you don't have to keep it should you not fancy it. It's nothing, really."

"You got me a gift?" she asked, the surprise in her face genuine. "Piers, I didn't expect—you were so sick, I—"

He cut off her words by reaching into his tunic and withdrawing her gift. He shoved it toward her.

"Just take it." He glanced self-consciously at the crowd of people gathered around them. "Merry Christmas."

She looked at the small cluster of wooden beads now tangled in her palm. She huffed a laugh and brought the fingertips of her other hand to her mouth.

Tiny pushed into her arm, craning her neck to see, as did several of the other closest villagers.

"What is it?"

"It's a bracelet!"

"Are those onions?"

"No, I think they must be lilies."

"Little birds, mayhap?"

Piers's face burned. He should have never given it to her.

Alys raised her eyes to his, and he saw a welling of tears there. "No. They're pomegranates."

Chapter 18

Alys wanted to throw her arms around Piers's neck and weep with joy when he looked relieved and nodded.

She knew where the materials for the bracelet had originated: the old strand of wooden beads and cross from his pack. Piers had taken the large beads and carved them down to resemble the round fruits, complete with fluted and puckered ends. She recalled their first afternoon together, when Piers had been so completely outraged that Alys was saving the last pomegranate for Layla when they were both starving. That was also the day he had agreed to take her back to Fallstowe, and then they had both been sent to flight by the arrival of Judith Angwedd.

It seemed so long ago, now.

She knew he was waiting on a reaction from her. She handed the bracelet back to him. He took it hesitantly, his brow lowered. She pushed up her sleeve, held out her wrist, and smiled up at him.

"Would you tie it on for me?"

Around them, the villagers once more took up their applause. Just as Piers was finishing the knot and preparing to draw away, Alys reached up with both palms and framed his face. She leaned in quickly before he could retreat and pressed her lips to his.

The applause quickly turned to hoots and shouts of encouragement, and beneath her lips, Piers's mouth softened. She pulled away.

"That is the most wonderful, beautiful, perfect gift I have ever received," she whispered against his mouth and looked up into his eyes. "Thank you, Piers."

He swallowed. "You're welcome."

The next handful of hours were filled with a happiness unlike any Alys had ever known. She and Piers joined in the woodland villagers' feast with enthusiasm, singing along with songs they knew and those they quickly learned, listening raptly at the retelling of the old legends, and drinking copiously of the strong, bitter mead of the folk. The children of the village were sent reluctantly to bed, and with each song, each tale, each mug, Piers and Alys sat closer, touched longer, smiled more deeply.

He had changed into his new suit of clothes, and Alys could sense a difference in him as soon as he'd donned the tunic and hose. He stood taller, his jaw out and his shoulders back. He was more forward with her, touching her low back, pulling her along gently with him. His hand gripped her waist, and with each touch, Alys became more drunk with desire. And so she returned each touch he gave her with one of her own. Running her palm across his wide shoulders, raking her fingers through the short hair over his ears, smoothing a palm up the padded velvet covering his chest. She could smell him, feel him, see this brilliant white glow around him that had nothing to do with their close proximity to the bonfire.

At Alys's side sat Ella, and in a moment the woman's

husband stood before her, presenting his wife with a sprig
of mistletoe whilst bowing low. Ella took it with a girlish giggle and then rose to her feet when her husband
took her hand and the two disappeared into the shadows
beyond the fire.

Alys looked around and noticed Ira circulating quite
drunkenly amongst the revelers, one crooked elbow full
of little sprays of the plant. The old man made his way to
Piers and then shook his head and tsked.

"None for you, lad. Not married," he said with a wink
for Piers and frown for Alys.

After Ira had moved on, Piers turned to look at her.
He glanced down at the mug in her left hand, its base
resting on her knee. Her right hand was presently inter-
twined with his.

"More drink?" he asked in a low, relaxed voice.

She shook her head. Then she licked her lips and
leaned toward him. Piers met her more than halfway, kissing her fully at last, pushing his tongue past her lips, the
bitter taste of the mead sweetened exponentially with his
desire.

All around them, married couples were stealing away
into the forest. Alys pulled away reluctantly, but only because she knew it was a temporary separation.

"Piers," she whispered. "You have no mistletoe to
give me."

He shook his head. "You heard Ira: we're not married."

Alys let a smile curve her mouth as she pulled her right
hand free from his. She reached up to the back of her
head and then held her fingers out to him.

"I say we are."

He looked at the tiny plant in her hand and then back
into her eyes. She could see that the happy ease he'd possessed only a moment ago was now gone.

"I need to talk to you, Alys. Will you come to the tree with me?" he asked.

She said nothing, only nodded.

He followed her closely up the ladder, his weight allowing her to climb more securely, his arms on either side of her hips steadying her. Her legs were trembling, from both nerves and the nature of her ascent. She stopped, her eyes closed, clinging to the rough ropes.

He nudged her with his head. "Go."

Alys went.

The interior of the tree house was pitch, and after the bright contrast of the bonfire, Alys couldn't see anything. She went instinctively toward the center of the shelter, where she knew the tree's trunk would be. Piers's footsteps whickered past, and in a moment, the bright flare of a candle sprang to life, illuminating the narrow cot that was, thankfully, not suspended by ropes.

She watched him crouch down and fill and light the small brazier. He replaced the lid with a scrape and then stood, staring at her. Dressed as he was, he could have stepped from the crowd of Sybilla's well-heeled friends, stood at the king's side, sat the throne himself. His clothing was refined, his body large and intimidating, his expression feral. The candlelight gave the hard planes of his face depth and mystery; his eyes glittered, colorless. Alys's heart beat with the rhythm of a thousand primitive drums.

He continued to stare at her, saying nothing, but she could feel his hesitation.

"Piers, do you want me?"

"I do," he replied. "But there are things I must tell you."

"What is there of such import that you would deny me?"

"Once I tell you, you may well deny me."

Alys shook her head with a smile. "Never."

"Ira is my grandfather."

Perhaps it was only the wind, but Alys felt the floor under her feet sway. "Surely that's impossible. Does he claim this?"

"'Twas I who discovered it, when he took the signet ring from me. It belonged to his daughter—my mother, Elaine. When my father got a child on her, he had the signet ring made for her. When Ira found out his daughter was carrying the lord's child, he tried to kill Warin Mallory. My father and Judith Angwedd had Ira banished from Gillwick. He was told that I succumbed to the same illness that claimed her, twenty-four years ago."

Alys could only blink. "Piers, that—it's so fantastical. Are you very sure?"

He nodded. "I am."

Suddenly, Ira's increasingly foul disposition toward her made perfect sense. She was noble, and she wanted a member of his family. The last time that happened to Ira, he had lost all. His home, his daughter, his grandson.

Piers broke the weighty silence. "He gave me back the signet ring, of course. And some information that I believe solves my father's deathbed riddle—Bevan bears a mark on his chest. One that I have seen with my own eyes. Bevan's true sire bears the mark's twin."

"The proof you need?"

"Mayhap. I still do not know for certain who fathered Bevan, but it is considerable more evidence than I possessed before you found Ira."

Alys brought her hands to her mouth. "You have a grandfather," she whispered.

He gave her a slight, crooked smile. "Thanks to you. I owe you a great deal, Alys. That's why I must lay all of my plans out in the open."

Alys dropped her hands from her mouth and held them out, walking toward Piers. "Why would such happy news give me pause? In truth, it only makes me more certain that we are meant—"

He grabbed her forearms, keeping her from embracing him as she wanted to do.

"Wait. There is more."

Alys let herself be held captive by him, relaxing and looking up into his face. She would be patient.

"Whether the king grants me Gillwick or nay, I know that I will encounter both Bevan and Judith Angwedd in London." She waited. "And once Edward's decision is reached, I fully intend to see Bevan dead. By my own hands," he added.

Alys's heart skipped a beat. "You would kill him for what he has stolen from you."

Piers shook his head. "He has played a part in stealing much from me, true: my father, my childhood, my self-respect—nearly my life. But more than that, he is a vile pestilence upon this earth, and I cannot abide him to live. You know not what he is capable of, Alys. And should I triumph in London, I would never rest easy in my own home while he lives. And neither would he. His entire life, Bevan has begrudged me the very air I breathed."

"Piers, you are no killer."

His eyes glinted in the candlelight, and for a moment, Alys was not quite certain that was true.

"Even if Edward sides in your favor, I doubt he would stand aside wordless while you take another man's life," Alys reasoned. "He could retract Gillwick the moment after you've won it."

Piers had no reply.

"Perhaps there is another way." Alys twisted her arms in his hands and he released her. She stepped to him fully, placing her hands on his chest. "We shall speak to the king, and—"

"I do not tell you these things so that you might try to reason me out of them," Piers said. "But I would not hide it from you, no matter how ugly."

He was very, very serious. He meant to kill Bevan Mallory, and any resistance Alys put up to the idea would only be met with rejection. She could not change his mind. At least, not tonight.

"I accept what you are telling me," she said at last. "I don't necessarily agree that it is your only recourse for justice, but I see why you might feel thusly."

He nodded.

"Is that all?" she asked, praying it was, but fearing in her heart that he had saved the worst of the lot for last.

"No. I will not hold you up before Edward in order to aid my cause. It is too dangerous for you, with the game Sybilla plays. When we reach London, I want you to use what coin you have left to send to Fallstowe for someone to come and fetch you home."

Alys nodded, relieved. "Alright."

Piers seemed to be about to say something else, but stopped mid-word. He closed his mouth and frowned. "Alright?"

"You have been right all along, Piers," Alys said, curling her fingers into his tunic, drawing the warmth from him. "The way I left Fallstowe was stupid and childish. Sybilla was only trying to do what was best for me, for the family. I know she must be very upset with me right now. I owe it to her—and to my parents, who left our family in Sybilla's hands—to return, and do whatever I can to help right things."

Piers was very still. "Even if that means marrying Clement Cobb?"

"Whatever I can, save that." Alys smiled briefly, but then let it fall from her mouth as she looked up into Piers's eyes. "I love you, Piers. I want to be with you for the rest of my life, whether that life is at Gillwick, or Fallstowe, or even here, in your grandfather's woodland village. Once I've settled things with Sybilla, I will come to you, wherever you are."

Piers shook his head. "No. Alys, it might mean losing your family if I fail to gain my father's title. Think of the children you might one day have—would you keep them in a tree, like this? Like Tiny? Stealing from travelers and digging in the dirt for roots when there is no food, no coin?"

"I don't think that will happen," Alys insisted. "I believe in you, Piers! I know that whatever you will say to the king will make him see reason!"

"You don't know that!" Piers shook her. "I don't know that! It is my word against Judith Angwedd's."

"Take Ira!" Alys said, hope filling her. "He can be your witness."

But her optimism was dashed. "Oh, Alys—you are so used to being listened to, catered to! Think you the king would take the word of a commoner, living illegally in the wood with a band of peasant brigands, over a noble's word? Even one as disgusting as Judith Angwedd? Ira would likely end up in the dungeon for his trouble. Ira is no one. And right at this moment, even in this fine suit of clothes, I am equal only to him in the king's eyes. In the eyes of the law."

"Then reconsider telling Edward of the Foxe Ring!" Alys insisted. "It may not help, true, but what then could it harm?"

"It could harm you. It could harm your sisters," he

said quietly, and Alys felt as though her heart was being squeezed.

"Alright." She licked her lips. "But what if you do succeed with the king? Will you come for me then? Make me your lady, in truth?"

"Gillwick is no Fallstowe, Alys. Even if I gain my father's place, I cannot offer you a crumb of the life that you are accustomed to." He averted his eyes. "I cannot say what I will do."

"You cannot say?" Alys stepped away from him. "You mean no, don't you? You don't plan to come back for me, no matter the outcome in London. Piers, do you care for me at all?"

His eyes flew back to hers and his anger was apparent. "Yes! If I did not, you would not be here with me now!" He turned with a terrible blasphemy on his lips, one hand on his hip, the other swiping across his face. "I could have left you alone in the wood long ago. Carried on without you."

"And you would have sickened and died! Never known your grandfather!" Alys tried not to shout, remembering the quiet of midnight that was all around the tree house, but tears filled her eyes. Why was he being so cruel? "You said yourself that you owe me a great deal—does that not include the truth of your feelings for me?"

Piers nodded. "I do owe you a great deal. Which is why I cannot allow any misunderstandings between us."

"Misunderstandings?" Alys threw her arms out to her sides. "How can you misunderstand me? I love you! I want to be with you, no matter what happens! I care not that you are rich or poor, that you're titled or common. We can live in a castle or a tree or a cave, what little it matters to me! The only misunderstanding is why you would readily throw that kind of love and loyalty aside as though it's rubbish!"

"I want," Piers said slowly, looking at her, "what is best for you."

Alys quieted and stepped to him once more. "*You* are what is best for me." She clasped his face in her hands, forced him to continue to look at her. "You've taught me to take nothing and no one for granted. You've shown me what it feels like to want a man, to want him for a husband, to love him as if he is the only man on earth. The way you *should* feel before you enter into a marriage."

"I won't let you throw away your life."

So there it was. There was his true reason.

Alys felt her brows lower, and she welcomed the anger. Perhaps it would smother the heartbreak she felt at his professed self-loathing.

"I am not a child," she said shaking him once for emphasis. "And it is *not* your decision to make." Then she brought her lips to his and kissed him with all the passion she felt, her anger, her fear, her love. She wrapped her arms around his neck, standing on tiptoe, and kissed him and kissed him, trying to erase his doubts. He did not deny her, although he did not encourage her.

At last she leaned back, her hands coming to rest on either side of his neck. Her heart pounded in her breast, and she could feel the reverberations of its thumping against Piers's solid chest.

He stared down at her, his eyes black and starving for what was before him. If only he would reach out and take it, take her . . .

"We should try to get some rest. We'll leave as soon as it is light."

Alys felt tears press against her eyelids and she shook her head faintly as she stepped back from him.

"You don't love me at all, do you?"

His throat worked as he swallowed. "I simply can make you no promises."

Alys rolled her lips inward and bit down on them to still their trembling. "Very well, Piers. Have your time in London to do what you feel you must do. No promises. I think we understand each other quite clearly now."

"I don't mean to hurt you, Alys," he said in a low voice.

She walked around him and paused at the side of the cot to slip out of her shoes. She crawled beneath the covers, not bothering to take off her cloak. She turned on her side to face the skin wall, her body feeling stiff and sore, as if she had sustained a great fall. After a moment, she heard Piers sigh softly and then the light from the candle went out, draping the shelter in darkness. The cot dipped as Piers joined her.

Alys didn't know how they managed to not touch on such a narrow bedstead.

Tiny knew that if she was caught down from the tree in the middle of the night, her Papa would switch her legs raw. But she thought there might be some pudding left from the feast, and she knew there would be mead, and any matter, Layla was restless. Lady Alys would take the monkey with her on the morrow when she and Piers left the town, and Tiny wanted to savor every moment she could steal with the marvelous little animal, and breathe the air that was scented with the presence of a real lady, for as long as possible.

The bonfire was no grand flame now, but its coals were lively and licking in a wide bowl that radiated a welcome heat onto Tiny's shins and face as she sat on a log, Layla on her shoulder. She was scraping the last cold, congealed dregs from a forgotten bowl with her fingers when Layla started, shrieked, and leapt away into the shadows. Tiny jumped to her feet, the bowl tumbling to the ground, and looked around for what could have startled the animal. She saw nothing.

"Oh, bugger!" Tiny huffed. She bent at the waist and tried to peer into the darkness. "Layla! Layla, come here, you naughty monkey!" She would be switched for certain now, being down from the tree at night alone, *and* having lost Lady Alys's pet. She heard a rustle behind a nearby tree and crept toward it.

"*Layla!* Oh mercy, you're going to get me switched! Come out right now!"

She was just about to peer around the wide gray trunk when a hand reached out and jerked her forward, spinning her around so that she could not see the face of the person who held her. One arm braced across Tiny's chest and a hand gripped her upper arm, while another hand clapped over her mouth. Tiny could smell heady cologne and then a voice whispered in her ear.

"I have no desire to harm you, child." It was a woman's voice, and finely accented. "But I cannot turn you loose for obvious reasons, and you do seem quite frail. So if you struggle, it is likely that I will break your arm. Do you agree?"

Tiny nodded. The arm across her chest was draped in a rich, heavy cloak material, and Tiny could see part of the massive hood out of the corner of her right eye. The woman holding her was not large, but her captor was right—Tiny was frail. With one twist, her arm would separate from her shoulder with a familiar snap.

"Good. Now, listen to me, very carefully, and you need only nod yes or nay: Lady Alys Foxe, she is still here, yes?"

Tiny hesitated, but then nodded.

"But she is to leave soon? With a man?"

Tiny was motionless. She didn't know who this strange woman was, or in what kind of jeopardy Lady Alys would be placed if she answered the questions.

As if the woman could hear her worried thoughts, she offered. "Had I ill intent, I could have acted any number of times she strayed to the fringe of the village." She paused, letting the fact sink in that the woman had known Alys had been residing at the village, had possibly been watching her for nigh on a week. "Now, is she to leave?"

Tiny nodded.

"On the morrow?"

She nodded again.

"Good. Well done. Now, I will remove my hand so that you may speak aloud your next answer. If you betray me, everyone in this village shall pay for your mistake. Do you understand?"

Tiny nodded.

"To where do Lady Alys and the man hie?"

The hand slowly eased away from Tiny's mouth, just enough for her lips to move, and the hooded head leaned closer, pressing into the side of Tiny's face.

"L-London," she whispered.

The woman seemed to give Tiny a squeeze, and instead of the hand clamping back across her face, it disappeared for a moment.

"Good girl," the woman whispered. "The lady's pet has scampered up the tree where she is sleeping. You are safe from your parents' wrath as long as you don't turn 'round until I am gone, and then you scurry up to your own bed. Tell no one I was here, and you may keep this for yourself."

Tiny's wrist was seized and a hard, flat object was forced beneath her fingers.

With a rush of cold air and snow, Tiny was free. She closed her eyes and counted twenty before turning around, and even then, she only cracked one eyelid at first.

She was alone.

Her heart began beating so fast in her chest that she thought her ribs might break, and she began to cry quietly. She swiped at her face and then looked down at the object in her hand.

She stared at it for a long time, the wind chilling her until she shivered. Then she began to walk slowly to her family's tree, to go to bed as she'd been told.

Chapter 19

Piers was already dressed and moving about the frigid tree house when Alys awoke the next morning. She opened her eyes and he was the first thing she saw—folding his new clothes and placing them carefully in his pack, which he had set on the edge of the cot.

She lay there for several moments, watching him silently. He was dressed in his old tunic once more, and as he put the fine costume away, Alys couldn't help but feel a sharp stab of fear—it was as if he was already putting away the days and nights they had shared on their long journey together. But she would not yet give up. She was still to travel the remainder of the way to London with him. Perhaps it was only a matter of days before a brighter, easier future was laid out surely before them both.

His eyes caught a glimpse of her watching him and he paused in his chores.

She gave him a little smile. "Good morrow."

"Sleep well?" he asked lightly.

"Not really," she said and felt a strand of her hair being pulled.

"I'd set out as soon as you are ready," he said, cinching

up the straps of his pack and then glancing beyond her shoulder. "Little wonder neither one of us slept—that cot is hardly big enough for two, let alone three."

Alys realized the pulling on her hair was Layla. She turned her head. "Hello, traitor," she said in a cool voice.

Layla reached out with lightning speed and tweaked her nose—hard.

"Ouch! The thanks I get for saving your life. Ungrateful little beast." She turned a smile to Piers, hoping he would be amused by her play, but he had already turned away, throwing the straps of his bag over one shoulder.

"I'd seek Ira before we depart," he said. "Come down when you're ready." He walked to the flap in the sidewall.

Alys sat up, pulling the blanket around her shoulders and knocking Layla from her perch. She pushed the long strands of hair escaped from her plait from her eyes. "Piers?"

He paused, turned his face halfway to her, his eyebrows raised in question.

Alys swallowed, tried to keep her voice light. "We're going to be alright. Aren't we?"

He nodded. "I'll meet you below."

Then he sidled through the wall and was gone, leaving Alys alone with a monkey in her lap and the cold, cold wind in her ears.

Piers's heart sank lower with every rung of the rope ladder he descended. Suddenly, he dreaded London, and all that it stood for: the uncertain as well as certain paths of his future. A future without Alys.

Ira was waiting for him at the bottom of the tree, as Piers had known he would be. The old man had terrible disapproval in his eyes.

"You're a fool and an idiot," was the old man's greeting.

"Good morning, Grandfather," Piers said lightly, as he reached the ground and turned to face Ira. It was obvious Ira suspected that he and Alys had spent the night together in an intimate manner.

Around them, the woodland village was alive with the chores of the day, and people tended their work as they must, but Piers caught their furtive glances of curiosity. They, too, suspected. Even Tiny, assisting her mother at the fire, stared at him, her small brow wrinkled with worry.

"You didn't tell her, did you?" Ira accused.

Piers dropped his pack to the ground. "She will send for her sister once we reach London."

The old man's hairy eyebrows shot up. "She agreed?"

"It was her plan before I mentioned it. She acknowledges that she must answer the betrothal."

Ira's eyes narrowed. "I cannot imagine it was that easy."

Piers sighed. "Let it be, Ira. What is done is done, and we will not know the outcome of it until I have my audience with Edward."

"Very well," the old man acquiesced. "But I would speak my mind to her all the same. Is her ladyship dressed to receive visitors yet?" he mocked.

Piers leveled a look at his grandfather. "Ira, I warn you now—nothing untoward happened between Alys and me last night, and you will say naught to upset her. I ken that the pair of you are not fast companions, but that is largely your own fault. Whether you believe it or not, Alys is a good woman, and this journey has not been an easy one for her. She deserves your respect. If not for her, the two of us may not ever have met."

"Until Edward dubs you a knight of the realm, you don't command me, pup," Ira said gruffly. "And even if he did, you still wouldn't! I'll speak my thoughts to whom and as I please."

"You heard me, Ira," Piers said. "I do not jest."

"And neither do I," Ira growled, leaning toward Piers and squinting one eye at him. "You're just like your mam—always making excuses for 'em."

Piers stared at the old man, his expression set.

Ira eased off. "It is a fair thing to have a bit of her returned to me."

Piers caught glimpse of the girl, Tiny, making her way ever closer to him, casting her mother furtive glances. It was as if she was trying to catch Piers's attention, and he thought it strange that she did not simply walk to him and greet him as she normally would.

Ira had already started climbing the ladder, like an ancient yet still nimble spider—all bony joints.

When Piers looked around once more, the small village girl was nearly upon him.

"Good morrow to you, sir," she called out gaily, and rather loudly, Piers thought. "Are you readied for your journey?"

"Good morrow to you, Tiny. I am all but," he replied with a faint smile. It amazed him how this small, frail girl had managed to survive these many years in the hard wood, let alone thrive.

"Is Lady Alys about yet?" she called, with a bit more put-on nonchalance than was necessary. Everyone in the village knew how the girl worshipped Alys.

"Ira's speaking to her now. I expect her shortly."

She came to stand before him, looking around her pointedly and swinging her arms at her sides. "Oh, that's grand. Grand!" Tiny turned a wide smile to him, but Piers could see the purple shadows under the girl's eyes. "Can you keep a secret?" she whispered, the smile falling from her mouth and her eyes darting side to side.

Piers raised his eyebrows. "I suppose I can, yes."

"A deep secret," Tiny emphasized, and her brow furrowed. "If you told anyone, I—I don't know what would happen."

"Alright," Piers said, growing serious at the girl's desperate tone. "What is it?"

"Swear to me," Tiny insisted. "Swear you won't tell. Papa would switch me to ribbons."

He crouched down. "I swear. What is it, child?"

Piers saw the slight tremble in her chin—the girl was terrified. "A stranger came into the village last night, looking for Lady Alys."

Piers's heart skittered to a halt. "You saw him?"

Tiny nodded hesitantly. "'Twas a woman, but I didn't see her face. She kept behind me. I snuck down with Layla to see what was left of the feast, and she came upon me."

"What exactly did she say?" Piers asked, trying to keep his voice level.

"She asked if the lady was still here, with you, and when she was leaving." Tiny glanced around again. "She asked me where the pair of you were going and"—her chest hitched, her eyes welled—"I told her. I had to, else she would have broken me arm."

Piers's heart was beating again, now in triple time. "You told this woman that Lady Alys and I were going to London?"

Tiny nodded, as if the motion pained her. "I'm sorry, Piers. Truly. I was so frightened though. Please tell me that you won't let her harm Lady Alys!"

"I wouldn't let *anyone* harm Lady Alys, Tiny," Piers said solemnly. "And you did the right thing in coming to me. Did she say anything else?"

Tiny shook her head. "No. But she gave me something, in payment for my answers." The girl looked around once more before digging her hand into her apron pocket and pulling out her small fist. She held it toward Piers, and he took it without allowing the object to see light while stretched between him and the girl.

Once Piers had the item close to his chest, the girl looked relieved. "You can keep it," she said, her mouth turned down with distaste. "I don't want a traitor's payment. It's filthy."

Piers frowned, and then looked down at his hand as he uncurled his fingers.

A gold coin lay in his palm, its likeness he had seen before in Alys's own embroidered purse. An ornate F curled handsomely on the backside of the coin.

Piers gripped the coin in his hand, closed his eyes, and breathed a sigh. He opened them again after a moment and held the coin back to the girl. She shrank away.

"Don't fear it," Piers said easily. "Take it in good conscience, child, and be glad. This coin came from no one who would harm your friend—see this here?" He pinched the coin between his fingers, and a figure of Edward stared at him as he showed Tiny the other side. "It's an F. For Fallstowe."

Tiny's worried face softened and her eyes raised to Piers's. "Lady Alys's home?"

Piers nodded. "The woman who visited you was likely Lady Alys's own sister. Neither you—nor Lady Alys—have anything to fear from her."

He saw the girl's flat chest rise and fall. She snatched the coin from Piers's fingers and it disappeared back into her apron pocket.

"But it should still be our secret," Piers warned. "Lady

Alys would be upset that her sister is following her, even with good intentions."

Tiny nodded. "And my Papa would still switch me for being down from the tree."

Piers nodded solemnly and held out his hand. "A bargain?"

Tiny shook his hand. "Indeed." Then the girl unexpectedly threw her other arm about Piers's neck and embraced him. "I do hope you return soon, Piers. And Lady Alys with you."

Piers patted Tiny's back awkwardly. "Run along now."

She released him, and Piers rose to stand as the small girl ran on swift feet back to her family's fire.

Sybilla Foxe was following them.

Piers turned and looked up at the underside of the tree house, where Alys was hidden away with his grandfather. He had heard no shouts, and no body had been tossed to the ground as of yet. 'Twas just as likely though that the two were simply engaged in the slow process of strangling each other to death simultaneously.

He looked to the woods that led away from the village. Somewhere, Sybilla Foxe was watching them, waiting for them. He stared through the trees for a long time.

Alys had not expected to get away from the village without Piers's grandfather cornering her, and she had been right. The old man had given her the courtesy of a warning before coming above, and Alys was dressed in her old gown and ready for him when he ducked through the wall. He came no closer to her than the flap that served as a doorway.

"Good morrow, Ira," Alys said mildly, folding the blue perse gown into her bag.

"Are you going back to your family?" he asked bluntly.

She took her time in answering him, cinching her bag closed carefully.

"After Piers and I gain London and he does what he's set out to do, yes. For a while, any matter."

"Set him free."

"Piers is free. Freer by far than I, and even you." Alys turned to face the old man. "He is not your daughter, Ira. And I am no Warin Mallory. I love him, and I will stand by him."

"You'll be his ruination," Ira said sadly.

"I love him," Alys repeated.

"Love him or nay," Ira insisted, "if he is refused his birthright by the king and returns to us here, *you're* not welcome."

Alys swallowed, blinked. Stared at the old man. "Is that supposed to frighten me?"

"I'm only warning you."

"And I hear you." She began to walk toward him. "But I am not troubled by the hateful things you say to me, Ira. I don't believe them."

"You're a fool not to," the old man sputtered, eyeing her suspiciously as she came ever nearer to him.

"Do you know why?" she asked as if he hadn't spoken. "I'll tell you: because I know you love him, too. And I know that the most important thing in your life now must be that Piers is safe and happy and well." She stopped, standing before the old man now, and realizing how stooped he was, how gray, how weary.

"Is that so wrong?" Ira demanded, squaring his shoulders as if the suggestion that he possessed such tender feelings was an insult.

"Quite the contrary," Alys said. "I want those things for Piers, too. He is the most important person to me, as well.

And I will do everything in my power, to my last breath, to help him gain what he desires. I swear it to you."

The old man stared at her with watery eyes. "See that you do," he said hoarsely at last. "You just see that you do. And then mayhap . . . well." He said no more, only nodded once firmly as if whatever he'd left unsaid was agreed upon.

Alys understood. She nodded, then leaned forward and kissed Ira's wrinkled, leathery cheek. "Thank you."

The old man bristled and harrumphed. "Get your things and I'll take you below. The man's anxious to meet the trail."

The farewells were so short that there was barely time for emotion to build. Ira was right in his report that Piers was anxious. He barely looked at Alys as they were wished well from the villagers. Tiny did cry a bit when she and Alys embraced, and for a moment, Alys thought that Layla would forsake her for the miniature girl. But at the last moment, the monkey scrambled back into Alys's arms.

Ira gave them both a final tutorial on the way out of the village and to the London Road. As they left, waving to the shouts of farewell that lifted them away from the village, Alys was thankful for the thick snow that would clearly show she and Piers if they were being followed once they were away from the village's familiar trails. She had to nearly run to keep pace with him as he led her away on an already well-worn path through a drift of white, and it made her smile, reminding her of their start together. He was not talking again, but it did not trouble her overly. Piers was quiet when he was thinking, and they had certainly given each other enough to think upon for the next several hours.

Alys was certain that they would air their concerns with each other when they made camp that night. The most important thing now was to get to London, and to get there as quickly as possible. They had only two days.

She frowned at the increasing number of horse tracks their path crossed over, and snow trampled by what seemed many feet. But Piers, ever wary, did not seem concerned, and so she held her tongue. Even when they took to the wider thoroughfare of the road rather than stay to the trees, Alys did not argue. 'Twas likely Piers thought that they could move faster beyond the danger of the snow-camouflaged debris of the forest floor. And anyone who had at one time been following them would have passed this way long ago, while they were hidden away in the trees of Ira's village. Wherein lay the danger that Judith Angwedd and Bevan had already bent the king's ear during the delay.

Alys trudged on, her spirit determined. The way ahead of them was—if not easy—at least clear.

Piers could have let them rest while they ate the noon meal, but he chose to keep going, ignoring Alys's grumbles about his swift recovery and her already sore feet. He didn't want to look at her, sitting across from him or next to him, her eyes bright with excitement and optimism. Piers felt weighted down enough with guilt at what he planned to do with Alys, and she was too perceptive of him now. He could not risk talking with her.

And besides, he didn't want to give her an opportunity to change his mind. He knew what he was doing was the right thing for her. Sybilla Foxe's quarrel with the king must be deadly indeed, for Alys's sister to be so desperate to reach her before London. Alys could be in as much danger in Edward's presence as her sister.

Piers could not allow her to carry on with him to London.

Perhaps he was already too late to plead his case with the king, any matter. The best he could hope for then was a portion of coin to take back to Ira and the villagers, and then he would be free to seek out Bevan. If he was lucky enough to gain that opportunity, he wanted Alys nowhere near that taint.

He loved her. He loved her, and he knew he was a poison to her very existence. He only hoped that Clement Cobb would love her, too.

So Piers pushed on with his heart aching like a bitter wind, farther into the late afternoon than he normally would have, and much farther than was likely wise considering his recent illness. He wanted dusk on their heels when they made camp, with only enough daylight left to gather wood for a fire. He spied a likely alcove off the road, just into the wood, where their location would be easily seen. He veered from the snow packed road and into the trees without warning to Alys.

"Thanks be to God," he heard her sigh behind him. She was cross with him again, he knew. Let her hang on to her anger for as long as she could.

"I'm going for wood," he called over his shoulder to her as he dropped his pack in the snow.

"We're to have a fire?" she asked incredulously. "Piers, do you think that's wise? What if—"

"It's fine, Alys," he said curtly. "Let me worry about it."

He heard her make a dubious comment to Layla about the surety of his relation to his grandfather.

By the time night fell, a blazing fire warmed them nicely while they ate in silence. Well, Piers was silent, any matter.

"What have I done to offend you so that you will not speak to me?" she demanded, feeding Layla bits of turnip from her fingers.

"I've a lot on my mind," Piers said, not meeting her eyes.

"I understand that," she said with forced patience. "But is that any reason why you must behave so boorishly?"

"Forgive me if I do not engage in frivolous banter," he said. "I'm trying to gather my thoughts before I try to convince the king to grant me that which is rightfully mine. Unlike *some*," he emphasized, "'tis not every day that I am engaged at court."

"Oh, come now. I've never been to court, either, and well you know it, Piers Mallory," Alys defended. "Don't be so prickly." She suddenly looked up and smiled at him. "I know—why don't you practice what you will say to Edward?"

"No."

"I could help you," she pressed. "Even if you wish me not to accompany you, we could prepare your argument together, and—"

"No," he repeated.

She finished her meal with the monkey in brooding silence. She disappeared into the wood, he guessed to relieve her bladder before going to sleep, and Piers held his breath while she was gone.

But she returned, and he did not know if he felt relief or frustration.

She stood across the fire from him. "Piers, are you angry with me?"

He glanced up at her from the blankets he was unrolling. "No," he answered gruffly, but honestly.

"Are you certain?"

He paused, sighed, and squeezed the bridge of his

nose. "I am quite certain, Alys. I'm only occupied. I'll be better in the morn. London is on the horizon."

She was quiet for a moment. "Alright. I'll leave you alone with your brooding." She approached him and crawled into the blankets he had prepared on a bed of boughs near the fire. "Are you coming?"

"In a bit," he stalled. "I'd clear my head before trying to sleep."

She nodded while she yawned. Piers felt a twinge at how hard he'd pushed her today. "Wake me if you need me." After a beat of silence, "I know you don't want to hear this now, but I love you, Piers."

He fussed with arranging the fire so that it continued to blaze. He had to swallow and clear his throat before he could answer her.

"Good night, Alys."

She was soundly asleep before a half hour was past. Piers stood over her for a long while, his back to the fire, watching her, committing her face to memory. He crouched down, remembering the first time he'd seen her, asleep much in the same position on the stone slab in the Foxe Ring. Then, as now, he reached out a hand to smooth the hair away from her face, but this time Layla tried only to grasp at his finger sweetly with her own warm, leathery palm.

He stood swiftly. He retrieved his long knife from near the fire and then swung his pack onto his shoulder.

He picked up one end of the long, slender log that rested in the center of the fire. It broke easily in half at its charred center with only a hushing crackle. Alys did not stir. Piers headed toward the road, and to the pile of tinder he had made earlier. He laid the smoldering log atop the tinder, setting a small fire in the center of the road with little coaxing. After looking both directions, he went back into the woods just past where Alys slept, to wait and to listen.

He heard the muffled hoof beats first, the mounts walking, being led on with caution. Then the crunching of snow, and each footfall seemed to crush his heart. Like the loyal sentry she was, Layla's screams shook the still blackness of the cold wood, and soon after, Alys's strident shouts. She cried his name only once, and Piers squeezed his eyes shut, hung his head and turned his face to the side.

Sybilla Foxe would not bother with a commoner such as he, and neither should her sister. In a few days, Alys would be back at her home, and well-begun the process of forgetting that Piers Mallory ever existed.

In moments, the wood was silent once more. He walked slowly toward the camp, his heart somewhere near the soles of his boots. But his mind telling him he had, for once, done the right thing. The noble thing.

He chuckled darkly to himself.

The fire still blazed. The blankets where Alys had lain were knotted and tangled in the snow. Of course Layla had vanished with her mistress.

Piers sat down on the snow rumpled blankets, staring at the fire.

And he was alone once more.

Chapter 20

Although she never would have thought it possible, Alys arrived in London before Piers. Carried through the city gates at dawn with her hood covering her face and a cold warning in her ear to not draw attention, she had been hesitant to assume she knew the identities of her captors. But once she was safely away from curious by-standers, the interrogation had begun, and she was left with no doubt as to who had kidnapped her.

"Where is he?" Judith Angwedd demanded, walking in a slow circle around the stool where Alys sat in the middle of the chamber. The gag had been removed from her mouth to allow her to answer the questions, but Bevan stood uncomfortably close by, his willingness to silence any outbursts dangerously clear by the way he watched her, his small eyes continually darting over her.

"I don't know," Alys said.

"You're lying," Judith Angwedd accused mildly. She had removed her riding gloves and was now smoothing them between her hands, over and over. "I would think you eager for your revenge—he gave you up to us to save his own skin, after all."

Alys forced a laugh, although the comment struck very close to her heart. Where had Piers been when the pair had snuck into camp and stolen her away? Why had he not come at her cries for help?

But she would not let them see her doubt. "Why would you think he gave me up to you?"

"Oh. You poor, spoiled, naïve little girl." Judith Angwedd cocked her head pityingly. "He led us straight to you. Even went so far as to set a beacon in the middle of the road a stone's throw from where we found you—we could see the blaze of your camp even through the trees. He *wanted* you to be found. I'm certain that if he hadn't thought you'd awaken and protest, he would have dragged your sleeping body to the road instead."

Alys could not think of a thing to rebut this, her head was spinning so with the dastardly information being relayed to her. He had truly abandoned her. Why?

Because he doesn't love you, a bitter voice in her head advised her. *He had taken to the trail by the time you had begun to foolishly dream of him. He is well rid of you, at last. What he wanted from the start.*

Outwardly, she held her tongue.

"Nothing to say for that, eh?" Judith Angwedd paused in her circuit to stand before Alys. "So you see, you may as well tell me what you know. He's obviously not going to rescue you if he intended you to be captured in the first place. And no one knows your whereabouts now—not even that cold bitch, Sybilla."

Alys looked away toward a bank of windows across the room. The blue sky stuffed the panes and mocked her.

"She doesn't care, I should tell you. I went to Fallstowe looking for Piers, and when it was ascertained that you were missing and could possibly have gone with him in your childish pique, do you know what she did?"

Alys refused to turn her head.

"Naught. She did naught. So no one is looking for you, and no one will know if you continue to disobey me and I am forced to . . . *punish* you." Judith Angwedd, obviously weary of addressing Alys's ear, came to stand between her and the windows. Alys turned her head, but when faced with Bevan's leering countenance, she dropped her eyes to the wooden floor below.

"Why would you protect him?" the woman continued in an interested tone. "You obviously know nothing about him, so let me enlighten you: He is no one. Worthless, common trash, that would steal my son's birthright with his lies."

"You mean your lover's son, do you not?" Alys shot back, no longer able to control her tongue when faced with such outright slander against Piers. She didn't know why he had left her, but she knew the things Judith Angwedd was saying were evil falsehoods. "I know about your cuckold of Warin Mallory, and how it is you who is trying to steal Gillwick. When the king finds out, it is *you* who will be punished, Judith Angwedd."

The redhead's already high set eyebrows nearly disappeared into her hairline before drawing down in warning slashes. "And who is going to punish me, hmm? You?" Her beady eyes looked Alys up and down with disdain. "I hardly think that likely."

"Piers has the ring Warin had made for Elaine as proof." Alys was pleased to see the white hot fury wash over Judith Angwedd's face at the very mention of Piers's mother's name. "And I will tell everyone who will listen what I know."

Judith Angwedd rushed her unexpectedly, struck Alys soundly in the face so that she toppled off of the stool and onto the floor, her hands bound behind her. *"Then it is very unlikely that you shall leave this room alive!"*

Judith Angwedd took several deep breaths, and in those moments, Alys realized too late the folly of her impetuousness.

"Pick up the pig and put her back," Judith Angwedd commanded, once again in control of herself.

Alys was roughly shoved back on the stool. She flung her hair from her eyes.

"Piers would not intentionally lead you to our camp. He would never intend for me to fall into your clutches," Alys said levelly. "And I know that he will come for me, because you see, he will not stand before the king as a common man. In truth, he will hold more sway with Edward than the pair of you could ever dream of possessing."

"Lies. Foolishness," Judith Angwedd scoffed on a braying laugh. "You're only trying to buy yourself time."

Alys shrugged. "Think that if you will, but it is to your own folly. Piers and I met at the Foxe Ring, after he had barely escaped with his life from the beating Bevan dealt him." Alys let a smile crawl over her lips as Judith Angwedd blanched. "Yes, two unmarried people, at midnight, during a full moon, at the Foxe Ring. And in keeping with the grand old tradition of the land, we are now married. Your stepson is presently kin to the most powerful house in all of England, and he outranks you by leagues."

Judith Angwedd turned abruptly away and for a moment, Alys savored her victory. Bevan seemed quite disturbed, his fists clenching and then unclenching, his heavy brow drawn down, his eyes flicking anxiously to his mother.

But when the redhead turned to face Alys once more, she was smiling, and Alys's dread increased.

"Perhaps you are telling the truth." She shrugged. "It matters naught. Piers could be married to one of Edward's own daughters, and it would not change the fact that Bevan is still known as Warin Mallory's first born. My husband never denied him, in all his many years. Bevan will gain Gillwick. The king has a love of the law, and he will uphold it."

Judith Angwedd paused, and her expression became perplexed. "But if that whore's spawn is now a husband of Fallstowe, why does he not simply give me back my husband's ring and be content with the life of luxury you will so foolishly bestow upon him, hmm?"

"Because—unlike you—Piers only wants what is due him. No more, no less." Alys prayed her next ploy would work. Her life—and Piers's—depended on it. "Were I you, I would not be at all certain that the king will grant Bevan anything. Because Piers knows who Bevan's true sire is—as do I."

Judith Angwedd rolled her eyes. "Impossible."

"Is it? Piers's own grandfather seems quite certain of it."

"Now you are inventing relatives for the bastard scum?" Judith Angwedd smirked.

"How quickly you seem to have forgotten about the man who was your wedding gift to Warin Mallory," Alys said, her disgust at the woman's self-absorption clear in her tone. "He is very much still alive, you know. Ira himself told us of the birthmark. I can hardly think it a coincidence, and I believe the king will share the opinion."

This time it was Bevan who charged at her, and Alys was spared her life in the last moment by Judith Angwedd's screech.

"Bevan, no!" She threw herself onto her son, causing him to stumble from his intended course. "If what she says is true, we must be very deliberate and very clever with our next move."

"He couldn't know!" Bevan choked. "He's never laid eyes upon John Hart!"

The room went grave quiet. Alys let her breath shudder out of her soundlessly.

Lord John Hart. The gray-haired old widower had been at Fallstowe's winter feast. He had offered for Alys, the same night that she had been betrothed to Clement Cobb.

Judith Angwedd slapped her son's face, and Bevan brought a hand to his wide cheek.

"Mother," he whined pitifully.

"You don't deserve even half of everything I have done for you," Judith Angwedd spat. "You ungrateful, drunken idiot!"

Alys tried to keep her face composed when Judith Angwedd swung around to her, her flat chest rising and falling with great effort. She stared at Alys, stared with her hard, beady eyes so that Alys wanted to flinch and look away. But she would not.

"Bind her completely and lock her in the wardrobe. Put the beast's crate in there with her."

Bevan yanked Alys from the stool, tossed her to the floor, and straddled her. He began lashing her legs together from ankle to thigh, as Judith Angwedd stepped nearby to look down upon her.

"If you are such a fool as to think yourself in love with him," she said coldly, "then you should know that it will be you who costs him his life." She leaned down abruptly, her arm stretched out, and Alys closed her eyes against the blow she felt certain would come.

But there was only a sharp jerk near the bonds at her wrists, and so she opened her eyes once more to see Judith Angwedd turning away.

Bevan had secured her arms at the elbows, so tightly that Alys could feel her chest muscles on the verge of tearing. Then he forced her mouth open and replaced the gag deep between her teeth before picking her up by her restraints as though she was a sheaf of grain. He dropped her into the bottom of the deep wardrobe, her skull banging against the thick lip of wood. She heard Layla's muffled scream, and then a moment later, the woven basket containing the monkey was tossed atop Alys's head. The doors swung shut solidly, leaving her in complete blackness, and Alys heard the scraping of the lock.

It sounded like a blade being honed.

The forest rang with the sound of the soldier beating his sword against his shield, and Sybilla felt made of stone so still was she astride Octavian.

"Rebels, come out!" the soldier commanded in a voice that carried with it the hard experience of many battlefields.

Sybilla looked up at the undersides of the well-camouflaged dwellings hung in the trees. Not a whisper was heard from any of them, although around her on the forest floor, fires still blazed, pots bubbled, chickens scratched the ground where snow had been scraped away.

They would not deny her.

Sybilla took a deep breath. "It is Sybilla Foxe who commands you, Lady of Fallstowe Castle, and sister to Lady Alys. You are surrounded by armed soldiers. You will bring the girl to me—the runted child with the yellow hair. You will bring her to me now, *or I will burn this village to the ground!*"

The only reply she received was the wind in the branches,

and then the sudden, muffled sound of perhaps a woman's fearful sob.

Sybilla waited for a count of ten. Then she called out to the soldiers, "Fire the trees."

Her men surged forward without hesitation, torches ready. They quickstepped through the village, going to the ground level huts and the bases of trees, kicking through and scattering piles of dried hay and thatching, touching their contagious flames to anything consumable. The smoke was instant, thick and black.

"Call your dogs off, you heartless bitch!" an old man shouted hoarsely, his bent and pointed backside the first thing appearing from the underside of one of the tree huts. A rope ladder unfurled beneath him and he began to climb down, glancing hatefully at Sybilla. *"I said call them off!"*

"You do not command me, old man," Sybilla replied calmly as her soldiers never paused. "Where is the girl?"

"Her family'd rather die than hand her over to the likes of you!" The old man said, reaching the ground with both feet in a stomp and then striding toward Octavian. The horse tensed and raised his muzzle slightly.

A soldier stepped to the front of Sybilla's mount and leveled a crossbow at the old man's chest. "One step more and you're a dead man."

Sybilla heard the click of mechanism as the soldier readied to fire. The old man stopped in his tracks, a tic wrinkling his already weathered cheek. He stared at the deadly, pointed end of the weapon.

"No!" a little voice shouted, and then the tree tops came alive with long tongues of ladders, and leather-clad legs appeared through the growing cloud of hovering smoke.

In moments, no fewer than three score people—men, women, children—haggard and dirtied and clothed in what appeared to be the forest itself had gathered together at the center of Sybilla's crackling and smoldering threat. Sybilla recognized the diminutive child, her shoulders clasped by a grown woman, moving to the fore of the crowd.

Sybilla gathered her skirts to one side and shook her boot free from the stirrup, then swung down from Octavian. Her soldiers had left their arsonistic duties to truly surround the destitute people, their attention focused on their lady.

Sybilla approached the crowd and stopped only six feet away from the girl and her glowering mother.

"You lied to me, child."

The girl shook her head, her eyes wide and bulging, her white face highlighted by the scarlet patches on her cheeks. "I'm not a child! I'm thirteen!" In that instant, Sybilla was reminded of Alys so clearly that it pained her.

"What do you mean, she lied to you?" the girl's mother accused. "She's never laid eye upon your cruel self!"

Sybilla raised her eyebrows. "That's not true, is it, girl? We met the night of the feast."

The girl's mother's eyes went to the top of her daughter's head. "Tiny?"

"I'm sorry, Mam," the girl croaked. "Truly, I am! I wouldn't have told her anything, but she was to break me arm!"

"No," Sybilla interrupted. "No, I would have never deliberately hurt you, Tiny, and I told you as much. I could not have turned you loose until I had the information I sought, and I could clearly feel your frailty beneath my fingers. Had you struggled, your arm would have given way." Sybilla looked to Tiny's mother. "Hmm?"

The woman nodded.

Sybilla looked back to the girl. "I didn't harm you, and in fact, I paid you a fine piece of gold for your cooperation."

Tiny's mother gasped. "You said the coin was from Lady Alys!"

"But you lied to me," Sybilla continued. "Lady Alys did not go to London. Piers Mallory walked into that city alone."

The old man's face fell from the hateful scowl into genuine surprise. "What do you mean he entered the city alone?"

"Just what I said, old one," Sybilla turned her head fully to him. "Have you any guess as to why that was?"

He frowned and shook his head. "They . . . they left here together, only yester morn. They knew the route, they had plans to—Alys, she was to send word to you once they gained the city."

Sybilla was stunned into silence for a moment. She spoke carefully. "I have watched your town the whole of the time my sister was obliged to stay here. The night before she and Piers Mallory left, Tiny confirmed to me where they would go next. We rode ahead to the city to wait for them, so that I could intercept my sister and bring her home before she acted foolishly before the king and found herself imprisoned. But when Piers Mallory arrived, he was quite alone."

"Did you speak to him?" the old man asked.

"No. He is not my concern. Only my sister."

"Mayhap you are the one who is lying, and you wish to harm Lady Alys," Tiny piped up suspiciously. "Ira's always said that nobles' favorite sport is spinning falsehoods—and you don't look a bit like Lady Alys!"

"And you don't look to be thirteen," Sybilla countered. "But I can assure you that I am indeed her sister, and that my utmost priority is her safety." Tiny properly chastised, Sybilla looked once more to the old man. "And as it was you who sent them, *Ira*, perhaps you had better tell me what you know before your village is naught but a smear of charcoal on the forest floor." She flicked her eyes upward. "One of your nests is on the verge of catching."

"I already told you, viper," Ira snarled. "They left together. And Piers, fool that he is, would never let harm come to your spoiled brat sister. For a reason known only to God, he's in love with her. He took her to wife at the Foxe Ring."

Sybilla swallowed, nodded, and then looked to the ground for a moment. When she again met the old man's eyes, she was heartened by the concern she saw, lurking just beneath the put on disdain.

"If their plan has wandered so far from the course they both intended, then I am inclined to believe that they are both in great danger."

Ira's hairy brows drew downward. "Judith Angwedd."

Sybilla was more than a little surprised to hear the old man speak that name. "He told you of her?"

Ira nodded once sharply. "He did. But I know enough of the bitch personally to last me the rest of my miserable life." The old man's mouth thinned, and Sybilla thought she saw his shoulders square. "Piers Mallory is my grandson, lady. My grandson, and the sole heir of Gillwick Manor."

Sybilla drew a quick breath. She was very rarely ever surprised, but this piece of information shook her. She looked around her to the soldiers and the crowd of villagers. "Do what you can to put out the flames, all of you—go!" she shouted. Then she looked back to Ira. "You'll be coming with me, Ira."

"You're no mistress here, woman, and I am not your subject to be ordered about," the old man sneered.

Sybilla simply waited.

He fidgeted for a moment, crossed and then uncrossed his arms. "I'll get me bag."

Chapter 21

The guards had admitted him into the palace.

Up until the instant he'd received the approving nod, Piers had doubted they would. His entire scalp was covered in perspiration beneath the weak glow of the late afternoon sun, his stomach knotted, the muscles of his legs shook. He was certain it was the suit of clothes that Alys had gifted him with that had swayed the guards—they'd looked him up and down and obviously believed his claim to be the Lord of Gillwick Manor, and for the brief instant their eyes had inspected him, Piers prayed they would not notice his old, worn boots that would clearly mark him as common. Even with the costly signet ring on his smallest finger—perhaps even because of—had he worn his old clothes, they would have likely turned him away, or had him seized for a thief.

But now he strode down the receiving hall, trying to stymie his sense of curiosity and his sense of overwhelming at being in the king's very home, but his eyes glanced around furtively at the lavish residence, the milling nobles preening before each other. He hoped to seek audience with the king immediately—as unlikely as that notion

was, else he did not know where he would pass the night.
He certainly was no royal guest, and he had not one
single coin to spend. He'd given his leather pack and all
of its remaining contents to a beggar just inside the city
walls, so now Piers had naught but the clothes upon his
back and the signet ring on his finger.

Perhaps he could feign his way around the stables, if
his audience was delayed.

Every time a man let out a shout of laughter, or a door
slammed, Piers had to fight his urge to jump and swing
around with his fists readied. His nerves were like a rope
being rubbed over a sharp rock.

He spotted a man near a set of ornate double doors,
who received people in turn, spoke with them briefly
before scribbling on a sheet of parchment with a quill and
sending them away. He was a large man, taller than Piers,
and looked more to be a soldier than a court servant. His
hair was longer than was fashionable, and fell away from
his face like a tawny lion's mane. Piers guessed that he
was looking upon Edward's own gatekeeper, and it was
that man he would have to first convince.

Piers turned away for a moment, pretending to admire
a tapestry on the wall, and he summoned Alys to his
mind. His eyes closed as her sparkling brown eyes and
impish grin flooded his consciousness, and his heart
kicked petulantly. He was a fool for sending her away
from him—he needed her brazenness now, her fire and
fearlessness. She had always had faith in his dreams and
abilities, even when Piers had not, and now he was determined to live up to her high opinion of him.

He wrapped the image of her in his soul, took a deep
breath, and opened his eyes. Turning with his head up and
eyes forward, he marched toward the lion at the gate.

The man looked him up and down with the merest flick

of his eyes before meeting Piers's gaze directly. "Good day, my lord."

"Good day," Piers said firmly. "I am Piers Mallory, lord of Gillwick Manor. I have a request to speak with the king this day. As soon as possible." Piers cleared his throat. "Now, actually."

The man's tawny eyebrows barely rose. He looked down at the parchment before him. "His appointments are filled for the next pair of days, and then there will be no further court until the year is new. Mayhap you could persuade your mother to speak on your behalf—she arrived only this morning with your brother, and will see the king on the morrow."

Piers shook his head once, little more than a jerk. Judith Angwedd was already here, somewhere, and Bevan with her. He had arrived in time, thank God. But only just, and his nerves sizzled and popped. He had to fight himself not to glance over his shoulder and look for them. "No. Forgive me, but it cannot wait."

Again, the man's eyebrows rose, and he seemed to present an expectant expression on his square face.

Piers clenched his teeth together, and he spoke low so that no other could eavesdrop. "The woman you named as my mother is not. She is my father's widow, and she has come to Edward so that he will bequeath Gillwick Manor to her son, Bevan. But I tell you, Bevan is not my father's child. Judith Angwedd Mallory is attempting to steal the lands that are rightfully mine, and is prepared to bear false witness to His Majesty in order to do so. I am the only true heir of Gillwick, and I can prove it." Piers held up his right hand, his mother's signet ring on his littlest finger flashing briefly in the dull light of the hall. He let his hand fall back to his side. "If the king hears

Judith Angwedd in his court without my witness, he will be making a grave mistake."

The man's eyebrows had slowly descended and then drawn downward as Piers spoke. He seemed to appraise Piers once again before saying, "Wait here." He turned, rapped three times on the door, and then disappeared between them. Raucous laughter escaped the seam of the doors before they shut once more.

Piers let out a tight breath he hadn't realized he'd been holding. Even though he knew in his gut that Gillwick was rightfully his, that Judith Angwedd was naught more than a lying, conniving, mad bitch, Piers felt extreme unease with his surroundings and with the task before him. He longed for the humid peace of Gillwick, or the quiet forest he had traveled through and lived in for so many days. He wanted Alys, needed her. God, how he loved her! And with that thought, he realized now that he was not fighting to gain Gillwick for himself any longer, or even to give peace to his long-dead mother. He was doing it for Alys.

Perhaps once she returned to Fallstowe, she would not want the humble life Piers could offer her. But he would offer it any matter. He could not help himself. He needed her and he loved her, and he knew that he would for the rest of his life. If there was any chance that she truly loved him, Piers planned to seize that love with both hands and never let her go. That damned monkey which had nearly killed him could also come, if Alys wished. After all, Piers had invited Ira, so it was only fair that Alys should have her own sort of cross beast at Gillwick.

He felt the faint impression of a smile twitch at his lips at the thought, but the very idea of joviality was killed with the cold words he heard spoken directly behind him.

"Hello, Piers. Stealing clothes now as well as land, I see."

Piers turned slowly, uncertain at what would happen once he faced the wretched woman who had tried to destroy his life.

She was actually smiling at him, her large, square teeth glistening in the festive gloom of the receiving chamber.

"It's over," Piers said, refusing to stoop to ridiculous, barbed banter with the madwoman. "I've just spoken to Edward's man. I will see the king on the morrow."

"Marvelous!" Judith Angwedd gushed, and clapped her hands together twice, as if in anticipation. "Just as I'd hoped."

Piers was wary. Although Judith Angwedd had a penchant for the cruelly dramatic, he didn't think she was being sarcastic.

"I would not be so enthusiastic, were I you," Piers warned. "I have proof of your treachery, and once the king hears of it you will lose all."

Judith Angwedd wrinkled her nose and shook her head. "No. I think not, really. I'm rather looking forward to you disavowing your claim to Gillwick before the king."

"There is naught you could say that would sway me," Piers growled. "You are a liar and a thief, and you will get exactly what you deserve."

"Oh, I am certain I will," she parried. "And I don't have to utter a single word to convince you to make way for Bevan and me. I'm actually going to give you a gift, and then you may decide on your own. You are completely and utterly in control of how this all plays out. I am more than willing to negotiate with you, which is why I brought you" —her teeth sparkled like ivory blades—"a peace offering of sorts."

"You mean a bribe," Piers snorted.

Judith Angwedd conceded with a slight tilting nod.

Piers shook his head. "Whatever it is, you can keep it. Nothing you could give me, promise me, will convince me to let you have my father's home. *My* home."

Her smile was secret and small now. "Nevertheless, it would be foolish of you not to at least consider it. But before I give it to you, I only ask that you realize that Bevan is not with me at the moment. You will be able to guess his company soon enough though. Only keep that in your thoughts before you would do anything foolish. If you try to cheat the negotiations in any way, my offer will become immediately void, and Bevan will have my blessing to do as he pleases. You know how . . . *spirited* he can be."

She held out her arm, her fist clenched palm down.

Piers didn't want to extend his hand. He looked down at her fist, white with bulging blue veins, cold, like a swirl of milk caught in a block of ice. He looked up into her eyes.

"Take it," she said softly, teasingly. "It won't bite you, foolish boy."

Piers held out his hand, and Judith Angwedd pressed something small and light into his palm. Her smile widened.

"Think well upon it," she advised. "I shall see you in the morn, when we shall both hear what you will tell Edward. I am simply *alive* with anticipation!" She swept away from him, and Piers watched her go. She gave him not another glance as she waggled her fingers at this person or another while she walked through the hall. No one returned her greeting.

When she was gone, Piers looked down at the object she'd placed in his hand.

It was a bracelet, its wooden beads carved inexpertly into crude renditions of little pomegranates.

Alys's bracelet.

All the air left Piers's body and his face raised slowly, looking for Judith Angwedd to be standing across the room, beaming in triumph. But she was truly gone.

"My lord," a voice behind him called, but it seemed too far away, and Piers was not accustomed to people addressing him by that noble title.

I only ask that you realize that Bevan is not with me at the moment. You will be able to guess his company soon enough though. Only keep that in your thoughts before you would do anything foolish. You know how . . . spirited he can be.

"Lord Mallory," the voice said again, and Piers turned. He knew his lips were slack, his eyes wild. At the man's wary look, Piers closed his mouth.

"Sorry. Yes?"

"The king will indeed hear your plea on the morrow, along with your stepmother's," the keeper of the doors advised with a frown as he glanced down at the wooden beads dangling over Piers's fist. "But I am to warn you that if you are playing about with something you are not lawfully entitled to, he is prepared to see you punished straightaway. He does not well tolerate having his time wasted."

Piers nodded faintly. He barely comprehended what the man was saying to him.

Bevan had Alys. Piers recalled the fleshy boy who had gleefully tormented and tortured Piers after he'd lost his mother, when Piers had been too small and frightened to fight back. And now the drunkard, who had once kicked a dog to death when it had dared to sniff at his boots. Bevan, whom Piers suspected had raped more women than he'd ever spoken to, and who not even the most heartless lords in the land would accept as a husband for their daughters. Piers knew nothing weaker than Bevan was safe in his presence.

And that man was now holding a delicate and innocent woman such as Alys in his evil and depraved clutches. Piers's Alys. His wife.

"I understand," Piers said and nodded again. He understood too well, perhaps. "My thanks." Piers began to turn away, feeling as though he were lost in a thick fog the color of terror.

"My lord," the man called Piers's attention once more. Piers half turned.

"Have you secured shelter for the night?" he asked in a lowered tone. The lion's eyebrows were drawn together, and had Piers been in possession of his capacities, he might have seen the concern there.

"Ah . . . no. No, I'm afraid not. I've"—he cleared his throat—"I've only just arrived in the city."

The lion-maned man seemed to think for a moment, debating something behind his golden eyes. "My wife bears our first child even now. I do expect it will be some time before I see my court suite or my own bed." He reached into a slit in his tunic and withdrew a key on a ribbon. He held it out to Piers.

Piers frowned and took it as if in a dream. If he could only think straight for one moment. "Forgive me, but—"

"Go above. Show the guard this key and tell him you have Lord Julian Griffin's permission to pass the night in his rooms."

Piers stared at the man for several moments. "Why are you doing this?"

Julian Griffin looked at Piers, and there was no ulterior motive in his eyes, no trickery. Only truth.

"Because I saw your boots," he answered low. "And the little strand of beads you now hold was not in your possession only a moment ago. I believe you have a great battle before you."

Piers nodded faintly. "I will one day repay you for your aid."

"Good day, Lord Mallory," Julian Griffin said dismissively and directed his eyes over Piers's shoulder. "Good day to you, my lady. How can I be of service?"

Piers turned to see the frowning woman behind him, obviously impatient to speak with the keeper of the king's court. Piers sidestepped out of the way, nearly stumbling. The woman swept past to take his place.

"Is there any time to spare today, Lord Julian? I fear my grandmother is—"

Piers dragged his feet back down the length of the receiving hall toward the wide stairs he'd seen when he'd arrived.

Somewhere, somewhere close, Alys was being held by a madman. And it was all Piers's fault. Sybilla Foxe had not been the only spy tracking them after leaving Ira's village, and Piers's innocent beacon to alert Alys's rescue had brought hell down upon her instead.

He looked to the ornate ceiling above his head, as if by concentrating he could discern Alys's location amidst the warren of rooms stacked atop him. Was she even being held in the king's home, though? Or an inn nearby? He did not know where or how to begin to search. Should he tear the stones apart and still fail to locate her, should he raise alarm to the king's guards—mayhap even the lion-maned Julian Griffin—Judith Angwedd would surely hear of it. She would hear of it, and then Alys's life would be forfeit.

He had but one recourse.

He would disavow his claim before the king. Gillwick had just slipped out of his fingers, for good this time. He would truly never have anything to offer Alys. Nothing but her life, which was in his hands now. And Piers was determined to move very slowly, act very carefully in the next several hours. There would be death in London, but Piers would breathe his last before he allowed that death to be Alys's.

He forced his feet to move him from the hall and climb the steps mechanically, the worn soles of his boots slapping marble. He jostled people he passed but he could not care. He did not see them.

Chapter 22

After straining her neck to push the basket containing Layla from the side of her face—with a silent apology to the monkey who screeched indignantly—Alys began concentrating on her breathing. Deeply in, slow and easy out through her nose. Her tongue felt as though it was being forced down her throat, blocking her airway. She could not swallow properly. She knew that if she let herself succumb to panic, she would faint at the very least.

In, out.

She turned her head to the side, to give some sort of escape for the saliva in her mouth. Her jaws ached. In her futile struggle with the gag, she had managed to swallow more air than she had breathed, and so a sharp pain now stabbed at her midsection, so intense that she could feel it in the muscles of her back.

Breathe. In. Out.

She closed her eyes against the seemingly cavernous dark. And when she felt the hot tears streak down her cheeks, she realized that all was not yet lost. She was breathing. She was crying. She was still alive. And that was just enough to calm her to where she could begin to think.

She had initially thought that Judith Angwedd and Bevan had both quit the chamber. But after perhaps a half hour, she could hear disgusting, muffled grunts from beyond the thick wardrobe doors. Bevan. After only a few minutes, the noises stopped on a hoarse exhalation of choking breath. The pain in Alys's stomach sharpened and swelled. Thank God, Judith Angwedd had said she was taking the key to the wardrobe with her when she'd left.

It wasn't long afterward when Alys heard the red-headed woman enter the chamber once more. She strained to hear the conversation, but only caught fading and swelling pieces.

"—she sleep—"

Mumbling, and then, "—'s'here . . . quested audience. Shh!"

Alys heard the key scraping in the lock again, and she forced her face to relax into some parody of sleep. She felt a release of pressure in the close air around her face, a slight puff of breeze, and then the lock was clicking once more.

"Asleep or dead," she heard Judith Angwedd say in a fading voice. "Saw him . . . keep watch . . . John Hart."

Bevan's voice reached her ears, shockingly clear and close. He must have stood at the seam of the doors.

"I say we simply go on and kill her."

There was a sharp, muffled reply from Judith Angwedd.

Bevan grunted. Then said, "If you're so fearful of being caught, why not just let the peasant bastard have Gillwick? Hart Manor is twice its size, and I will have it regardless of Edward's decree."

Judith Angwedd must have taken offence to her son's

reasoning, for Alys could feel the sharp reverberations of the woman's approaching footfalls through the wood of the wardrobe.

"Why settle for ten of something when you could have twenty? Why take some, when all is within your grasp?" she demanded in a raspy whisper, and Alys could sense her mad passion for which she spoke. "I came to Warin Mallory as a girl, in good faith."

Bevan snorted.

"Shut your foolish mouth! John Hart was married, and he used me, just as I used him. I was determined to make a prosperous life at Gillwick, give Warin the children he desired, increase the worth of his farm. *He* cuckolded *me* with a *commoner*! It was simply my misfortune that I got with child by the wrong man."

"Why, thank you, Mother."

"But now," Judith Angwedd continued, in a somewhat placating tone, "John Hart is widowed, with no heirs to leave his fortune to. You have two feasts spread before you now, Bevan—we both do! Once Gillwick and Hart Manor are joined together under us, we will have a veritable empire! Think of the power that will wield!"

Alys was aghast. Lord John Hart's possessions were more than Gillwick's, for certain, but it was not of such import as to be considered the basis of an empire. The woman was obviously delusional, and truly mad with greed.

"I fucking hate cows," Bevan grumbled.

"That's simply too bad. Now, go and do as I've asked. If Piers leaves the chamber, follow him. If he comes within beckoning distance of John Hart or this floor—"

"I know—kill him," Bevan said wearily.

Alys's throat threatened to close once more. Piers was here. Not only in London, but in a chamber not far from her, right at this very moment. He was here, and possibly in greater danger than Alys herself.

"What of her?" Bevan pressed, sounding unenthusiastic about his mother's plans. "She may try to free herself once we are both gone."

"And then she'd do what? Beat through the doors with her skull? The bonds would need be cut to be removed, which I don't plan on doing regardless of the outcome at court. I shall dine with John Hart this night. And shortly after the morrow's audience, we shall be rid of bastard Piers and his pagan princess bride. Sybilla Foxe shall have her right comeuppance as well, and that thought does please me greatly."

Alys waited until she was absolutely certain that both mother and son had departed before trying to sit upright. Her spine creaked, and as she pushed with both feet and slid up the side of the wardrobe it felt as if all the bones in her shoulder and back were laid bare to the wood.

Layla's basket tumbled from her shoulder to her midsection and arrived upside down on her thighs. The exertion had caused Alys to break into a sweat, and she sat for several moments, slowing her breathing once more. Bevan had bound her hopelessly. There was no chance of her working her hands free—she couldn't so much as feel them at this point. And without her hands, there was even less chance of her freeing her legs, which were bound to her knees so tightly that they could barely bend. But her feet tingled now that her legs were stretched out along the floor of the wardrobe, and that little thing heartened her.

On her lap, Layla shifted within the basket and Alys felt it move. Layla cooed sadly, and Alys wanted to comfort her pet, but the best she could manage was a strangled caw, which nearly choked her. The basket on her legs began to rock, and from within, Layla screeched in agitation. There was a terrible flurry of sound, crackling and splitting of the basket, and Alys hoped desperately that the monkey wouldn't hurt herself. In a moment, the basket tumbled down toward her feet, and then four little appendages pummeled back up Alys's body.

Layla was free. Alys could feel the little animal's huffs of breath on her cheek as Layla inspected the gag in her mouth. The monkey forced dainty fingers between the rope and Alys's skin and yanked, tugged, jerked back and forth wildly. Alys squeezed her eyes shut at the dizzying shaking but made no sound that Layla might mistake for disapproval. Layla climbed over Alys's head, worried at the knot at the base of her skull, relieved her of several pieces of hair, bringing sharp tears to Alys's eyes.

Then the monkey was back at her shoulder, and this time, Alys felt Layla's mouth, and the scrape of little teeth against her skin. She kept her eyes shut and held very, very still, barely daring to breathe as the *chick-chick* sounds and humid breaths brought out a blanket of gooseflesh over her body. She felt the gag give infinitesimally, and had to steel herself against pushing at it with her tongue. It gave again, jerking once sideways in her mouth. In the next instant, Alys realized the rope was now slack between her teeth. She shook her head with a cry, spitting to eject the gag from her mouth.

"Good girl, Layla," Alys praised. "Good girl!"

The monkey was now perched on her knees, as if waiting for Alys to take over the task of freeing them both. Alys sat for a moment in thought. But only for one moment. She began to scoot and turn her bottom, until she was wedged perpendicular to the floor of the wardrobe, her feet against the deep lip below the doors. Then she pushed with all her strength, sliding her back up the rear wall. For the first time in her life, Alys blessed her lack of height. When she finally stood, swaying in the black on legs effectively turned into one tapered post, her head only whispered against the shelf above.

She turned sideways, leaned into the wall, and then threw her left shoulder into the doors. Her back and chest muscles screamed, but the doors did not so much as bulge. She leaned against the wall again, pushed into it, gathered herself, and threw herself again. The doors stood firm, but an unexpected vertigo overtook Alys as the blackness inside the wardrobe seemed to lean toward the floor.

Alys gasped and flung her weight toward the back once more. If she toppled the large piece of furniture on its face, she would never get out.

"Oh God, help me," she breathed. "Come *on*!" She flung sweaty tendrils of hair from her forehead and cheeks with a frustrated toss of her head. She tried to think of something—anything—else she could do.

Then she heard the distinct *chud* of the chamber door beyond the wardrobe. The sound of feet approaching.

It could be Bevan. It could be Judith Angwedd. It could be a common thief, come to rob the apartment, or it could be no one save a simple chamber maid. Alys couldn't risk calling out. If it was one of her captors returned, they might punish her, hurt her—

Kill her.

As it was, if Judith Angwedd opened the wardrobe to check on her prisoner, she would likely be much displeased to see the gag missing and Alys standing upright.

Layla chose that very moment to begin jumping up and down at Alys's feet, screeching, and it sounded to Alys like the monkey was pounding on every surface of wood her hands or feet touched.

"*Layla, no!*" Alys whispered. "*Shh! No!*"

The monkey quieted, but so did the footsteps beyond.

To Alys's utter and complete dread, the lock in the doors began to scrape. She pressed her bound arms against the back wall of the wardrobe, prepared to launch herself in attack. She would be bested, helpless as she was, but before she died, that redheaded bitch would know forever more that a Foxe never surrendered.

Both doors swung wide, and Alys opened her mouth to give a battle cry.

Her "Aagh!" quickly turned into a shout of *"Ira?"*

The old man, stingy as a leather strap and twice as tough, stared back at her mildly. Layla launched herself at Piers's grandfather, and Alys had to give the old man credit when he caught the monkey deftly and hefted her to his shoulder.

"You're welcome," he said gruffly, nodding once at Alys.

"Alys," another voice called, and even as Alys was turning her head to take in the person standing slightly behind and to the side of the old man, she couldn't believe it. Her eyes traveled up the worn leather boots, rough woven leggings, long tunic that was frayed and stained. The leather coif hid the hair that was beneath it, but the face, the sparkling eyes . . .

"Sybilla," Alys choked on a sob, and then her sister was there, catching her, holding her.

"Her hands, Ira," Sybilla said over Alys's shoulder, and Alys heard the ripping of the linen binding her.

"Sybilla, how did you find me? What is Ira doing here? If Edward learns that you are in London—not to mention his very home—he'll have you arrested!"

"I would not let another come for you in my place," Sybilla said calmly. "As for the rest, I will answer you when we are safely away. We must hurry."

Alys's elbows fell free from each other and she gave a soft cry, bringing her arms around before her gingerly and rubbing at them. She looked down at Ira, who was releasing the bonds from her legs as Layla clung to his head like a skullcap.

"Have you seen the lad?" Ira asked, his eyes flicking up at her.

"Piers is here, but I don't know where," Alys said. Her eyes went to Sybilla's. "Judith Angwedd and Bevan were using me to force Piers to relinquish his hold on Gillwick Manor. They're planning to kill him!"

Sybilla shook her head matter of factly. "No. Ira will find him and tell him that you're safe. There is no need to retract his claim. Once in the king's court, he will be free to tell of their dastardly plans. Thank you, Ira. You're free now, Alys. Let's go." Sybilla took Alys's elbow and began pulling her toward the door. "Night has fallen, and if we can escape the castle undetected, we'll be through the city gates in moments."

Alys began to resist, but then quickly acquiesced. "Alright, I'll go with you to the gates, but then I'm returning."

Sybilla halted, spun to face her, the laces from her assumed coif whipping across her cheeks. "You're *not* returning."

"Yes, I am," Alys insisted. "I will not leave Piers here to defend against such wolves with no other witness save a woodland rebel. Forgive me, Ira," Alys tossed to the old man with a sympathetic look.

"You will be thrown in jail, after which guards will be set to my trail back to Fallstowe, finding me in the open. Do you wish to see Fallstowe ripped from us?"

"No!" Alys said, and pulled her elbow from Sybilla's grip in order to seize both of her sister's hands. "Once you are through the gates, I will hide myself—somewhere—

until the morn. You'll be too far out of Edward's reach by then."

"Hide yourself? In London?" Sybilla sighed. "Alys, this is no gentle city. You'd be set upon by the parasites that prowl the streets, looking for an innocent young girl to feed upon. You'd be dead by sunrise—or wishing you were!"

"I'm not a girl," Alys said calmly. "I'll go with Ira then, help him find Piers. Piers will protect me."

"Protect you like he did in the forest? When Judith Angwedd kidnapped you?"

Alys's face burned.

Sybilla gave her no time to speak. "You couldn't re-enter the palace alone without revealing your identity. Ira's not leaving, so he only needs not be caught while within. You are coming *home*, with *me*, right *now*." Sybilla began to pull again.

Alys jerked her hands free. *"No, I am not."*

Alys could feel the fury radiating from her sister, and she wanted to step back, but she would not. Sybilla was her sister, and she had come for Alys by herself. They did truly love each other. And, like magic, Alys finally understood the seemingly bottomless depth of that emotion in her sister: Sybilla felt things so deeply, so sincerely, her concern and her protectiveness came out as demands.

"I am risking my life for you at this moment—risking our very home—when it was your childishness that got you into this situation," Sybilla accused. "I will not further jeopardize Fallstowe, Cecily, or our people be-cause of your girlish fantasies of fated love supposedly blessed by some goddamn ring of stone! Alys, you are so irresponsible—"

"I am not irresponsible!" Alys shouted, having enough of the listing of her faults. She knew them better now than

Sybilla could ever guess. "I've only never had anything to be responsible *for*!"

The chamber was silent. Sybilla stared at Alys with no expression.

"Until now," Alys said quietly. "I know the truth, and my station could lend veracity to Piers's claim."

"It will not change the fact that he doesn't want you, Alys," Sybilla said, and Alys could see the rare softening of her sister's eyes. "He wanted you to go home, to Fallstowe. He never meant for you to be captured by Judith Angwedd, but he did mean for you to be found. He knew I had been following you, and he thought it would be me that came upon you at your camp."

Alys looked to Ira, whose head was tilted slightly to the side, eyeing her with pity. One bony finger combed through the hair on Layla's arm.

"Ira?" Alys asked. "Is it true? Piers knew Sybilla was following us, and he left me for her to find?"

He nodded once. "He's always wanted you to go home. I think you already know that though, do you not?"

The truth of it fell upon Alys with the crushing weight of an undermined tower. Since the night they'd met, Piers had done little else but try and persuade her to return to Fallstowe. He had not kept it secret. He had never played her false.

And now, she was ready to risk her family's home, her own freedom and perhaps even her life, to return to the side of a man who had set her free. In truth, Alys couldn't even predict whether Judith Angwedd's threat on her life would persuade Piers to disavow his claim. He had been denied what was rightfully his his entire life and now it was within his reach. Why would he forsake it all for a woman he never wanted in the first place?

Sybilla was right again. But this time, Alys was not

bitter. Perhaps, she thought, it was hard truths like this, the acceptance of them and the pain they brought, that gained a person wisdom. She thought fleetingly of the enormous heartbreak Sybilla must be hiding. And the idea of such untold pain horrified her.

"Alright," Alys said quietly. "Let's go then, before Judith Angwedd or Bevan return."

Sybilla's eyebrows rose and she drew her head back. Then her eyes narrowed. "Is this some sort of trick? You'll wait until I'm in the corridor and lock the door behind me, like you did when you were a child?"

Alys smiled at the bittersweet memories that hung between them right then . . . *when you were a child.* Perhaps at last her sister no longer thought of her in that manner. "No, Sybilla. No tricks this time. Let's go." She turned and held out a crooked elbow toward Layla, who still perched on Ira's shoulder. "We're off, girl."

The monkey leaped the distance to Alys's shoulder, and gained a firm hold by twisting her little fingers in Alys's hair.

"I wish you well, Ira," she said to the old man. "Both of you."

Ira stared hard at her for a long moment. "As I do you. Both of you," he clarified, his eyes flicking to Sybilla. Then his body seemed to spasm, jerk forward, and Alys realized he was bowing. "Ladies."

Alys tried to restrain the sob that knotted in her chest. She stepped to the old man quickly, leaned up on tiptoe to press her cheek into his and grasp both of his shoulders with her hands.

"Take care of him," she choked. "He has been alone for so long."

His only answer was a quick nod.

"Alys," Sybilla called gently.

Alys stepped away and swiped at her eyes quickly while

she turned toward her sister. She saw her bag crumpled on the floor near the hearth and swiped it up with one hand.

Atop the deep, reddened grooves on her wrist, she noticed her pomegranate bracelet was gone, and it caused her heart to clench.

She did not look back as she followed Sybilla into the corridor.

Chapter 23

He didn't sleep.

Piers was grateful for the generosity of the stranger, Julian Griffin. If not for his keen eye, and perhaps a bit of intuition, as well, Piers would have been forced to wander the palace grounds, searching for some place to hide away during the night. But the suite of rooms he'd been lent was opulent beyond anything Piers could have ever imagined. He'd been loathe to touch anything for fear that he would break it—and he imagined he would be unable to afford to replace so much as a single thread in the intricate, embroidered coverlet, especially since he would now never see a farthing of Gillwick's earnings.

So he passed the night on the floor, his back against the bolted door. He lit not one candle, only sat in the pitch blackness, the smell of privilege all around him, cloying and invisible in the night, and thought of Alys. Prayed for her safety. Begged God's forgiveness for the jeopardy he'd placed her in, because he knew he would never forgive himself.

And he prayed for his own soul, because Piers knew that God knew him, and knew his heart. God knew that

Piers meant to kill Bevan, and now Judith Angwedd, as well, regardless of Edward's decision. They had wronged him, stolen from him, defamed him, cursed him, beaten him, tried to kill him. And yet before today, they both might have lived.

But not now. No, not now that they had touched Alys. Alys would be happy. Alys would not know fear of them again, for the rest of her long life. Wherever she made her home, wherever she would lay her pretty head down to sleep, she would never again worry that the ones who had taken her, held her, threatened her—all because of Piers— were out in the land somewhere.

Alys had risked her own life to save Piers. It was because of her unselfish heart that he now had Ira. She had sworn to stand by him, even in defiance of the king. When Piers had faith in nothing, no one, Alys had placed all of hers in him, and he had denied her at every turn. His father's rejection of him at the insistence of Judith Angwedd had ensured that Piers would never know the privileges of his father. His hard labor at Gillwick had labeled him common, just as surely as it had labeled his very body by the scars and calluses and muscles it bore. Piers Mallory was not known for his lands or his title, but for his fists. He was no one. And yet Alys had loved him.

And so now he would sacrifice all that he had or might have had for her. She would never forgive his betrayal of her in the forest, his arrogant stupidity that had placed her in the teeth of danger, but Piers would at least be certain that from this night on, he did everything he could, gave everything he had for Alys.

When the windows behind the still-open draperies began to brighten with gray fog, Piers was dry-eyed and calm. He stood slowly, his body stiff and sore from his travels and his still pose on the hard floor.

He rinsed his mouth and washed carefully in the basin, wincing when the lip of the pitcher trembled against the bowl. He brushed at his tunic with a damp rag, swiped the cloth over the tops of his boots. Piers noticed with irony how he could feel the plush towel through the thin leather. He washed his hands and beneath his fingernails, polished the stone in the signet ring.

Then he went to stand before one of the windows, looking down on a brightening courtyard, quiet and still and bare with winter's breath. He tried to summon his mother's face in his mind's eye, but the best he could muster were dim memories akin to something once sweet on his tongue and the rich smell of hay.

Then, as if someone had called his name, Piers turned suddenly and left the room.

He went purposefully down the wide flights of stairs, passing servants bearing trays and candle snuffers and stacks of folded linens. He bid each good morn, and most gave him a started look before returning the greeting, adding "milord" to the end.

No one of station had ever deigned speak to Piers outside of a barked command before. He had been part of the invisible machinery that enabled Gillwick to prosper, much as these servants did for the king's home, and Piers wanted to acknowledge them as he had never been acknowledged.

He reached the grand receiving hall, and was surprised to see a crowd of people already gathered around the gilded double doors at the far end. Some sort of commotion was being raised, and Piers heard a man's shouts from the center of the crowd.

"I've had many a year to dream of the day you'd receive your comeuppance, and thanks be to God that day is nigh!"

Piers's footsteps faltered when the old man's statement was met with a female's gay laugh. Then Piers charged, his heart galloping to match his footfalls. He met the wall of the crowd and muscled to its center forcefully, pulling people out of his way by their arms like scarves from a basket, while the old man still invisible to him continued.

"Laugh now, heifer! I'll be drinkin' to your tears with me supper!"

"Ira," Piers said, as he at last reached the center of the crowd and stood a pair of steps from his grandfather, as well as the same distance from Judith Angwedd and Bevan. "What are you doing here? How did you—?"

"Piers!" Ira shouted and rushed to him, gripping his arm with one bony hand. The old man continued to speak, but Piers heard him not, his eyes having locked on to Bevan's.

Red, boiling, bloody hate swelled up in Piers's veins. It burned beneath his skin, caused his muscles to twitch, his teeth to grind. Bevan was smirking below his red-lined nose and the dark circles beneath his small eyes. But Piers could only see the man's thick neck, his adam's apple bulging grotesquely. Piers fantasized briefly at the gristly cracking noise it would make when he crushed it in his fist.

"Alys," was Piers's only word.

"Dunno, mate," Bevan snorted, then after another deep smirk, he shrugged his big, dumb shoulders. "Alys who?"

"Where. Is she?" Piers enunciated, slightly louder.

"Yes, who is this Alys you speak of?" Judith Angwedd asked stridently, and then gave another cawing laugh. "I vow I have no idea who you mean. A scullery maid you're fond of, mayhap?"

Piers heard a growling, and only faintly realized the sound was coming from his own throat. His eyes never left Bevan. He felt his back tense, the muscles bunch. He couldn't wait.

"Piers. Piers!" Ira was shaking his arm. "They don't have her! Listen to me—Alys is safe."

His grandfather's words were slowly penetrating the haze of rage that had enveloped Piers's head. He turned his head minutely, listening.

"Me and"—Ira glanced toward Judith Angwedd— "*a friend* freed her last night. She's gone home, Piers. She's safe."

Now Piers did let his eyes flick to his grandfather's face. "You're certain?"

Ira nodded once and then leaned in, whispering harshly. "They want you to attack—don't! Stand firm! Let the king be your witness, lad."

Piers had no comment to Ira's advice, although he recognized the wisdom of the old man's words. Alys was *free*. Piers could now do his best to strip the pair of Gillwick before the king, but then—*then* . . .

Bevan snorted again. "Fine boots you have there, *Lord Piers*."

Piers let his eyes bore into Bevan's, and he hoped even a fraction of the hatred he felt was evident. When he spoke, his voice was low and deadly. "Enjoy the air you now breathe, Bevan. Savor it. You shall not be earthly witness to another sunrise."

"Oh!" Judith Angwedd screeched, seizing Bevan's arm and pulling him toward the doors that were now opening. "Did you all hear that? He threatened my son's life! You . . . you base criminal! Thief! Liar!" she continued to shout as she slipped into the king's private court.

Bevan held Piers's eyes as he was dragged along by his mother. "A fine piece of ass she was too," Bevan said and then waggled his fat tongue at Piers.

Piers lunged and Ira threw all his bony weight onto him.

"No, lad! No, he lies!" The other nobles—their numbers more than tripled in the time since Piers arrived in the receiving hall—swarmed cautiously around and past them into the chamber as Ira held Piers back. "Lady Alys was untouched when we found her. She is safe with Lady Sybilla. She's safe, Piers! For the love of God, would you concentrate on what you came here to do!"

Piers looked down at Ira, nodded hesitantly. "She must hate me for what I did. Did she . . . did she ask of me?"

Ira's brows lowered into a pained looking frown. "She wished you well, my lad. There is no malice in her."

Piers swallowed and then nodded again, this time more resolutely. "Alright," he said. He looked to the open doors as if they were a portal to his eternal judgment. In a way, they were just that.

"Let's go."

It was yet an hour before the king presented himself to his court, and in that time, Piers let Ira fill his ears and mind with meaningless chatter. Grandfather and grandson stood alone on one side of the narrow room, while Judith Angwedd and her son stood opposite the long center aisle. The nobles gathered together to plea their own claims or simply to witness the goings-on approached neither group, only stared at the individuals with blatant curiosity. And this pleased Piers, because he knew it vexed Judith Angwedd.

Then everyone in the chamber was sinking suddenly into low bows. Piers felt Ira jerk on his sleeve, and then he realized Edward had come upon the rear of the dais. Piers too paid his homage, and did not rise until the rest of the chamber had, at a loss for the mannerisms of court.

The king was a tall man, pale, with a pointed face. His clothes fit his long, slender limbs closely, and when he sat in his ornate, marble throne, he leaned on an elbow and stretched one leg out before him, as if it was stiff.

A richly-dressed man with a rolled scroll stepped to the front of the dais. "Before the court of our sovereign lord, His Majesty King Edward, this day: Lady Judith Angwedd Mallory of Gillwick Manor and her son, Lord Bevan Mallory of Gillwick Manor. Regarding the estate and inheritance of the late Lord Warin Mallory of Gillwick Manor. Denied by Piers Mallory, a commoner unknown to the realm." The man looked up from his scroll and eyed the sea of people. "Persons step forward."

As Piers made his way to stand before the dais, perhaps only six feet separating him from Judith Angwedd, he noticed the man sitting just behind Edward at a little table, scribbling with a quill.

The court's agent spoke again. "Let it be known that the matter with which you present the king this day will be irrevocably decided, and that your witness is your solemn vow. Perjurers will be held up to the law." The man stepped back to the king's side.

Edward raised his chin from his hand long enough to flick a long finger at Judith Angwedd. "You."

The redhead stepped forward and curtsied so low Piers thought her forehead would bounce off the floor. She rose.

"Your Majesty, my husband, God rest his soul, was a good man. He naturally wanted our son, Bevan, to succeed him. This . . . commoner," Judith Angwedd spat in Piers's direction, "is a bastard from the village whore. He stole the Gillwick crest from my husband's hand before his body was cold. His claim is a false one, and I would humbly ask that he be punished for not only his theft, but the humiliation his accusations have wrought."

Edward's eyebrows rose. "Is that all?"

Judith Angwedd bowed deeply once again. "There is simplicity in the truth, your majesty."

Then the king's eyes turned to Piers. "This crest, you have it with you?"

Piers nodded. "Yes, Sire." Then without hesitation, he pulled the ring from his finger and began to approach the dais.

From either side of him, armed guards previously unnoticed rushed to block Piers's advance. The court's agent stepped from the platform with a disapproving frown and held out his hand. Piers heard Bevan's snort as he placed the signet ring in the man's palm. When Piers stepped back, the guards retreated.

Piers watched as the king held the ring between long forefinger and thumb and turned it this way and that, inspecting it. Then Edward looked to Piers once more.

"You claim that you are also Warin Mallory's son?"

"Yes, Sire," Piers said, and gave a hesitant half-bow, only because he knew not what else to do. "But let it be known to all who gather here that my mother was no whore. She was common, yes—the daughter of a simple dairy man who served Gillwick." Piers glanced around and saw Ira's shoulders square. "My grandfather, there."

Edward said nothing for several moments, only looked between Piers and Bevan. Then he addressed Piers once again. "Who is the elder?"

"Bevan is, Sire," Piers offered. "By not quite one year."

Edward's eyebrows rose again, this time in genuine surprise. "Then your claim is dismissed, man. By the very nature of primogeniture, the eldest son shall inherit his father's estate. It would be highly unusual in any matter for a man to bequeath his home to an illegitimate heir when he clearly has another son to which his estate is legally entitled, even should the illegitimate son be the elder. Which you, by your own admission, are not."

Judith Angwedd squealed and clapped her hands. "Thank you, your majesty! Your wise and—"

"Silence," Edward threw at her. He looked to Piers. "Why would you bring such a frivolous claim to my court, knowing that you could not win?"

Piers swallowed. "My father bade me, Sire. On his deathbed. Bevan was born before me, yes. But not of my father's loins." Behind him, the court gasped. "Bevan Mallory is not my father's son at all."

Edward sat up in his chair and threw an annoyed look to his agent.

"Silence in the hall!" the man demanded.

"How do you know this?" Edward asked, his head tilted, an intrigued look on his face.

"He is a liar and a thief, your majesty!" Judith Angwedd screeched. "He threatened Bevan's life before all who are gathered here!" She spread her arms wide and indicated the crowded chamber. "Only ask any of them!"

"I do not lie, Sire," Piers said, his teeth aching in response to his clenched jaw. "That woman and her son attacked me just after my father died. They were looking for the ring you hold in your hand, suspecting that my father had warned me of their duplicity and knowing that its value had increased to far more than the weight of its gold. I survived their attempt on my life only in thanks to the charity of the monks at Alcester Abbey. One of them fished my body out of the River Arrow."

"Is that how you came to bear the scars on your face and the wound upon your left hand?" Edward asked, a thoughtful expression still on his face, although his chin was propped once more.

"On my face, yes," Piers answered.

"Not your hand though?"

"No, Sire." Piers hesitated only an instant. "I was bitten."

"Lady Mallory set hounds to your trail?" Edward guessed.

"No." Piers lifted his chin. "'Twas a monkey, sire."

Behind him, the crowd of nobles twittered.

Edward frowned crossly. "Go on."

"I shall say again, I do not lie. Judith Angwedd herself approached me only last eventide, while I was consulting with your man, Julian Griffin. She and Bevan had gone so far as to have kidnapped my . . . my traveling companion, and were holding her with my retraction of my bid for Gillwick Manor as ransom for her life."

"That's a lie!" Judith Angwedd nearly screamed.

"I beg you, ask your man, Sire—I would thank him myself for his generosity." Piers reached into his tunic and withdrew the key to his borrowed quarters. Knowing better now than to approach the dais, he held it toward the court's agent, who stepped forward and took the key. "Lord Griffin lent me his rooms last night, and he saw the proof of my companion's captivity—a string of beads crafted with my own hands—which Judith Angwedd presented to me." Piers now held up Alys's bracelet with thumb and forefinger.

"Filthy liar!" Judith Angwedd's face looked ready to explode.

"Additional outbursts of that nature, Lady Mallory, shall win you dismissal from my court," Edward said curtly.

Judith Angwedd bowed, shallow and stiff. "Forgive me, your majesty."

Edward turned back to Piers. "Lord Griffin is otherwise detained this morn, else I am certain he would readily support or deny your claim." A shadow seemed to pass over Edward's face momentarily, but then he was back to the matter at hand. "This mysterious companion of yours—she is less valuable to you than a potential demesne, obviously. Where is she now? Shall I have the Mallory rooms searched for her?"

"My grandfather freed her in the night," Piers said. "But no, Gillwick is not more valuable to me. There is naught more important to me than her safety. I was fully prepared only this morn to resign Gillwick to secure her release."

"Hmm." Edward sat up once more. "I must know— who *is* this companion you hold in such high esteem?"

Piers swallowed, and it felt to him as if the entire hall was holding its breath in anticipation of his answer.

"Alys Foxe, my liege."

The audience behind him broke into roaring chatter and gasps. Before Piers, the king's expression darkened.

"Alys Foxe?" Edward asked slowly. *"Lady* Alys Foxe, of Fallstowe Castle?"

"Yes, my liege."

"I have had enough!" Edward roared, ending the rumblings of the court. He looked to Piers, leveled a long finger at him, his ire unmistakable. "I wanted to believe your tale, and until this last admission, I was for you. But now you stand before me and claim that you have traveled from the north of the land with a woman belonging to a family that even I cannot reach, with your injuries sustained from a monkey attack, and claiming to be the sole heir of a dead man! With no proof outside of a ring that is likely only stolen, as is charged against you!"

"My father swore it, my liege," Piers said. "The truth pained him greatly."

"Your father swore it," Edward repeated. "Your *dead* father, who cannot testify to your statement, swore it."

Piers nodded. "Yes, Sire."

Edward sighed. "Were it later in the day and my patience more run out, I would have you thrown in the dungeon straight away. Without any proof—"

"I have that proof, your majesty!" a woman's voice called out from the rear of the chamber.

Everyone in the hall turned toward the gilded double doors which now stood open. A guard pursued the woman now walking down the center aisle, half running after her, holding his banging sword against his thigh. The woman wore a blue perse gown and a monkey rode jauntily on one shoulder, and she paid the bumbling guard no heed. Her hair was the color of sun-bleached straw, her stature delicate and regal, her stride efficient.

Piers felt his knees spasm, as if he would fall to the floor before her, worshipping her.

On the dais, the agent called out in a threatening voice, "Declare yourself and your purpose before your king, young woman!"

She stopped in the aisle, standing precisely juxtapose to Piers, Judith Angwedd and Bevan, and the king himself. She didn't so much as glance at Piers before sinking into a low curtsey, Layla clinging to her shoulder. She rose, and her chin lifted.

"Your majesty, I am Lady Alys Foxe. And I am his *wife*."

Chapter 24

Alys ignored the uproar from the assembled nobility behind them and at last turned to Piers. God, he looked terrible, pale, haggard—his appearance reminded her of how he'd looked at the height of his illness, before they had traveled to Ira's treetop village.

Nonetheless, he would be held accountable.

"Traveling companion?" she said through her teeth.

"Alys," Piers said in a choked whisper, and Alys liked the way his eyes seemed to be devouring her face. "I—I . . ."

"I am your *traveling companion*, Piers? Really?"

"Alys, I—"

Piers's explanation—which Alys very much wanted to hear—was cut short by the king, whom Alys had very nearly forgotten was present.

"Lady Alys Foxe," Edward said, in a tone that was neither pleased nor impressed.

Alys turned and bowed once again, taking that spare instant to compose her face. What she wanted to do was to throw herself upon Piers and kiss him, over and over. *Gillwick is not more valuable to me. There is naught more important to me . . .*

"I heartily beg your pardon for my unannounced appearance in your court, your majesty," Alys said, hoping that her tone conveyed the proper deference and humility of a loyal servant. "I mean you no disrespect."

"I will have a private audience with you when this business concludes—ken you my meaning?"

Alys swallowed and nodded, and Edward, placated momentarily by her meek cooperation, continued. "Is what this man—Piers Mallory—says true? Were you abducted and held against your will by Lady Mallory?"

Alys curtsied again. "Yes, my liege. All of what he claims is true. We were en route to London when I was abducted from our camp by Judith Angwedd and her son. They carried me to London, and I was kept prisoner in their suite here, in your home."

Judith Angwedd screeched with rage. "I've never laid eyes upon you in my life!"

"They held me locked in the wardrobe, Sire," Alys continued, as if Judith Angwedd had never spoken. "You need only bid a servant check the lock—Piers's grandfather had need to break it in order to free me. And there is a basket within where they caged my girl, here." Alys jostled her shoulder to indicate Layla.

Edward's eyes flicked to Piers's hand. "The purveyor of the bite, I assume?"

Piers bowed.

"If what you say is true, the charges of kidnapping a peer of the realm are serious enough," Edward mused. "But you also said you have proof of this man's claim to Gillwick Manor?"

"I do, my liege," Alys said, and then at last turned to face Judith Angwedd and Bevan boldly. "At least, I know why Bevan Mallory is not entitled to one blade of grass belonging to Gillwick. He is not Warin Mallory's son, as evidenced by a birthmark he bears upon his chest."

"Shut up, you bitch," Bevan growled at her.

"Such a mark can mean anything, nothing," Edward said mildly. "It is ambiguous at best."

"Not this mark, your majesty," Alys offered. "It is quite unique, so I've been told, to the man who bears its twin, as well as a descriptive surname."

"Shut up!" Bevan insisted again.

Alys smiled at Bevan. "Bevan's true sire is alive and well and in this very chamber. Judith Angwedd dined with him only last night."

"Take care with your claims, littlest Foxe," Edward warned sternly. "I will not have a peer maligned by gossip or hearsay."

"As my presence must assure you, I am willing to stake my family name on what I know, my lord. Bevan Mallory's true sire is Lord John Hart."

Alys would have never dreamed that a man would be foolish enough to attack a woman before the very king, but Bevan charged at her in that moment, his face a swollen mask of hate and rage. His meaty fingers reached for her, and Alys screamed, several nobles shouted, the court agent called out—

And Layla lunged at Bevan, her hands circling in a blur, her teeth bared in a primal and very deadly scream. The monkey landed on his face, clawing, biting, and Bevan grabbed Layla, tried to push her off while he screamed and screamed.

"My face! My face!"

Alys rushed forward, feeling more than seeing Piers at her back. She beat Bevan's hands away while Piers seized his arms, and then Alys was pulling at Layla, who clung to Bevan's tunic. Alys at last succeeded in separating the monkey from the man with the sound of rending fabric, and the left side of Bevan's chest was laid bare to the sunlight filtering through the high windows of the chamber.

Barely touching the inside of Bevan's left nipple, and as big as a fist, a raspberry colored patch stained his skin. Two rounded humps at the top, a tapering point at the bottom.

The shape of a heart. And Alys thought in that moment that it was the only one the evil man would ever possess.

She gasped and held the trembling Layla to her breast as she stepped back and watched the guards separate Piers from Bevan. Alys looked down and saw that Judith Angwedd had collapsed to her knees on the floor, her face frozen in shock and fear. Her bulging eyes blinked repeatedly.

"You fucking pig," Bevan shouted at Piers. "I had you bested. I had you!"

"You've never bested anyone in your life," Piers spat as the guards shoved him away and stood as barriers between the two men. "You and your mother are naught but scavengers."

One guard lay hand to the hilt of his sword, and nodded at Piers in warning. Piers lifted his chin in answer and came to Alys's side, and when his forearm braced against her lower back, Alys wanted to melt into him and weep.

"Good girl, Layla," Piers whispered, and scratched the monkey's head. Alys could feel the solid rise and fall of Piers's chest at her shoulder and for the first time since her mother had died, she felt she had come home.

After several moments, the guards had the scandalized crowd and Bevan under control, and Edward rose from his throne.

"John Hart!" the king called out. In moments, a tall, gray haired bear of a man, whose face Alys now recognized was an older, sagging replica of Bevan's, reluctantly stepped forward at the urging of two guards. "Do you deny that this man is your son?"

John Hart's eyes narrowed. But then perhaps thoughts of defiance left him. "I have never claimed him," was all he would concede.

Edward ignored the strangled murmurs of the audience who were all but swooning with the excitement afoot at a simple morning court.

"Bare your chest, Lord Hart."

The man hesitated for a long moment. "May my dead wife forgive me." He began to slowly unlace his tunic, only far enough so that he could pull down at the neckline, revealing a faded burgundy patch, like bloody angel's wings, beneath sparse gray chest hair.

The crowd was oddly silent, as if they were witnessing an execution. Perhaps it was only now that they realized the gravity of the situation beyond the mere sensation of gossip.

Lord Hart returned his tunic and then suddenly looked to Piers. "I am sorry for your plight, Lord Mallory. I knew naught of you before this day, and I have had no hand in any of the wrongs done to you. I vow now before the king, it was never my intention to acknowledge this viper's offspring as my heir. She was trying to woo me with Gillwick as late as last evening, when she accosted me in the dining hall, but rather would I take my own life than give either of them my home or my name. Your father was a man who lived his convictions. I regret that I have never."

Alys knew her mouth was hanging agape when Lord Hart turned to the king, assumedly to receive Edward's next command. She noticed with a pang of sympathy that the man had refused to meet her eyes.

"Is that all you have to witness, Hart?" the king asked.

John Hart nodded once, his mouth set, his cheeks flushed and quivering. Alys could not help but think the man might not survive the humiliation he'd been dealt, and she was amazed at the idea that only weeks ago, this lord had been a guest at Fallstowe, with intentions of taking Alys for his own wife.

"Your wishes as to your estate have been duly recorded. You are dismissed," Edward said mercifully.

John Hart bowed low and then turned on his heel and strode quickly down the aisle, his head up, despite the on-lookers who followed his exit, gaping openly at him.

The king remained standing, and once the chamber was properly silent, he spoke. "I have arrived at my verdict. Lady Judith Angwedd Mallory, for your perjury, kidnapping and imprisoning of a peer, and false witness in order to hold lands, I hereby strip you of your title as Lady of Gillwick, and sentence you to one year in prison."

Judith Angwedd cried out faintly as the guards approached her.

"Bevan, son of Judith Angwedd Mallory, for your collusion and the attempted murders of two peers of the realm," Alys gasped at this, and wondered if Piers had caught the king's meaning. "You shall die by beheading in one week. May God have mercy on your soul."

"I cannot be imprisoned! No!" Judith Angwedd shrieked as she was pulled to her feet. "Bevan, save me!"

Alys winced. Bevan had made no move, his eyes were trained on the floor between his feet, blood trickling down his still cheek.

"Do you understand, man?" the king demanded.

Slowly, Bevan brought his head up. He looked at the

king for a moment, his face an expressionless mask. "Why wait out the week?" he asked levelly.

Then in the next moment, he had reached into his torn tunic and pulled out a short dagger. Without so much as a shout, Bevan turned and dove at Piers.

Alys was shoved aside, falling to the floor and rolling to protect Layla. She flung herself onto her back to find Piers with her eyes and screamed his name.

Bevan's arm was raised, the blade arcing down. Piers, weaponless, threw up a blocking hand.

And then Bevan crumpled to the floor, following his clattering blade with a hoarse cry. One of the king's guards stepped away, pulling his bloodied sword free.

Judith Angwedd gave an eerie, keening wail as she was dragged away. From somewhere in the crowd of witnesses, someone retched.

Edward looked down on the body from his dais as guards stepped quickly to remove the lifeless bulk of a very disturbed man. "Why wait out the week, indeed."

When all that remained was a swash of bright blood, the king looked to Piers. "Piers Mallory, I dub thee, and rightly so, Lord of Gillwick Manor." Edward held out his hand, fingers first, palm down.

Alys felt the catch of breath in Piers's chest. He left her side to mount the dais and kneel before the king. Taking Edward's hand, he kissed the royal symbol. When Piers rose, Edward handed him the carnelian signet ring.

"I trust you will keep close watch over this particular piece in the future?"

Piers nodded and then after another bow, returned to Alys's side. She felt her heart would burst when he slid his fingers around hers.

Edward spoke in a low voice to his agent, who then addressed the hall. "No more audience this day. Come back on the morrow. Good day." His face swung around. "Save the pair of you," the man said pointedly to Alys and Piers.

Alys gulped. It was time to answer for Fallstowe, for Sybilla. And although Alys was in truth frightened of how the king might punish her in her sister's stead, Alys was ready to face the king. For the first time, it would be Alys who would protect Sybilla.

Chapter 25

The monkey had saved the day.

Piers waved Ira on with the rest of the crowd, signaling that he would join his grandfather as soon as he was able. In the last instant, Ira came back and took charge of Layla, who went willingly enough. Piers vowed silently that the monkey would have all the pomegranates that Gillwick could afford to buy her. Alys blew Ira and Layla each a kiss from her fingertips. Piers squeezed her hand as they turned in the emptying chamber to face the dais.

She had come back for him. She had survived Judith Angwedd and Bevan, grasped her freedom, and turned it away in favor of him. Piers did not know what her plans were, or in truth how she would feel about him once they were out of sight of the king, but he knew he loved her, more than he'd ever thought possible. And now he would stand with her before Edward, as she had stood with him.

Her lovely face was milk-pale, and he could feel her trembling. But other than those signs which only he, at such close proximity, was privy to, she appeared calm, confident. She was the Alys that Piers knew.

Edward fell back onto his chair and took a chalice from

a tray offered by a serving boy. The king took a long drink, and then appraised Alys over the rim.

"Where is your sister, Lady Alys, and why has she ignored my repeated summons?" he demanded straight away.

Piers felt rather than heard Alys's deep intake of breath. "Fallstowe keeps her very engaged, your majesty. The death of my mother was a sharp blow. She and Sybilla were very close."

"People die, Lady Alys. That is no reason to dismiss a direct command from the king."

Alys nodded. But all she said was, "I understand."

Edward stared at her. "Do you have her blessing to be here, with this man?"

Then Alys smiled. "No, Sire. In fact, I have done naught but disobey my sister's orders. I am in direct defiance of her at this very moment."

Edward returned the smile. "Then mayhap you are not the enemy I mistook you for, if you would go against one who defies *me* at every turn." He paused, as if thinking. "Is she taking up arms against me?"

Alys shook her head. "No, your majesty."

Edward's eyes narrowed.

"I swear it to you," Alys insisted.

Edward tapped the base of his chalice against the carved marble armrest for a moment. "I know things about your family, Lady Alys. About your mother, in particular. Things that perhaps you yourself have no idea about. Sybilla would deny me further investigation."

"I can assure you that what little I know is of no consequence, my lord," Alys said, without a trace of mockery.

"I agree, else you would not be risking your life by appearing in my court."

Alys's eyes widened and Edward nodded. "Oh, yes—

'tis indeed that serious." He took another drink. "You said you were Lord Piers's wife, and yet I cannot fathom how that is possible."

Now it was Piers's turn to speak for her. "We met at the Foxe Ring, my liege. 'Tis a stone ring at the old—"

"I know the legend, Piers," Edward interrupted mildly. "You both acknowledge the tradition?"

Piers looked to Alys, and she only stared at him.

"I do," he said, never breaking eye contact with her.

"I do," she replied faintly. "Of course, I do."

"And you also know," Edward said musingly, a touch of humor in his voice, "that Lady Sybilla will likely be much put-out at the thought of you, a Foxe, marrying a humble farmer, no matter that he is now titled."

Alys chuckled sweetly. "Oh, my liege, I indeed am aware of how displeased she would be. She had arranged a betrothal between myself and Lord Clement Cobb of Blodshire."

Edward winced. "That so? His mother is a beastly woman." Then the king shrugged, drained his chalice, and then set it aside, rising leisurely. "Regardless of your sister's notions, it is still I who rules this kingdom, and it is I who decides if a marriage shall be constituted binding or otherwise. You may tell your sister to pay the Cobbs your dowry for her arrogance."

Piers's heart dropped into his stomach.

Edward waved his hand at them nonchalantly. "Alys Foxe, Lady Mallory." He pointed to his agent. "Witnessed." And to the scribe behind him. "Witnessed. So be it, and my blessing on you both. It is my most sincere wish that your sister suffers a fit of apoplexy."

Piers heard Alys gasp and then she sank into a deep curtsey. Piers followed her lead with a bow of his own.

Behind the king, the scribe continued to scratch frantically at his parchments.

The king gestured to the court agent again, spoke low to him and then began to turn away, adding to the pair still below the dais, "Stay on for a fortnight if you wish, as my guests. But Lady Mallory," Edward said interjecting a heavy pause, and oh, but Piers thought that title was the sweetest pair of words he'd ever heard.

"Yes, my lord?" Alys said, sounding breathless.

"I am coming for Fallstowe. I am coming, and I will not be denied."

"I will give Sybilla the message, your majesty."

Edward nodded. "You are dismissed." He turned away and disappeared through a nondescript panel, his scribe scrambling to gather up the sheafs and sheafs of parchment scattered over the small table. On the floor before the dais, servants were already at work erasing the blood of Bevan Mallory.

The king's agent approached them and handed Piers the key belonging to Julian Griffin. "His majesty has granted you use of Lord Griffin's rooms. He shan't be needing them."

Piers smiled at the dour faced man, and wondered if his job was always so harsh that his face was permanently scowling. "Spending time with his new son, I'd wager."

The agent paused, looked up at Piers. "'Twas a daughter. Lady Griffin did not survive."

Alys gasped and whispered, "Oh, no!"

Piers felt an odd, heavy sense of loss for this man, Julian Griffin, who was little more than a kind stranger to him.

"I am most saddened by that news. Please give him my—"

"Our," Alys interjected.

"Yes, our regrets," Piers amended. Was it 'our' now? Piers had never been an 'our' before.

The agent looked to Alys briefly and his eyes narrowed. "Likely you will be able to make your regrets personally." He bowed slightly. "Good day, my lord. My lady." He turned and was off on swift, clicking feet.

"A damned shame," Piers murmured.

"Heartbreaking," Alys agreed. "But I wonder what he meant when he said we'd be able to make our own regrets? He was looking at me when he said it."

"I suspect Lord Griffin carries a heavy responsibility for Edward," Piers guessed. "My thought is that 'twill be none other than Julian Griffin whom he sends after Fallstowe."

"Surely it won't be soon—the man's just lost his wife."

Piers shrugged because he had no answer for her. Then turned to look down at Alys. In that instant, Julian Griffin and his misfortune were forgotten, as was the fate of Alys's childhood home. He was faced with a woman he had nearly lost himself. His own wife now, was she? Was she, truly?

She looked up at him. And then she smiled.

"I told you we were married."

Piers didn't know what to do, how to react. He wanted to grab her, kiss her, beg her to come home to Gillwick with him and Ira. But although her smile was sweet and relieved, he didn't know how she felt about their hasty and very legal marriage that had just taken place.

"I'm certain there is still time to have it retracted if you wish," Piers said, more gruffly than he'd intended.

Alys's brows lowered and she drew her head back. Then her fist. She dealt him a blow in the soft spot between his left breast and shoulder, and although it barely rocked Piers, he knew she'd intended for it to hurt him.

"I can't believe you would even suggest that!" she said. And then she burst into tears, her hands flying up to cover her face.

Piers cursed softly and gathered Alys into his arms, as he'd wanted to do from the moment she'd stormed the king's court for him.

"Alys, Alys—forgive me. I am a fool, true," he murmured into her hair. Piers took a deep breath and, for the first time in his life, spoke unabashedly from his heart. "I love you so, my little wife. Please, please say that you will come home with me to Gillwick, and live with me forever."

She slowed her sobs with sniffling breaths and after several moments, looked up at him, wiping at her cheeks. Piers raised a hand and brushed at a rogue tear she'd missed near her chin.

"Will you?" he asked, pressed. He cared not that she might refuse him now. He was laying himself open to her, his heart, his home, everything he was and everything he owned. He would never be as wealthy as her family. Gillwick would never be as grand as Fallstowe.

But she was no child, and so she already knew this. Perhaps she had realized it long before Piers had ever thought to.

"I told you once that I would go with you to the ends of the earth," Alys said solemnly. "That was my vow, and I meant it. I am so proud to be Lady Mallory, Piers. Your wife. So much prouder than I ever was to be just Alys Foxe."

Piers huffed a laugh. She was remarkable. "You were never 'just' Alys Foxe," he said, smoothing back her hair from her face with his palm.

He released her suddenly from his embrace and grasped her left hand. He brought out the carnelian signet ring once more, and slid it onto Alys's longest finger. It fit perfectly. He heard her soft cry, and Piers raised her hand to his lips and placed a kiss atop the carved M, much as he had done with the king's royal crest.

"Thank you," Alys said softly, her eyes shining. She squeezed his fingers. "But Piers—"

"Shh," he said with a smile, and then produced the little string of wooden beads and tied them once more onto Alys's right wrist.

"Now I truly feel that we are married . . . again." She smiled up at him as he took her into his arms and kissed her mouth lightly.

"Tell me," he asked, pulling her more closely into him, "what outrageous excuse were you forced to concoct that convinced Sybilla to allow you to return?"

Alys shook her head and ran her hand up the fine velvet of the stolen tunic she had purchased for him. "No outrageous excuse. But let us talk about it somewhere else, Piers. The air here is . . ."

"Tainted, yes," Piers agreed, thinking of the ghastly culmination of Judith Angwedd's and Bevan's fates. He pulled the key from his belt and held it before her. "Allow me to introduce you to the luxuries of a royal apartment, my lady wife." He smiled, thinking it odd that it was he who had spent the night in the king's home before his privileged spouse.

Alys's eyes sparkled. "Ooh! Is the bed as soft as I imagine it will be?"

Piers chuckled and raised his eyes to the ceiling for an instant, his face flushing. "We will find out together, my love. I spent the night on the floor, too fearful of mussing the bedclothes."

Alys laughed and grasped his face with both palms, pulling his lips to hers for a firm kiss. "I love you, Piers," she said when she pulled away.

"Not nearly as much as I love you," he challenged.

She wrinkled her nose at him and began pulling him toward the double doors of the chamber. "Let us make provisions for your grandfather and Layla, and then we shall just see about that."

The suite of rooms was grand, Alys had to admit, but unlike Piers, she was unintimidated by the plush setting. And so she was determined to waste little time in teaching him how to muss the bedclothes properly.

"Alys, do you want me?" Piers asked, his voice low and, Alys thought, somewhat unsure. "I mean, now. You've been through a trial and—"

"I do," she interrupted him with the two words that had sealed their union before the king. She brought her fingertips to the clasp at her throat and undid her cloak, although she let it continue to hang on her shoulders. "I've wanted you since the night you came to me in the Foxe Ring."

No sooner had the whisper escaped her lips than Piers claimed her mouth with his own. He wrapped his arms around her and half lifted her off the floor, as if trying to absorb her.

His mouth was slick and cool and wet, and she met his passionate need with one of her own every bit as fiery and demanding. Her fingers clawed at his belt, and Piers turned them both until Alys's back was toward the bed. He let her down onto her feet and then brought his hands over hers, stilling them. She whimpered.

"I am unlearned in the manner of a lady's clothing— it would be best for your gown should you remove it yourself."

Alys glanced down at the perse gown which now held so

many memories. And now it would mark her emergence into her life as a married woman. "You mean this old rag?"

Piers only smiled, and took a step back from her to give them both room to move. She undid her laces quickly, and when she was to slide her gown from her shoulders, she noticed him watching her. She paused, her face pinkened, and then she lifted her chin minutely.

Her eyes never leaving his, she pushed the left yoke of her gown away from her collarbone with her right hand, slowly, slowly, the fabric bunching and damming before it finally slid away. She caught the right side of her gown quickly before it could fall, and bringing her left arm across her chest, she slid her right arm free.

She paused, glanced down at his hands which had frozen in the action of removing his belt. "I'm a bit ahead of you already," she said pointedly.

He was staring at her exposed skin above her gown. "I'm in no hurry," he said hoarsely.

Her eyebrows rose briefly and one corner of her mouth lifted. "Very well." She slowly, slowly brought her arms from her chest, and the gown slid away by its own sheer weight. In an instant, Alys stood naked before him.

"Alys," he choked. "You are so beautiful."

She smiled, feeling proud, powerful. Her eyes flicked to his chest. "Your tunic, milord."

Piers's hands started up the motion of undoing his belt once more. He dropped it to the floor with a dull clunk. His fingers found the ends to the intricate laces on his chest, and Alys was surprised at the ease with which he untangled them. Piers pulled the thick garment over his head, and she saw his nipples puckered in the cool air of the chamber. He glanced down at the erection deforming his hose, and then looked boldly to Alys once more.

Alys sat on the edge of the bed and raised each knee

in turn, removing her feet from the circle of gown on the floor before taking off her shoes. Piers gasped when she lifted her heels and slid beneath the heavy coverlet, the motion parting her legs for a brief moment. He lifted one leg and put his foot on the edge of the bed frame, untying his own boot, then the other. Alys watched him openly, her cheek propped on one hand, the other holding the blanket to her chest.

Piers stepped out of his boots and then began to unfasten and remove the expensive woolen hose. He stood a moment at the side of the bed he was about to share with Alys, naked, shivering. She looked at his body boldly, his manhood, and then back up to his face where the pupils of his eyes seemed to have doubled in size. Alys herself felt heated and flushed and ready to be loved.

Piers gave her a moment of pause. "Alys, have you ever—"

"No," she answered right away, saving him from asking fully. "Aren't you the fortunate man? A pure, sweet virgin in your bed on your wedding morning." Her smile grew with the daring and love she felt. "At least for the next few moments." She held the blankets aside, an invitation.

Still, he hesitated. "Are you frightened?"

Her smile faded away. "I'll never be frightened of anything ever again with you by my side." She gestured with the blankets. "Come."

He slid into the cocoon she offered, her slightly warmed skin feeling afire once pressed against his cold flesh. Her arms went around his neck and she pressed her breasts against him while her mouth sought his. Her nipples felt like hard little buttons, the hair between her legs whispered at his rock hard thigh as she drew her knee over his hip. His hands seemed to each span the width of her back and waist as he pulled her to him, pressed his hips forward. She groaned at the feel of his rough skin on her flesh.

He skimmed his right hand down over her buttock and then reached beneath it with his fingers to find her, and when he touched her with a firm swipe, she mewed into his mouth. Piers rolled her onto her back and pulled away from her mouth.

"Take hold of the blanket," he commanded. Then he slid beneath, backing carefully over her until his shoulders were between her legs. And then he tasted her.

Alys cried out, and she reached her hands down to find his head through the blanket. He nipped and licked and explored with his tongue until she was panting, and then he began to ready her with his finger.

"Piers," she gasped. "Please."

She was so close to achieving her own pinnacle, and she knew it even without ever having proper knowledge of it. He slid up her body once more, leaving his hand in place. When he was over her, her moist heat touching him, bucking against him, Piers arched his hips and used his hand to push the head of his penis into her. He left his hand between them, holding his weight on his other forearm, and continued to rub her with his thumb.

He licked her lips, sucked at her tongue. Alys raised her hips up and took an inch of him; Piers followed her motion back to the cot and gave her another. She knew she was small, and she had witnessed that there was still so much of him left to give her. She knew a moment of fear.

She whimpered and pressed upward once more, her passion urging her past the discomfort, opening to him, taking him in. He pushed forward and was at half.

Alys cried out and gripped his waist. Piers withdrew only slightly, enough to give his hand room to increase their ministrations for a moment. Then she was panting again, and Piers sank into her. Withdrew. Deeper now. His fingers moved faster.

Alys began to move in counter rhythm with him, her swollen flesh pulsating, crying out now with longing, and impatience. With two more thrusts, she took the full length of him. A pair more, and Alys felt a wild expansion in her, an explosion, and she arched away from the magnificent bed to gain every bit of him. While she held him like a grasping fist, he gave his length to her fully and hard, and a moment later he filled her.

Alys covered his face in tiny kisses as he panted into her ear, "I love you, Alys. I love you. I love you . . ."

They made love twice in as many hours, slowly, savoring the familiarity of the act more each time, as well as committing to memory those private details between lovers. The heat of a sigh, the length of thigh against thigh. The curve of a shoulder and the pattern of goose-flesh raised by a kiss and a breath. The reward of separate climax, and for Alys, a repeat of such a miracle before they collapsed together on the sheets a final time.

A servant had rapped on the door, offering food, which Piers had accepted with such effusive thanks that Alys had giggled while he shut and bolted the door, balancing the heavy tray on one hand. He slid the tray with exacting care onto the large square table near the hearth and then rejoined her beneath the thick blankets. They stared out the window, curled together, at the glow of afternoon sunlight—all they could see from their position on the bed. Simply blue sky and sunlight.

"Are you going to tell me now?" Piers prompted, rousing Alys from a half doze.

"Tell you what? I told you so?" she teased.

"I believe we've already covered that bit." His fingertips skittered down her side to pinch the curve of her buttock. "I want to hear the wild tale you told your sister that gained you return to court."

Alys smiled, although being behind her, Piers could not see. "I simply told her the truth—what had happened to you and to the both of us in the wood. That I loved you, and that you needed me."

She felt him go still behind her. "And that was it? Sybilla let you go without argument?"

"Not exactly," Alys admitted. "After I told her that, she still insisted that I return to Fallstowe. And so I agreed. Sybilla risked her life for me, risked Fallstowe, by coming directly into Edward's home. I owed her, for that and for many other things that I never even realized before you came into my life. And I thought you didn't want me—you did little else but try to get me to leave you for weeks. I thought mayhap it was because you didn't love me after all."

"Alys, I—"

"Shh," she interrupted, and patted his forearms, wrapped around her middle. "I'm not finished. When we reached the gates of the city without detection, Sybilla stopped. She turned to me and said, 'Alys, I want you to be happy. You have shown great bravery in standing by Piers alone these many weeks. You are not a child, and Clement Cobb is a piece of shit.'"

"She called him a piece of shit?" Piers said in a laughing voice.

"She did, although she did not explain her change of heart about him. She said she wouldn't allow me to marry him now were he the last titled man in the realm. She said she trusted my judgment, and if I found you worthy, then so did she."

"I'll be damned," Piers mused.

"It was also a fact of standing behind her vow," Alys admitted. "Remember, she'd told me when I left Fallstowe that if I found a man at the ring who would have me, he was welcome to me. Sybilla places great value on keeping her word."

"Thanks be to God."

"Indeed. She embraced me, kissed me, told me that if things did not go in our favor to come home to Fallstowe, and then she left me at the gates."

"I think I love her," Piers said, his amazement clear in his voice.

"I know I do," Alys said softly.

After a long, peaceful silence, Piers said, "On our return, I would go to Ira's town. See who would join us at Gillwick."

"I think that is a wonderful idea," Alys said firmly.

"It will be more difficult than just that," Piers said, and Alys could hear his doubt. "There are so many, and Gillwick is modest. I don't know how I will house them all, how much strain Gillwick's coffers can withstand."

"Worry not about it, husband," Alys said, squeezing his arms to her, snuggling her head into the pillow and closing her eyes with a sleepy yawn. "We'll visit Sybilla en route to Gillwick."

Piers was quiet for a moment before he gave a wary, "Why?"

"Besides the fact that I carry the king's message, you still have to claim my dowry," Alys murmured. "I'm certain Sybilla will have it ready for us when we arrive. It is quite a large amount."

Piers gave a disbelieving huff. Then he kissed Alys near her ear. "I will do whatever I can to help your family," he said. "I've never had one before. Barring an act of outright treason, I will stand with Fallstowe when the king sends his man."

"I know," Alys said quietly. Her eyes were open once more, and she was staring out the window. "I know you will, my love."

But there was much Alys had failed to ask Sybilla in all their years as sisters. The eldest daughter had kept her mother's secrets well, but if the Foxe matriarch was to survive the king's wrath, she would have to learn to trust someone other than herself.

Alys did not know if she honestly wanted to learn the truth.

Edward was coming for Sybilla, true, but that meant sweet Cecily was also at risk. The sooner Alys's quiet, pious middle sister was safely ensconced in her beloved nunnery, the better.

She closed her eyes again. No matter now. She had her husband, and at his side, they could do anything. Anything at all. She was drifting off to sleep now.

"I love you, Piers," she murmured.

"Love you, my woman." He kissed her temple.

That night Alys dreamed of sweet music, and her mother, and her husband's babies. And she dreamed of Fallstowe—beautiful, grand Fallstowe.

Please turn the page for an exciting sneak peek of
Heather Grothaus's

NEVER SEDUCE
A SCOUNDREL,

coming soon from Zebra Books!

February 1277
Fallstowe Castle, England

Cecily Foxe was fairly certain she was going to hell.

She had been standing alone for the better part of two hours following the lavish supper, struggling to maintain a serene expression while she watched the revelers and their atrocious behavior. It was proving increasingly difficult. Men drank so heartily and hastily that the fronts of their tunics were dark with wine, and most women recklessly attempted to match pace with them. Unmarried couples danced, although the lewd displays of bodies touching so intimately could hardly be defined as such a supposedly innocent activity.

Cecily bristled as she watched even the least of the nobility, the humble, the homely, the meek, carry on with members of the opposite sex. Even poor Lady Angelica, who had a lazy eye and spat upon anyone unfortunate enough to be engaged in conversation with her, was being twirled about Fallstowe's great hall with sordid abandon. Cecily had clearly seen the young man currently in possession of Lady Angelica unabashedly grasp the woman's breast.

Only Cecily stood alone.

No one had asked her to dance. No young lord dare come near and whisper lurid suggestions to her, proposing they steal away from the hall for an hour of private sin. She was a lady of Fallstowe, wealthy beyond comprehension, powerful by her connection to Sybilla, perhaps even wanted as a criminal by the crown. Unmarried. Both her eyes pointed in the same direction and she kept her saliva properly in her mouth when speaking.

And yet they all simply pretended she wasn't there.

To everyone who knew her—nay, even knew *of* her— she was Saint Cecily. Middle daughter of Amicia and Morys Foxe. Slated for a life of quiet, gentle sacrifice. Although she had yet to formally commit to the convent, Cecily already fulfilled many of the obligations put upon one under holy orders. Up to even the wee hours of that very morn, she had assisted Father Perry in the countless and tedious preparations for the Candlemas feast, and in general, she looked over Fallstowe's charitable responsibilities, tending the ill and dying, duteously prayed the liturgy of the hours.

Most of them, any matter.

She seldom raised her voice in a passion of any nature. She did not lie, nor indulge in gossip. She was obedient to her older sister, Sybilla, the head of the family now that both of their parents were dead. She was not ostentatious in either dress or temperament, preferring to wear costumes so closely akin to the habits of the committed that strangers to the hold often greeted her with a deferential incline of their heads and a murmured, "God's blessing upon you, Sister."

Cecily knew she was admired and even revered for her

restraint and decorum. She was not outwardly bold, like young Alys, seen now dancing gaily with her new husband in the middle of the crush of guests. She was not obviously ambitious like the eldest, Sybilla, who ruled Fallstowe with a delicate iron fist. Cecily had spent the greater part of her score and two years carefully cultivating her gentle qualities. Molding herself to them.

And yet, at that very moment, her supposedly meek heart was so full of discord, she was quite surprised that she had not already burst into flames where she stood.

The dancers continued to whirl past, little carousels of gaiety and color around massive iron cauldrons which blazed with fires fed by the brown and brittle swags of evergreen and holly that had festooned Fallstowe's great hall since Christmas. Although the blessed candles burned in their posts, the remainder of the celebration was largely pagan, bidding farewell to the barren winter while at once beckoning to the fertile light of spring. Cecily knew that her elder sister had purposefully sought to emphasize the heathen aspect of the celebration— unfortunately, Sybilla seemed to thrive on wicked rumor.

The Foxe matriarch herself weaved through the crowd now, both adoration and jealousy following close at her heels as she made her way toward Cecily. The men hungered for Sybilla—those few who'd once held her let their eyes blatantly show the aching memories of their hearts, and the many who had not been honored with the privilege of her bed pursued her without care for their pride. Sybilla was powerful, desirable; Cecily was not.

As if to emphasize this point, Cecily again caught a glimpse of the primary object of her bitterness.

Oliver Bellecote.

He could have been your husband, a wicked little voice whispered in her ear.

"Hello, darling." Sybilla had at last fought her way through the pulsating throng to stand at Cecily's side, her slender arm pulling the two sisters together at the hip. "I would have thought you to be abed an hour ago."

Cecily was careful to keep her tone light. "This may well be my last feast at Fallstowe, Sybilla. I would remember it."

Sybilla gave her sister's waist a gentle squeeze, but did not comment on Cecily's reference to Hallowshire Abbey. The two women observed the debauchery that ruled the supposedly holy day feast in silence for several moments. Then Oliver Bellecote whirled past once more, causing Cecily to lose control of her suddenly wicked tongue.

"I am quite surprised to see him," she said, thankful that, at least, her tone was casual.

"Who? Oliver?" Cecily felt more than saw Sybilla's shrug. After a moment, she said quietly, "I suppose I must call him Lord Bellecote, now."

Cecily's heart thudded faster in her chest, and her indignation made pulling in her next breath difficult. "August has not been dead a month, and yet he is here— still behaving as if he hasn't a care in the world or one whit of responsibility. It's indecent and disrespectful. To his brother and to you."

Sybilla drew away slightly, and Cecily could feel her sister's frosty blue gaze light the side of her face. Cecily's ear practically tingled. She hadn't meant for her comment to come out that way at all.

"I am not offended by Oliver's presence, Cee, nor by him enjoying himself at Fallstowe. Although 'tis no secret that Oliver oft exasperated him, August loved his younger brother. And Oliver loved August."

Cecily turned to look at Sybilla, the question out before she could restrain herself. "Did *you* love August?"

For the briefest instant, Sybilla's lips thinned and a fleeting fire came into her eyes. But then it was gone, replaced by a washed out melancholy that wrenched at Cecily's heart.

"No, Cee. I did not," she admitted as she turned her attention back to the crowd, now dispersing from the center of the hall as the music came to an end. The guests seemed only able to communicate in shouts and shrill laughter that sounded to Cecily like tortured screams. Yet she heard her sister's low murmurs as if the two women stood alone in a cupboard. "I'm certain you pity me now."

"No, not pity," Cecily insisted. "I only worry for you. I was with the two of you the last time August was at Fallstowe, Sybilla—I remember."

"As do I." Sybilla's eyes scanned the crowd disinterestedly. "I told him not to come back."

"You didn't mean it, though."

"Oh, but I did," Sybilla argued, quickly but with her signature coolness. "And now he never *will* come back. Now Oliver is Lord of Bellemont, a position I know from his brother that he never wanted, and is perhaps ill-equipped to fill. Oliver deserves a final farewell to his carefree existence before he truly dons the mantle of responsibility over such a large hold. Perhaps he'll marry Lady Joan Barleg now—Bellemont needs heirs." She paused as if thinking, and when she again spoke her voice was low. "It gladdens me to see him at Fallstowe."

"It wasn't your fault, Sybilla." Cecily had forgotten her selfish pity at the thought that she had caused her sister to relive such sad memories. "You did nothing to cause August's death. 'Twas a terrible accident, and that is all."

"Hmm. Well, perhaps you should pray for my soul, any matter."

Cecily tore her gaze away from her sister's pale, enigmatic

profile as the dancers reformed at the opening notes of the next piece. "I do hope he *does* marry Lady Joan," she said abruptly. "He's been toying about with the poor girl for the past year. She must be completely humiliated. Are they already betrothed?"

Sybilla chuckled. "Oliver took nothing from Joan Barleg that she didn't freely offer him, and now that he's Lord of Bellemont, she has chance to better her station immensely. Had Oliver been firstborn instead of August, Lady Joan would have had little chance of winning him." A faint smile remained on her lips. "You likely don't remember, but there was talk of a betrothal between you and Oliver when you were children."

Cecily indeed remembered, but she gripped her tongue between her teeth painfully. Should Sybilla continue to goad her so, Cecily would end up as Lady Angelica, spitting her words rather than speaking them.

Sybilla continued in a bored tone when Cecily gave no comment. "It would be quite the *coup d'etat* for Joan. But I have heard no formal announcement from either of them as of yet, so who can know?"

As if their talk had summoned him, Oliver Bellecote himself slid between a pair of dancers, becoming momentarily entangled in their arms. The three shared a raucous laugh as he extracted himself with a lewd pinch to the woman's buttock, his chalice held high above his head to preserve the wine contained within. Cecily felt her diaphragm shrivel up uncomfortably at his approach.

Then he was before them both, bowing drunkenly, his lips crooked in a cocky grin beneath the close shadow on his face. His brown eyes were like muddy pools powdered with gold dust—dark and dirty and deep, the bright sparkle hiding what lay beneath. His thick black lashes clustered like reedy sentries, both beckoning and guarding at once.

"Lady Sybilla," he sighed, drawing up Sybilla's hand beneath his face and kissing the back of her palm loudly three times.

Cecily rolled her eyes and sighed.

Sybilla only laughed. "Lord Bellecote, you flatter me."

He should have risen then. Instead, he dropped to one knee, pulling Sybilla's hand to his bosom and then lowering his chin awkwardly to kiss her fingers once more before raising his slender, strikingly handsome face to gaze adoringly at Cecily's sister.

"Lady Sybilla Foxe, my most gorgeous, tempting hostess! Won't you marry me?"

Cecily gasped.

Sybilla threw back her head and laughed even louder, and although it was likely only the candlelight and smoke, Cecily thought she saw a glistening of tears in Sybilla's eyes.

"Is that a no?" Oliver asked, feigning shock.

"Guard your honor well, Lady Sybilla!" a female's gay shout rang out, and Cecily looked up in time to see the comely Joan Barleg skip past them in the arms of her dance partner, her golden curls spilling recklessly from her simple crispinette. She looked so carefree and . . . at ease. Cecily's spine stiffened further.

Sybilla gave the woman a wink, and raised a palm in acknowledgement. She then looked back down at the still-kneeling Oliver Bellecote.

"It is a no," she affirmed.

To Cecily's horror, Oliver Bellecote gave a horrendous wail—as if he'd been shot with an arrow—and then collapsed fully onto his back, the drink inside his chalice still miraculously maintaining the level.

"I am crushed! *Defeated!*" he shouted in mock agony. Several guests were now pointing and laughing at the display he presented on the stones. He raised his head abruptly, took a noisy swallow, and then looked at Sybilla. "Will you at least sleep with me then? Completely inappropriate, I know, considering our very slight degree of separation, but I fear I am now considered quite eligible."

"Oh, this is truly too much," Cecily gritted out from between her teeth. Her cheeks felt as if they were on fire.

Sybilla cocked her head and gave him a sympathetic smile. "Sorry, Oliver."

His forehead wrinkled, giving him the appearance of a chastised pup. "Damn my slothly feet—you're already spoken for."

"I'm afraid so," Sybilla answered.

"Sybilla!" Cecily hissed, outraged that her sister would have such an inappropriate conversation—even in jest— with this man where any could overhear their lewd banter. This man *in particular*.

"Forgive me, Cee," Sybilla conceded, turning amused eyes to her sister while Lord Bellecote staggered to his feet.

Cecily squared her shoulders, somewhat placated that Sybilla had at last remembered both her station and her very public venue.

"How thoughtless of me," Sybilla continued. "Lord Bellecote, I *am* engaged with other business this night, but I believe Lady Cecily, however, is thus far unattended."

Cecily's entire body went ice cold. She was unsure whether she would cry or throw up.

Oliver Bellecote had tardily gained his feet, brushing at his pants with his free hand. Sybilla's flip invitation caused his movements to freeze. He slowly raised his face until his eyes met Cecily's.

She would have gasped had she been able to draw breath. His direct gaze was like witnessing lightning striking the ocean. The first thought that came into her mind was, *why, he's as lonely as I am.* Her stomach hardened into a pained little stone. She wanted to scream at him to stop looking at her, wanted to turn and berate Sybilla for drawing her into such an indecent exhibition—

—she wanted Oliver Bellecote to suggest something inappropriate to her so that she might agree.

Oliver's eyes flicked to Sybilla's and in that next instant, both the notorious nobleman and Cecily's sister burst out in peals of laughter.

"I am sorry to tease you so, Oliver," Sybilla chuckled, drawing her arm back around Cecily's middle, and Cecily hung a brittle, fragile smile on her numb lips. "My dearest sister would not have the likes of you wrapped up in the holy shroud itself."

"Nor should she," Oliver agreed with a naughty grin and deep bow in Cecily's direction, although his eyes did not look at her directly again. "Alas, I am not worthy of such a gentle lady's attention, as our wise parents decided so long ago."

Sybilla quirked an eyebrow. "Yet you are worthy of my attention?"

The rogue winked at Cecily's sister. "One must never cease to aspire to the heights of one's potential." He bowed again. "Ladies." And then he slipped back into the writhing crowd with all the grace of a serpent in the garden.

Cecily felt her eyes swelling with tears, and she swallowed hard.

Sybilla sighed. "Perhaps he—Cee? Cee, are you alright?"

"Of course, Sybilla. I'm fine."

Sybilla's expression turned uncharacteristically sympathetic. "I'm sorry. You appeared so forlorn standing there, I only wanted you to join in a bit of merrymaking."

How would you have me join in? Cecily screamed in her head. *No one will so much as speak to me, and I've just been rejected by the most notorious womanizer outside of London!*

But she pulled together every last scrap of her dignity to give Sybilla a smile. "I'm fine, Sybilla. Don't apologize. It was . . . it was amusing." She tried to laugh but it came out a weak, stuttering breath. Cecily pulled away from her sister slowly, deliberately. "It *is* late. I am off to Compline and then my own bed."

Sybilla's fine brow creased, and Cecily leaned in and pressed her cheek to her sister's. "Don't worry so. Would that you ask Alys and Piers to wait for me in the morn so that I might bid them farewell. I fear 'twould take me an hour to find them tonight in the crush."

"Of course," Sybilla promised. "Good night, Cee."

Cecily could not return the sentiment, as it had been anything but for her, and so she simply smiled again and walked away.

She made her way around the perimeter of the hall beneath the musicians' arched balcony, excusing herself quietly around little clusters of people oblivious to her passing, until she at last came to the lord's dais—Sybilla's dais now. The stacks of tables and benches cleared away from the great hall floor to give the dancers room felt like a haven, a fortress, shielding Cecily from the cruel celebration as she ducked through the hidden door set in the rear wall.

The stone corridor was cool and blessedly unoccupied, a welcome relief from the humid cacophony of the feast.

Cecily's footsteps were quick and quiet as she made her way to her rooms to fetch her cloak for the walk across the bailey to the chapel.

He hadn't considered her for one instant, even in jest.

She reached her chamber and stepped inside, forcing herself to close the door gently, when what she wanted to do was slam it loose from its hinges. She crossed the floor to the wardrobe.

She didn't understand why she was so completely and suddenly enraged. She had decided her path long ago, even if she had dragged her feet in formally committing. She loved the peace of a prayerful life, found meaning in service. The beauty and wonder of the world—and its wickedness too—explained and supported by faith. In pledging herself to the religious, her life would forever be simple, predictable. Peaceful.

Cecily found her cloak easily among her few gowns and pulled it out. She held the worn material in her hands and looked down at it, musing suddenly that the old cloak was not unlike her life in the present—the weave coming slowly apart, rubbed thin and transparent in places, the hem ragged and uneven. In truth, the garment was much too short for her now. She hadn't noticed before that moment how shabby it had become, although when her mother had sewn the final stitches, it had been quite enviable.

She realized that had been ten years ago. Had any at Fallstowe known peace since then?

Her parents had seen little peace while they'd lived. Morys Foxe had held Fallstowe against the Barons with King Henry III, and then after the weak monarch's death, as well as Morys's own, Amicia had seized the reins of Fallstowe in bitter defiance of the king's son, who thought her a spy against the crown. And now that Amicia was gone, Sybilla had taken up their mother's dangerous banner, rebelling against Edward so that Cecily was certain the consequences would be most dire.

Alys was safe now that she was married with the king's own blessing, yes. But what of Sybilla? Her pride would never allow for surrender to Edward's demands, no matter how rich and well-tended the monarch promised to leave her. Cecily did not often dwell on the possibilities that lay in store for her elder sister, although she knew they were quite real, and more pressing now than ever. Alys and Piers had carried rumors from London of a siege only two months ago. Sybilla could be imprisoned.

She could be put to death.

One of her sisters was a solitary warrior, the other now a simple farmer's wife. Cecily was truly in the middle, and not just because of the order of her birth. She could not choose either path—to fight or to surrender. And so she had chosen the only other option that was likely to bring her peace—

She had become invisible. And for years, her inconspicuousness had served her well.

Then why was she, this night, so very unhappy? So atypically discontent, and even envious of the carefree and pretty Joan Barleg, of all people? And why was she so put out at the thought that a man who would lie naked with a donkey paid her no mind?

Cecily wondered for the hundredth time this evening how her life would have been different if she and Oliver Bellecote had married. Would they be happy? In all likelihood, she would still be known by the hated moniker of Saint Cecily, if only because people would surely look upon her with pity at being married to such a scoundrel as Oliver Bellecote.

The terribly handsome, lonely scoundrel.

She sniffed loudly and then wiped at her face with the

hem of her cloak before swirling it around her shoulders. She turned to the little plain clay dish on the table near her bed to retrieve her prayer beads.

This will all have passed away by the morn, she reasoned with herself. After all, Alys had been in the very depths of despair when she thought she was to marry against her will, and Alys had gone on to meet her husband at the F—

Cecily's head came up. Her chamber was as silent as the bottom of a well.

"The Foxe Ring," she whispered aloud, and brought her fingers to her mouth, the smooth, round beads in her hand pressing against her lips, as if trying too late to stifle her words.

The old ring of standing stones at the crumbling Foxe ruin was rumored to be a magic place. Men and women throughout the land had used the mysterious circle for generations in order to find a mate. The legend was unlikely, yes, but Alys had gone, and Piers had found her in the midst of a very unlikely set of circumstances.

Perhaps . . . perhaps Hallowshire *wasn't* Cecily's true vocation, which might explain her sudden, fierce reluctance. Perhaps she, too, should visit the Foxe Ring. Perhaps—

Cecily dropped her hands and her gaze went to the floor while she shook her head. "Superstitious nonsense," she said sternly, quietly. "Likely a sin, as well." Hadn't she herself warned Alys of such on the very night her youngest sister set out for the ring?

But weren't you also wrong then? a little voice whispered in her ear.

She tried to ignore it.

Besides, the moon wasn't even full presently, as the legend commanded. It wouldn't be full again for a fortnight, and by that time, her letter of intent would be firmly in

the hands of the kindly and elderly abbess, and this inde-
cisive madness that had suddenly seized her would be
naught but a faint and unpleasant memory.

Cecily took a deep breath and blew it out with rounded
cheeks. Then she walked determinedly to the door and quit
her chamber, her feet carrying her purposefully toward the
wing of the castle that would allow her to exit in the
bailey closest to the chapel. The sounds of the feast
behind her—the shouts and laughter—chased her from
her home in diminishing whispers until she was running,
and she burst through the stubborn wooden door with a
gasp, as if coming up from the bottom of a lake.

The bailey was empty, the sky above black and pin
pricked with a hundred million stars. Her panting breaths
clouded around her head as she recalled her mother
telling her that the night sky was a protective blanket between the earth and heaven's blinding glory. Starlight was
angels peeking through the cloth.

The thought led Cecily's mind to another faded, bittersweet memory—herself and her two sisters, as girls, playing at the abandoned keep. It was springtime, and Cecily,
Alys—she could have been no more than four—and even
Sybilla collected long, spindly wildflowers, yellow and
white, while Amicia watched benevolently from the shade
of a nearby tree.

The girls weaved in and out of the tall, standing stones,
singing a song Amicia had taught them, their arms full of
ragged blooms.

One, two, me and you . . .
Tre, four, forever more . . .
Five, six, the stones do pick . . .
Seven, eight, 'tis my fate . . .
Nine, ten, now I ken . . .

Cecily stared up at the sky for a long time.

When her heart beat slowly once more, Cecily began walking determinedly toward the chapel—the exact opposite direction of the Foxe Ring, which seemed to be sending out ghostly echoes of that almost forgotten childhood song. As penance for her sinful thoughts and desires, Cecily decided then that she would specifically pray for Oliver Bellecote. Surely that would be akin to wearing a hair shirt.

Any matter, she would *not* be going to the Foxe Ring.

She stopped at the doors to the chapel, the night still around her, as if the angels above the blanket of sky held their breath and watched her to see what she would do. Her hand gripped the latch.

Cecily looked slowly, hesitantly over her shoulder.

About the Author

Heather Grothaus is the author of the internationally acclaimed Medieval Warriors Trilogy, and her novels have been translated into several foreign languages. When not writing, she enjoys gardening, studying French, and investigating real-life haunted locations. She lives in Kentucky with her husband, their children, and two enormous dogs. You can visit her online at www.HeatherGrothaus.com.

Romantic Suspense from
Lisa Jackson

Books by Bestselling Author
Fern Michaels

___The Jury	0-8217-7878-1	$6.99US/$9.99CAN
___Sweet Revenge	0-8217-7879-X	$6.99US/$9.99CAN
___Lethal Justice	0-8217-7880-3	$6.99US/$9.99CAN
___Free Fall	0-8217-7881-1	$6.99US/$9.99CAN
___Fool Me Once	0-8217-8071-9	$7.99US/$10.99CAN
___Vegas Rich	0-8217-8112-X	$7.99US/$10.99CAN
___Hide and Seek	1-4201-0184-6	$6.99US/$9.99CAN
___Hokus Pokus	1-4201-0185-4	$6.99US/$9.99CAN
___Fast Track	1-4201-0186-2	$6.99US/$9.99CAN
___Collateral Damage	1-4201-0187-0	$6.99US/$9.99CAN
___Final Justice	1-4201-0188-9	$6.99US/$9.99CAN
___Up Close and Personal	0-8217-7956-7	$7.99US/$9.99CAN
___Under the Radar	1-4201-0683-X	$6.99US/$9.99CAN
___Razor Sharp	1-4201-0684-8	$7.99US/$10.99CAN
___Yesterday	1-4201-1494-8	$5.99US/$6.99CAN
___Vanishing Act	1-4201-0685-6	$7.99US/$10.99CAN
___Sara's Song	1-4201-1493-X	$5.99US/$6.99CAN
___Deadly Deals	1-4201-0686-4	$7.99US/$10.99CAN
___Game Over	1-4201-0687-2	$7.99US/$10.99CAN
___Sins of Omission	1-4201-1153-1	$7.99US/$10.99CAN
___Sins of the Flesh	1-4201-1154-X	$7.99US/$10.99CAN
___Cross Roads	1-4201-1192-2	$7.99US/$10.99CAN

Available Wherever Books Are Sold!
Check out our website at **www.kensingtonbooks.com**

Discover the Magic of
Romance with
Jo Goodman